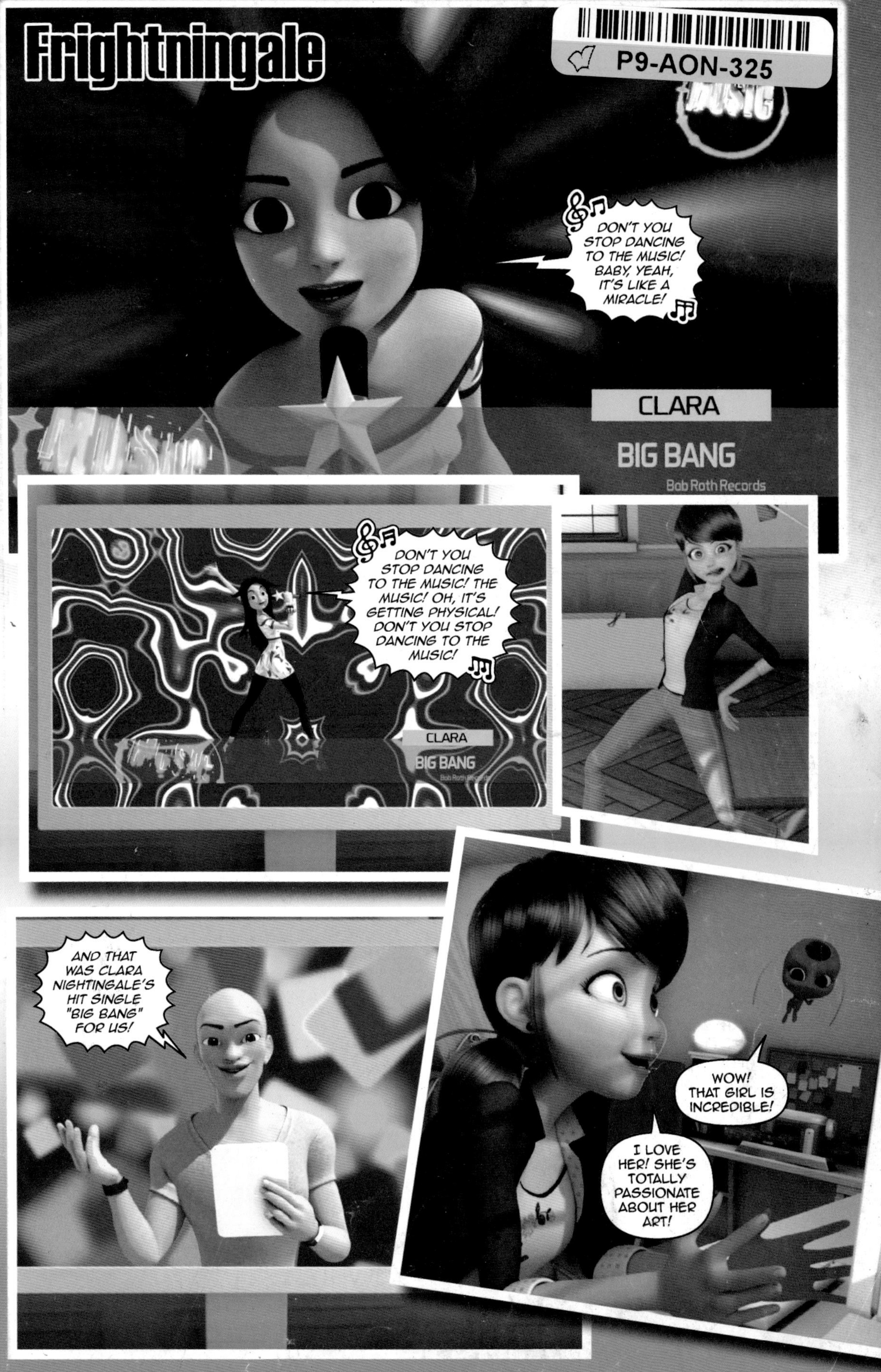
Frightningale
DON'T YOU STOP DANCING TO THE MUSIC! BABY, YEAH, IT'S LIKE A MIRACLE!
CLARA
BIG BANG
Bob Roth Records
DON'T YOU STOP DANCING TO THE MUSIC! THE MUSIC! OH, IT'S GETTING PHYSICAL! DON'T YOU STOP DANCING TO THE MUSIC!
CLARA
BIG BANG
AND THAT WAS CLARA NIGHTINGALE'S HIT SINGLE "BIG BANG" FOR US!
WOW! THAT GIRL IS INCREDIBLE!
I LOVE HER! SHE'S TOTALLY PASSIONATE ABOUT HER ART!

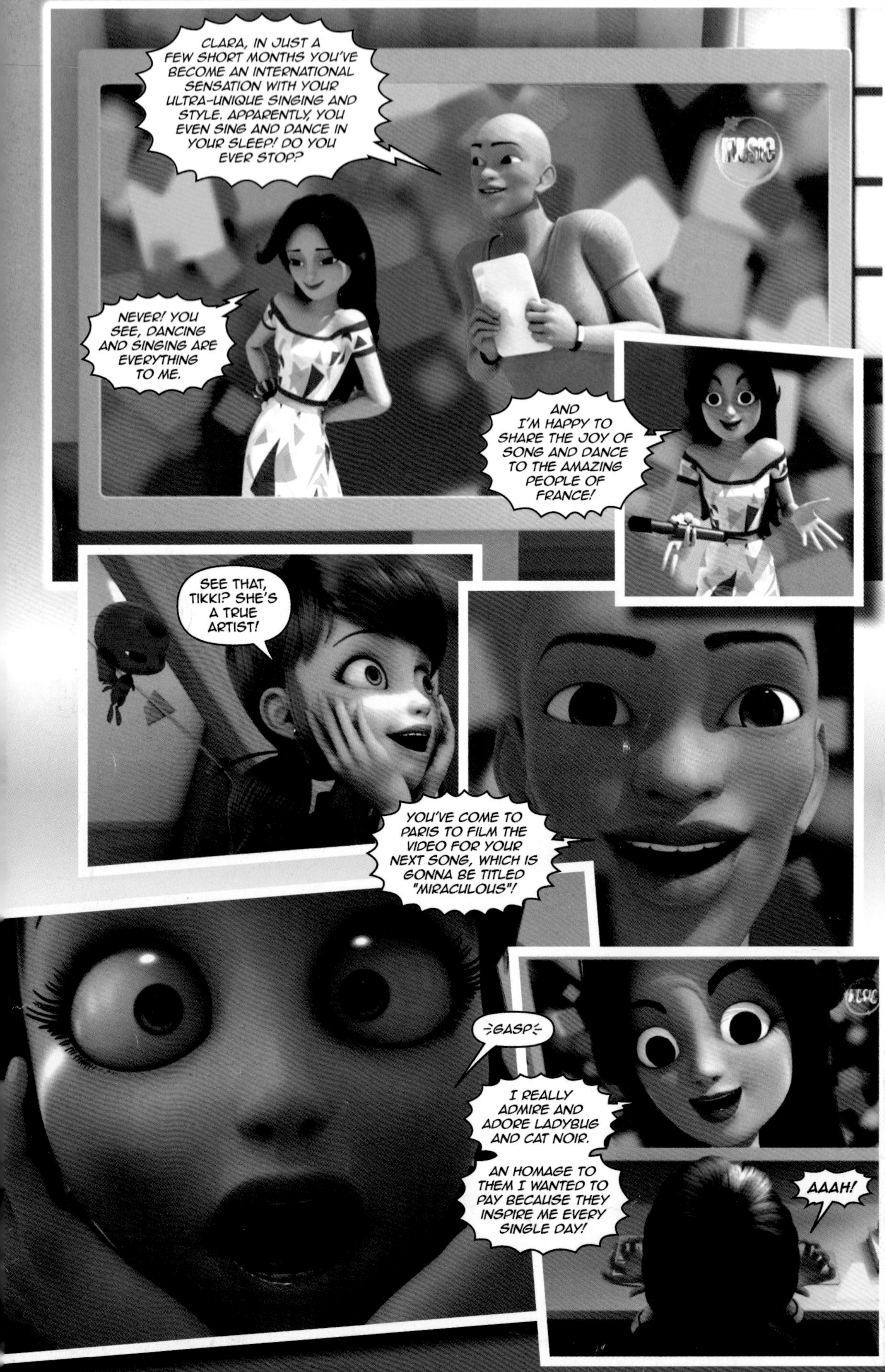
CLARA, IN JUST A FEW SHORT MONTHS YOU'VE BECOME AN INTERNATIONAL SENSATION WITH YOUR ULTRA-UNIQUE SINGING AND STYLE. APPARENTLY, YOU EVEN SING AND DANCE IN YOUR SLEEP! DO YOU EVER STOP?
NEVER! YOU SEE, DANCING AND SINGING ARE EVERYTHING TO ME.
AND I'M HAPPY TO SHARE THE JOY OF SONG AND DANCE TO THE AMAZING PEOPLE OF FRANCE!
SEE THAT, TIKKI? SHE'S A TRUE ARTIST!
YOU'VE COME TO PARIS TO FILM THE VIDEO FOR YOUR NEXT SONG, WHICH IS GONNA BE TITLED "MIRACULOUS"!
GASP
I REALLY ADMIRE AND ADORE LADYBUG AND CAT NOIR.
AN HOMAGE TO THEM I WANTED TO PAY BECAUSE THEY INSPIRE ME EVERY SINGLE DAY!
AAAH!

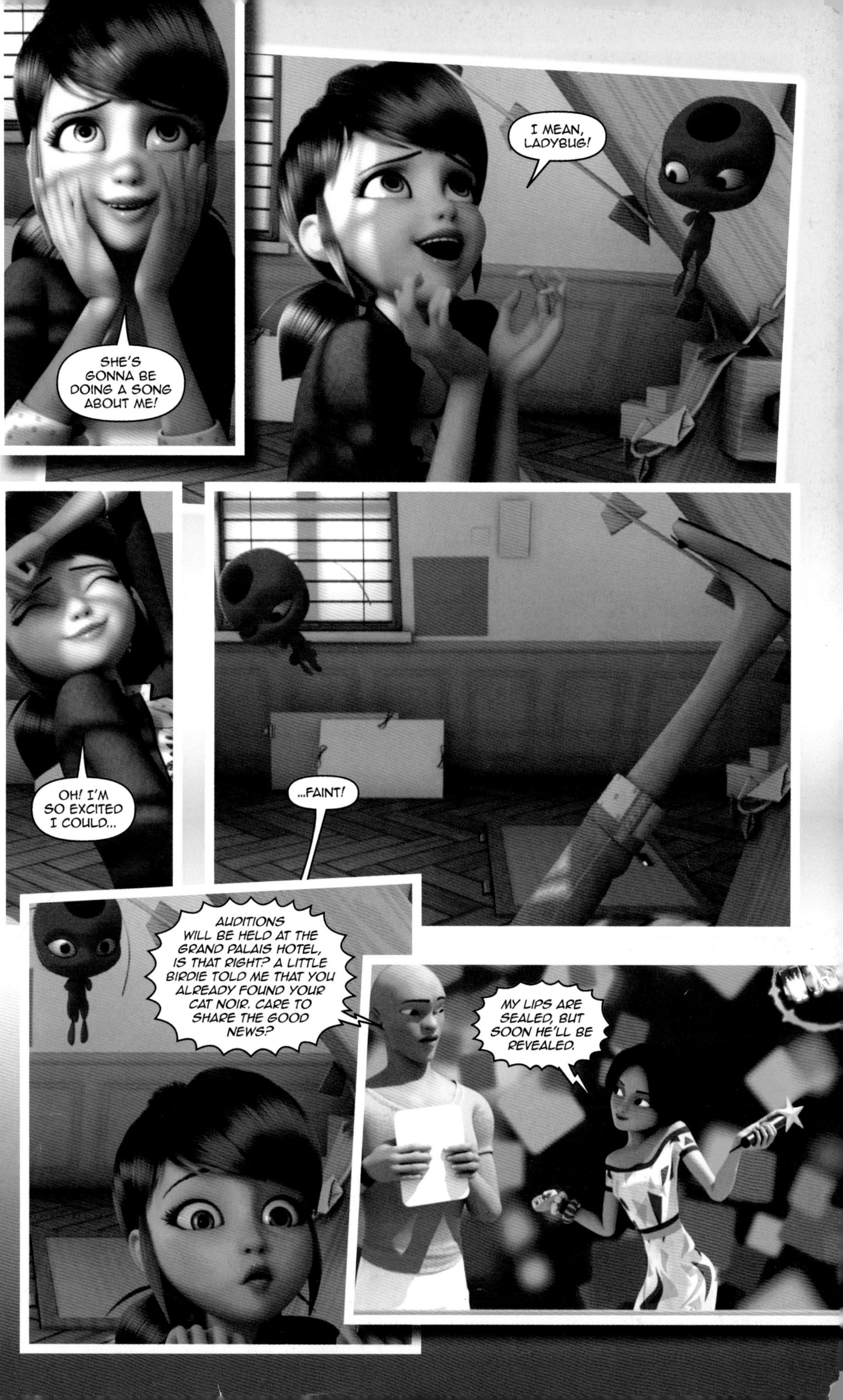
SHE'S GONNA BE DOING A SONG ABOUT ME!
I MEAN, LADYBUG!
OH! I'M SO EXCITED I COULD...
...FAINT!
AUDITIONS WILL BE HELD AT THE GRAND PALAIS HOTEL, IS THAT RIGHT? A LITTLE BIRDIE TOLD ME THAT YOU ALREADY FOUND YOUR CAT NOIR. CARE TO SHARE THE GOOD NEWS?
MY LIPS ARE SEALED, BUT SOON HE'LL BE REVEALED.

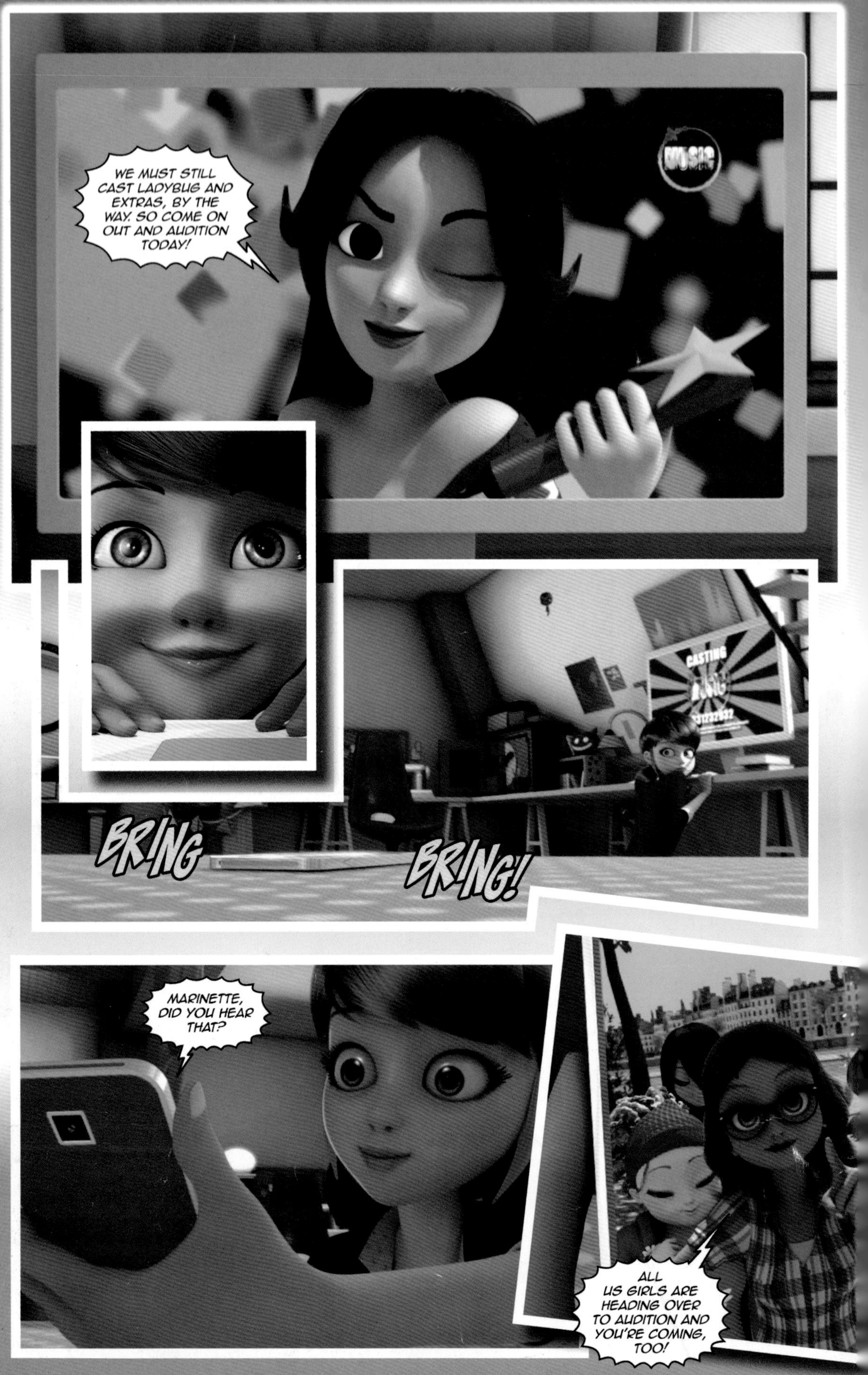
WE MUST STILL CAST LADYBUG AND EXTRAS, BY THE WAY. SO COME ON OUT AND AUDITION TODAY!
CASTING
BRING
BRING!
MARINETTE, DID YOU HEAR THAT?
ALL US GIRLS ARE HEADING OVER TO AUDITION AND YOU'RE COMING, TOO!

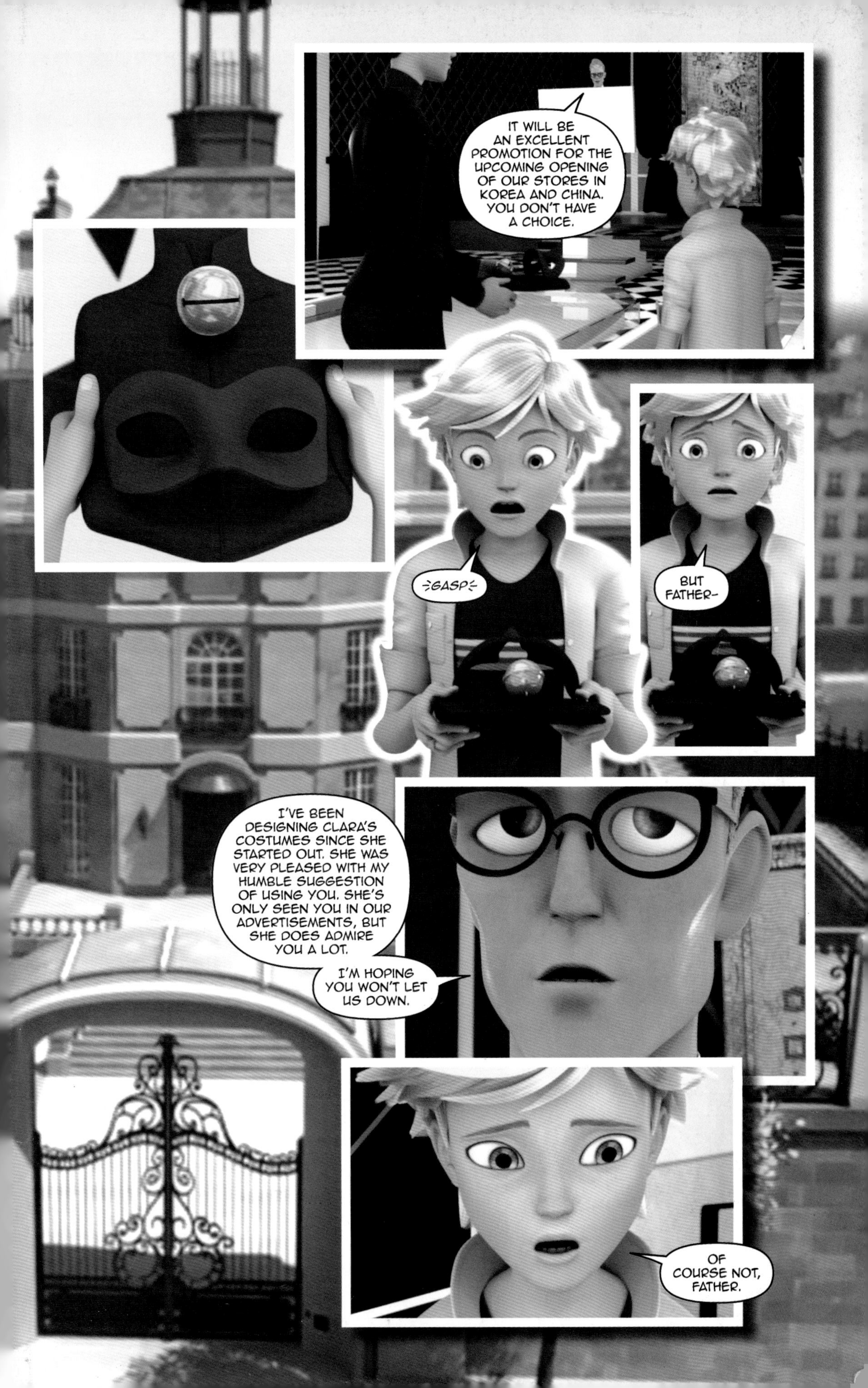
IT WILL BE AN EXCELLENT PROMOTION FOR THE UPCOMING OPENING OF OUR STORES IN KOREA AND CHINA. YOU DON'T HAVE A CHOICE.
GASP
BUT FATHER–
I'VE BEEN DESIGNING CLARA'S COSTUMES SINCE SHE STARTED OUT. SHE WAS VERY PLEASED WITH MY HUMBLE SUGGESTION OF USING YOU. SHE'S ONLY SEEN YOU IN OUR ADVERTISEMENTS, BUT SHE DOES ADMIRE YOU A LOT.
I'M HOPING YOU WON'T LET US DOWN.
OF COURSE NOT, FATHER.

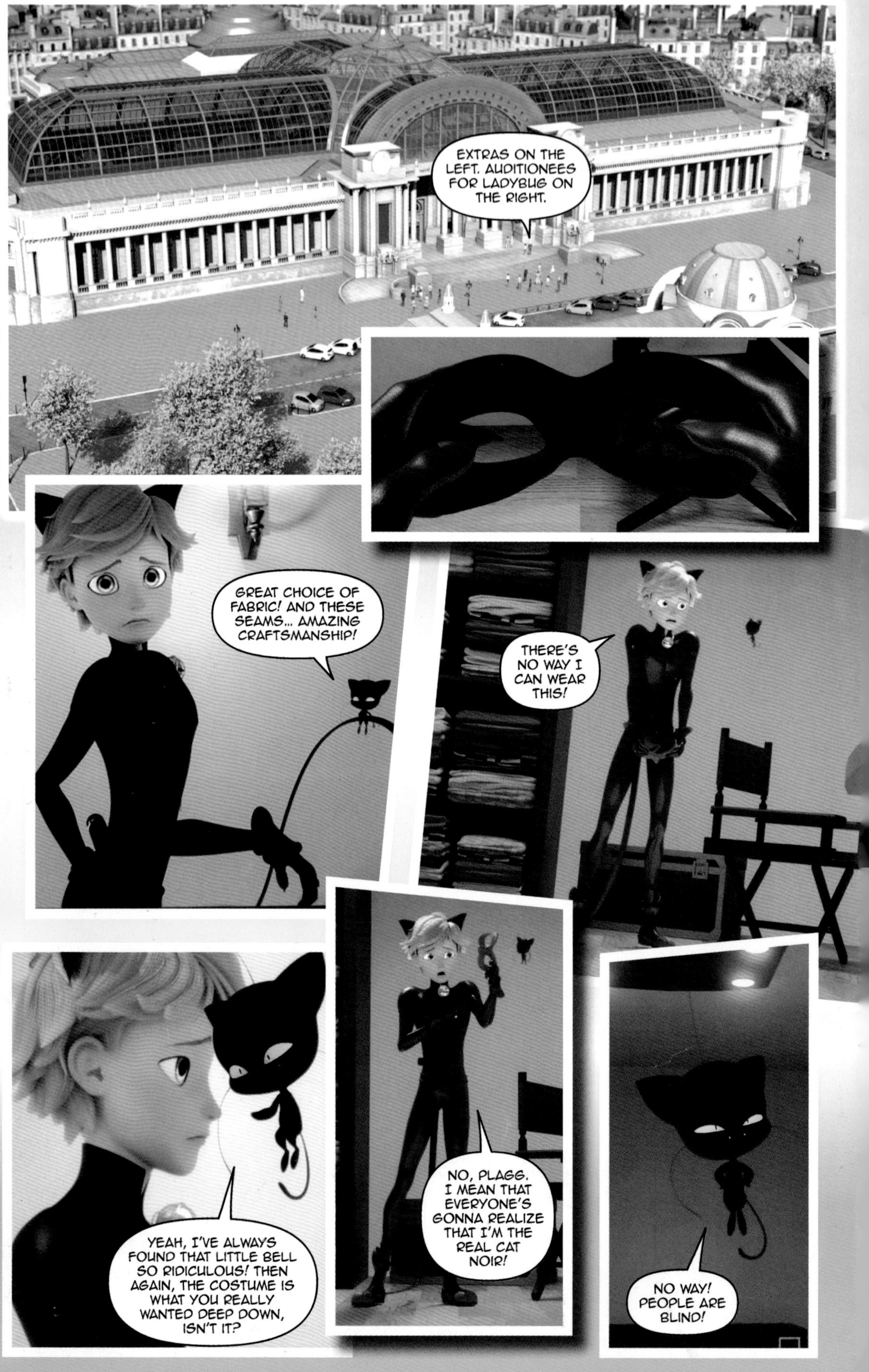
EXTRAS ON THE LEFT. AUDITIONEES FOR LADYBUG ON THE RIGHT.
GREAT CHOICE OF FABRIC! AND THESE SEAMS... AMAZING CRAFTSMANSHIP!
THERE'S NO WAY I CAN WEAR THIS!
YEAH, I'VE ALWAYS FOUND THAT LITTLE BELL SO RIDICULOUS! THEN AGAIN, THE COSTUME IS WHAT YOU REALLY WANTED DEEP DOWN, ISN'T IT?
NO, PLAGG. I MEAN THAT EVERYONE'S GONNA REALIZE THAT I'M THE REAL CAT NOIR!
NO WAY! PEOPLE ARE BLIND!

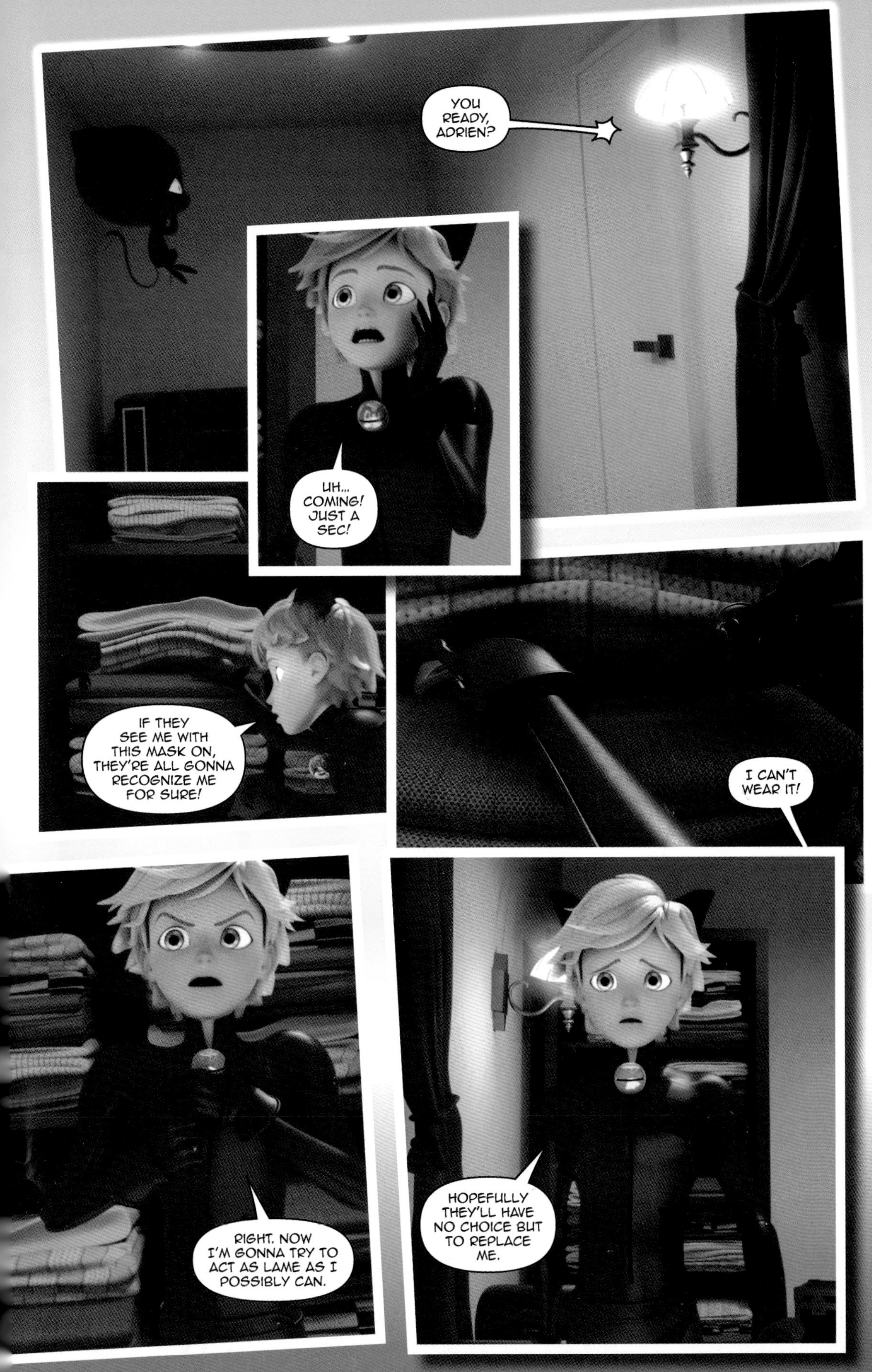
YOU READY, ADRIEN?
UH... COMING! JUST A SEC!
IF THEY SEE ME WITH THIS MASK ON, THEY'RE ALL GONNA RECOGNIZE ME FOR SURE!
I CAN'T WEAR IT!
RIGHT. NOW I'M GONNA TRY TO ACT AS LAME AS I POSSIBLY CAN.
HOPEFULLY THEY'LL HAVE NO CHOICE BUT TO REPLACE ME.

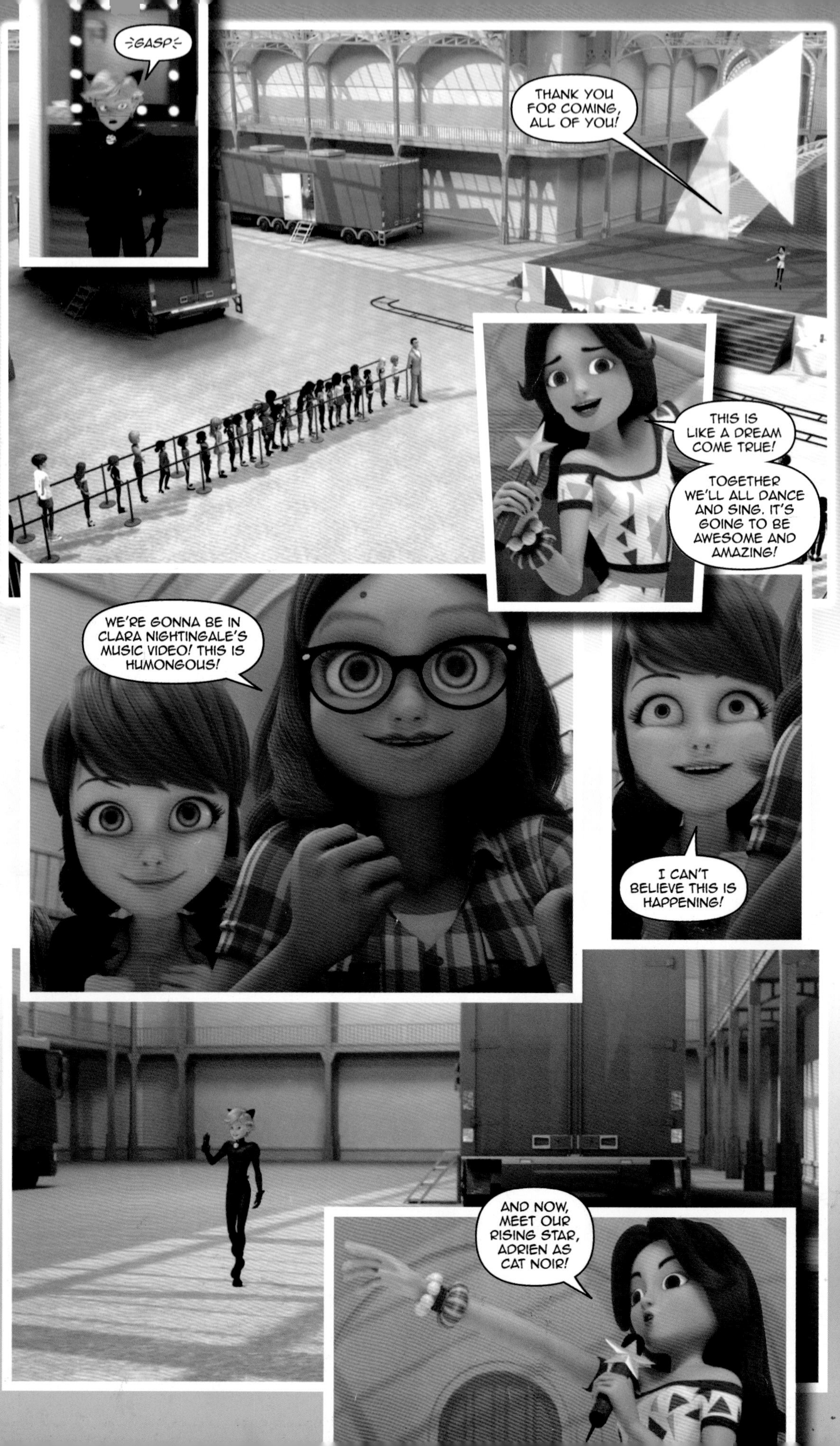
GASP
THANK YOU FOR COMING, ALL OF YOU!
THIS IS LIKE A DREAM COME TRUE!
TOGETHER WE'LL ALL DANCE AND SING. IT'S GOING TO BE AWESOME AND AMAZING!
WE'RE GONNA BE IN CLARA NIGHTINGALE'S MUSIC VIDEO! THIS IS HUMONGOUS!
I CAN'T BELIEVE THIS IS HAPPENING!
AND NOW, MEET OUR RISING STAR, ADRIEN AS CAT NOIR!

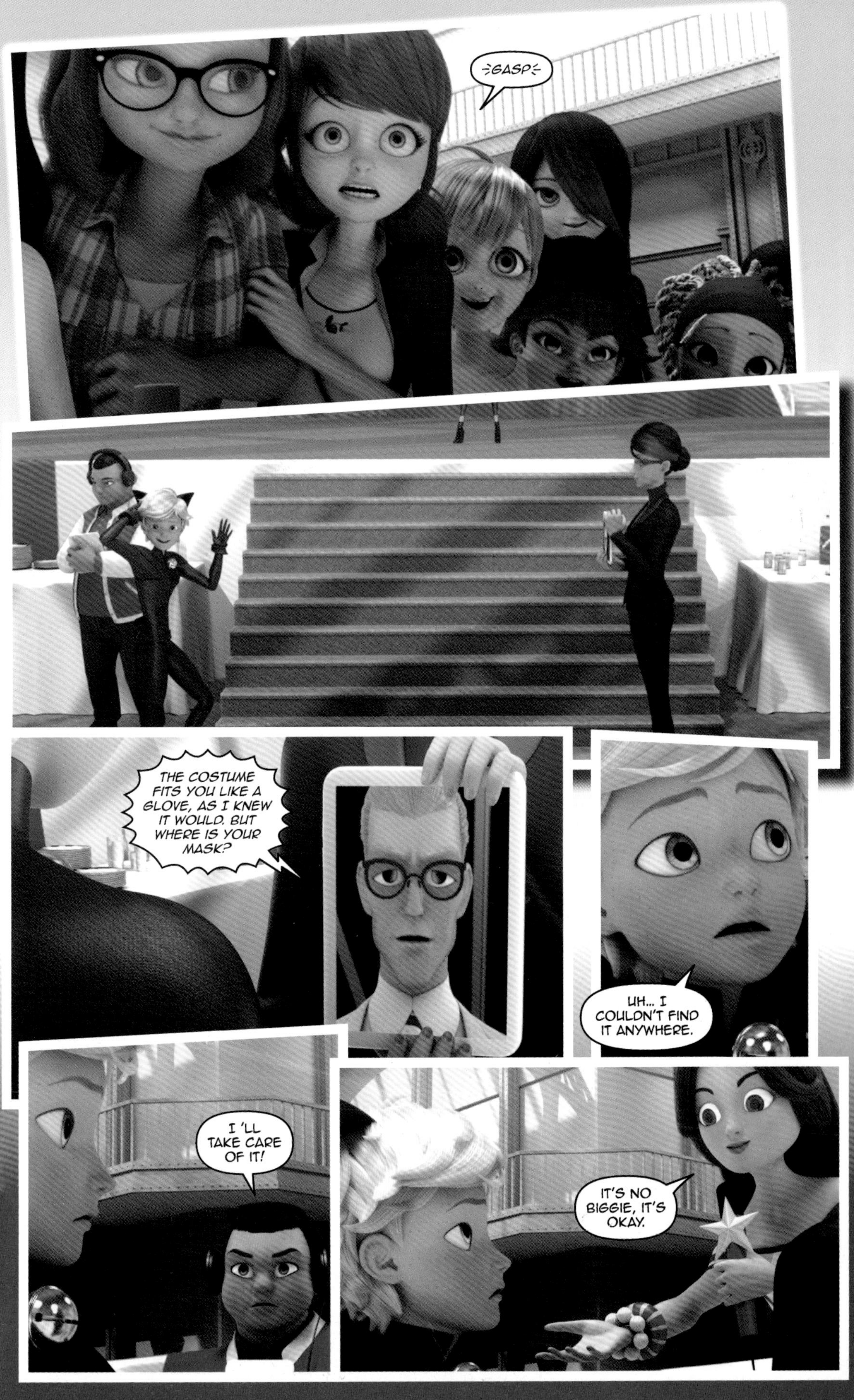
GASP
THE COSTUME FITS YOU LIKE A GLOVE, AS I KNEW IT WOULD. BUT WHERE IS YOUR MASK?
UH... I COULDN'T FIND IT ANYWHERE.
I 'LL TAKE CARE OF IT!
IT'S NO BIGGIE, IT'S OKAY.

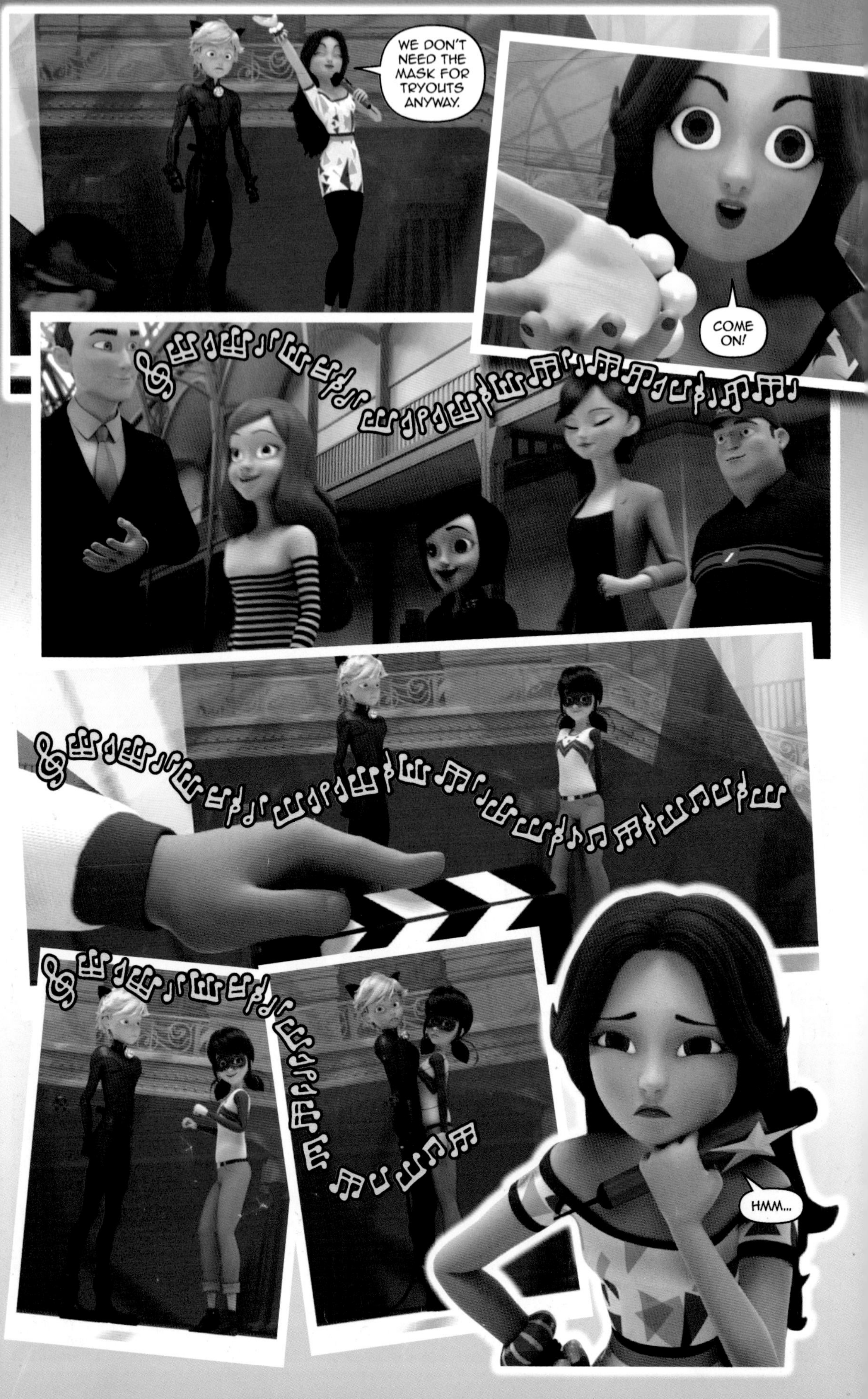
WE DON'T NEED THE MASK FOR TRYOUTS ANYWAY.
COME ON!
HMM...

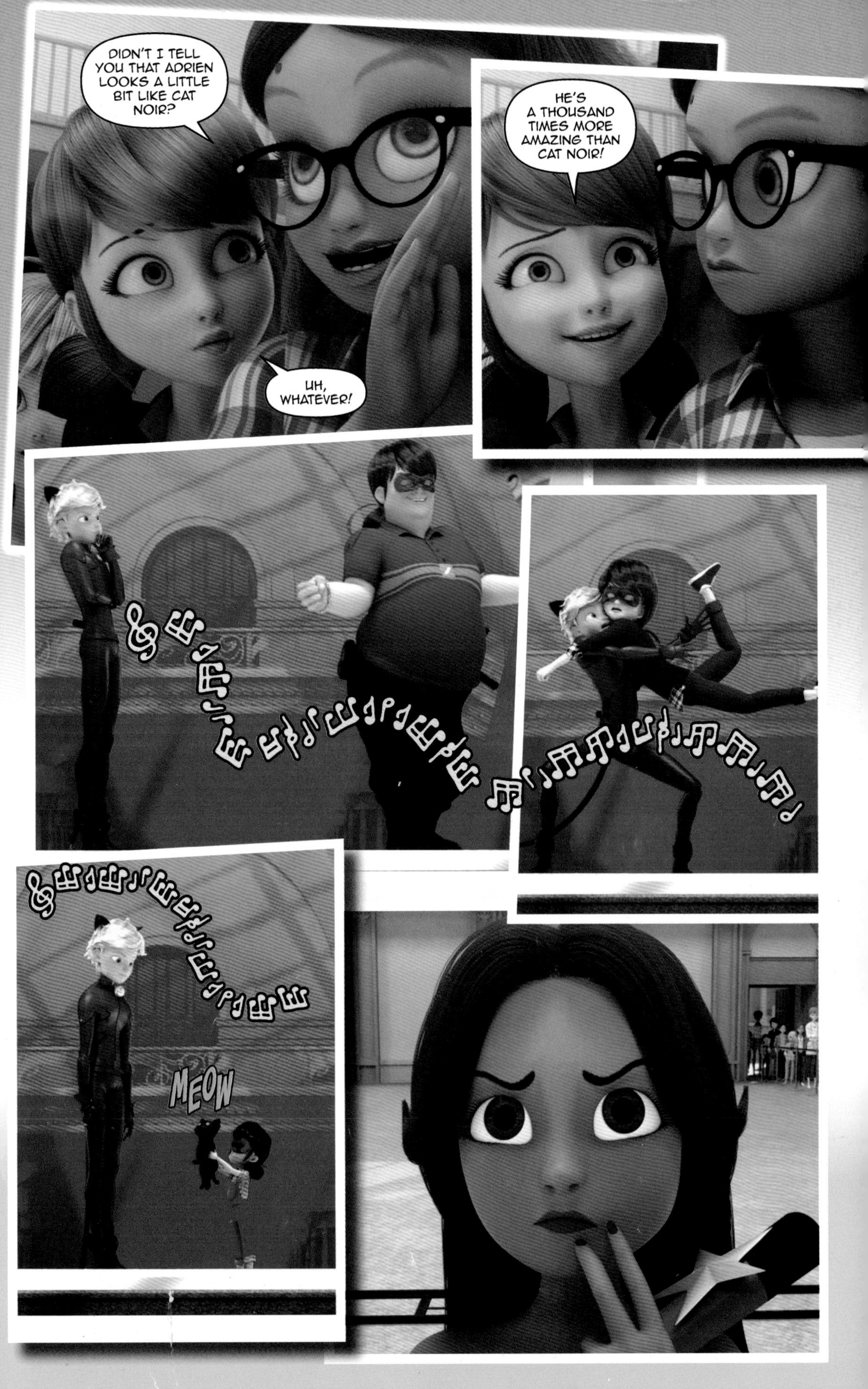
DIDN'T I TELL YOU THAT ADRIEN LOOKS A LITTLE BIT LIKE CAT NOIR?
UH, WHATEVER!
HE'S A THOUSAND TIMES MORE AMAZING THAN CAT NOIR!
MEOW

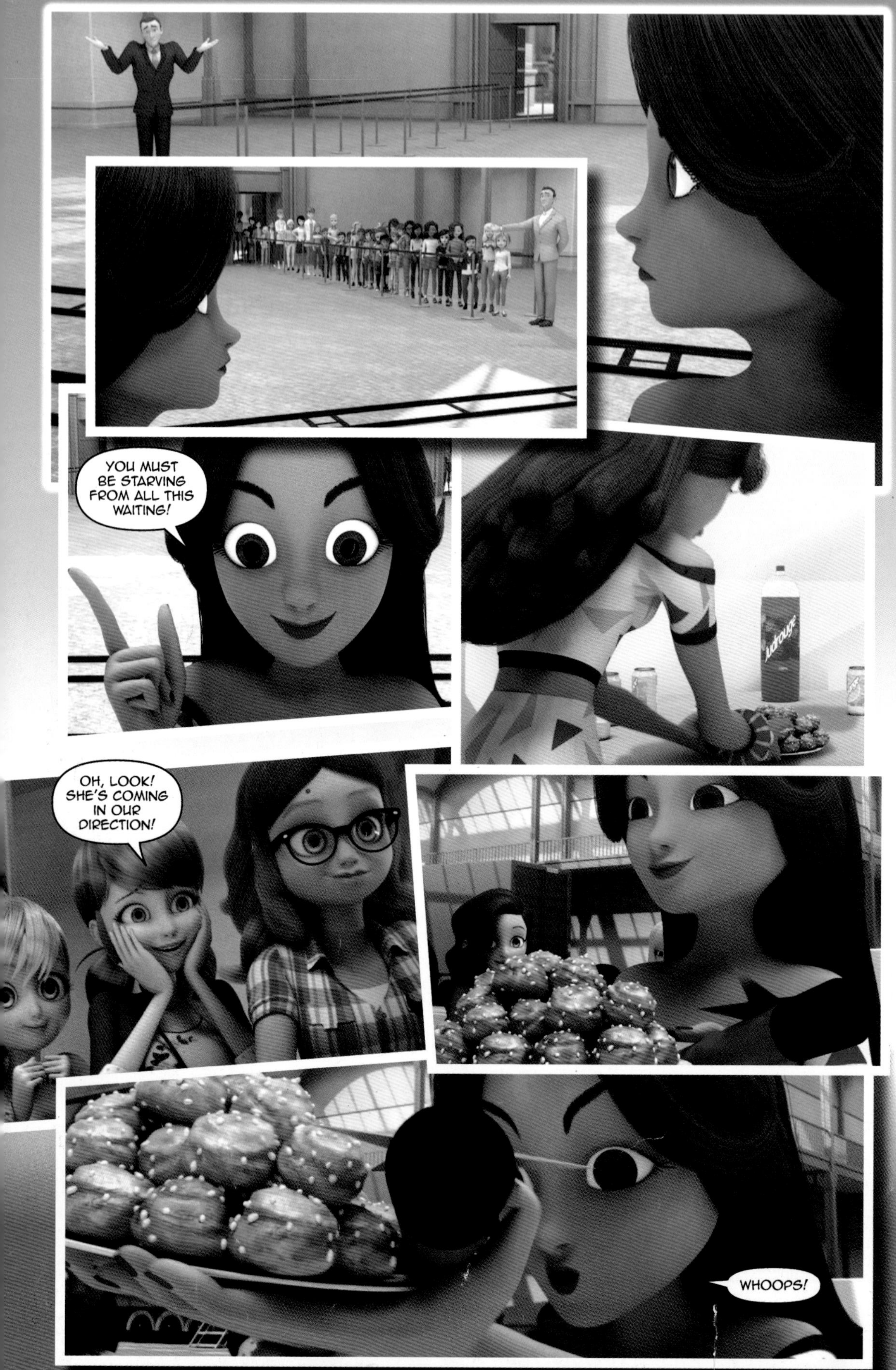
YOU MUST BE STARVING FROM ALL THIS WAITING!
OH, LOOK! SHE'S COMING IN OUR DIRECTION!
WHOOPS!

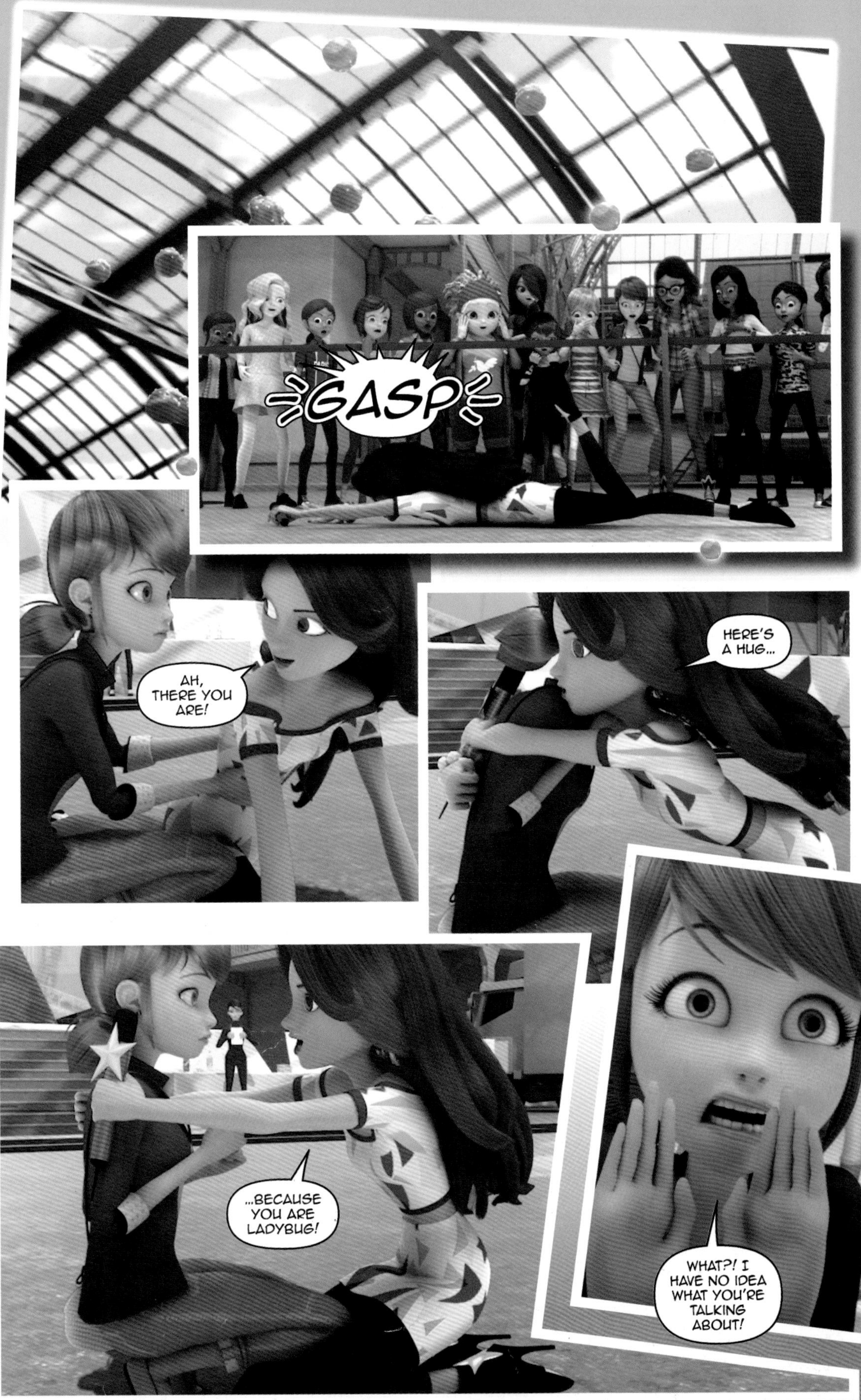
GASP
AH, THERE YOU ARE!
HERE'S A HUG...
...BECAUSE YOU ARE LADYBUG!
WHAT?! I HAVE NO IDEA WHAT YOU'RE TALKING ABOUT!

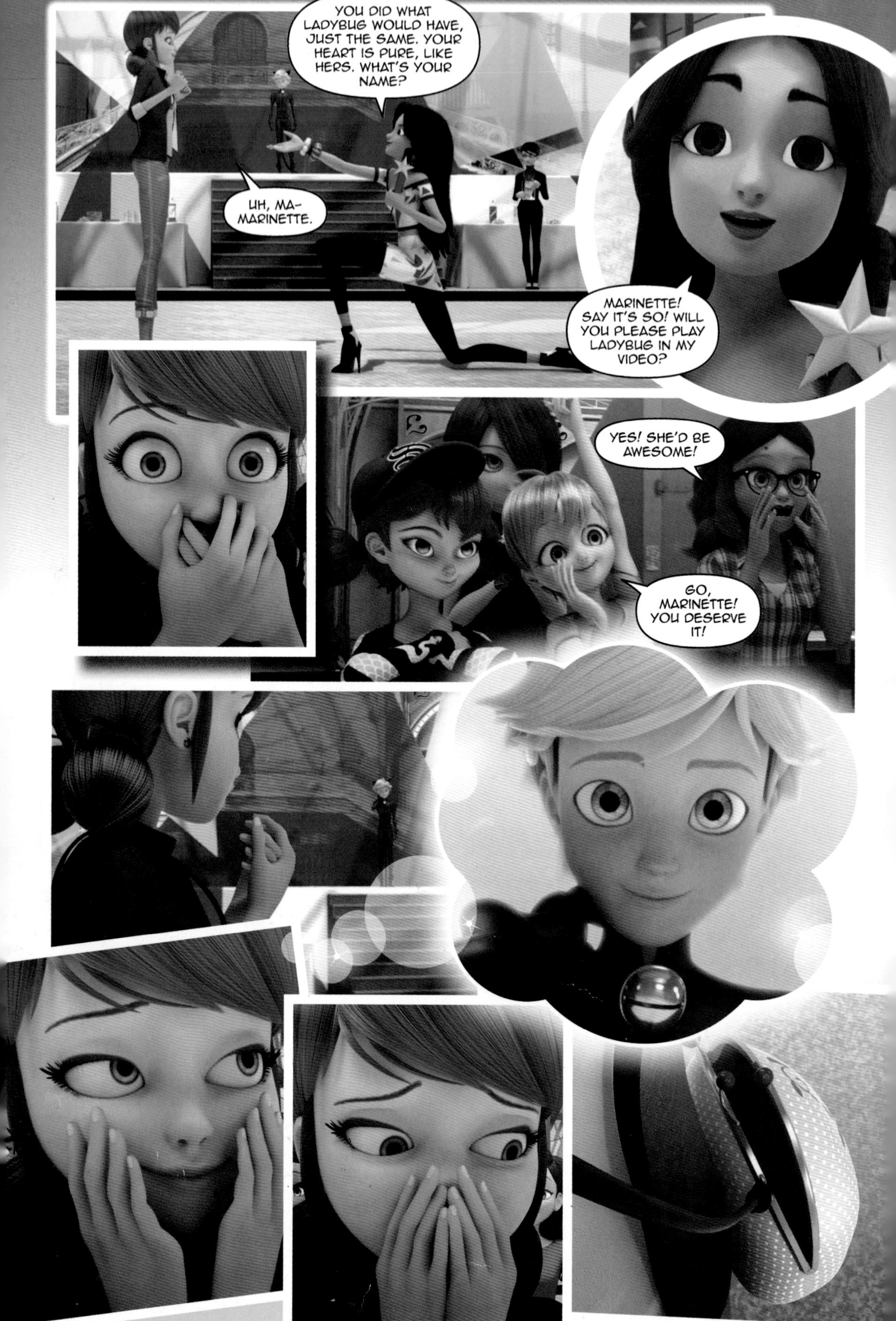
YOU DID WHAT LADYBUG WOULD HAVE, JUST THE SAME. YOUR HEART IS PURE, LIKE HERS. WHAT'S YOUR NAME?
UH, MA-MARINETTE.
MARINETTE! SAY IT'S SO! WILL YOU PLEASE PLAY LADYBUG IN MY VIDEO?
YES! SHE'D BE AWESOME!
GO, MARINETTE! YOU DESERVE IT!

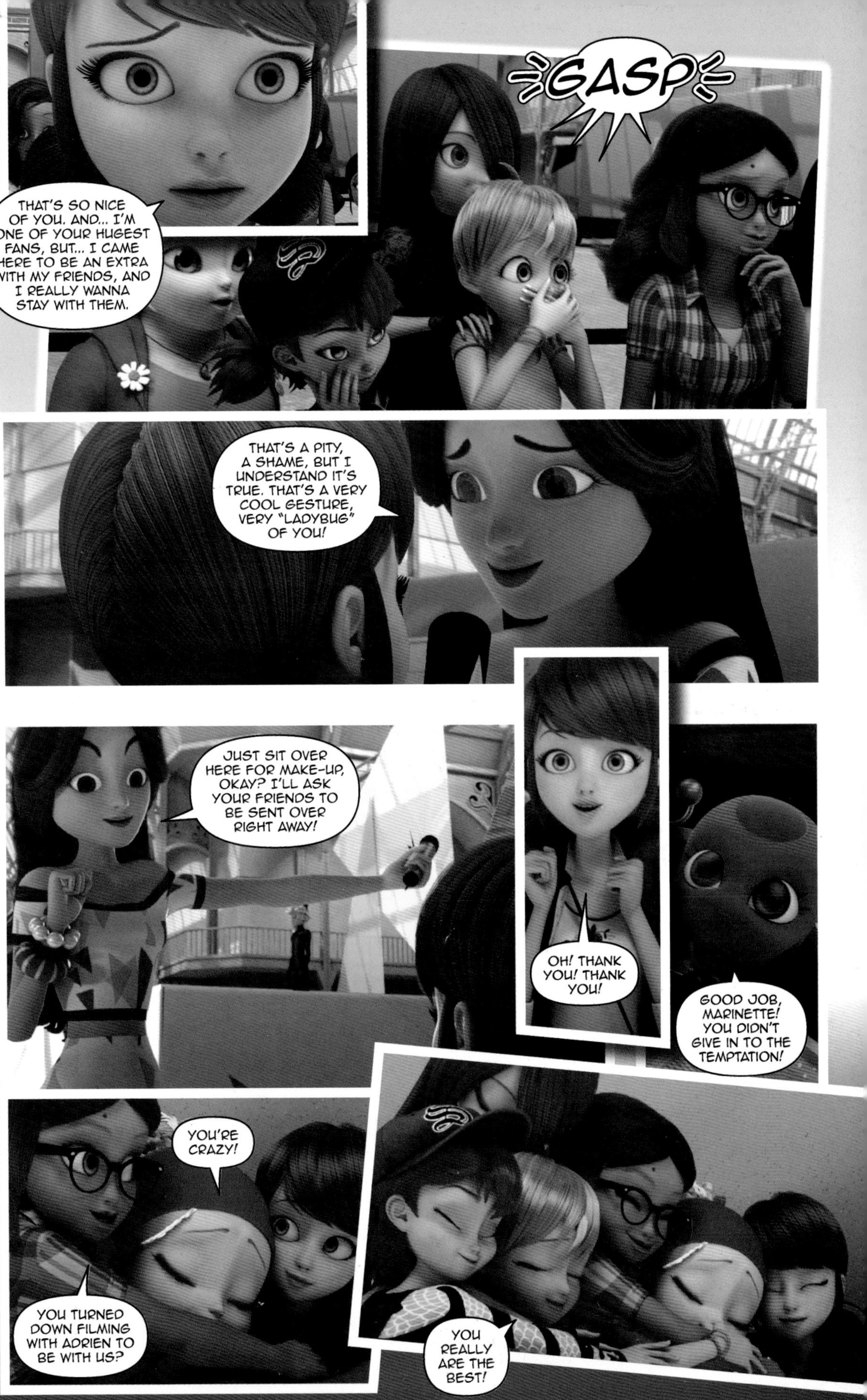
THAT'S SO NICE OF YOU. AND... I'M ONE OF YOUR HUGEST FANS, BUT... I CAME HERE TO BE AN EXTRA WITH MY FRIENDS, AND I REALLY WANNA STAY WITH THEM.
GASP
THAT'S A PITY, A SHAME, BUT I UNDERSTAND IT'S TRUE. THAT'S A VERY COOL GESTURE, VERY "LADYBUG" OF YOU!
JUST SIT OVER HERE FOR MAKE-UP, OKAY? I'LL ASK YOUR FRIENDS TO BE SENT OVER RIGHT AWAY!
OH! THANK YOU! THANK YOU!
GOOD JOB, MARINETTE! YOU DIDN'T GIVE IN TO THE TEMPTATION!
YOU'RE CRAZY!
YOU TURNED DOWN FILMING WITH ADRIEN TO BE WITH US?
YOU REALLY ARE THE BEST!

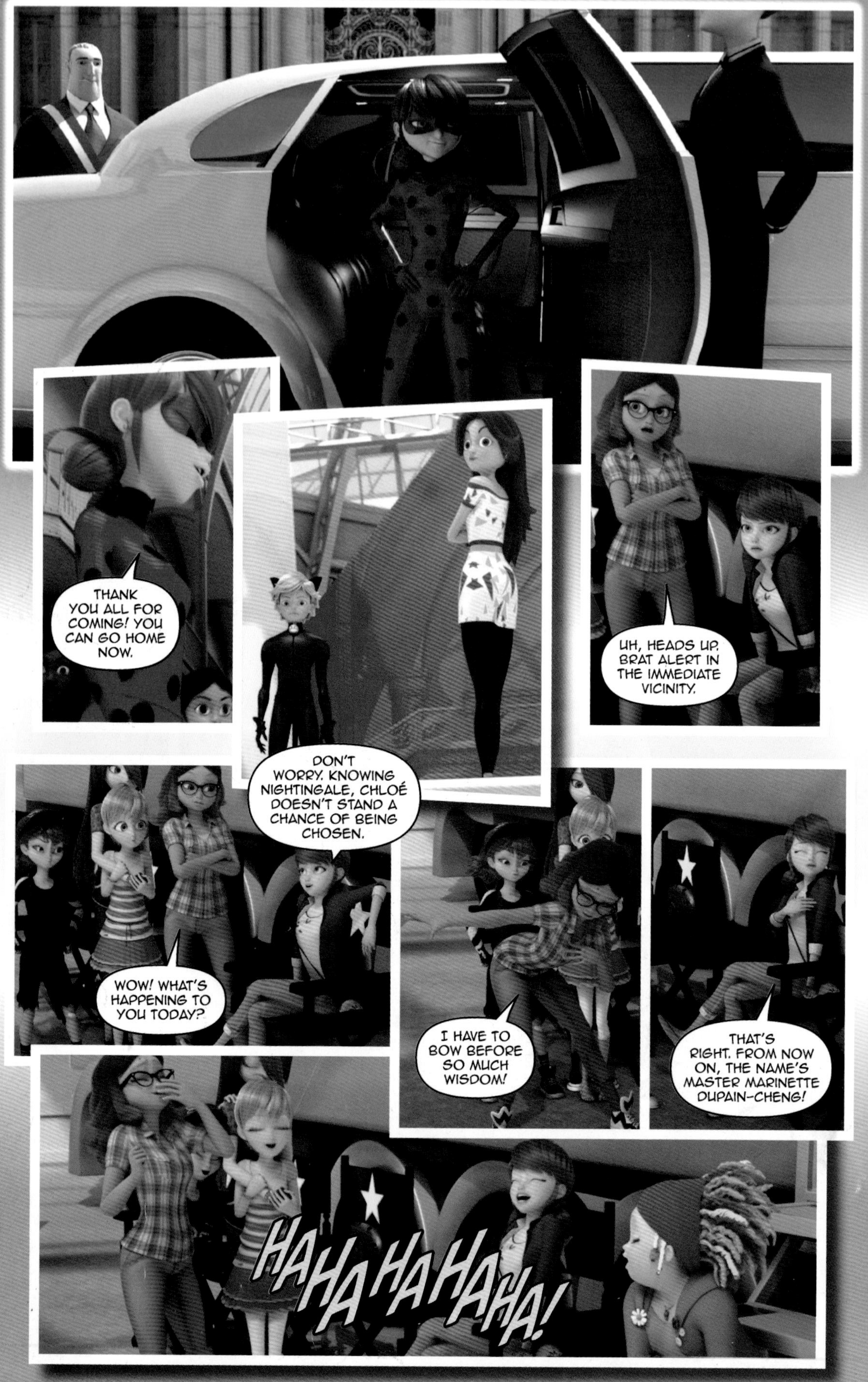
THANK YOU ALL FOR COMING! YOU CAN GO HOME NOW.
UH, HEADS UP. BRAT ALERT IN THE IMMEDIATE VICINITY.
DON'T WORRY. KNOWING NIGHTINGALE, CHLOÉ DOESN'T STAND A CHANCE OF BEING CHOSEN.
WOW! WHAT'S HAPPENING TO YOU TODAY?
I HAVE TO BOW BEFORE SO MUCH WISDOM!
THAT'S RIGHT. FROM NOW ON, THE NAME'S MASTER MARINETTE DUPAIN-CHENG!
HAHAHAHAHAHAHA!

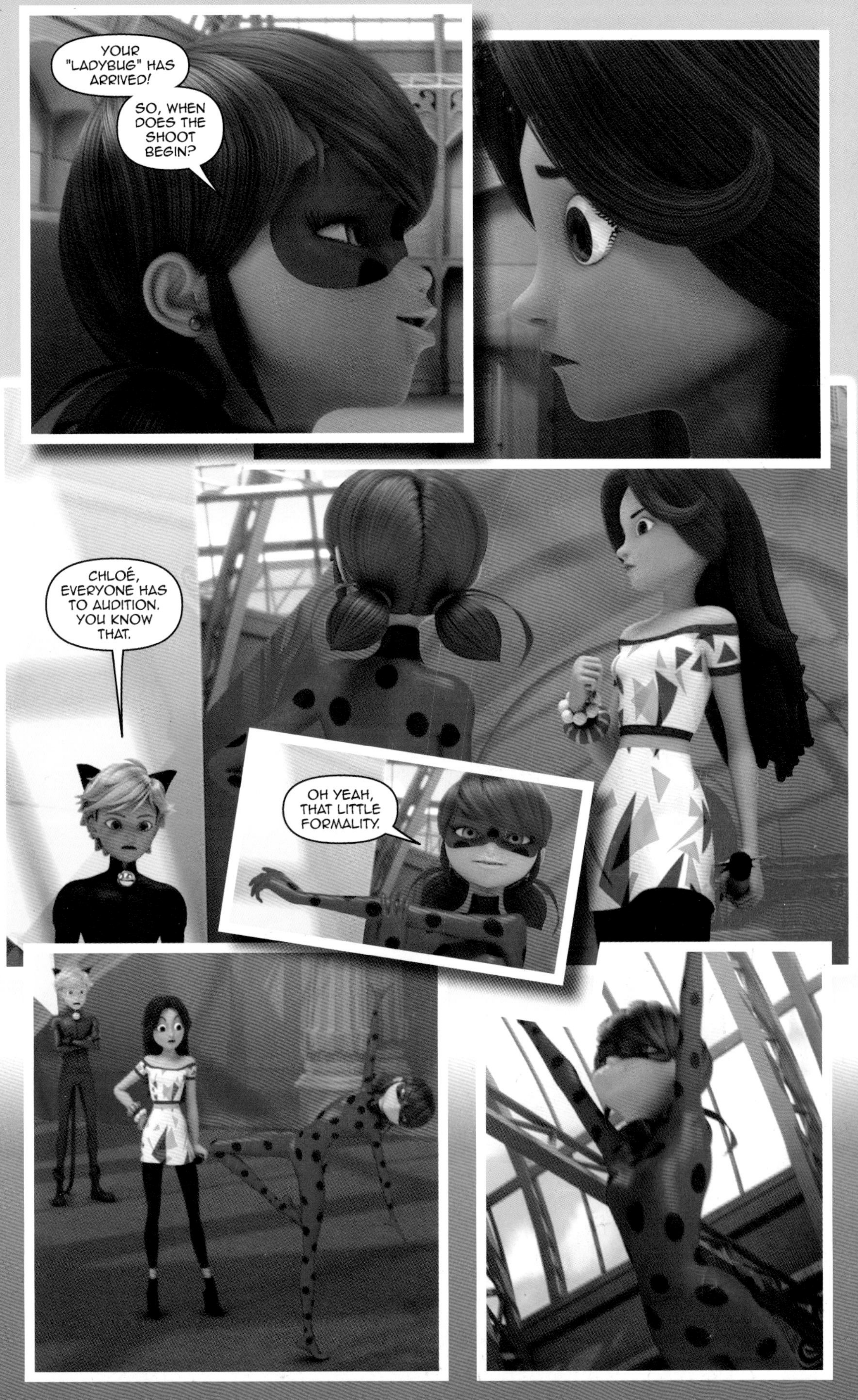
YOUR "LADYBUG" HAS ARRIVED!
SO, WHEN DOES THE SHOOT BEGIN?
CHLOÉ, EVERYONE HAS TO AUDITION. YOU KNOW THAT.
OH YEAH, THAT LITTLE FORMALITY.

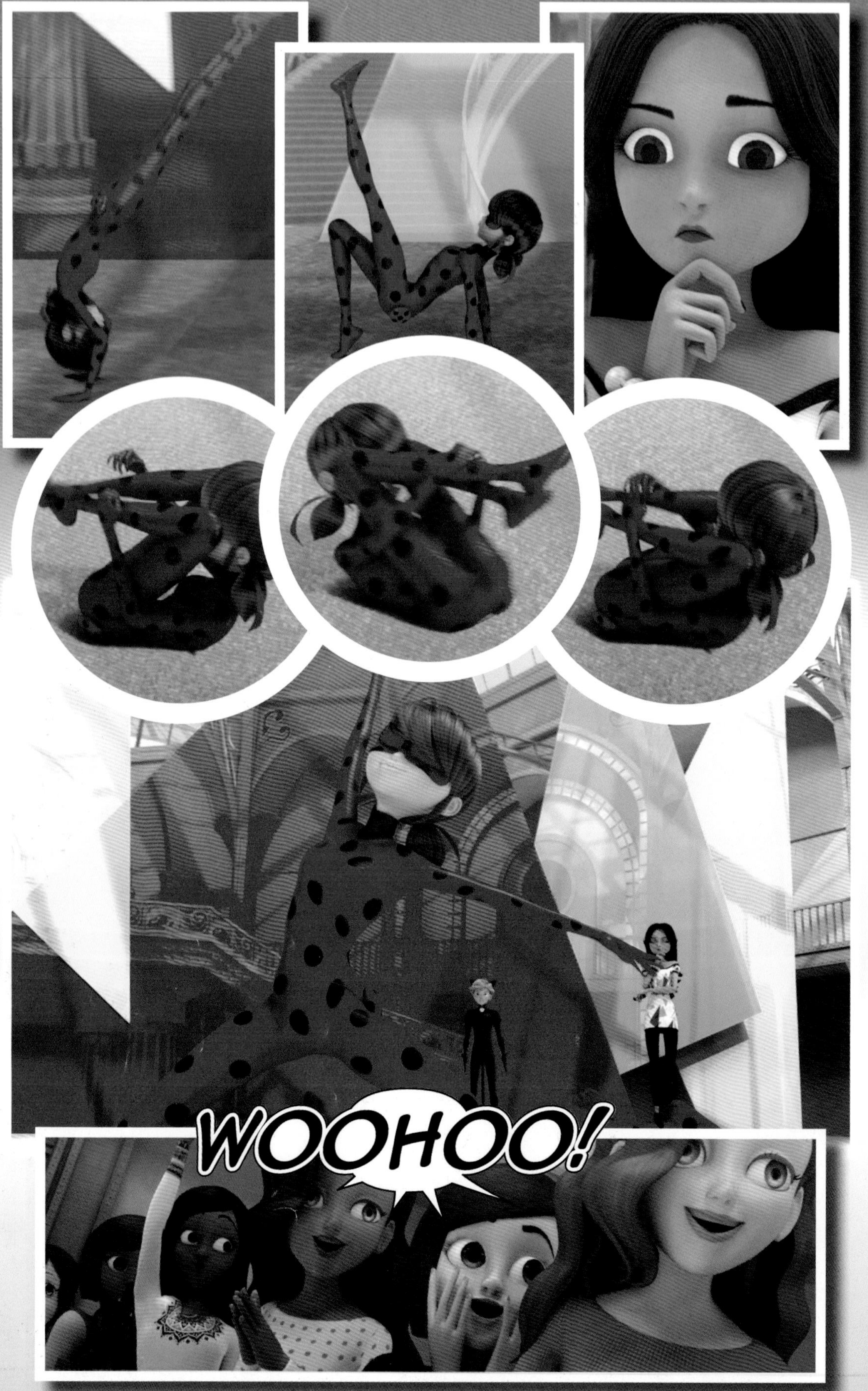
WOOHOO!

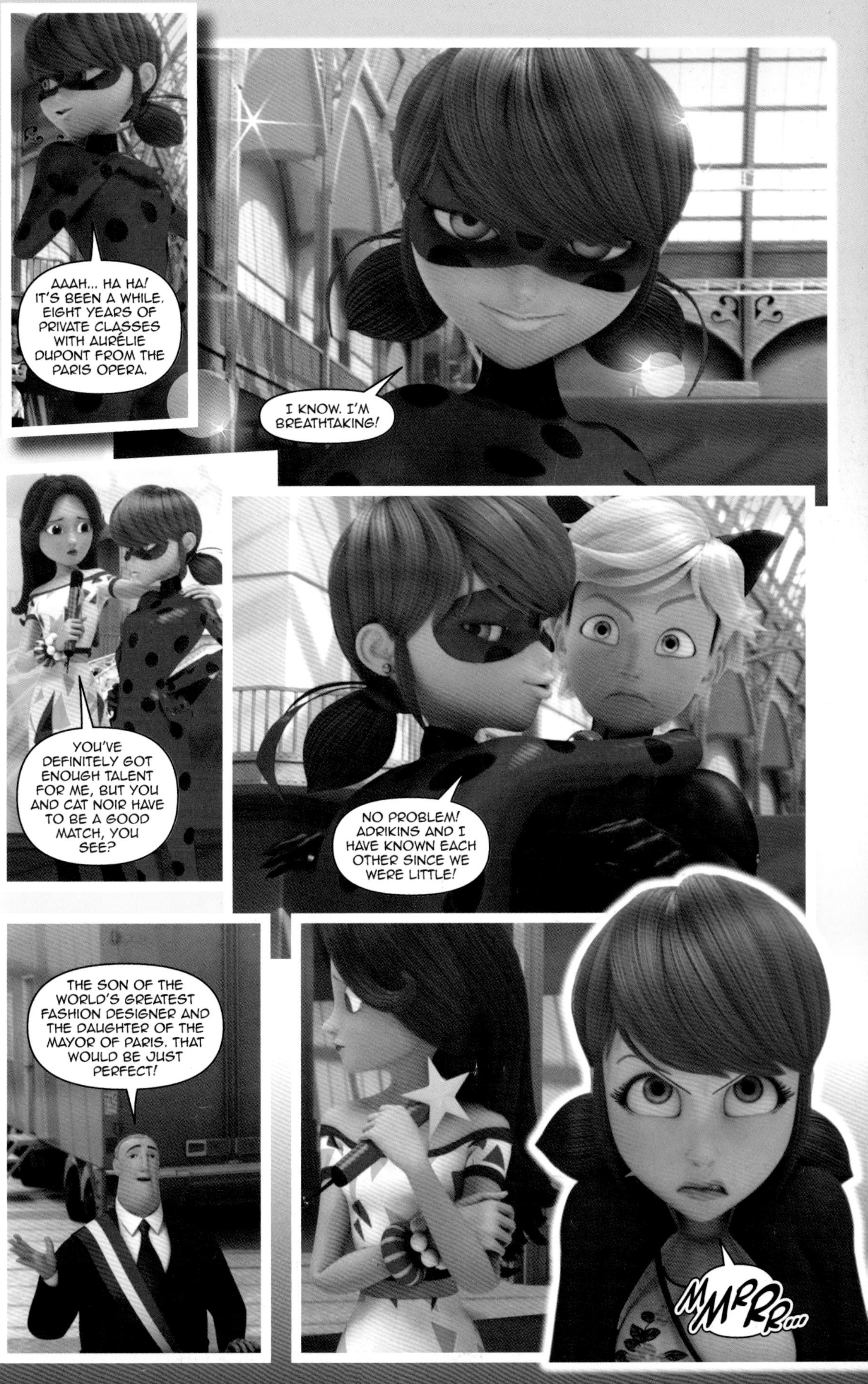
AAAH... HA HA! IT'S BEEN A WHILE. EIGHT YEARS OF PRIVATE CLASSES WITH AURÉLIE DUPONT FROM THE PARIS OPERA.
I KNOW. I'M BREATHTAKING!
YOU'VE DEFINITELY GOT ENOUGH TALENT FOR ME, BUT YOU AND CAT NOIR HAVE TO BE A GOOD MATCH, YOU SEE?
NO PROBLEM! ADRIKINS AND I HAVE KNOWN EACH OTHER SINCE WE WERE LITTLE!
THE SON OF THE WORLD'S GREATEST FASHION DESIGNER AND THE DAUGHTER OF THE MAYOR OF PARIS. THAT WOULD BE JUST PERFECT!
MMRRR...

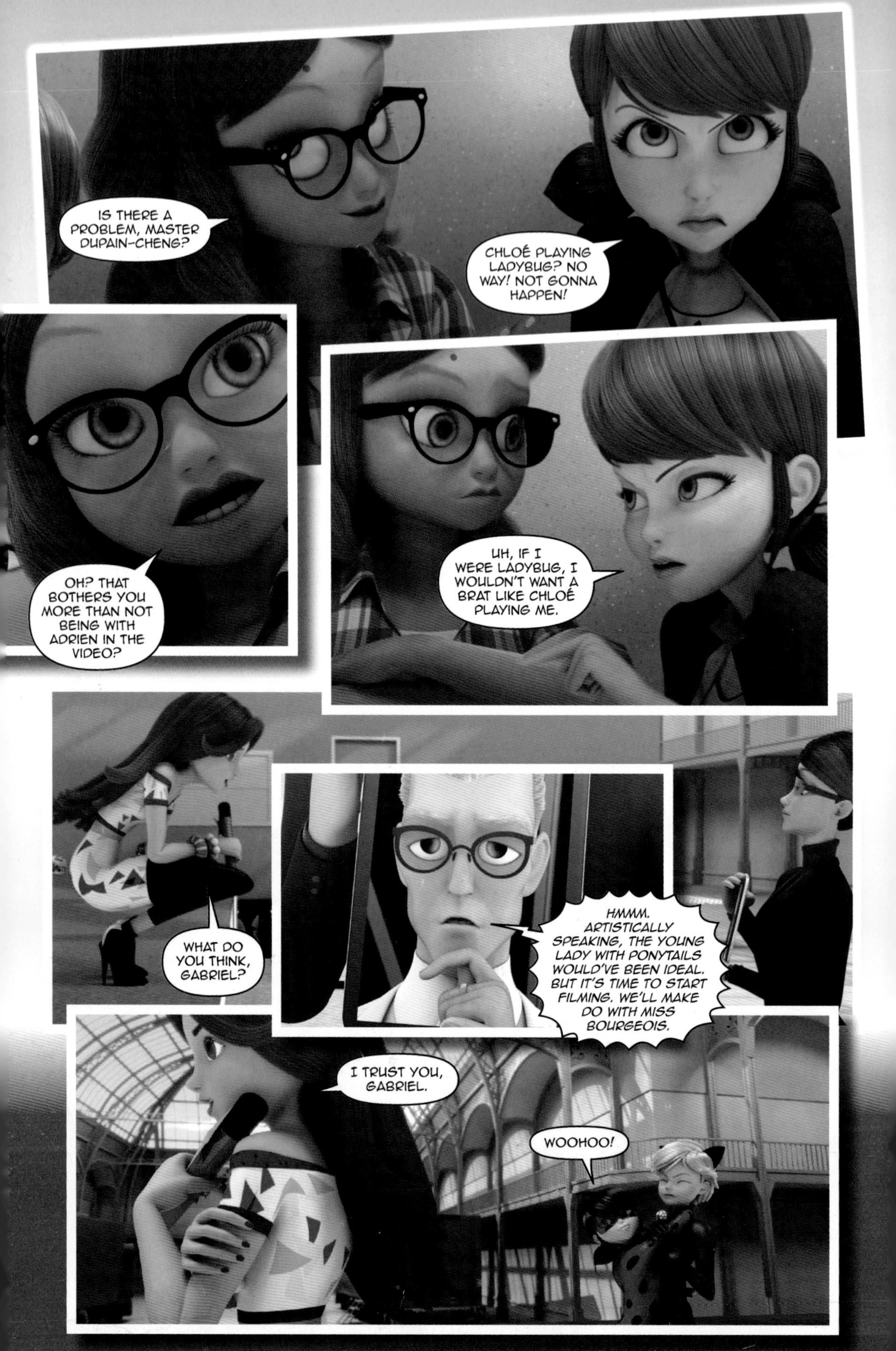
IS THERE A PROBLEM, MASTER DUPAIN-CHENG?
CHLOÉ PLAYING LADYBUG? NO WAY! NOT GONNA HAPPEN!
OH? THAT BOTHERS YOU MORE THAN NOT BEING WITH ADRIEN IN THE VIDEO?
UH, IF I WERE LADYBUG, I WOULDN'T WANT A BRAT LIKE CHLOÉ PLAYING ME.
WHAT DO YOU THINK, GABRIEL?
HMMM. ARTISTICALLY SPEAKING, THE YOUNG LADY WITH PONYTAILS WOULD'VE BEEN IDEAL. BUT IT'S TIME TO START FILMING. WE'LL MAKE DO WITH MISS BOURGEOIS.
I TRUST YOU, GABRIEL.
WOOHOO!

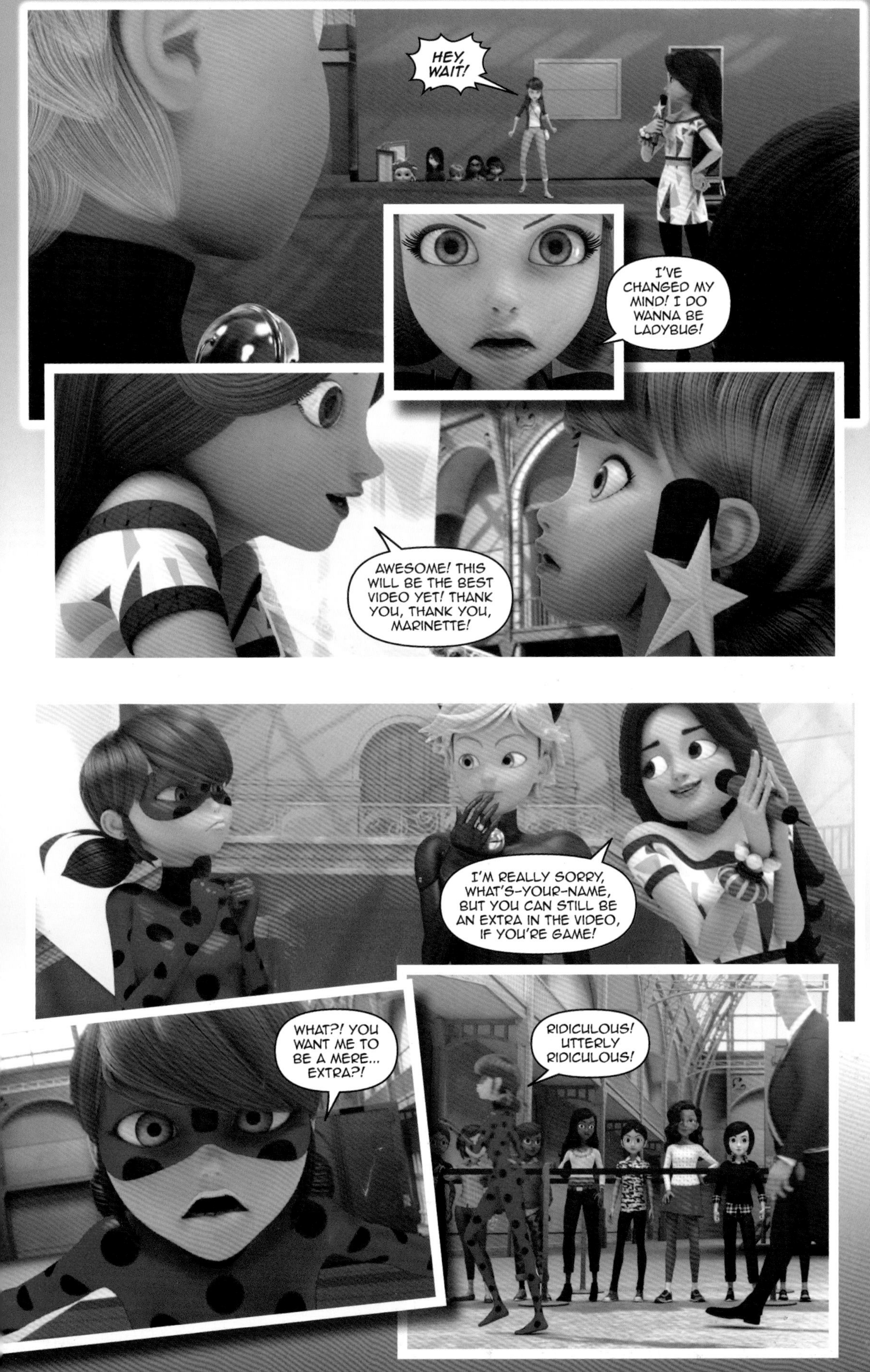
HEY, WAIT!
I'VE CHANGED MY MIND! I DO WANNA BE LADYBUG!
AWESOME! THIS WILL BE THE BEST VIDEO YET! THANK YOU, THANK YOU, MARINETTE!
I'M REALLY SORRY, WHAT'S-YOUR-NAME, BUT YOU CAN STILL BE AN EXTRA IN THE VIDEO, IF YOU'RE GAME!
WHAT?! YOU WANT ME TO BE A MERE... EXTRA?!
RIDICULOUS! UTTERLY RIDICULOUS!

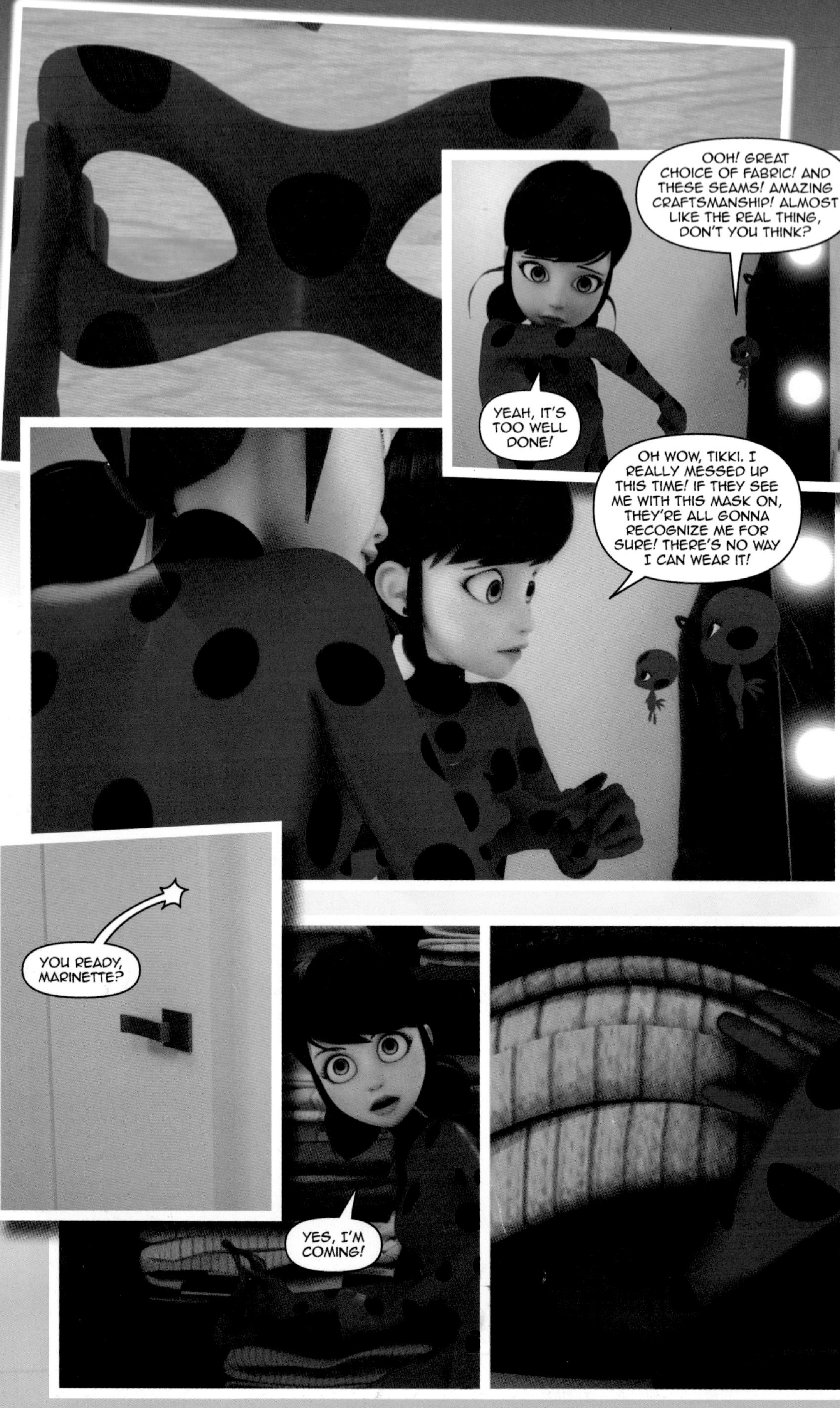
OOH! GREAT CHOICE OF FABRIC! AND THESE SEAMS! AMAZING CRAFTSMANSHIP! ALMOST LIKE THE REAL THING, DON'T YOU THINK?
YEAH, IT'S TOO WELL DONE!
OH WOW, TIKKI. I REALLY MESSED UP THIS TIME! IF THEY SEE ME WITH THIS MASK ON, THEY'RE ALL GONNA RECOGNIZE ME FOR SURE! THERE'S NO WAY I CAN WEAR IT!
YOU READY, MARINETTE?
YES, I'M COMING!

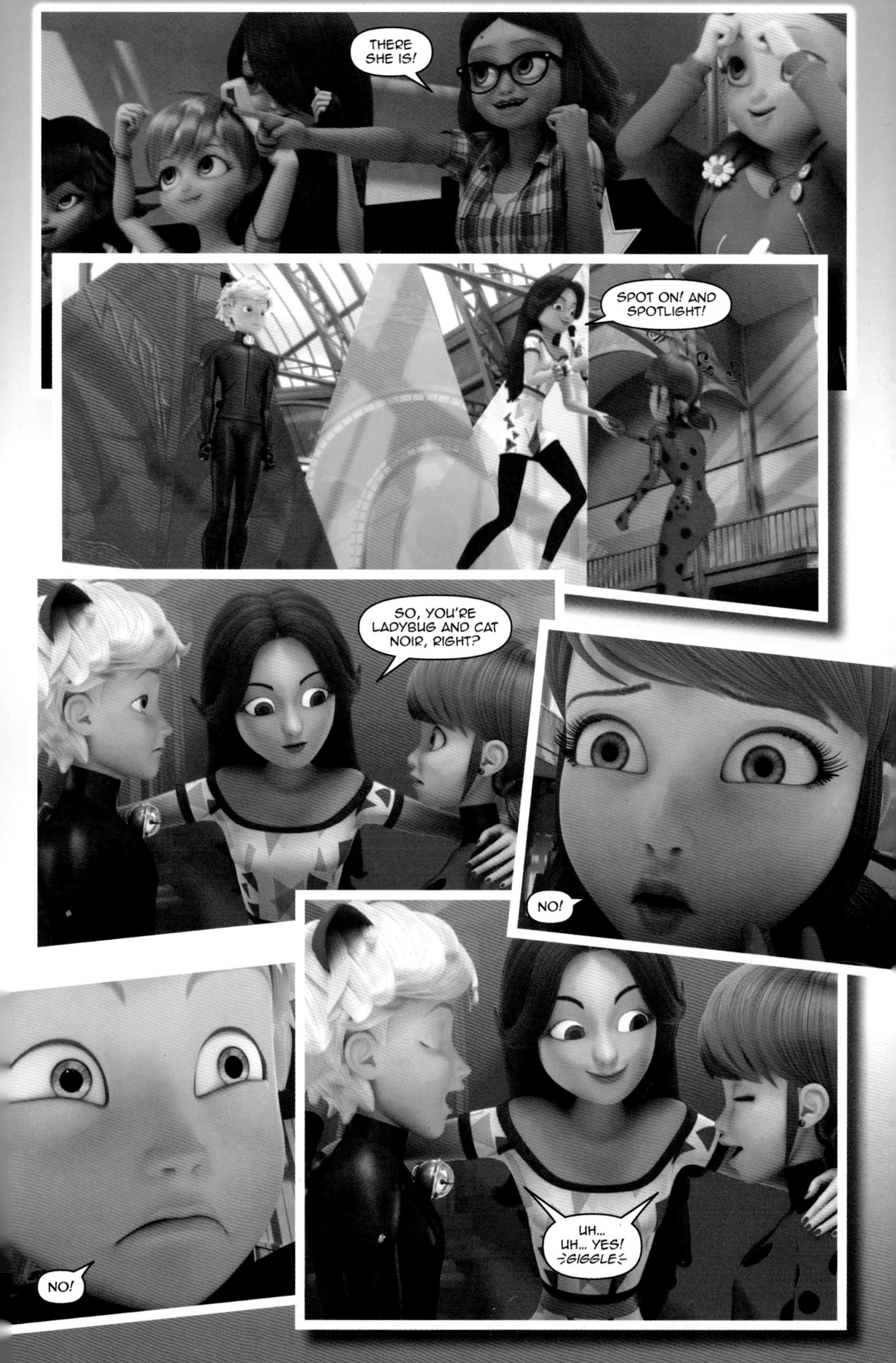
THERE SHE IS!
SPOT ON! AND SPOTLIGHT!
SO, YOU'RE LADYBUG AND CAT NOIR, RIGHT?
NO!
NO!
UH... UH... YES! GIGGLE

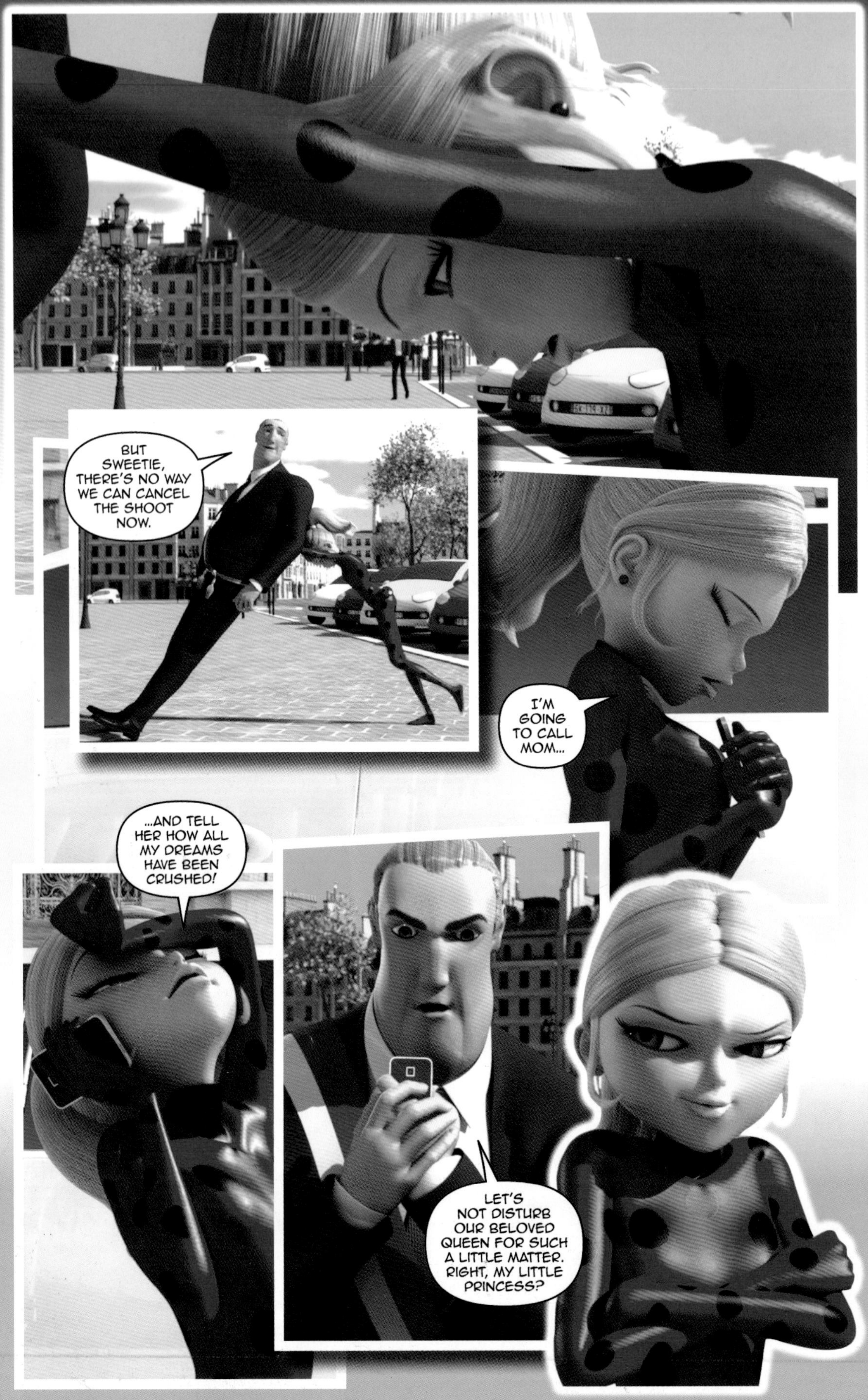
BUT SWEETIE, THERE'S NO WAY WE CAN CANCEL THE SHOOT NOW.
I'M GOING TO CALL MOM...
...AND TELL HER HOW ALL MY DREAMS HAVE BEEN CRUSHED!
LET'S NOT DISTURB OUR BELOVED QUEEN FOR SUCH A LITTLE MATTER. RIGHT, MY LITTLE PRINCESS?

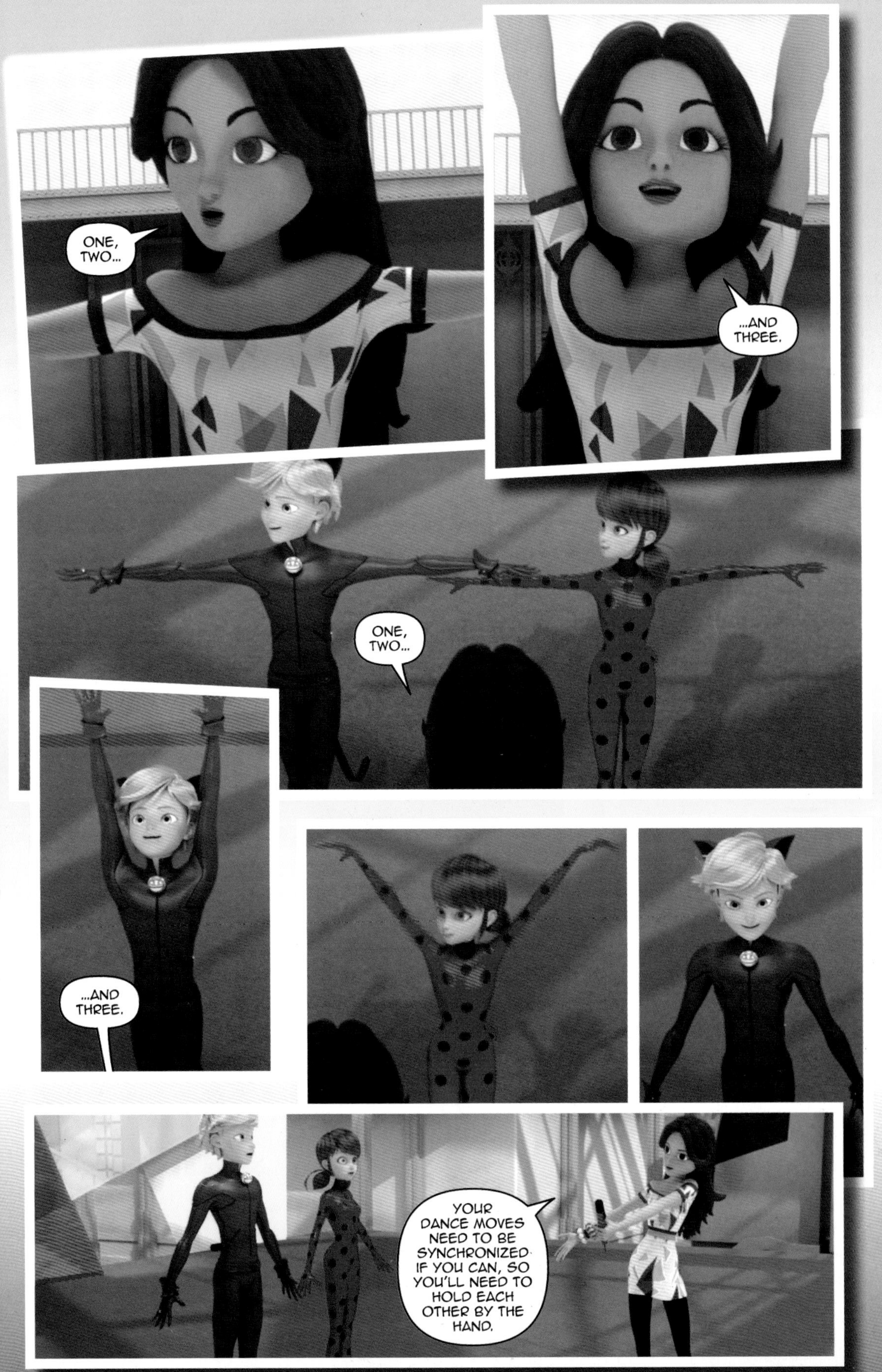

ONE, TWO...
...AND THREE.
ONE, TWO...
...AND THREE.
YOUR DANCE MOVES NEED TO BE SYNCHRONIZED IF YOU CAN, SO YOU'LL NEED TO HOLD EACH OTHER BY THE HAND.

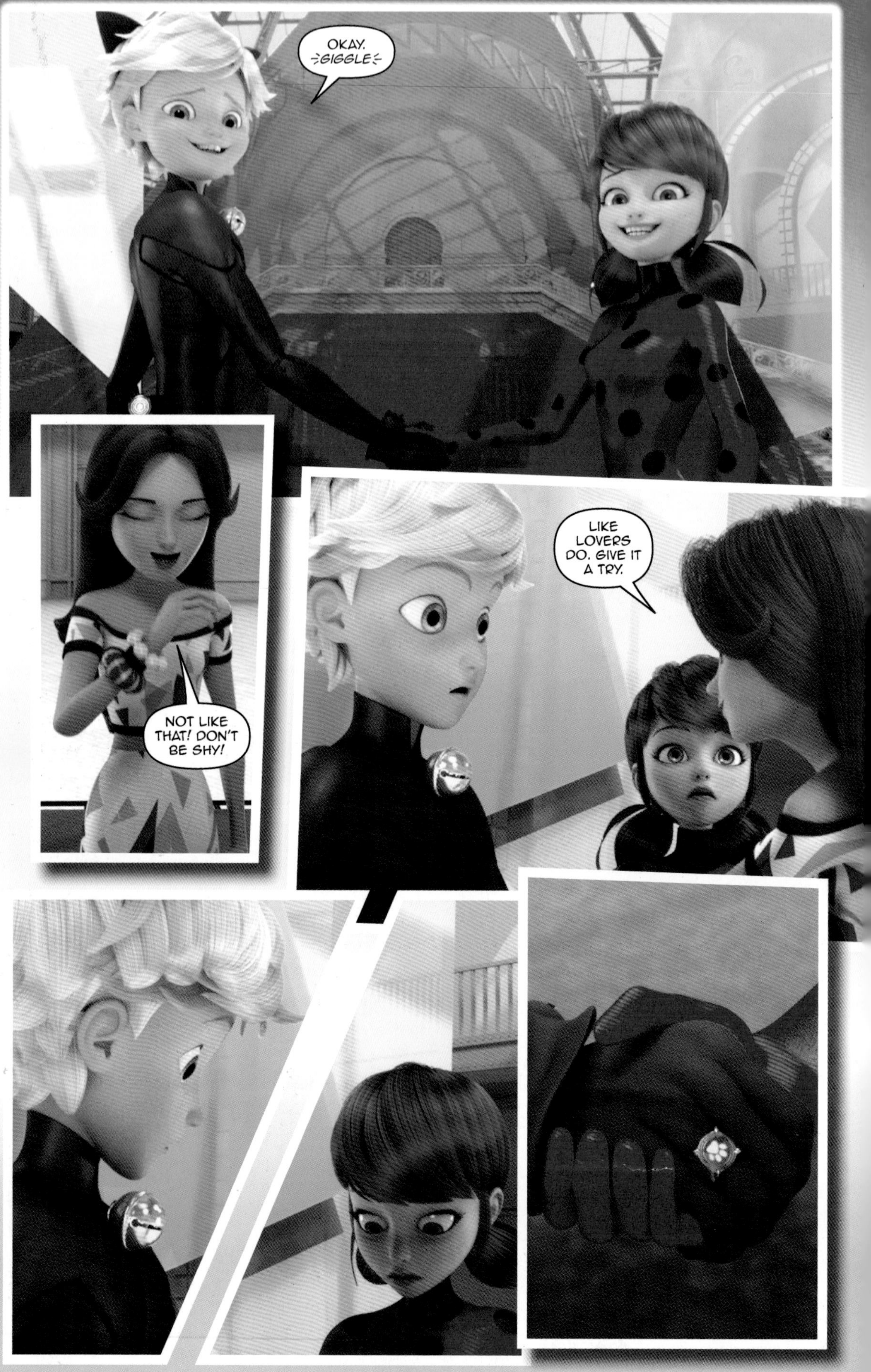
OKAY. -GIGGLE-
NOT LIKE THAT! DON'T BE SHY!
LIKE LOVERS DO. GIVE IT A TRY.

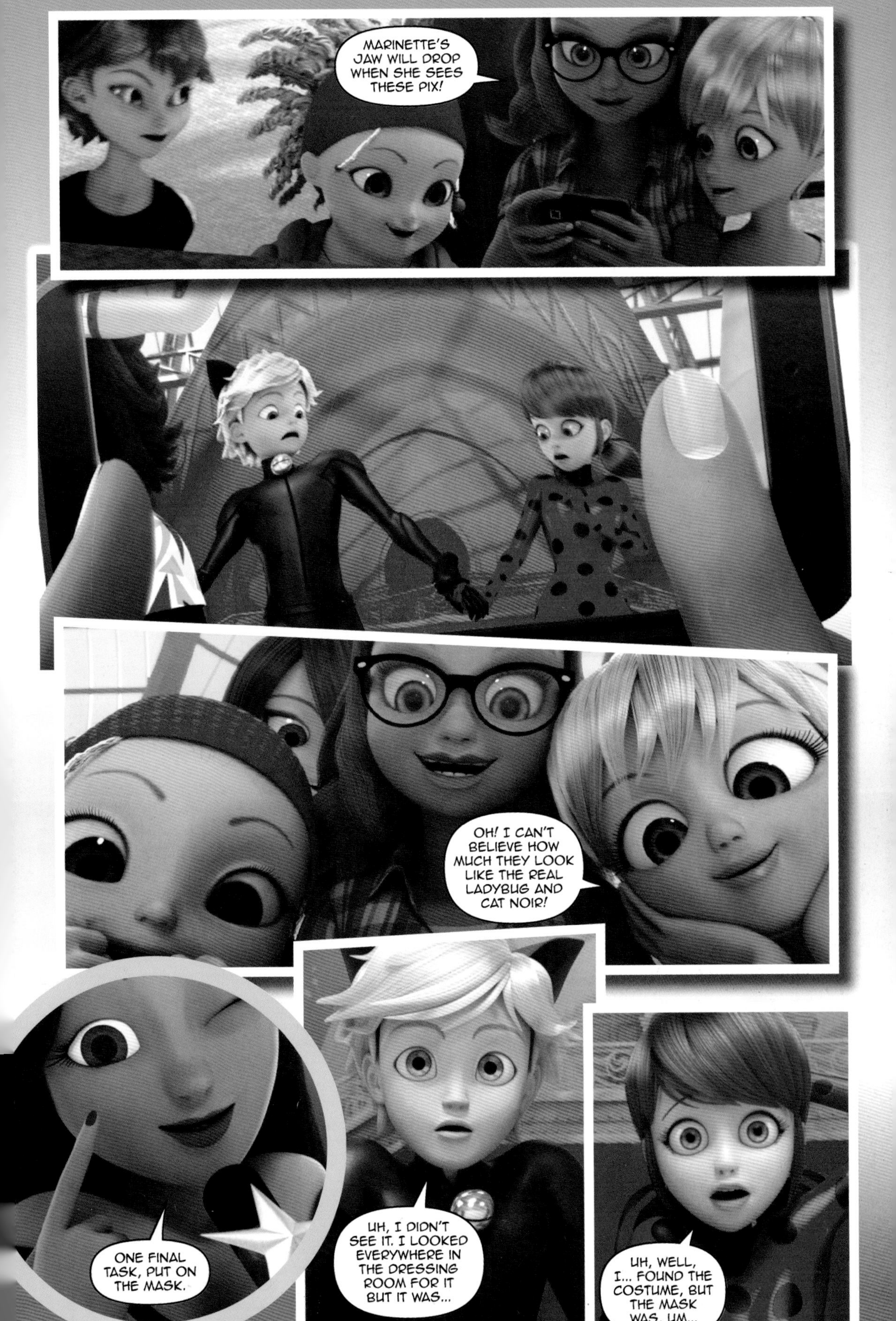
MARINETTE'S JAW WILL DROP WHEN SHE SEES THESE PIX!
OH! I CAN'T BELIEVE HOW MUCH THEY LOOK LIKE THE REAL LADYBUG AND CAT NOIR!
ONE FINAL TASK, PUT ON THE MASK.
UH, I DIDN'T SEE IT. I LOOKED EVERYWHERE IN THE DRESSING ROOM FOR IT BUT IT WAS...
UH, WELL, I... FOUND THE COSTUME, BUT THE MASK WAS, UM...

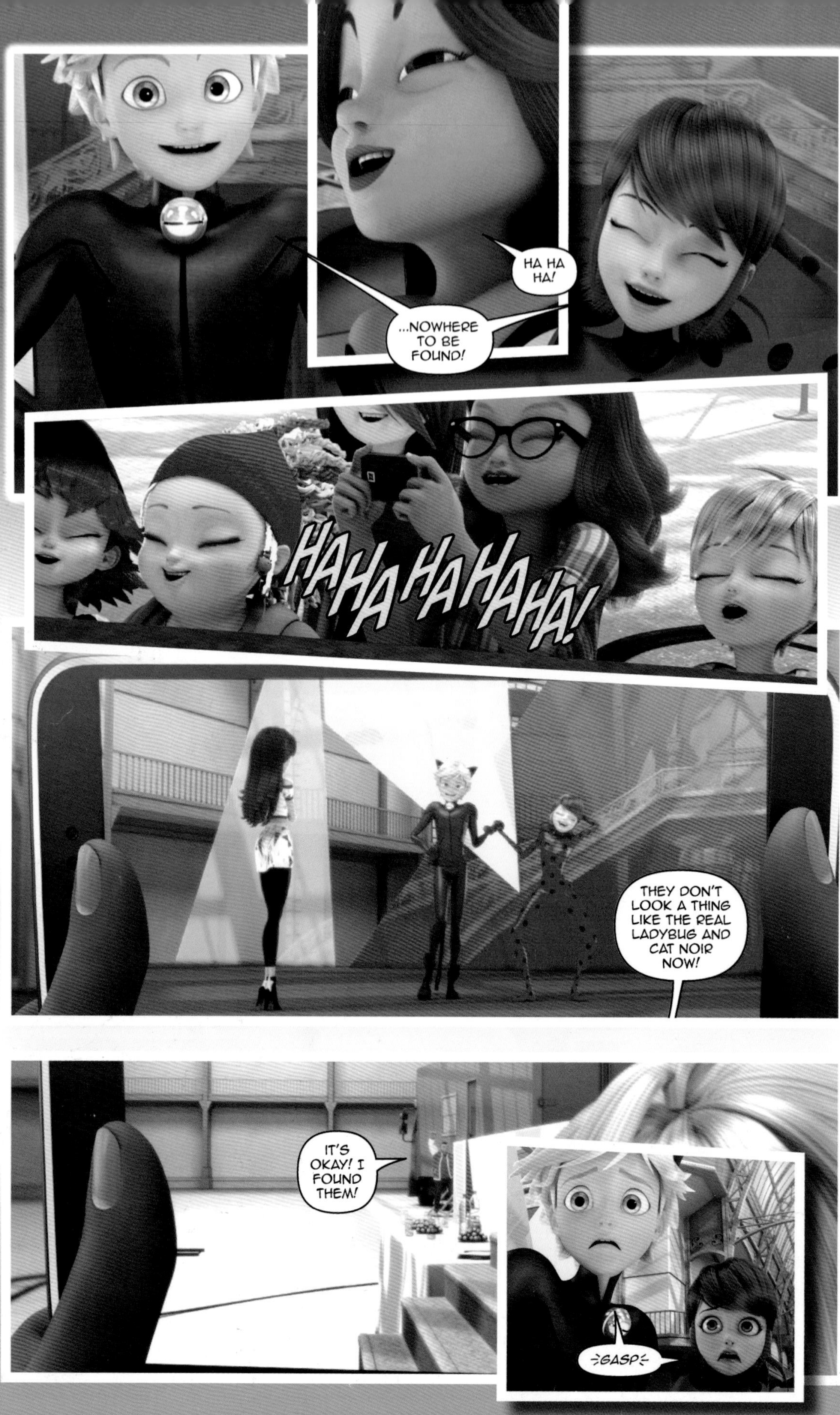
HA HA HA!
...NOWHERE TO BE FOUND!
HAHAHAHAHAHAHA!
THEY DON'T LOOK A THING LIKE THE REAL LADYBUG AND CAT NOIR NOW!
IT'S OKAY! I FOUND THEM!
GASP

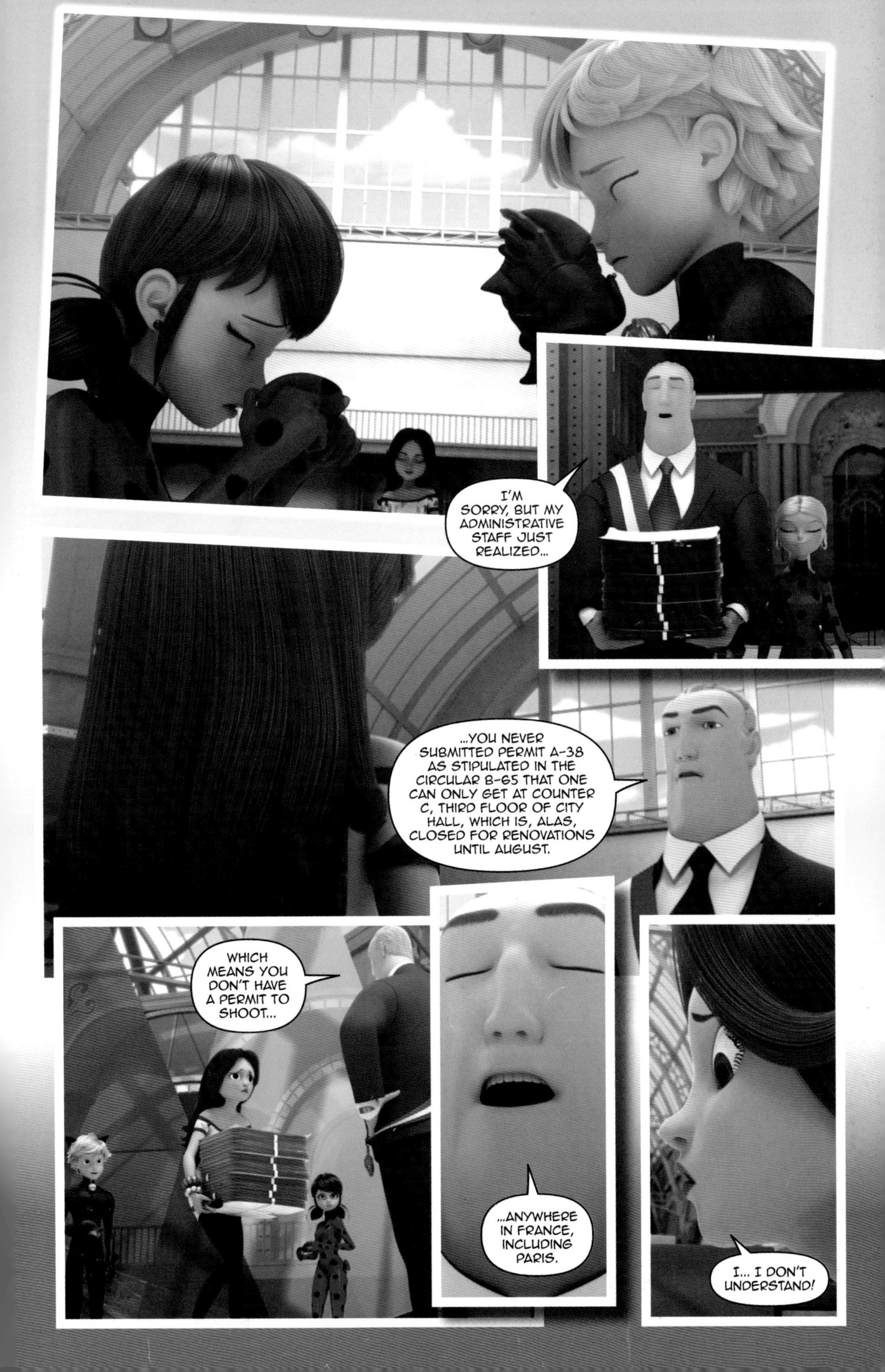
I'M SORRY, BUT MY ADMINISTRATIVE STAFF JUST REALIZED...
...YOU NEVER SUBMITTED PERMIT A-38 AS STIPULATED IN THE CIRCULAR B-65 THAT ONE CAN ONLY GET AT COUNTER C, THIRD FLOOR OF CITY HALL, WHICH IS, ALAS, CLOSED FOR RENOVATIONS UNTIL AUGUST.
WHICH MEANS YOU DON'T HAVE A PERMIT TO SHOOT...
...ANYWHERE IN FRANCE, INCLUDING PARIS.
I... I DON'T UNDERSTAND!

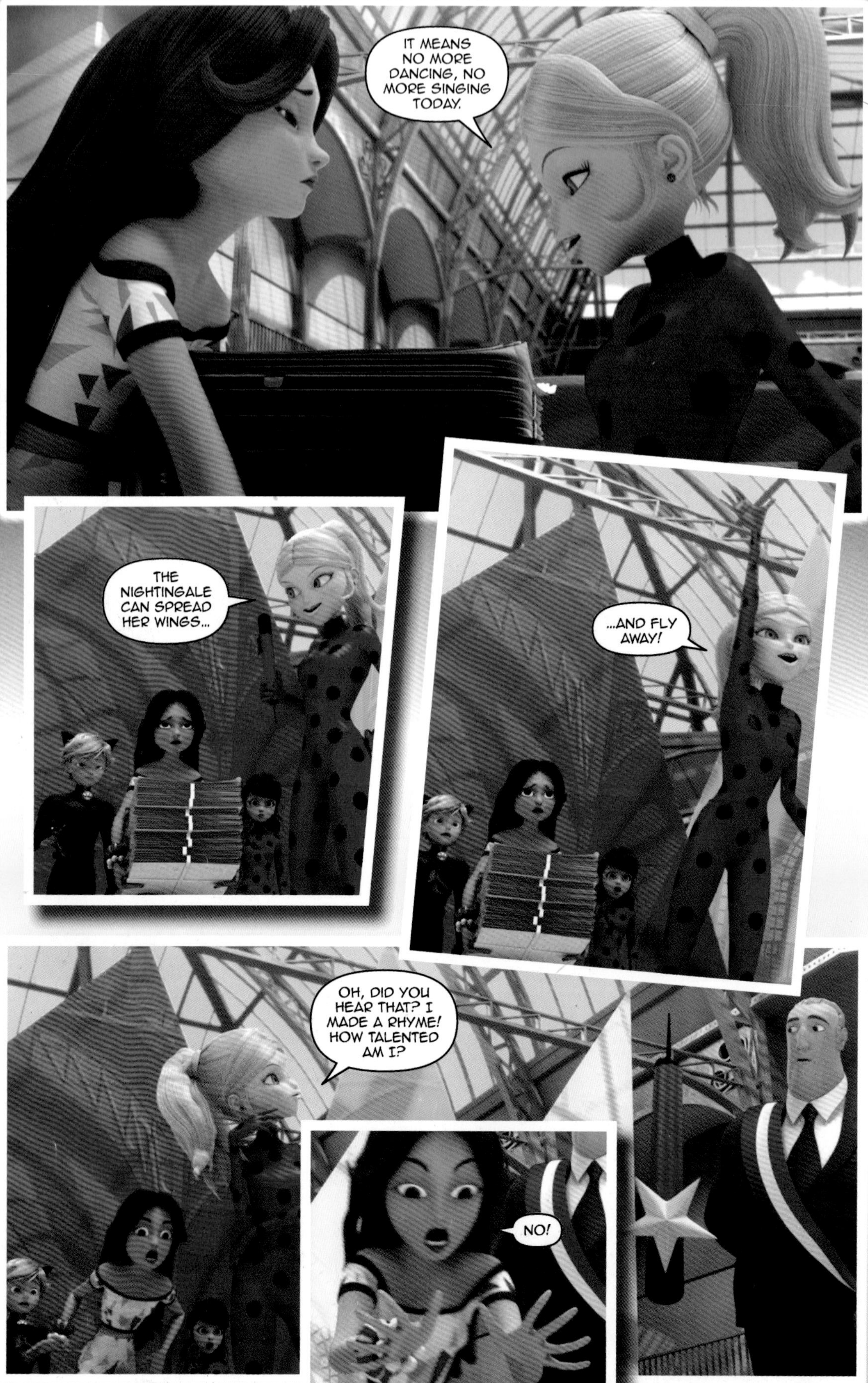
IT MEANS NO MORE DANCING, NO MORE SINGING TODAY.
THE NIGHTINGALE CAN SPREAD HER WINGS...
...AND FLY AWAY!
OH, DID YOU HEAR THAT? I MADE A RHYME! HOW TALENTED AM I?
NO!

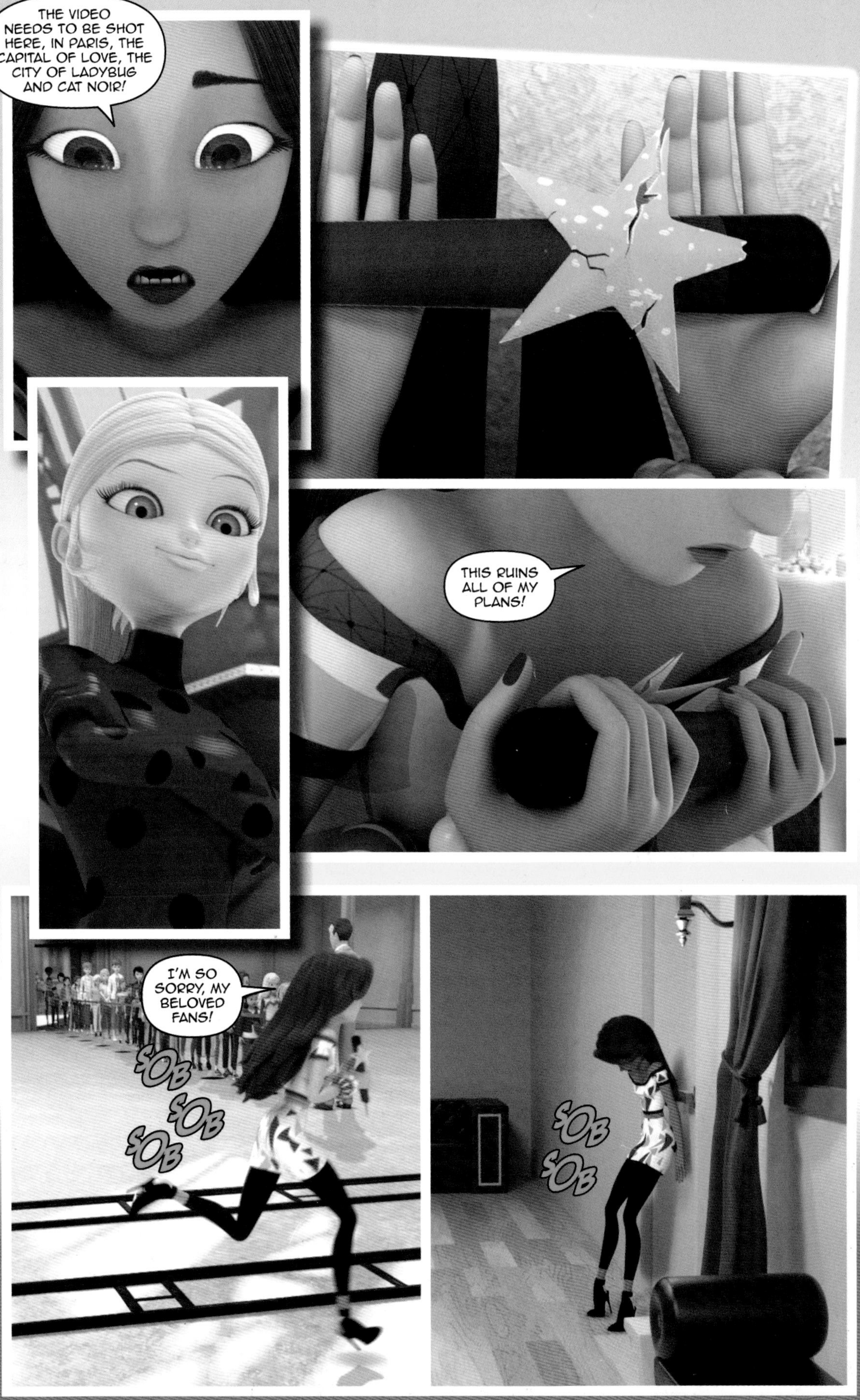
THE VIDEO NEEDS TO BE SHOT HERE, IN PARIS, THE CAPITAL OF LOVE, THE CITY OF LADYBUG AND CAT NOIR!
THIS RUINS ALL OF MY PLANS!
I'M SO SORRY, MY BELOVED FANS!
SOB
SOB
SOB
SOB
SOB

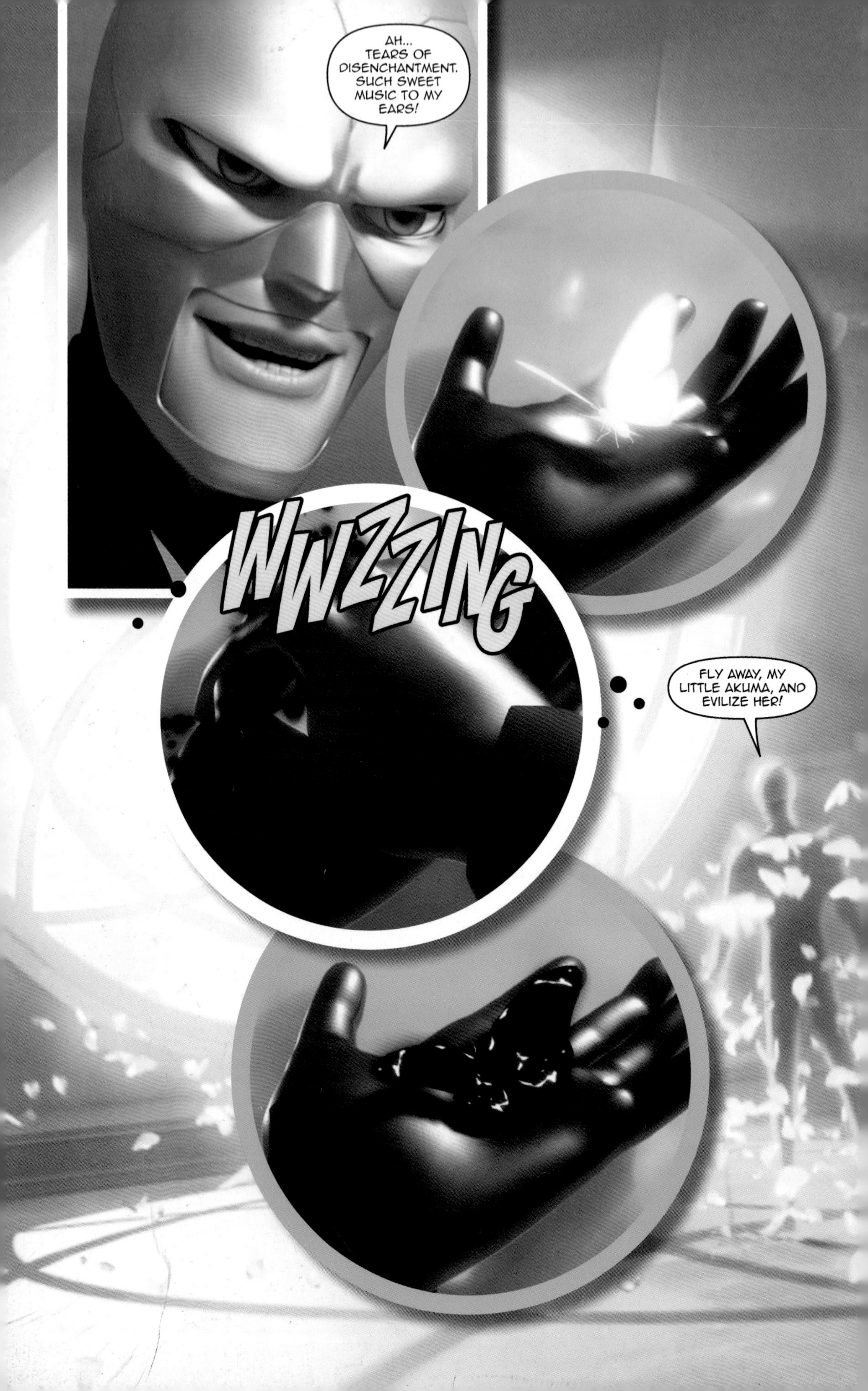
AH... TEARS OF DISENCHANTMENT. SUCH SWEET MUSIC TO MY EARS!
WWZZING
FLY AWAY, MY LITTLE AKUMA, AND EVILIZE HER!

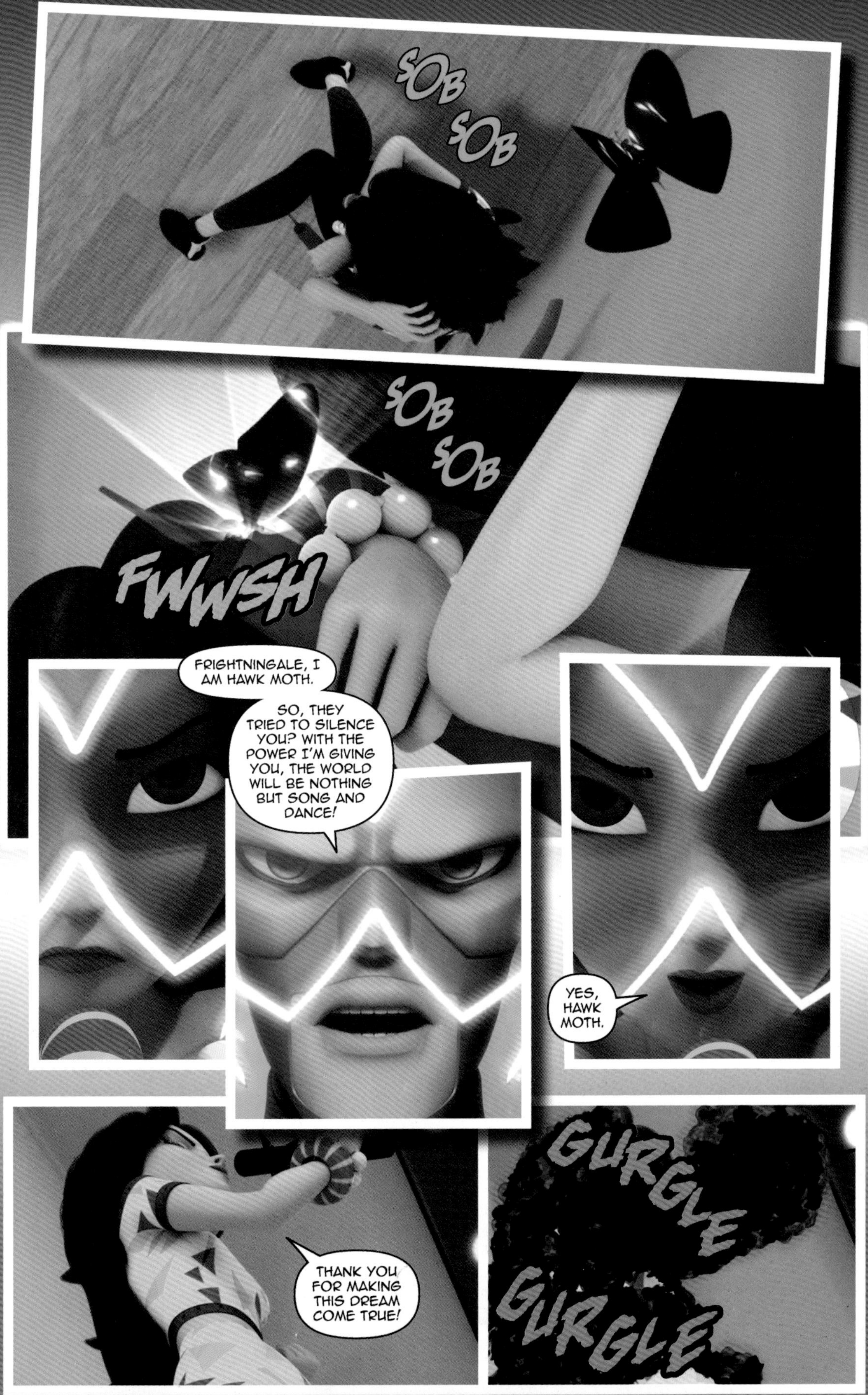
SOB
SOB
SOB
SOB
FWWSH
FRIGHTNINGALE, I AM HAWK MOTH.
SO, THEY TRIED TO SILENCE YOU? WITH THE POWER I'M GIVING YOU, THE WORLD WILL BE NOTHING BUT SONG AND DANCE!
YES, HAWK MOTH.
THANK YOU FOR MAKING THIS DREAM COME TRUE!
GURGLE
GURGLE

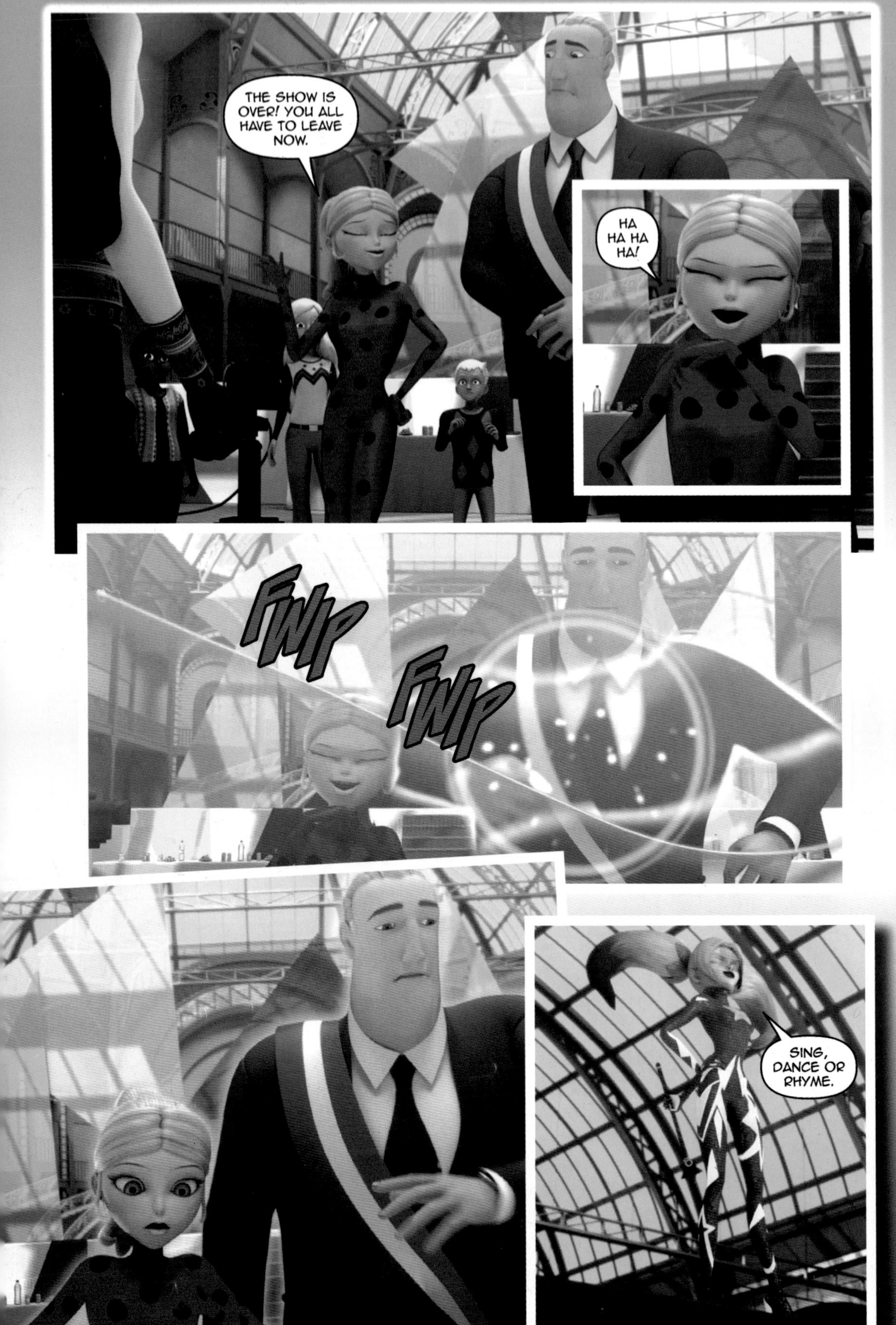
THE SHOW IS OVER! YOU ALL HAVE TO LEAVE NOW.
HA HA HA HA!
FWIP
FWIP
SING, DANCE OR RHYME.

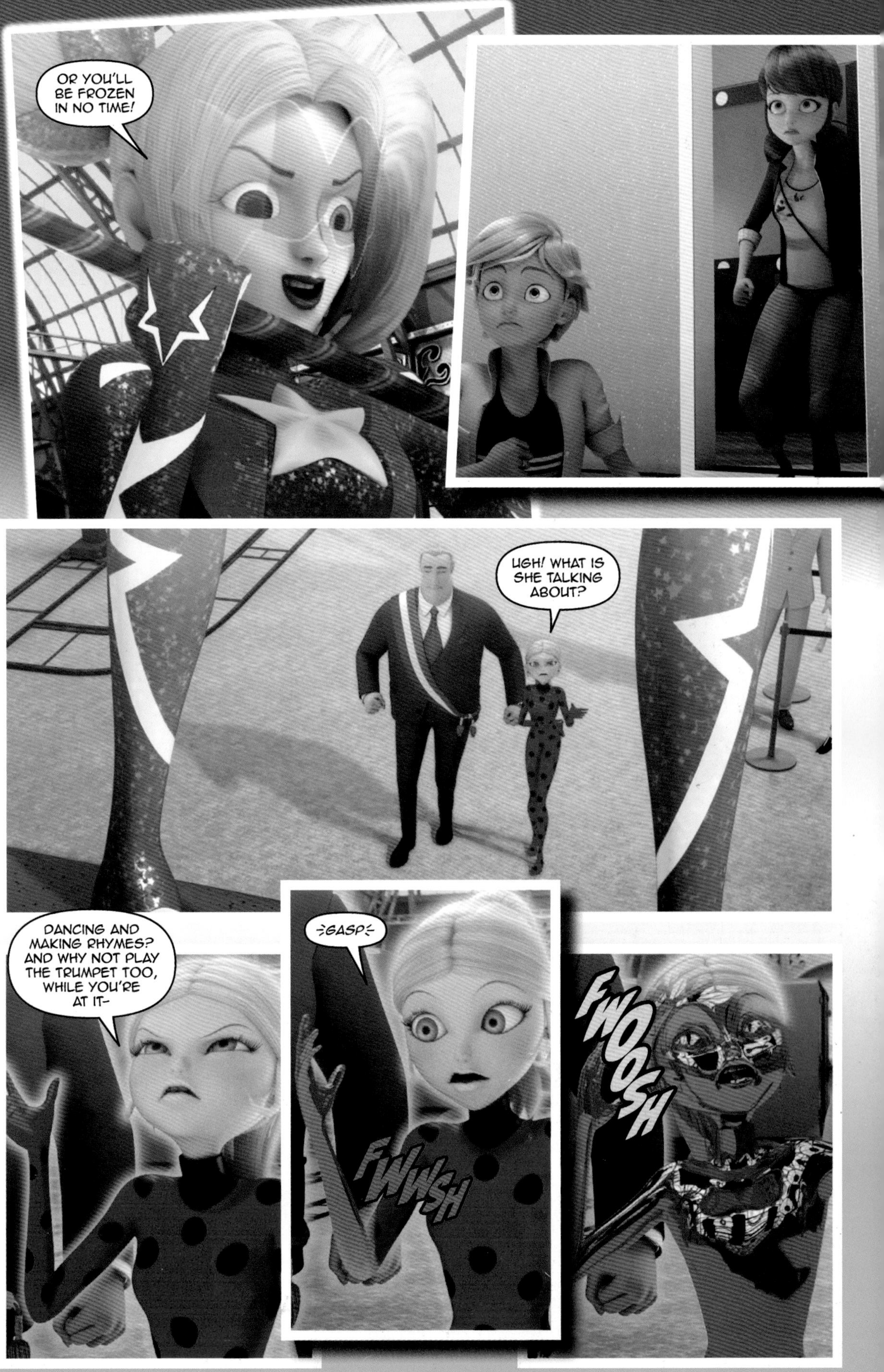

OR YOU'LL BE FROZEN IN NO TIME!
UGH! WHAT IS SHE TALKING ABOUT?
DANCING AND MAKING RHYMES? AND WHY NOT PLAY THE TRUMPET TOO, WHILE YOU'RE AT IT-
GASP
FWWSH
FWOOSH

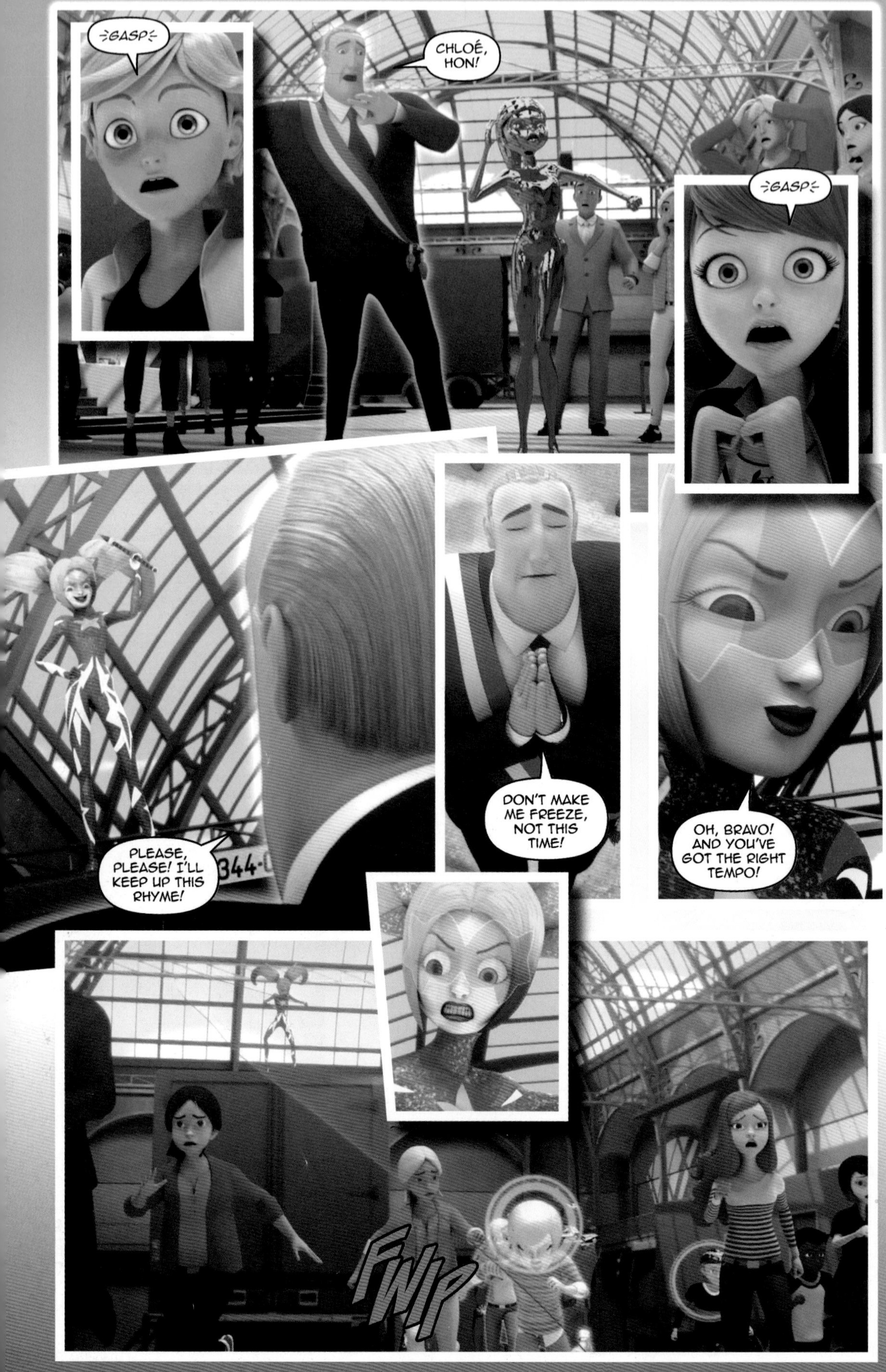
GASP
CHLOÉ, HON!
GASP
PLEASE, PLEASE! I'LL KEEP UP THIS RHYME!
DON'T MAKE ME FREEZE, NOT THIS TIME!
OH, BRAVO! AND YOU'VE GOT THE RIGHT TEMPO!
FWIP

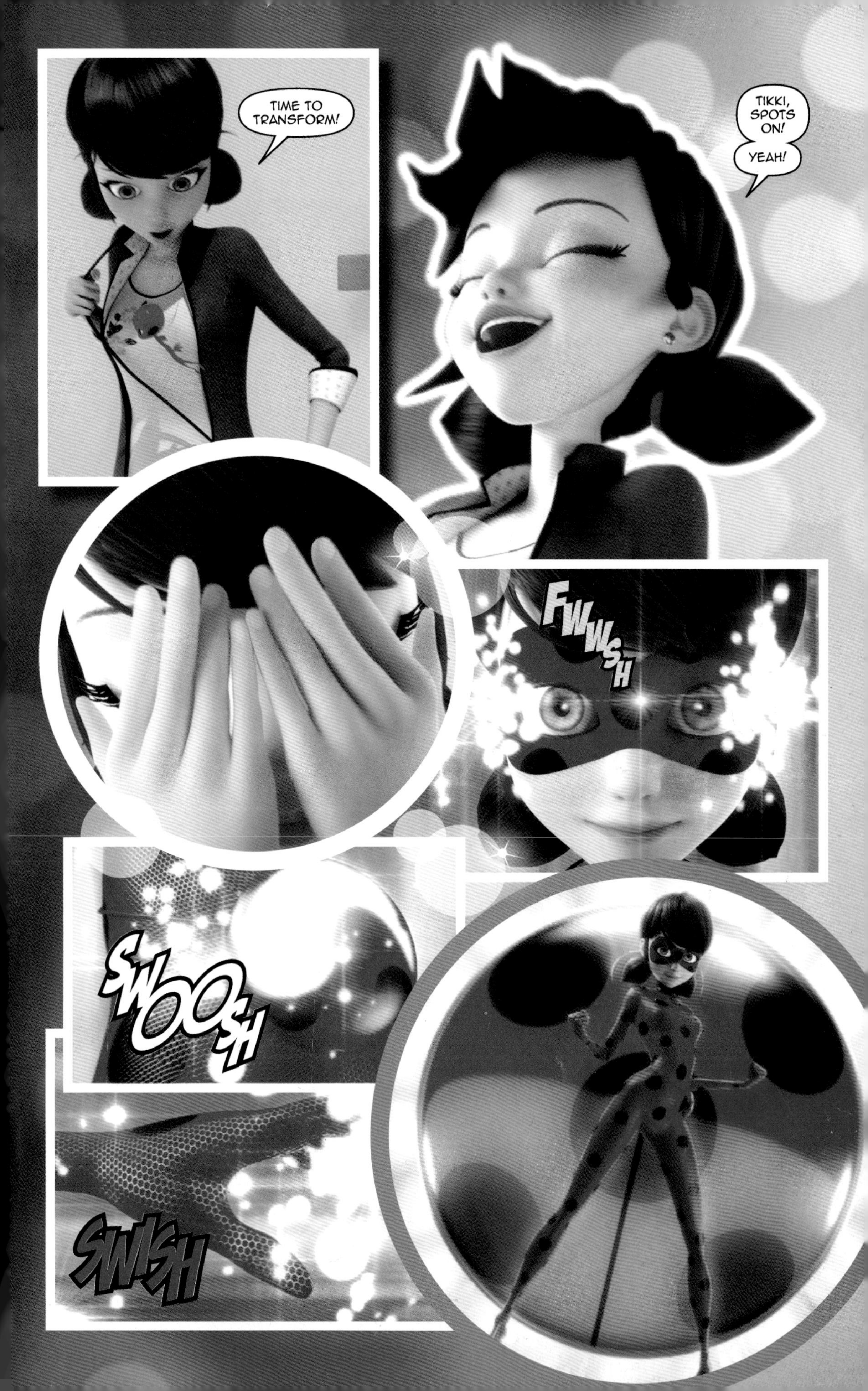
TIME TO TRANSFORM!
TIKKI, SPOTS ON!
YEAH!
FWWSH
SWOOSH
SWISH

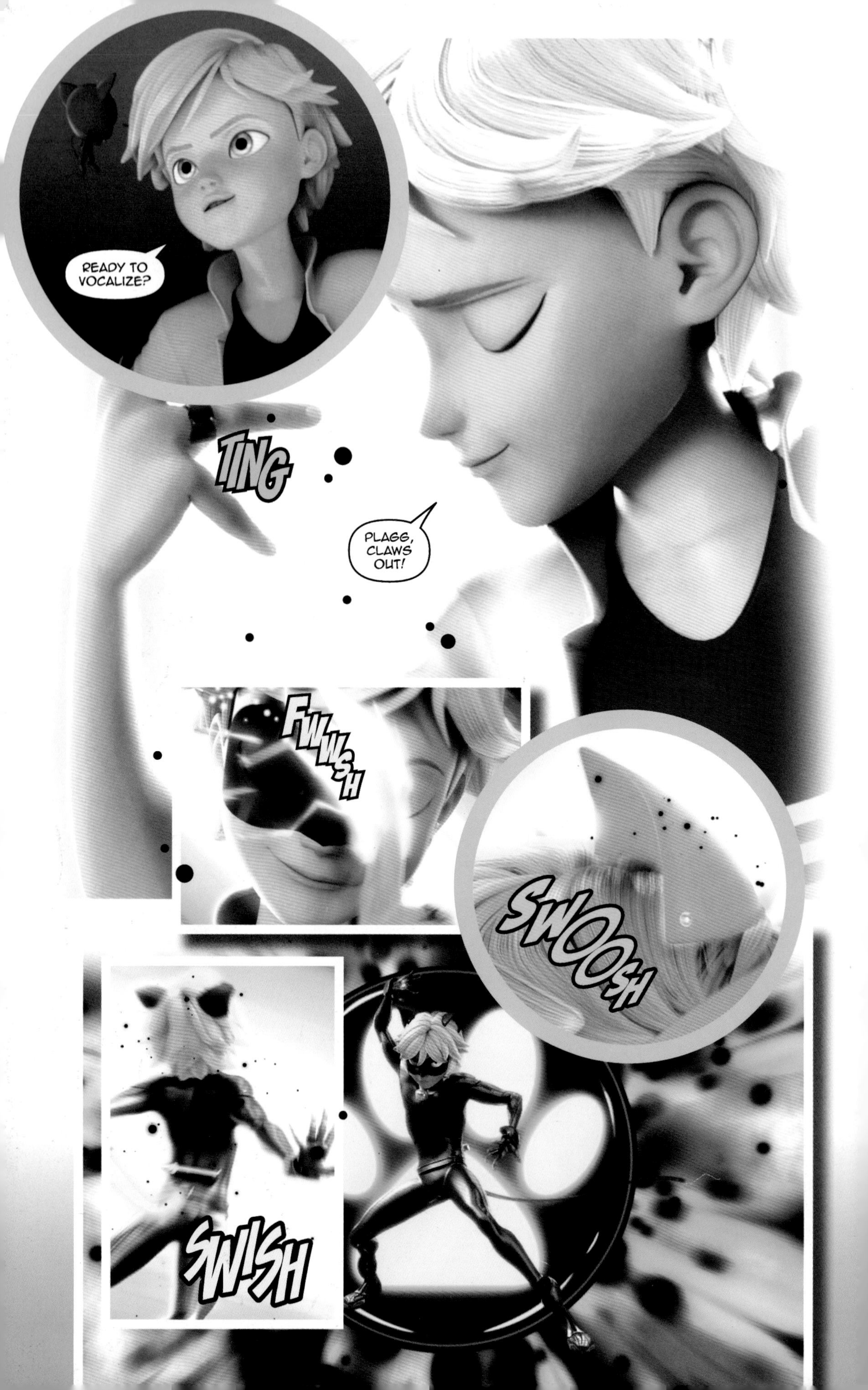
READY TO VOCALIZE?
TING
PLAGG, CLAWS OUT!
FWWSH
SWOOSH
SWISH

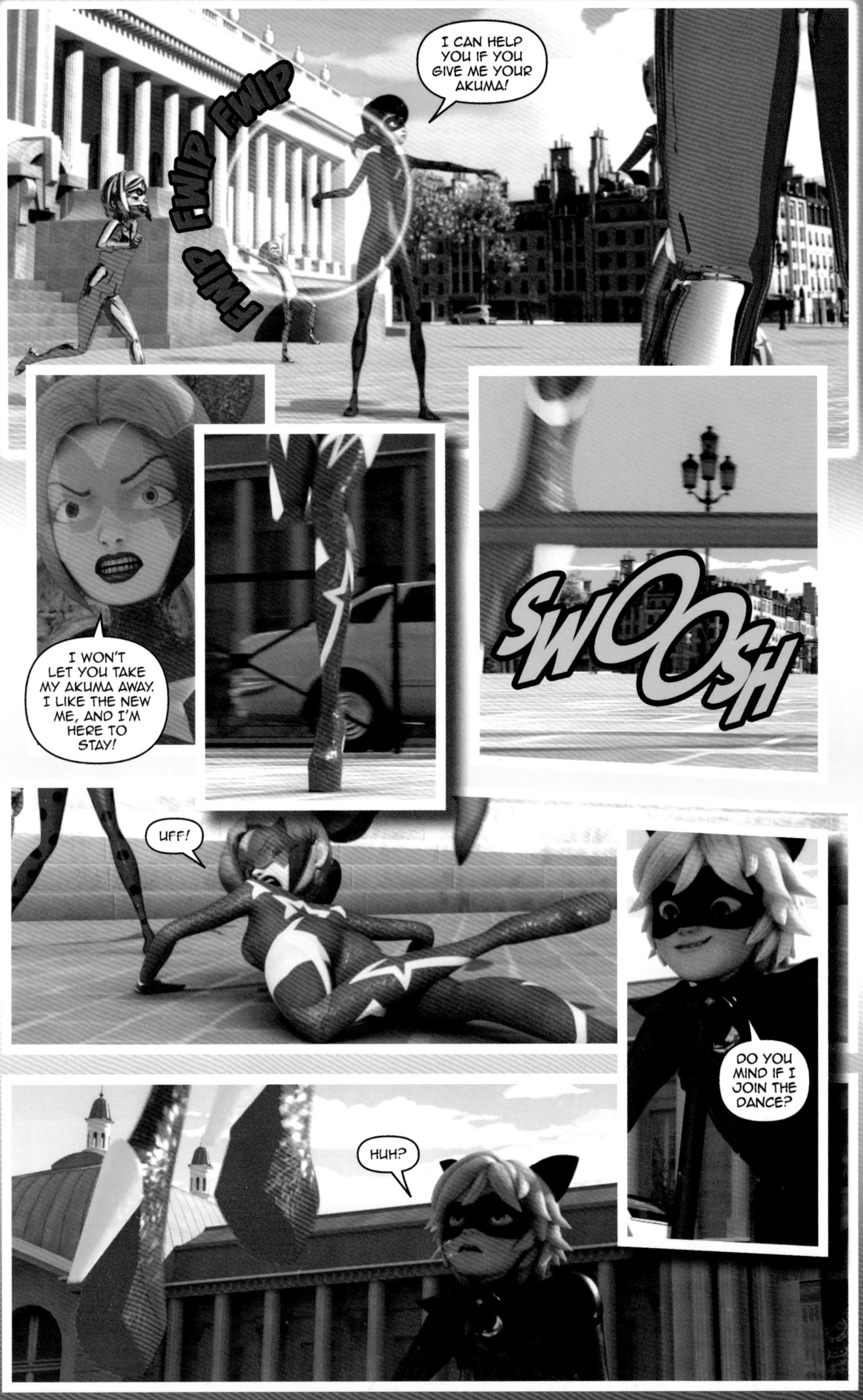
I CAN HELP YOU IF YOU GIVE ME YOUR AKUMA!
FWIP FWIP FWIP
I WON'T LET YOU TAKE MY AKUMA AWAY. I LIKE THE NEW ME, AND I'M HERE TO STAY!
SWOOSH
UFF!
DO YOU MIND IF I JOIN THE DANCE?
HUH?

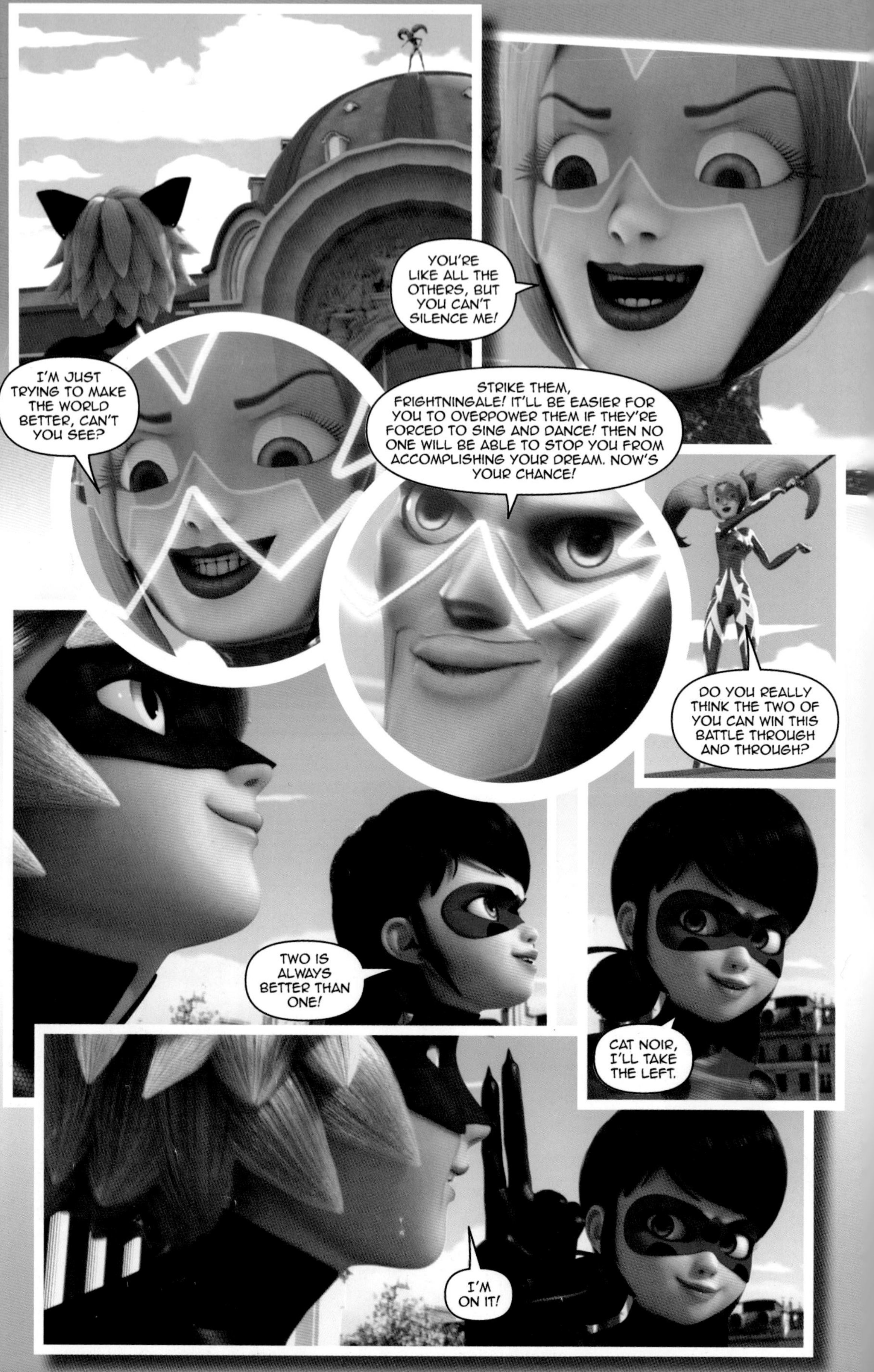
YOU'RE LIKE ALL THE OTHERS, BUT YOU CAN'T SILENCE ME!
I'M JUST TRYING TO MAKE THE WORLD BETTER, CAN'T YOU SEE?
STRIKE THEM, FRIGHTNINGALE! IT'LL BE EASIER FOR YOU TO OVERPOWER THEM IF THEY'RE FORCED TO SING AND DANCE! THEN NO ONE WILL BE ABLE TO STOP YOU FROM ACCOMPLISHING YOUR DREAM. NOW'S YOUR CHANCE!
DO YOU REALLY THINK THE TWO OF YOU CAN WIN THIS BATTLE THROUGH AND THROUGH?
TWO IS ALWAYS BETTER THAN ONE!
CAT NOIR, I'LL TAKE THE LEFT.
I'M ON IT!

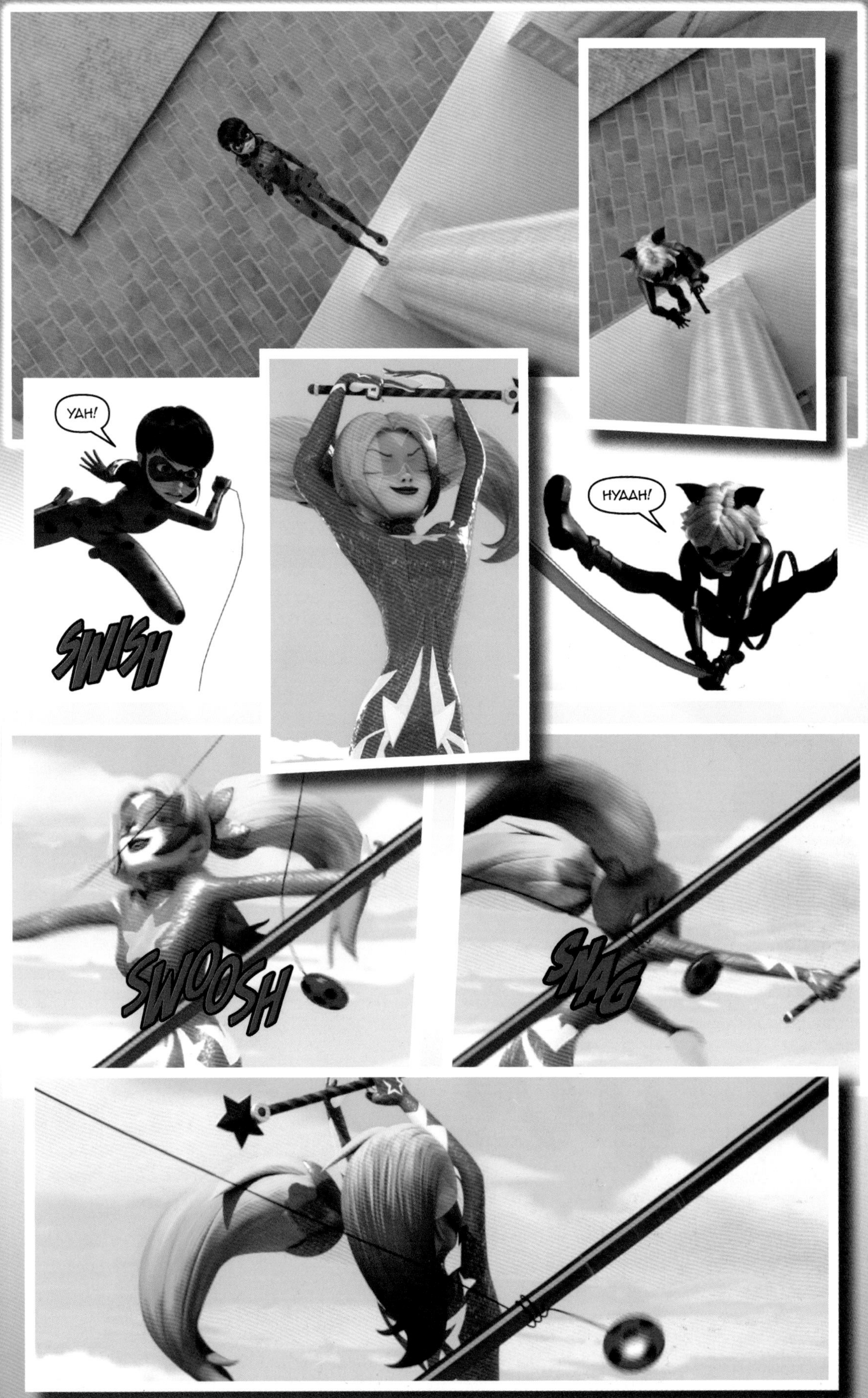
YAH!
SWISH
HYAAH!
SWOOSH
SNAG

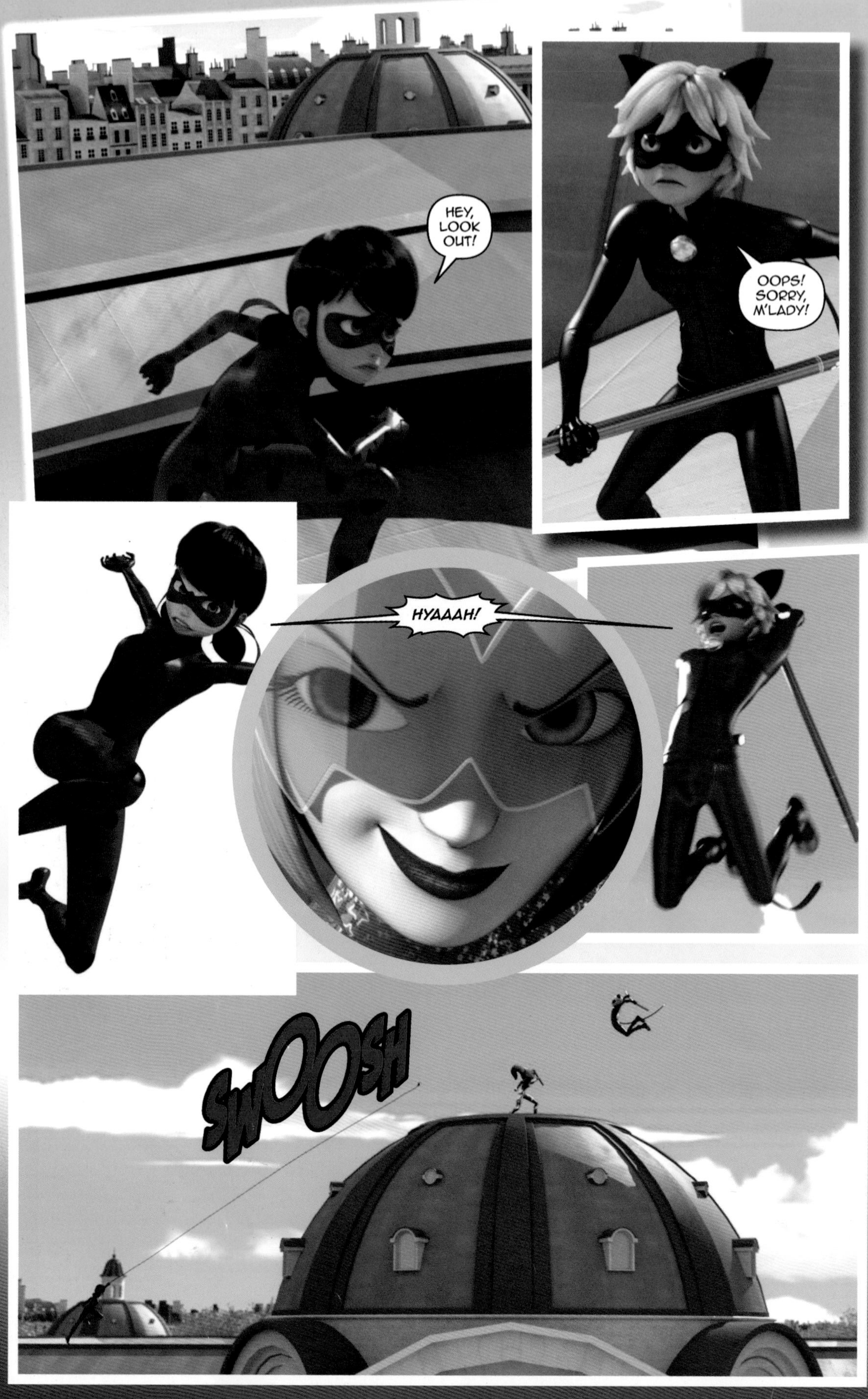
HEY, LOOK OUT!
OOPS! SORRY, M'LADY!
HYAAAH!
SWOOSH

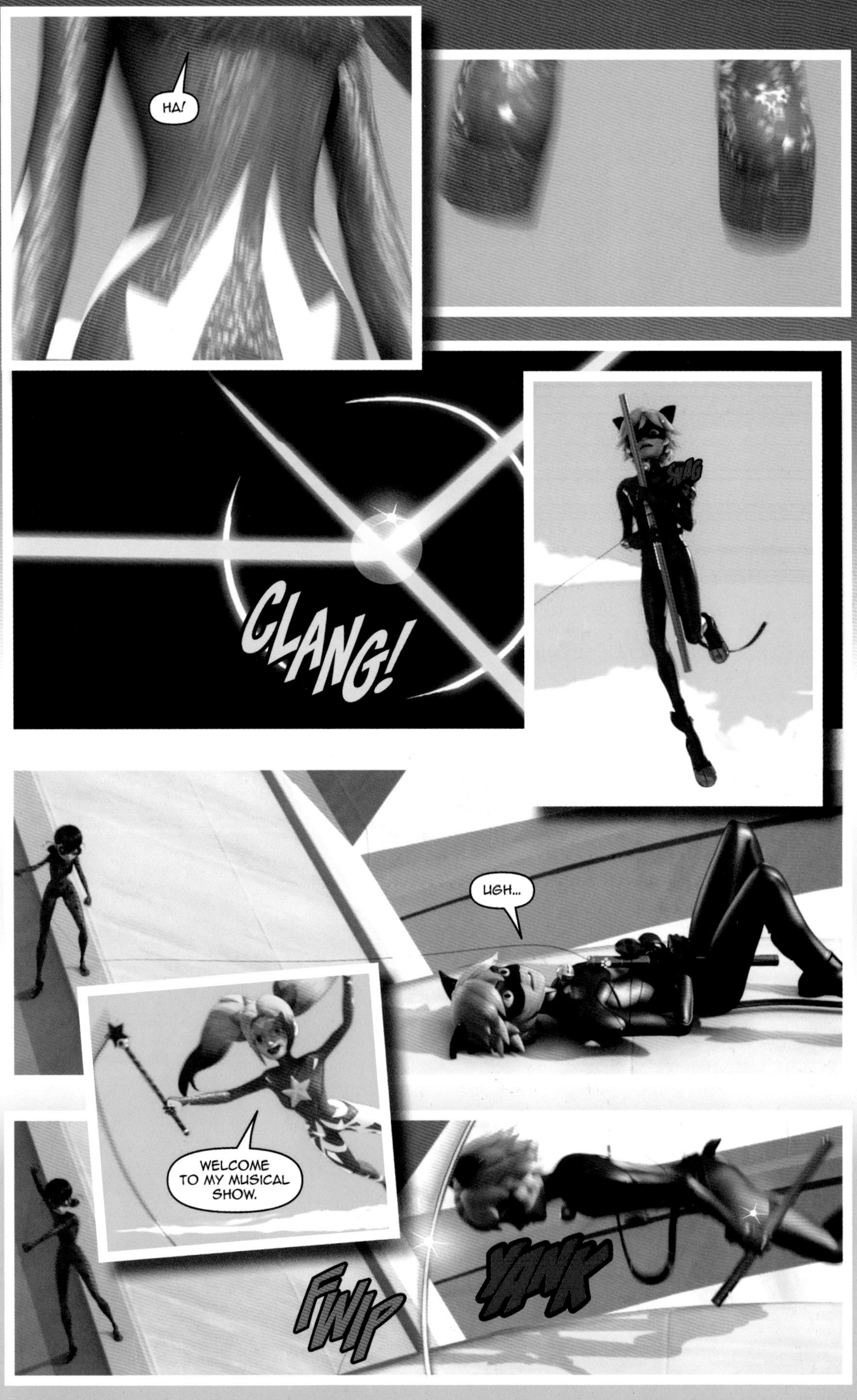
HA!
CLANG!
SNAG
UGH...
WELCOME TO MY MUSICAL SHOW.
FWIP
YANK

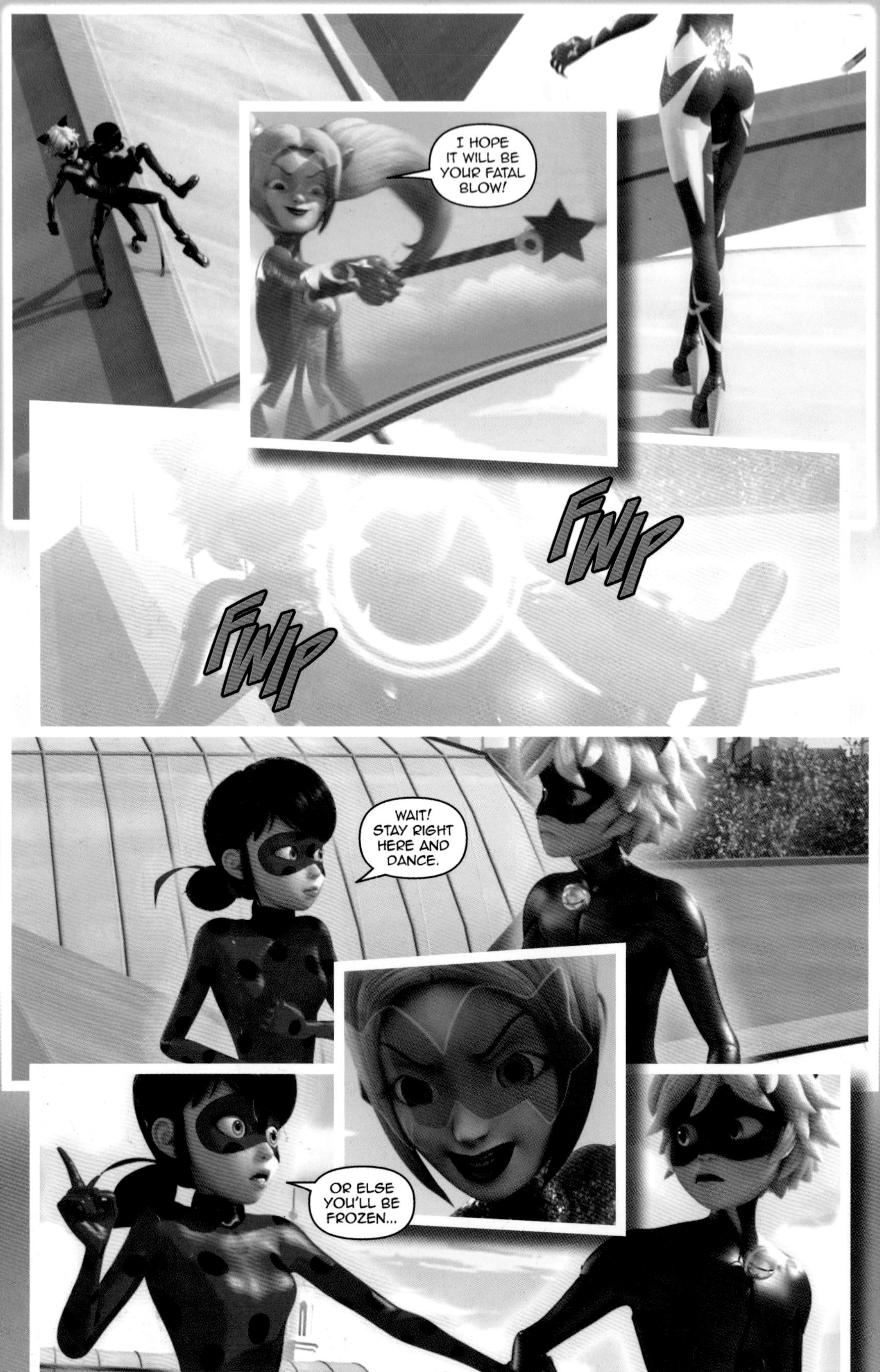
I HOPE IT WILL BE YOUR FATAL BLOW!
FWIP
FWIP
WAIT! STAY RIGHT HERE AND DANCE.
OR ELSE YOU'LL BE FROZEN...

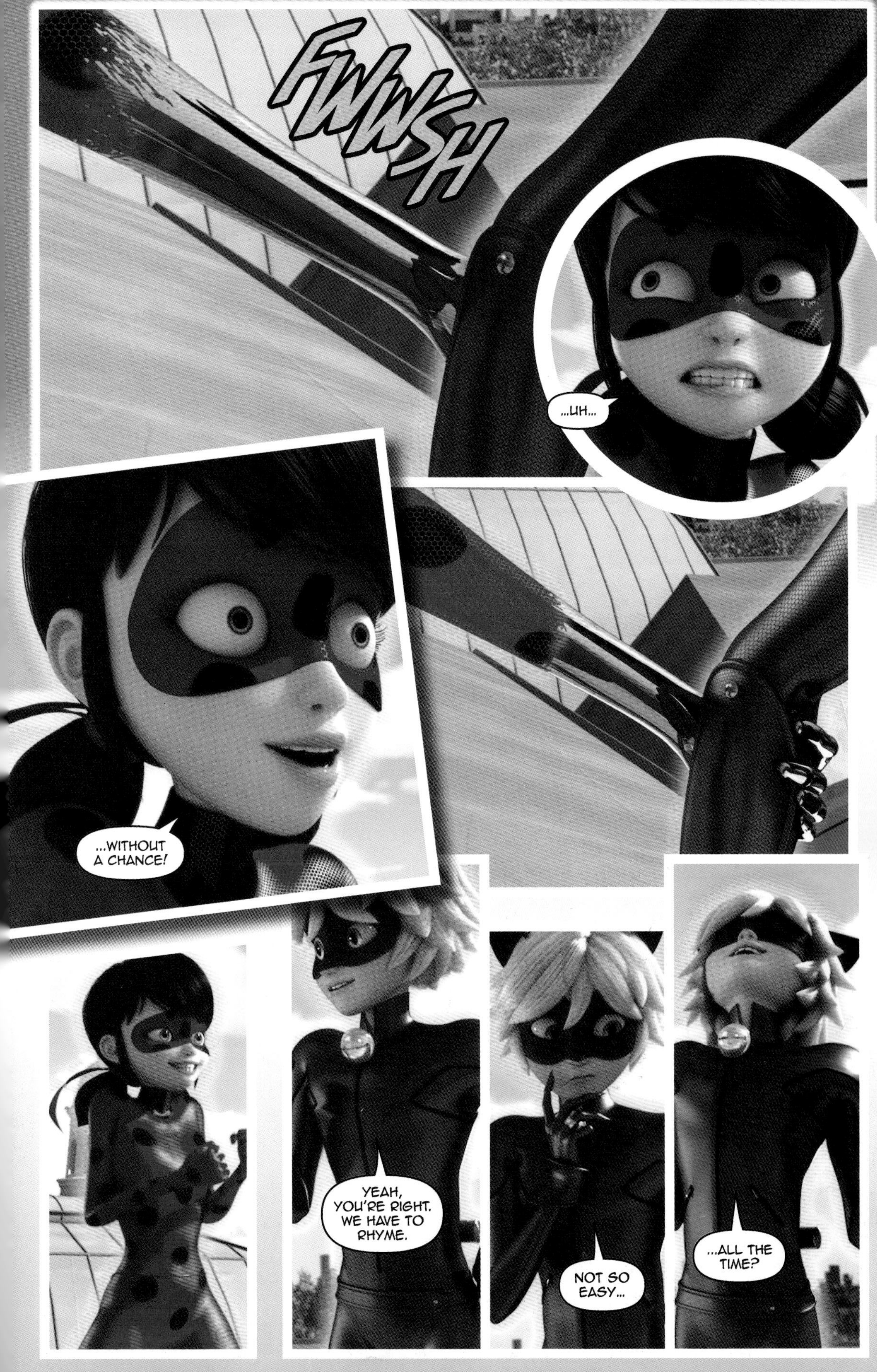
FWNSH
...UH...
...WITHOUT A CHANCE!
YEAH, YOU'RE RIGHT. WE HAVE TO RHYME.
NOT SO EASY...
...ALL THE TIME?

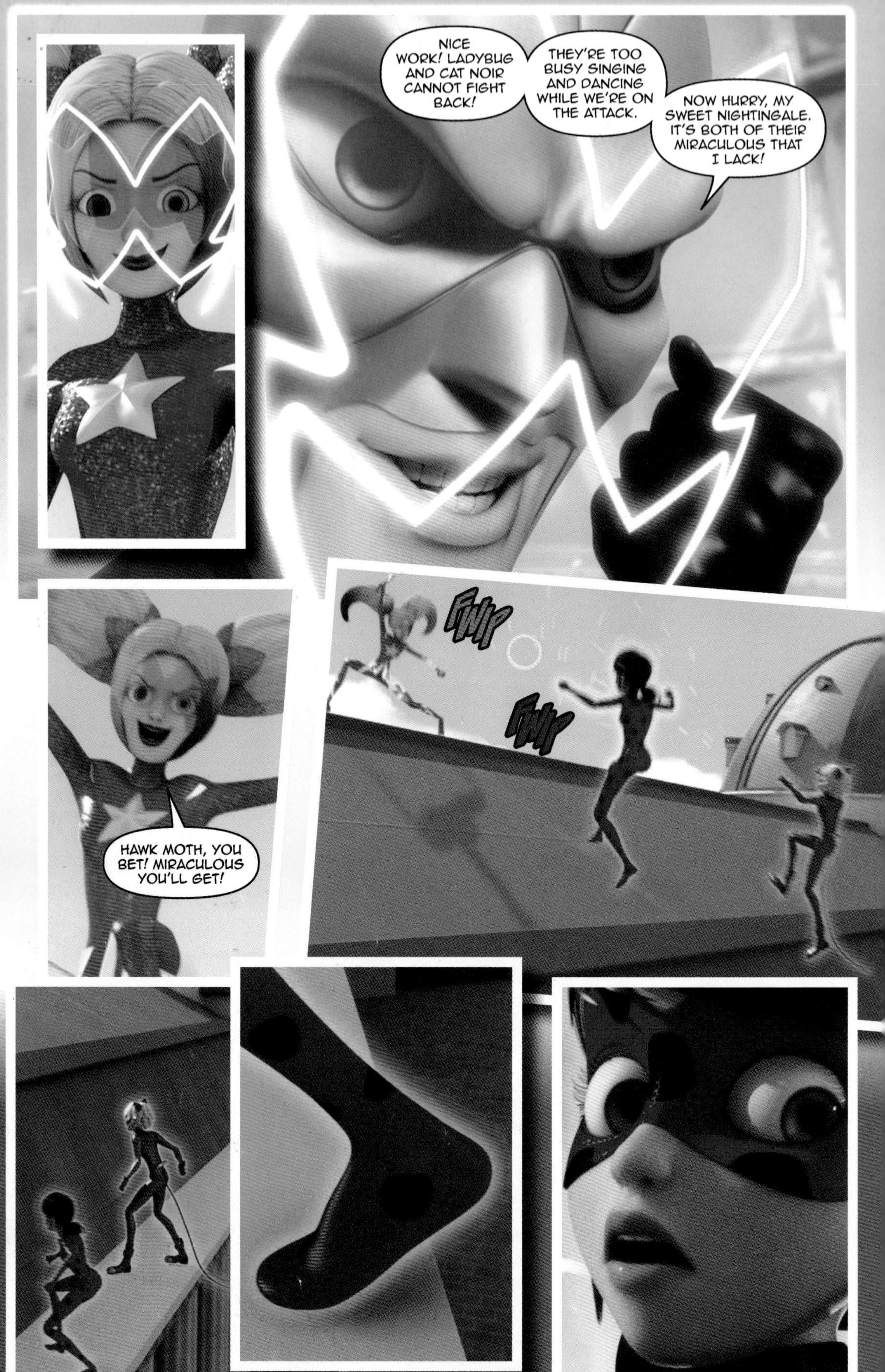
NICE WORK! LADYBUG AND CAT NOIR CANNOT FIGHT BACK!
THEY'RE TOO BUSY SINGING AND DANCING WHILE WE'RE ON THE ATTACK.
NOW HURRY, MY SWEET NIGHTINGALE. IT'S BOTH OF THEIR MIRACULOUS THAT I LACK!
HAWK MOTH, YOU BET! MIRACULOUS YOU'LL GET!
FWIP
FWIP

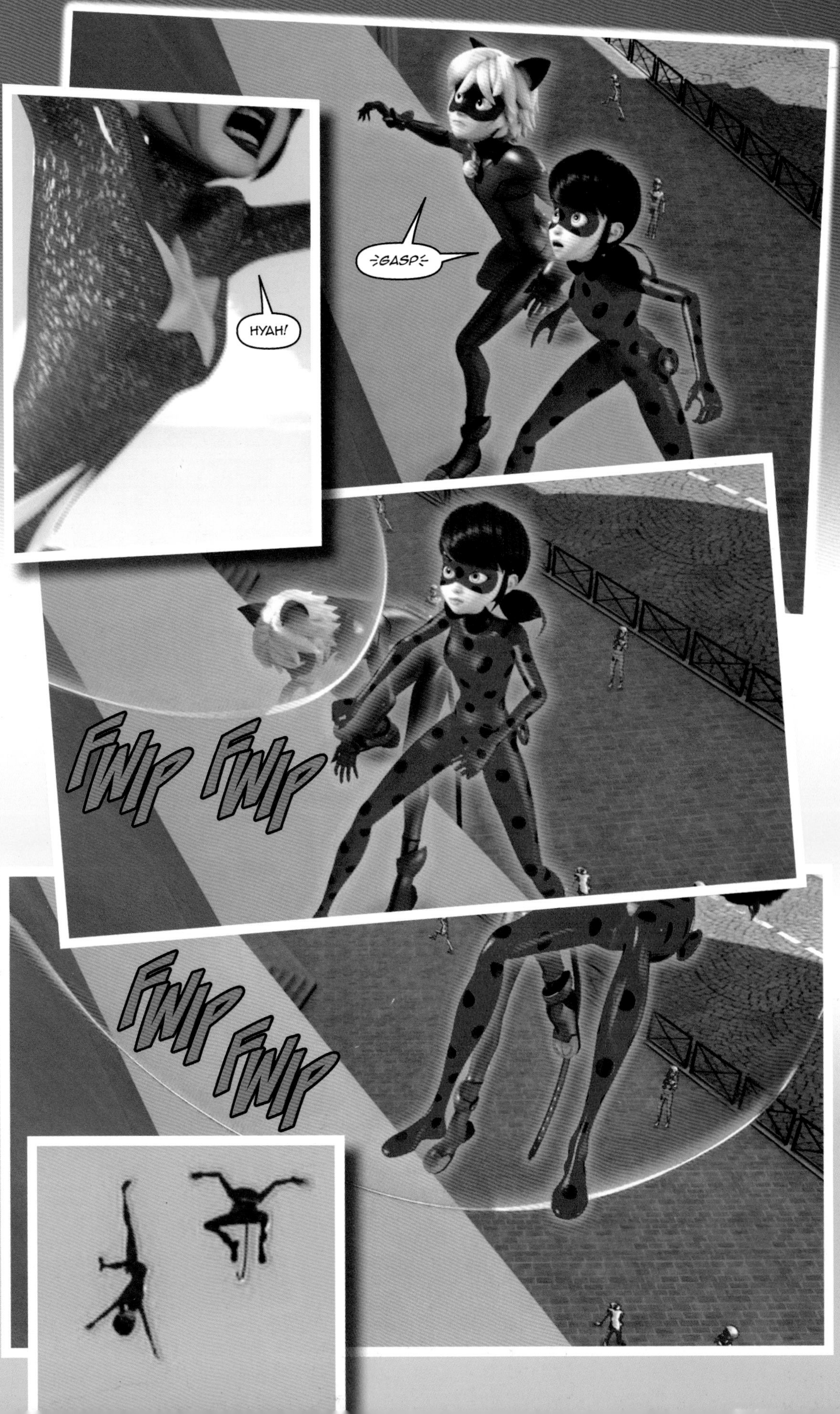
HYAH!
GASP
FWIP FWIP
FWIP FWIP

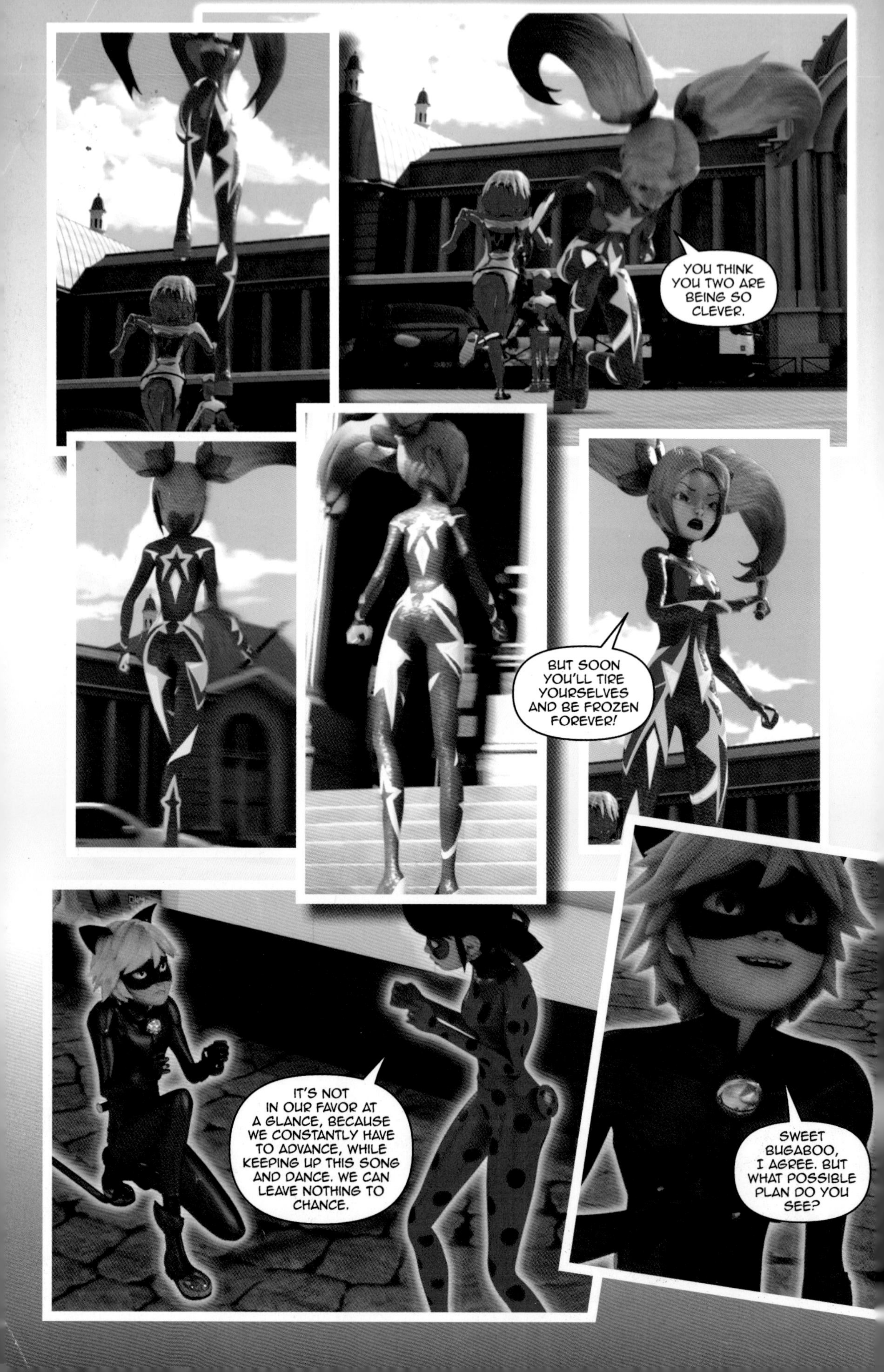
YOU THINK YOU TWO ARE BEING SO CLEVER.
BUT SOON YOU'LL TIRE YOURSELVES AND BE FROZEN FOREVER!
IT'S NOT IN OUR FAVOR AT A GLANCE, BECAUSE WE CONSTANTLY HAVE TO ADVANCE, WHILE KEEPING UP THIS SONG AND DANCE. WE CAN LEAVE NOTHING TO CHANCE.
SWEET BUGABOO, I AGREE. BUT WHAT POSSIBLE PLAN DO YOU SEE?

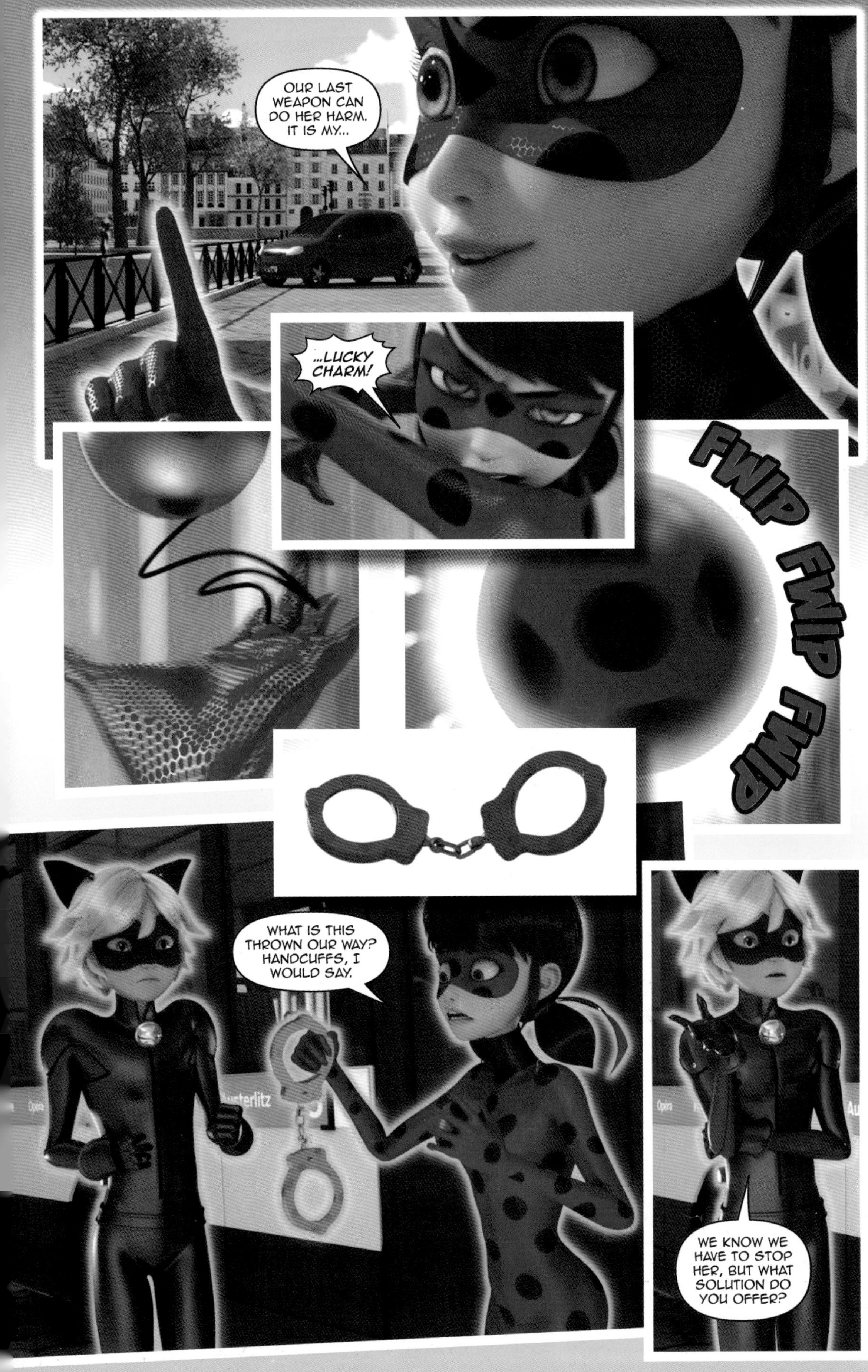
OUR LAST WEAPON CAN DO HER HARM. IT IS MY...
...LUCKY CHARM!
FWIP FWIP FWIP FWIP
WHAT IS THIS THROWN OUR WAY? HANDCUFFS, I WOULD SAY.
WE KNOW WE HAVE TO STOP HER, BUT WHAT SOLUTION DO YOU OFFER?

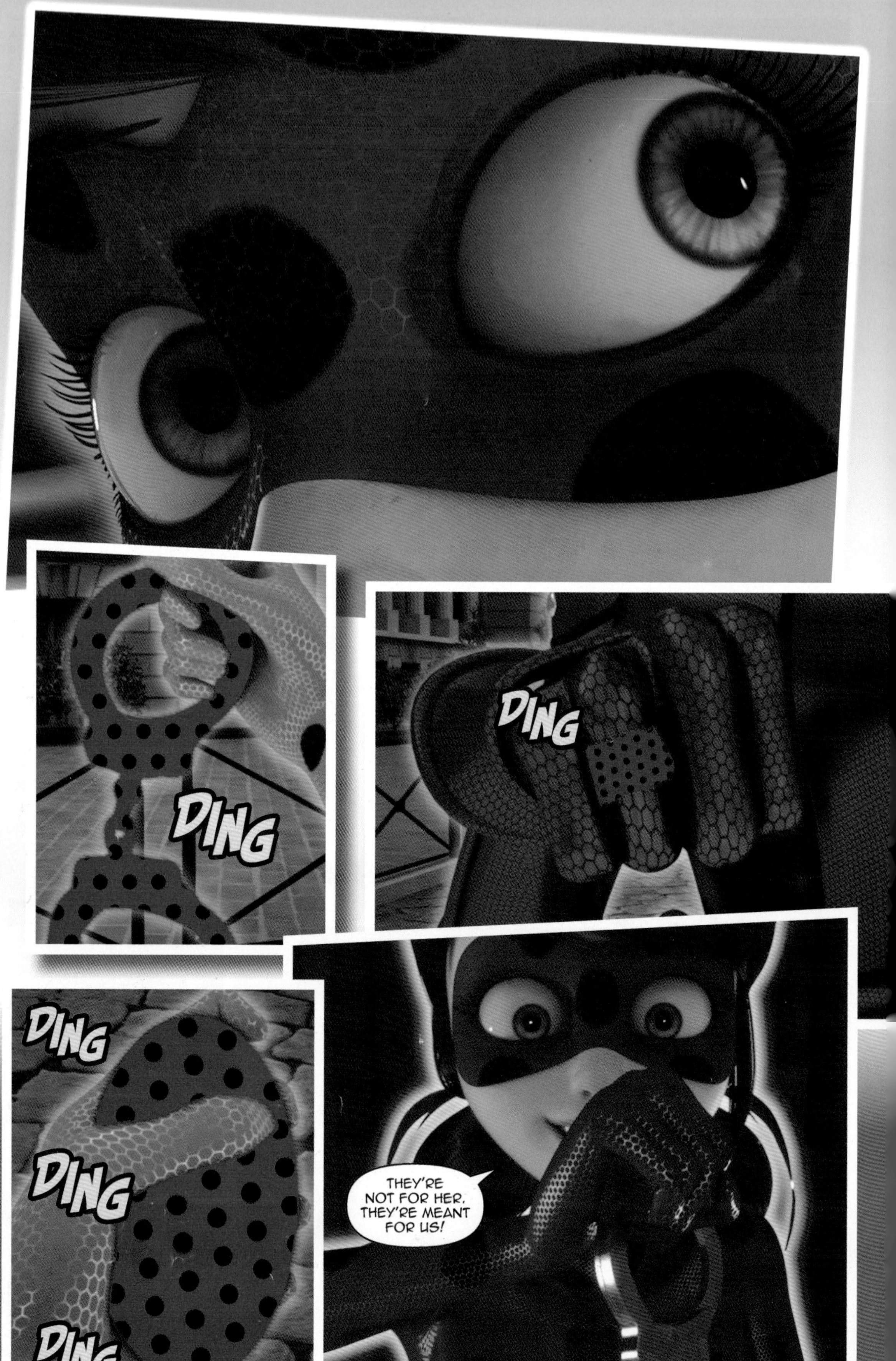
DING
DING
DING
DING
DING
THEY'RE NOT FOR HER. THEY'RE MEANT FOR US!

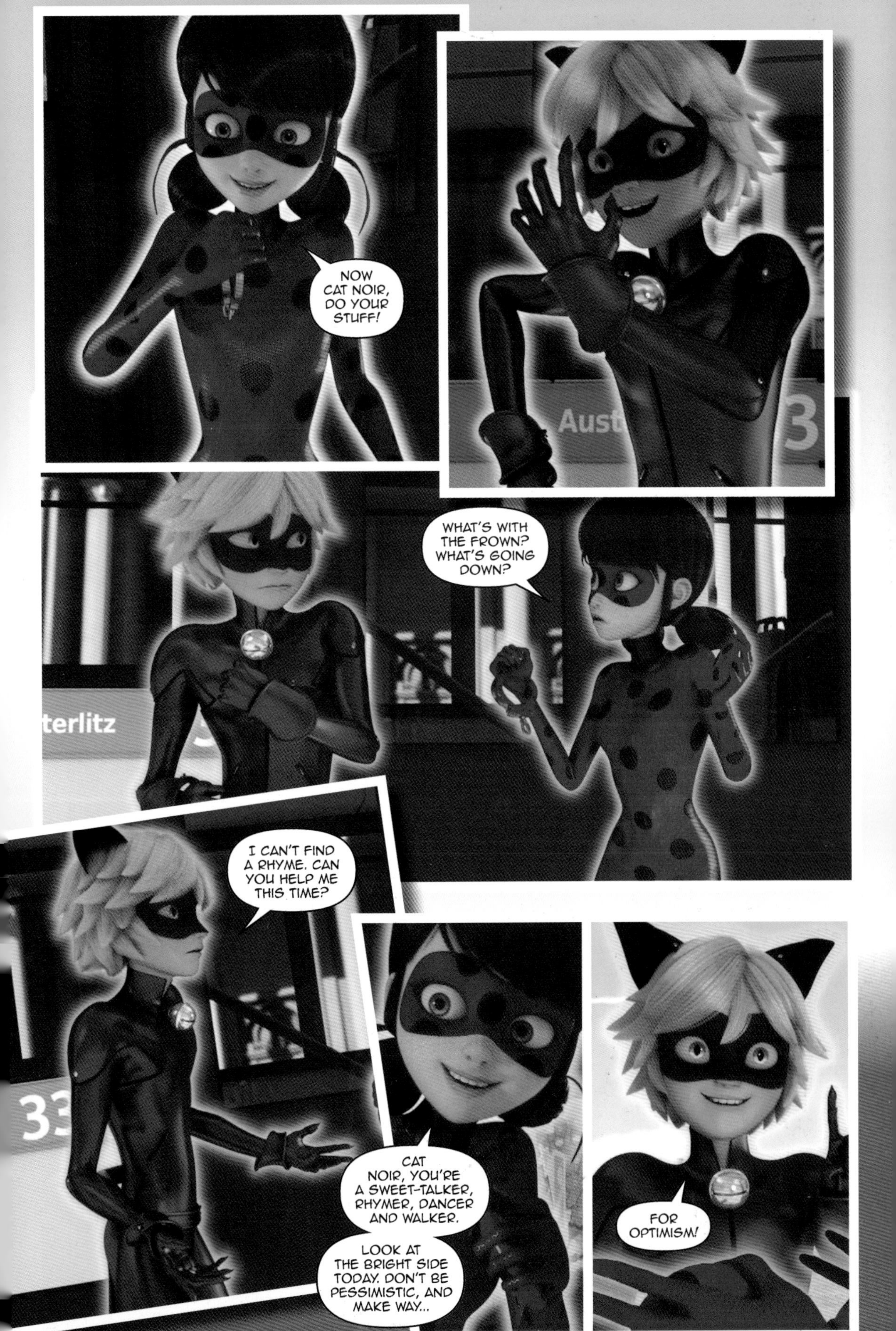
NOW CAT NOIR, DO YOUR STUFF!
Aust
3
WHAT'S WITH THE FROWN? WHAT'S GOING DOWN?
terlitz
I CAN'T FIND A RHYME. CAN YOU HELP ME THIS TIME?
33
CAT NOIR, YOU'RE A SWEET-TALKER, RHYMER, DANCER AND WALKER.
LOOK AT THE BRIGHT SIDE TODAY. DON'T BE PESSIMISTIC, AND MAKE WAY...
FOR OPTIMISM!

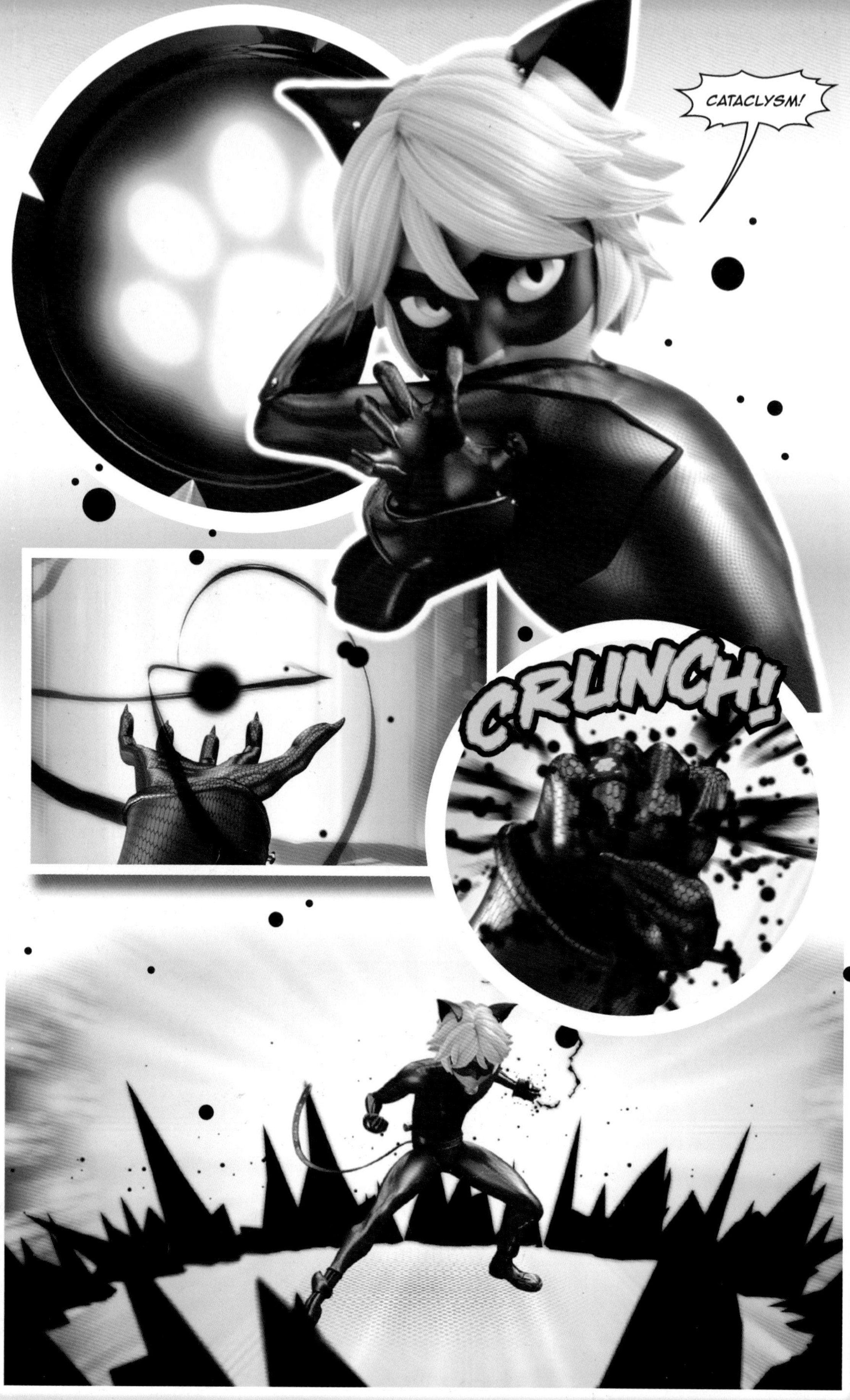
CATACLYSM!
CRUNCH!

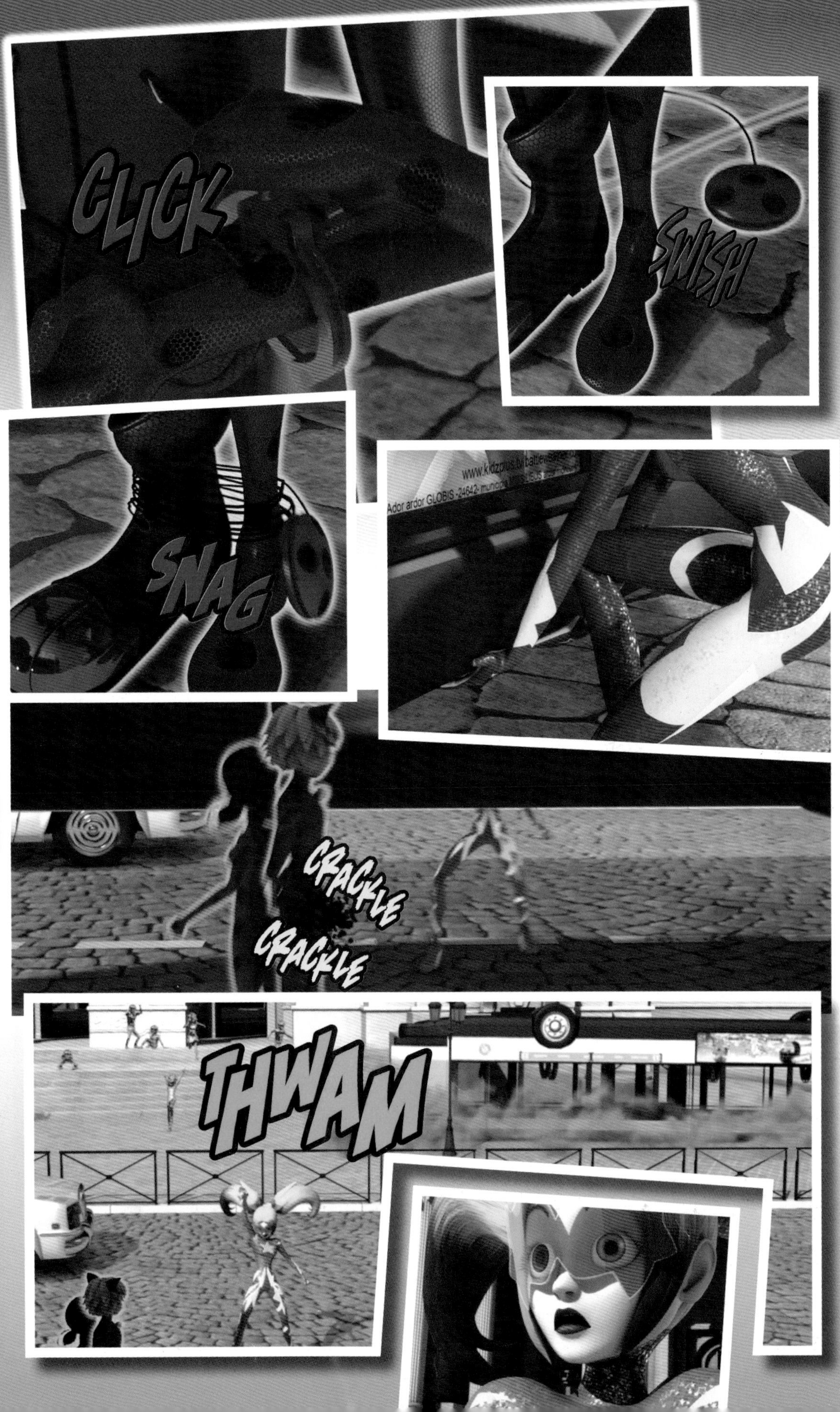
CLICK
SWISH
SNAG
CRACKLE
CRACKLE
THWAM

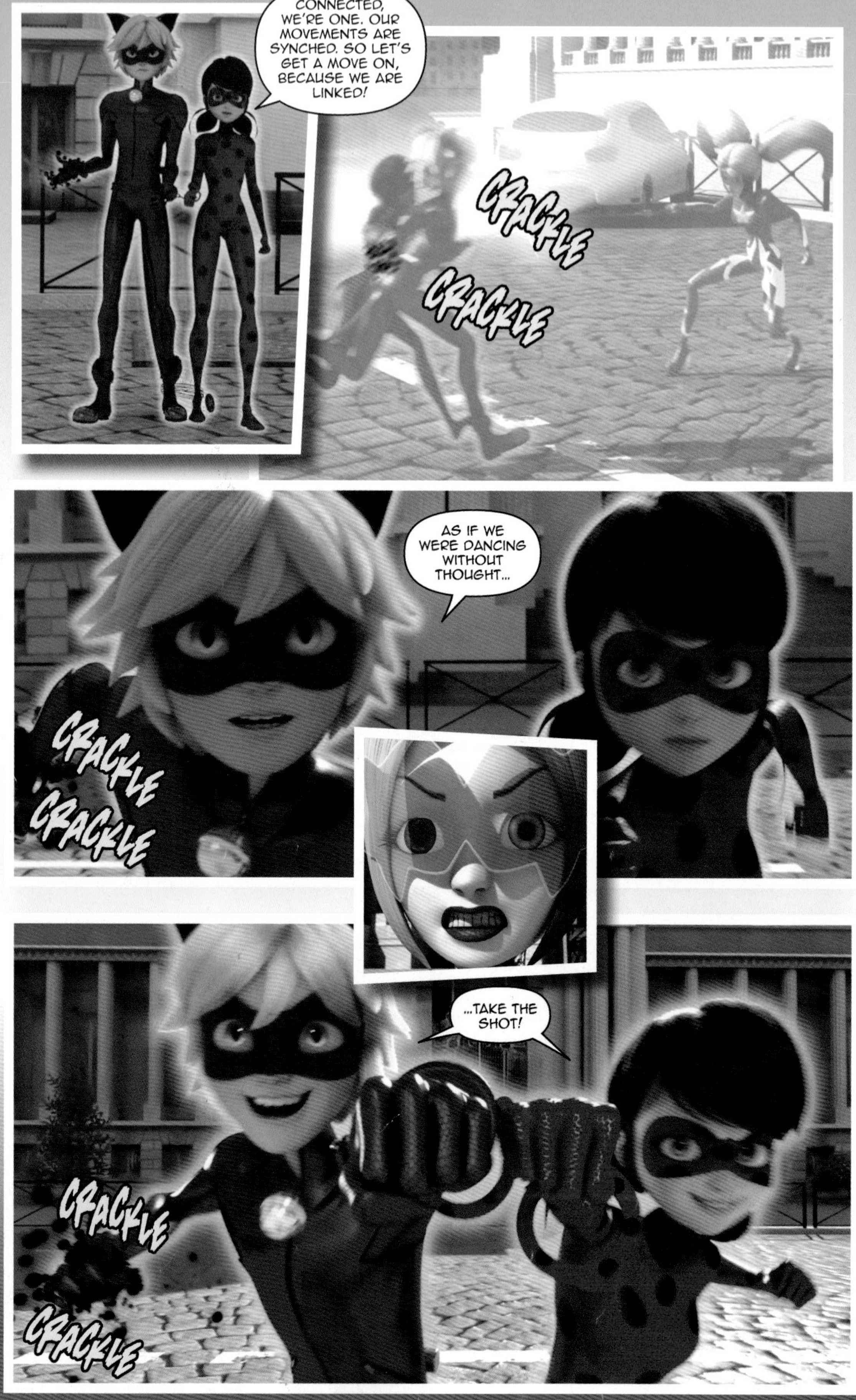
CONNECTED, WE'RE ONE. OUR MOVEMENTS ARE SYNCHED. SO LET'S GET A MOVE ON, BECAUSE WE ARE LINKED!
CRACKLE
CRACKLE
AS IF WE WERE DANCING WITHOUT THOUGHT...
CRACKLE
CRACKLE
...TAKE THE SHOT!
CRACKLE
CRACKLE

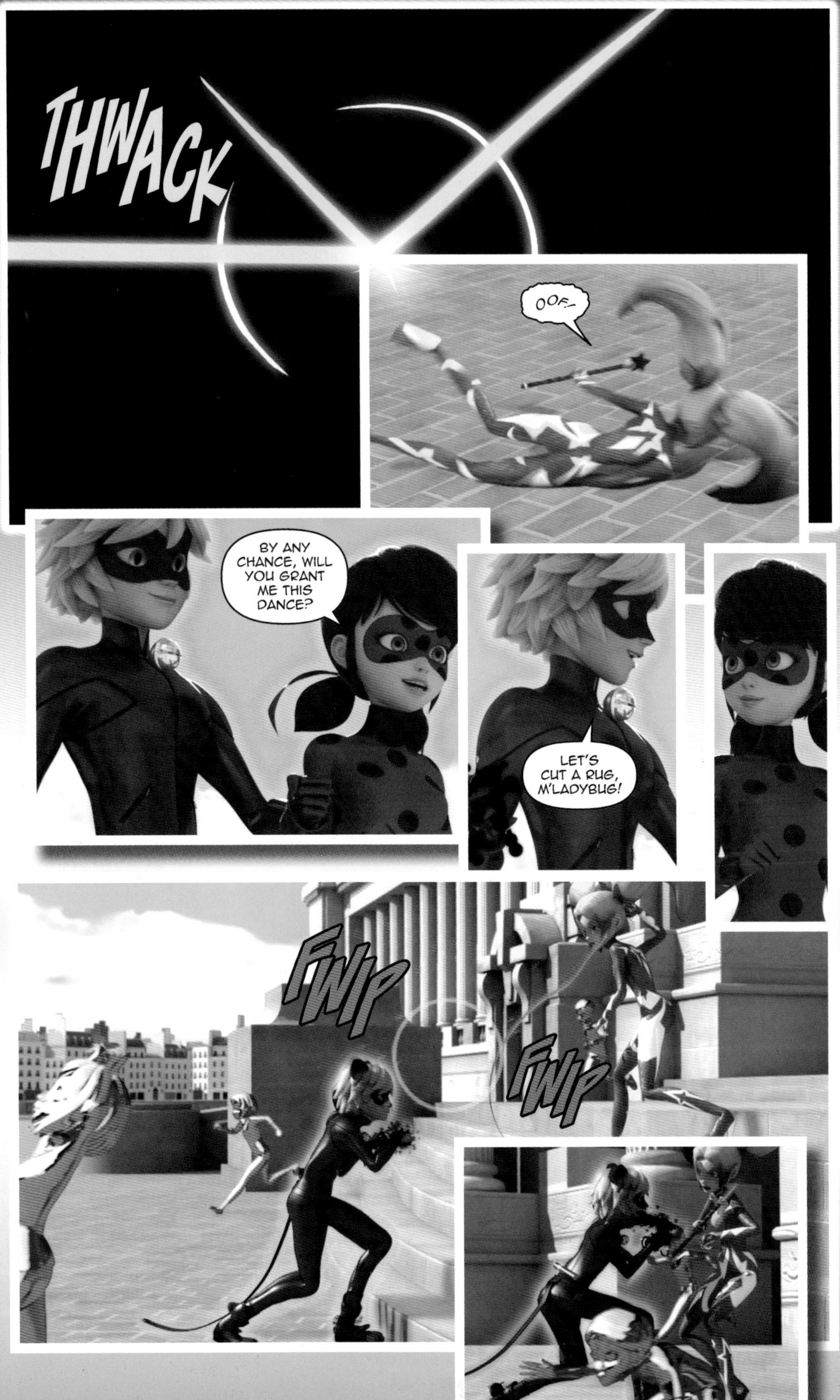
THWACK
OOF!
BY ANY CHANCE, WILL YOU GRANT ME THIS DANCE?
LET'S CUT A RUG, M'LADYBUG!
FWIP
FWIP

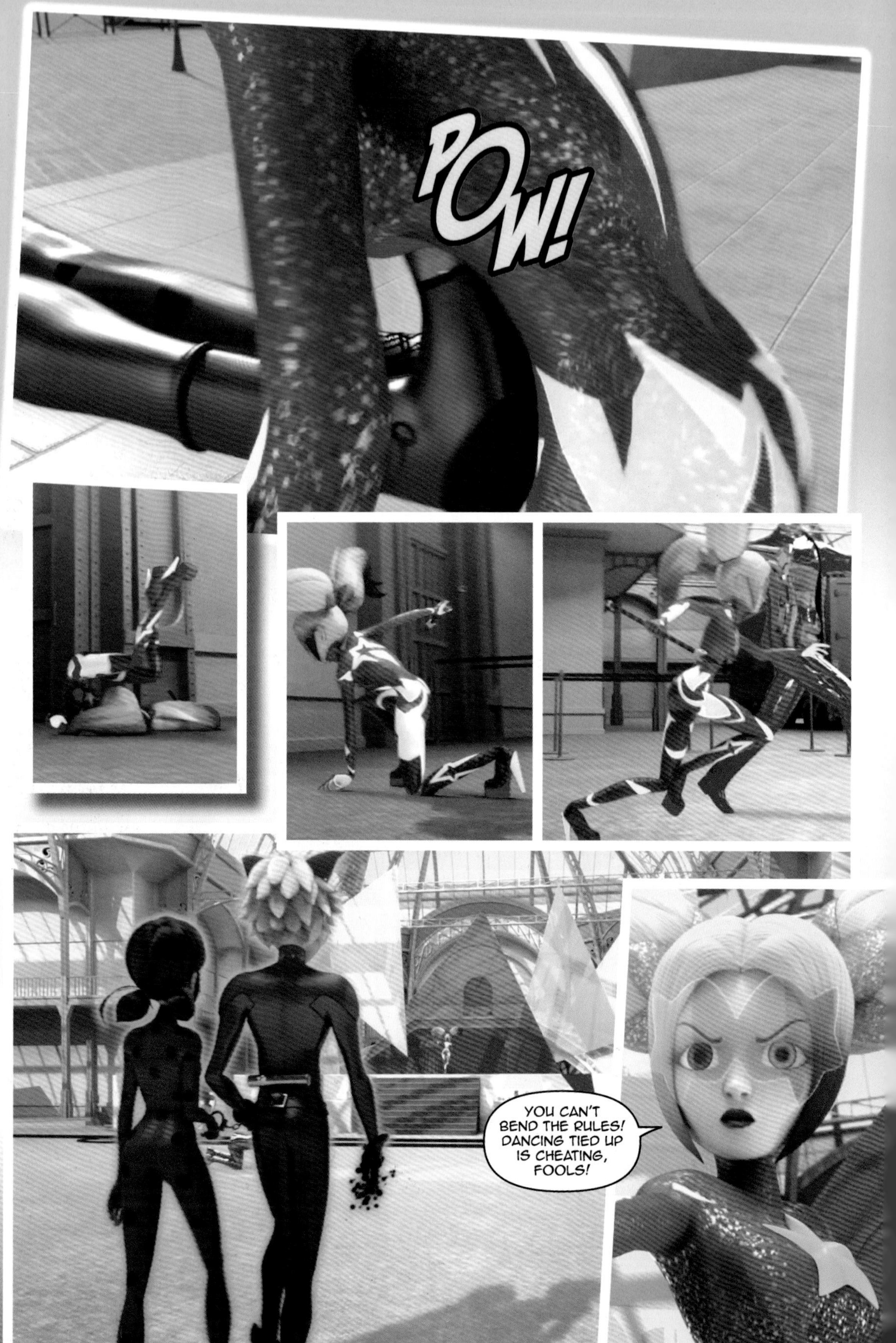
POW!
YOU CAN'T BEND THE RULES! DANCING TIED UP IS CHEATING, FOOLS!

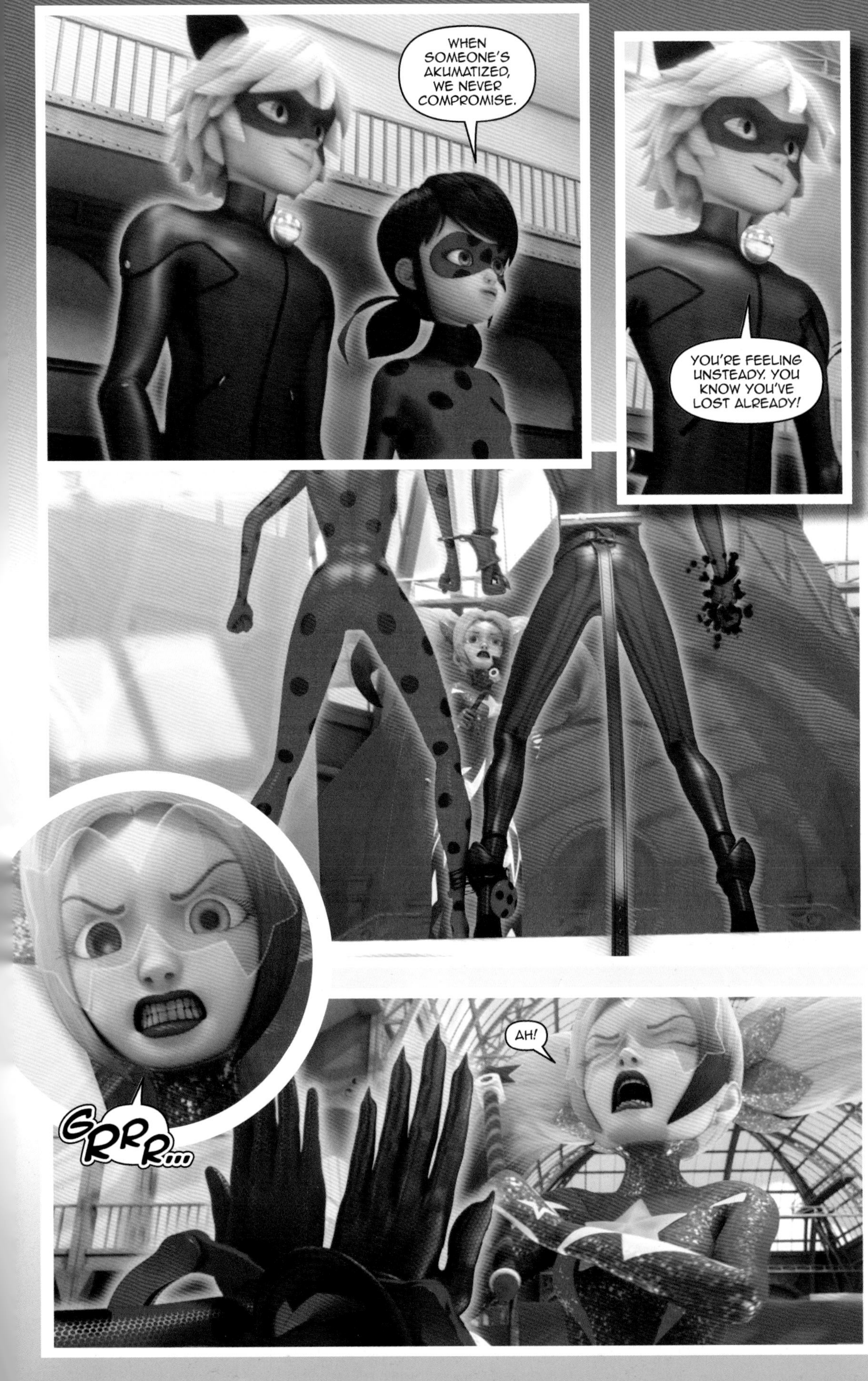
WHEN SOMEONE'S AKUMATIZED, WE NEVER COMPROMISE.
YOU'RE FEELING UNSTEADY. YOU KNOW YOU'VE LOST ALREADY!
GRRR...
AH!

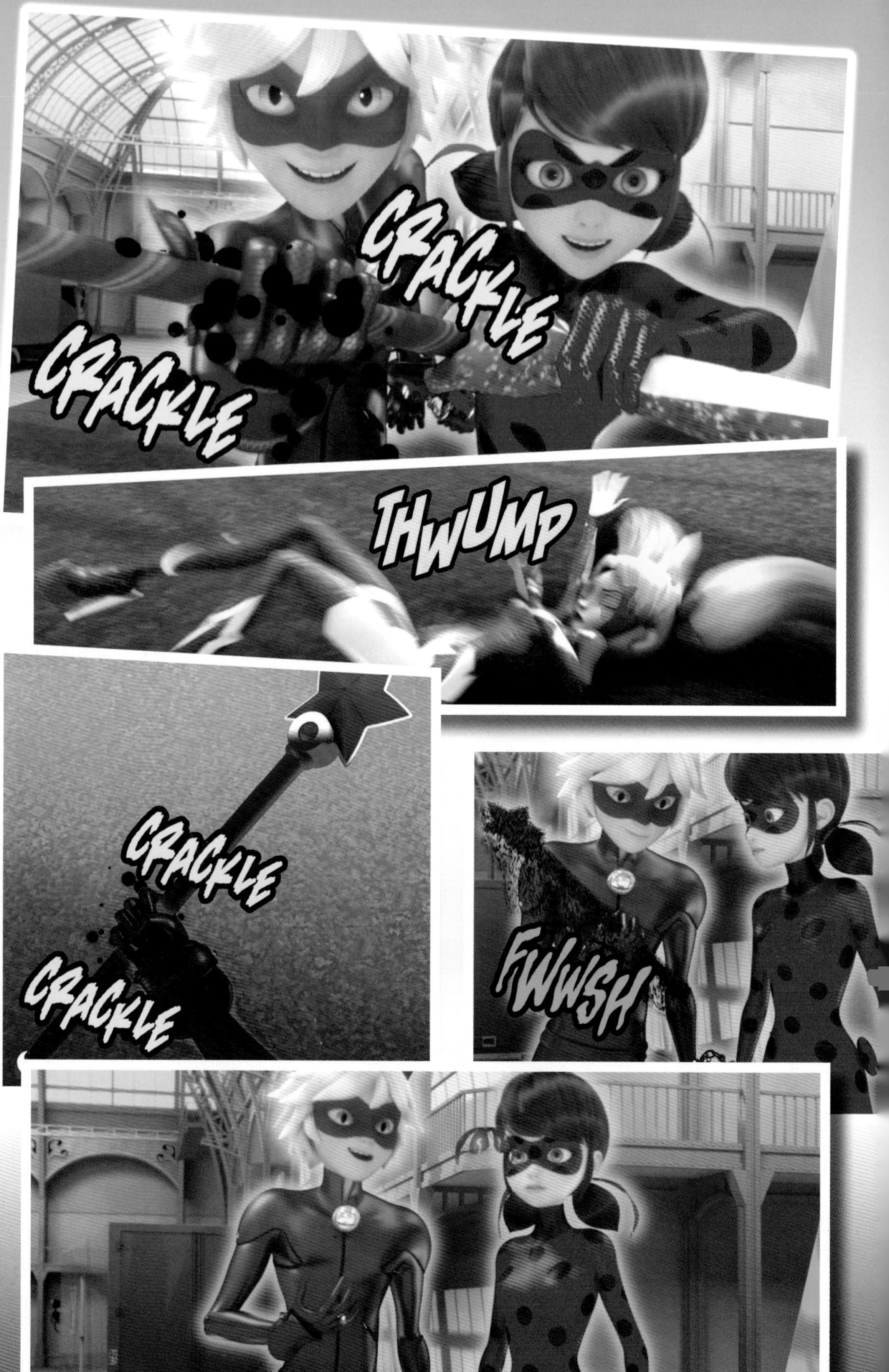
CRACKLE
CRACKLE
THWUMP
CRACKLE
CRACKLE
FWWSH

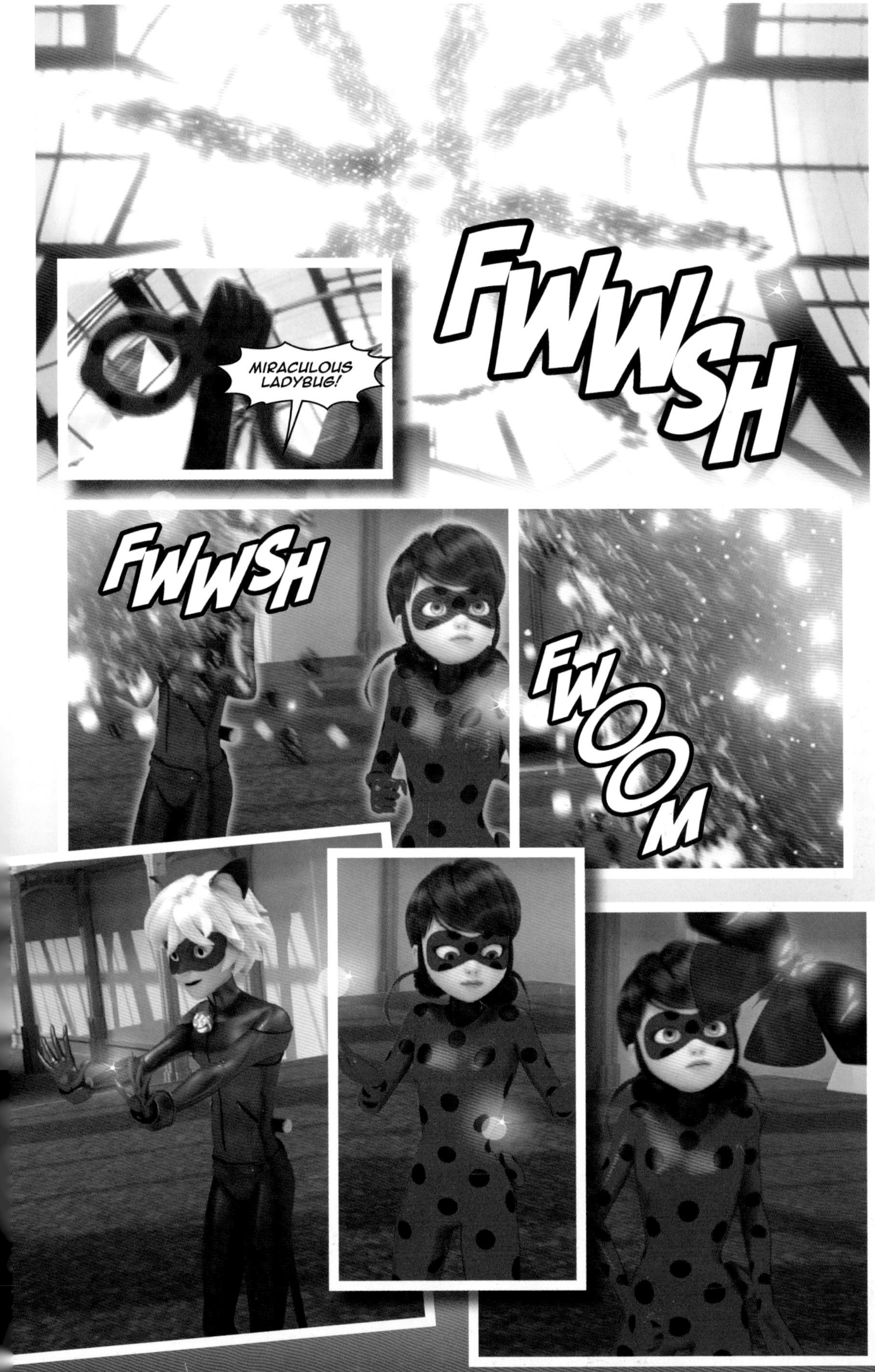
MIRACULOUS LADYBUG!
FWWSH
FWWSH
FWOOOM

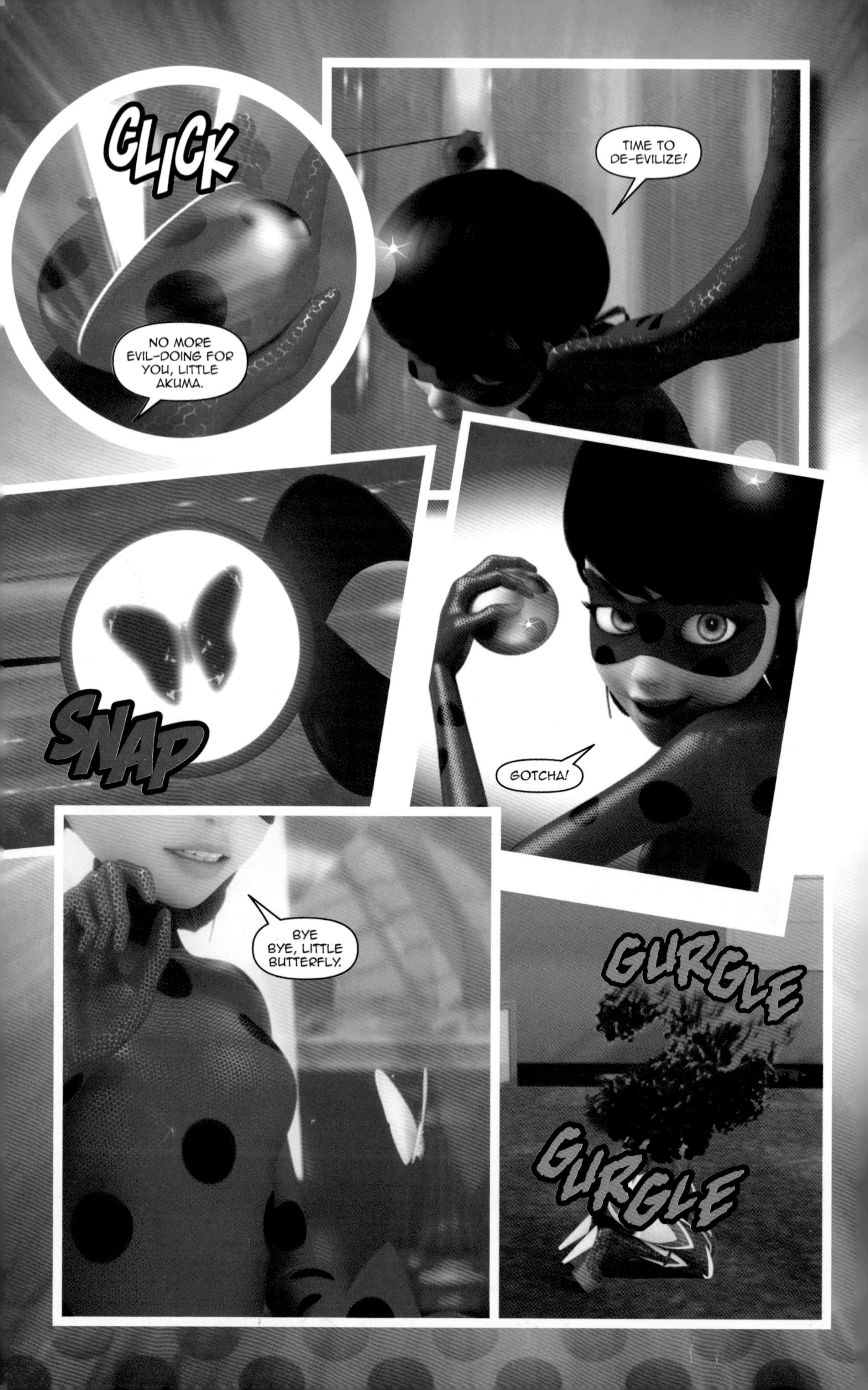
CLICK
NO MORE EVIL-DOING FOR YOU, LITTLE AKUMA.
TIME TO DE-EVILIZE!
SNAP
GOTCHA!
BYE BYE, LITTLE BUTTERFLY.
GURGLE
GURGLE

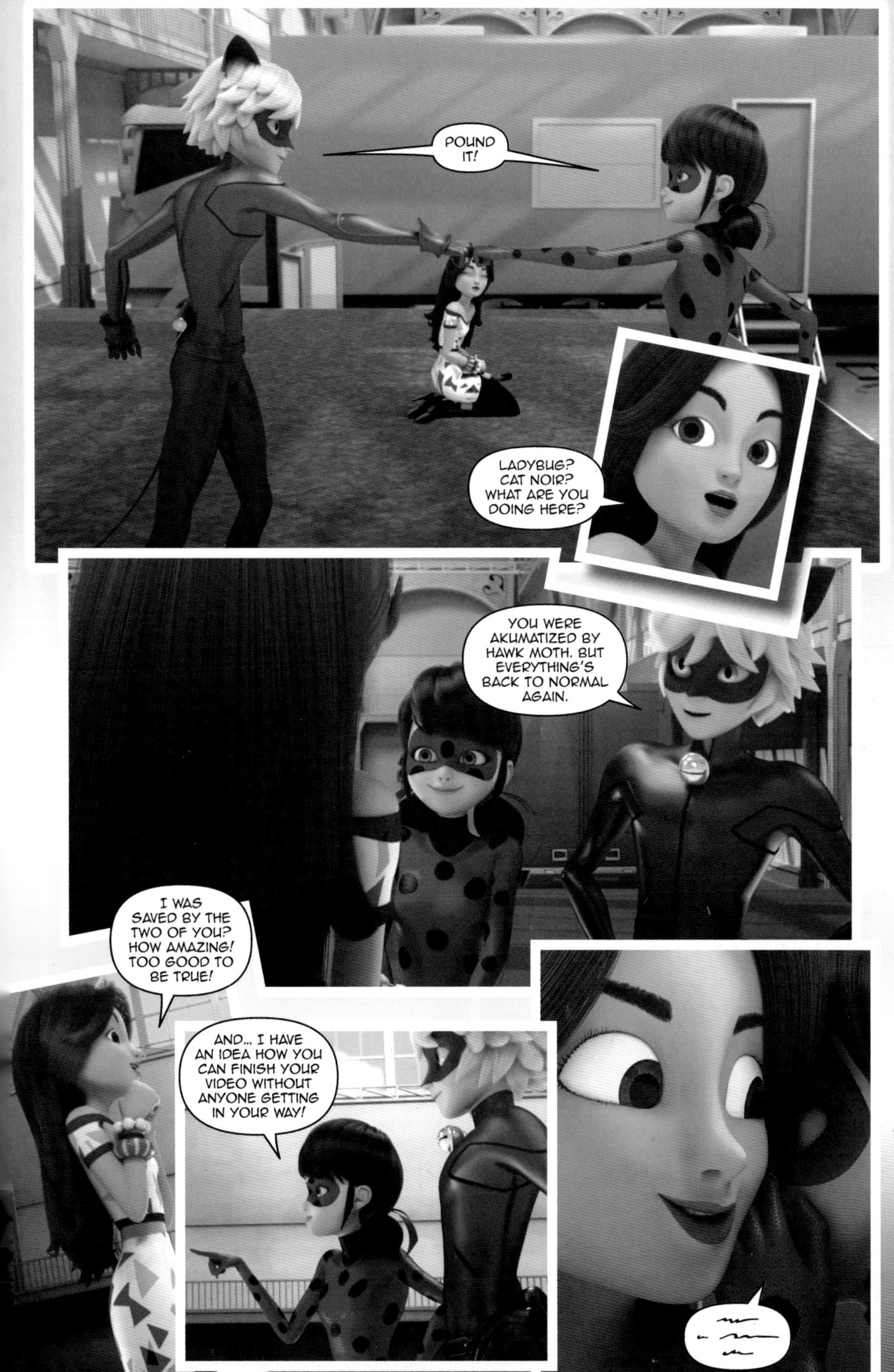
POUND IT!
LADYBUG? CAT NOIR? WHAT ARE YOU DOING HERE?
YOU WERE AKUMATIZED BY HAWK MOTH. BUT EVERYTHING'S BACK TO NORMAL AGAIN.
I WAS SAVED BY THE TWO OF YOU? HOW AMAZING! TOO GOOD TO BE TRUE!
AND... I HAVE AN IDEA HOW YOU CAN FINISH YOUR VIDEO WITHOUT ANYONE GETTING IN YOUR WAY!

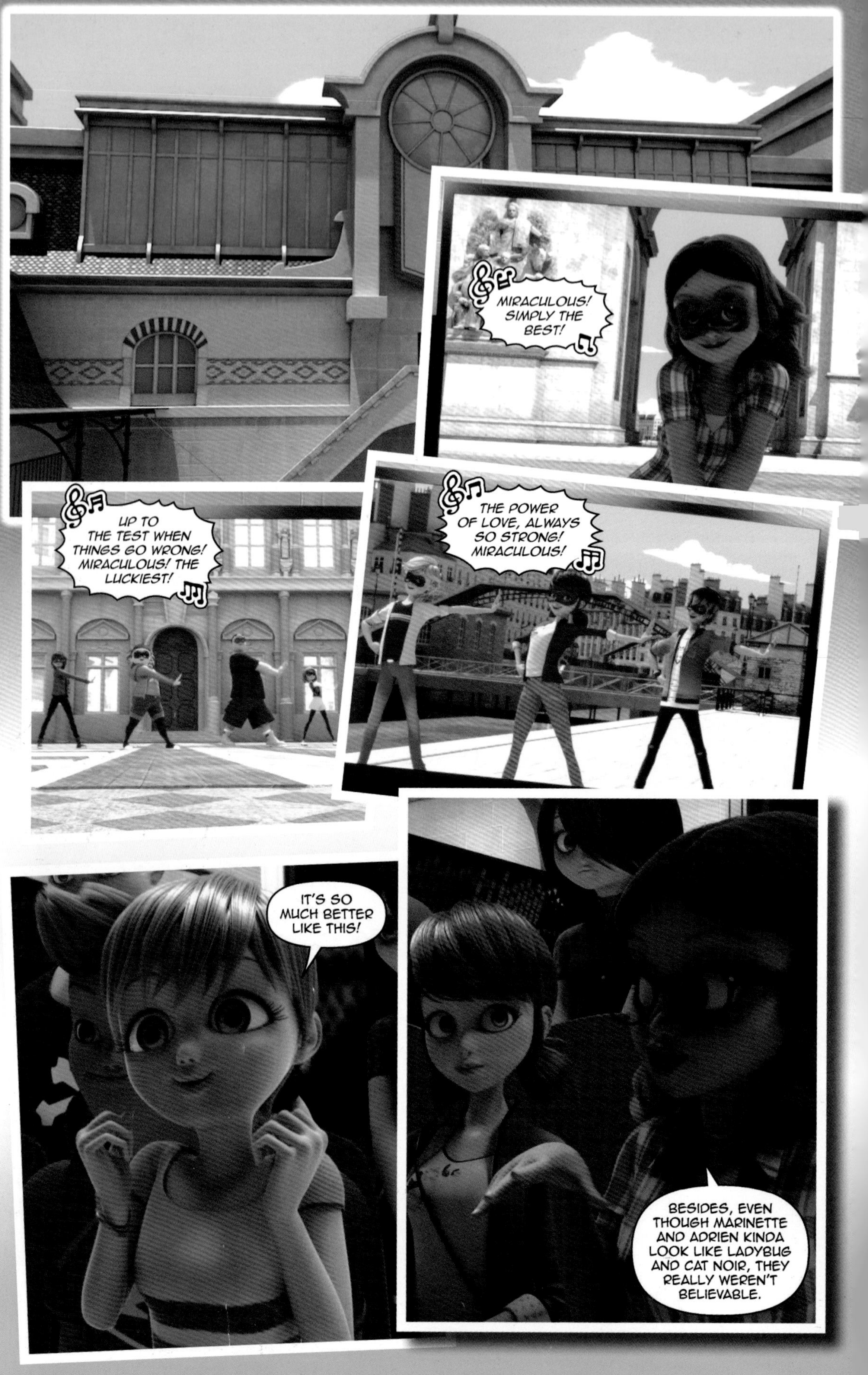
MIRACULOUS! SIMPLY THE BEST!
UP TO THE TEST WHEN THINGS GO WRONG! MIRACULOUS! THE LUCKIEST!
THE POWER OF LOVE, ALWAYS SO STRONG! MIRACULOUS!
IT'S SO MUCH BETTER LIKE THIS!
BESIDES, EVEN THOUGH MARINETTE AND ADRIEN KINDA LOOK LIKE LADYBUG AND CAT NOIR, THEY REALLY WEREN'T BELIEVABLE.

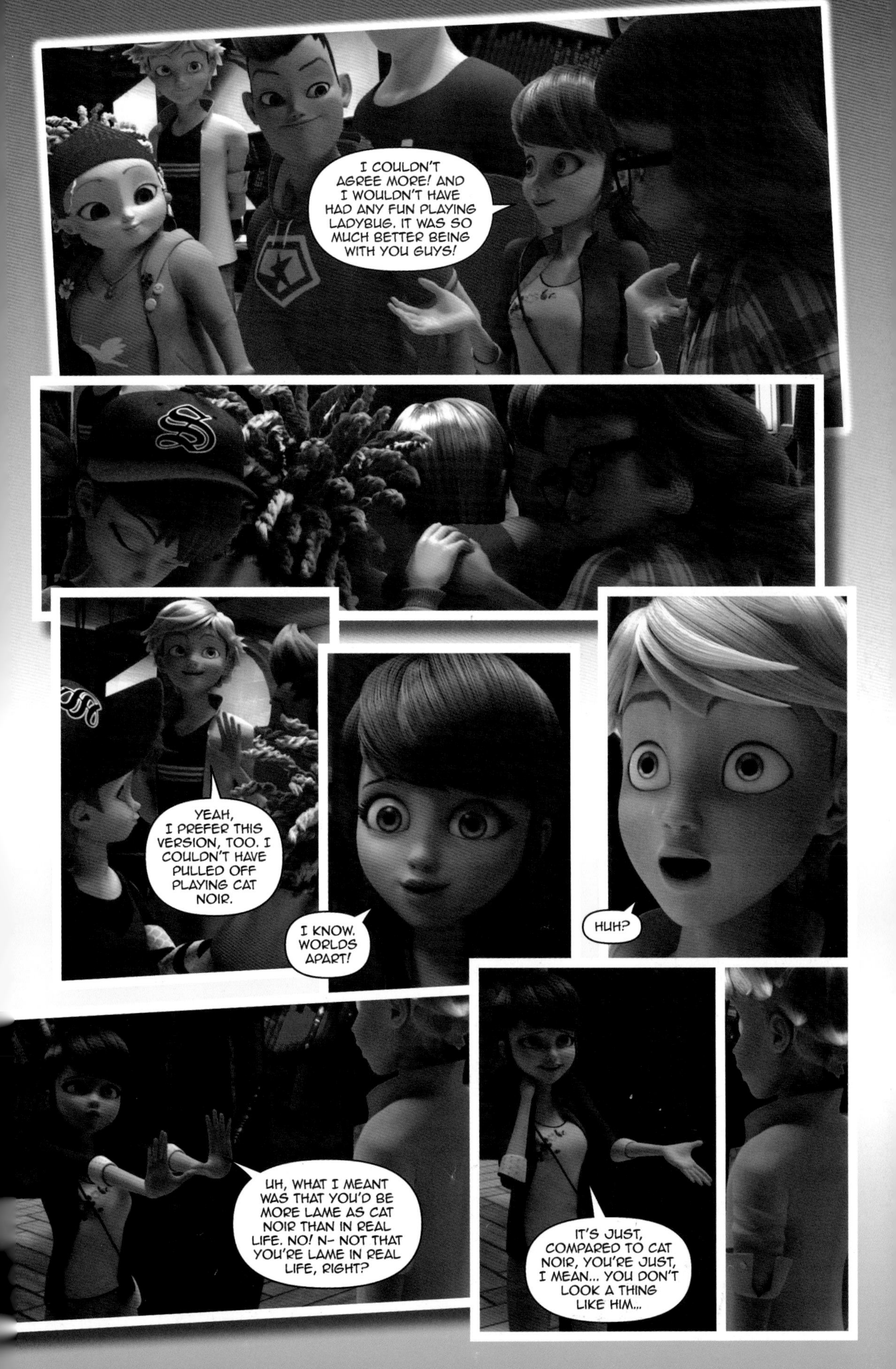
I COULDN'T AGREE MORE! AND I WOULDN'T HAVE HAD ANY FUN PLAYING LADYBUG. IT WAS SO MUCH BETTER BEING WITH YOU GUYS!
YEAH, I PREFER THIS VERSION, TOO. I COULDN'T HAVE PULLED OFF PLAYING CAT NOIR.
I KNOW. WORLDS APART!
HUH?
UH, WHAT I MEANT WAS THAT YOU'D BE MORE LAME AS CAT NOIR THAN IN REAL LIFE. NO! N- NOT THAT YOU'RE LAME IN REAL LIFE, RIGHT?
IT'S JUST, COMPARED TO CAT NOIR, YOU'RE JUST, I MEAN... YOU DON'T LOOK A THING LIKE HIM...

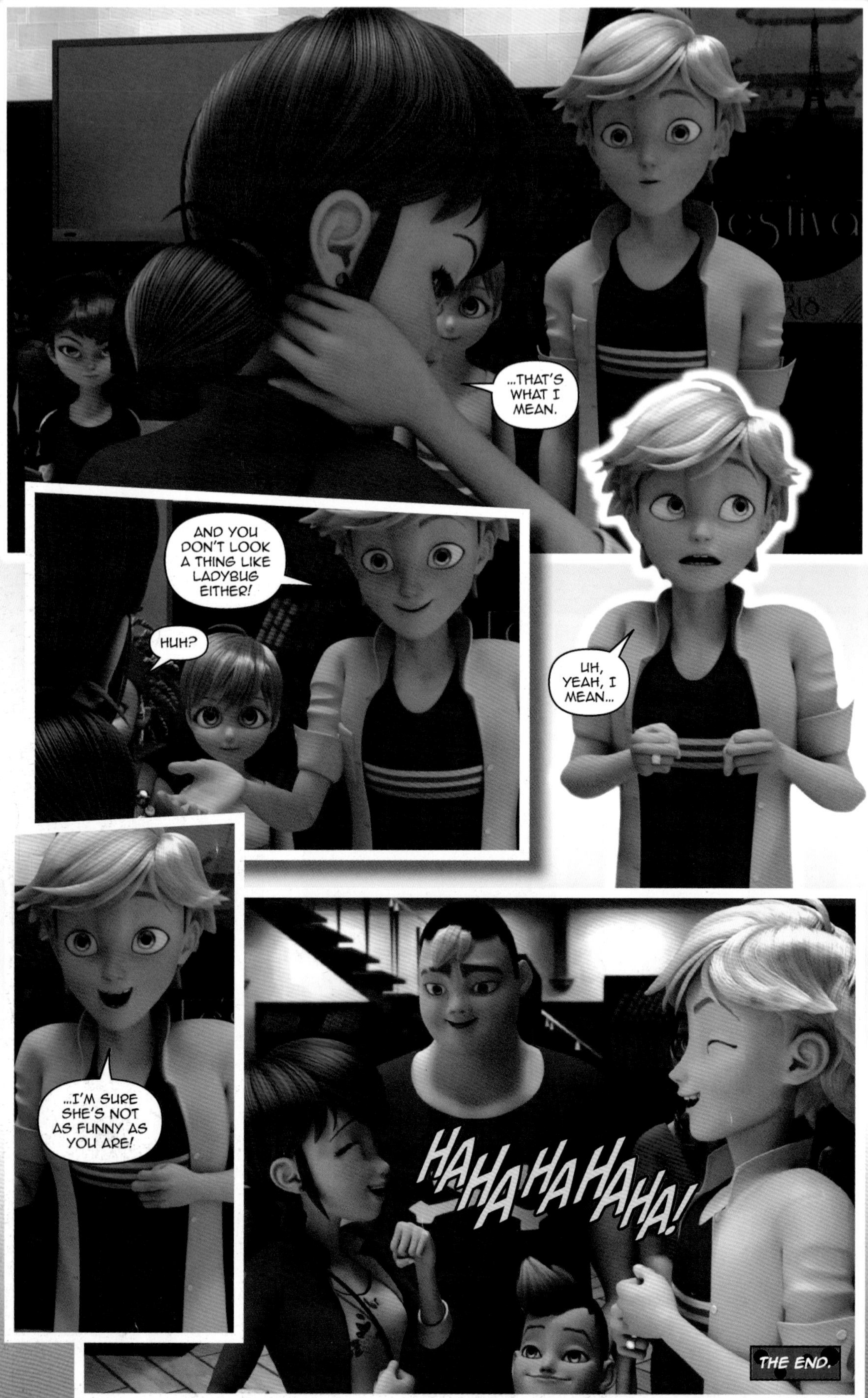
...THAT'S WHAT I MEAN.
UH, YEAH, I MEAN...
AND YOU DON'T LOOK A THING LIKE LADYBUG EITHER!
HUH?
...I'M SURE SHE'S NOT AS FUNNY AS YOU ARE!
HAHAHAHAHAHAHA!
THE END.

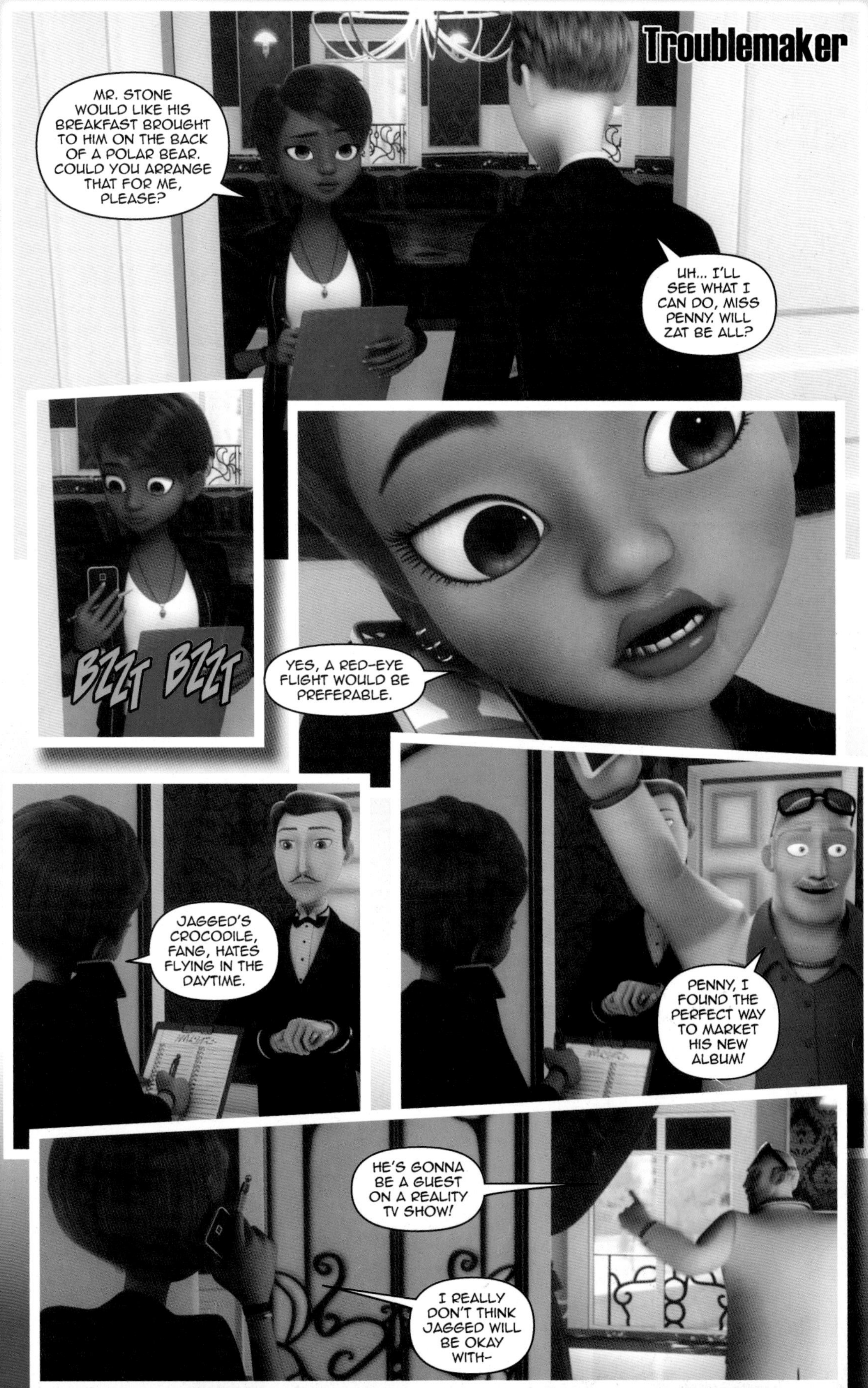
Troublemaker
MR. STONE WOULD LIKE HIS BREAKFAST BROUGHT TO HIM ON THE BACK OF A POLAR BEAR. COULD YOU ARRANGE THAT FOR ME, PLEASE?
UH... I'LL SEE WHAT I CAN DO, MISS PENNY. WILL ZAT BE ALL?
BZZT BZZT
YES, A RED-EYE FLIGHT WOULD BE PREFERABLE.
JAGGED'S CROCODILE, FANG, HATES FLYING IN THE DAYTIME.
PENNY, I FOUND THE PERFECT WAY TO MARKET HIS NEW ALBUM!
HE'S GONNA BE A GUEST ON A REALITY TV SHOW!
I REALLY DON'T THINK JAGGED WILL BE OKAY WITH-

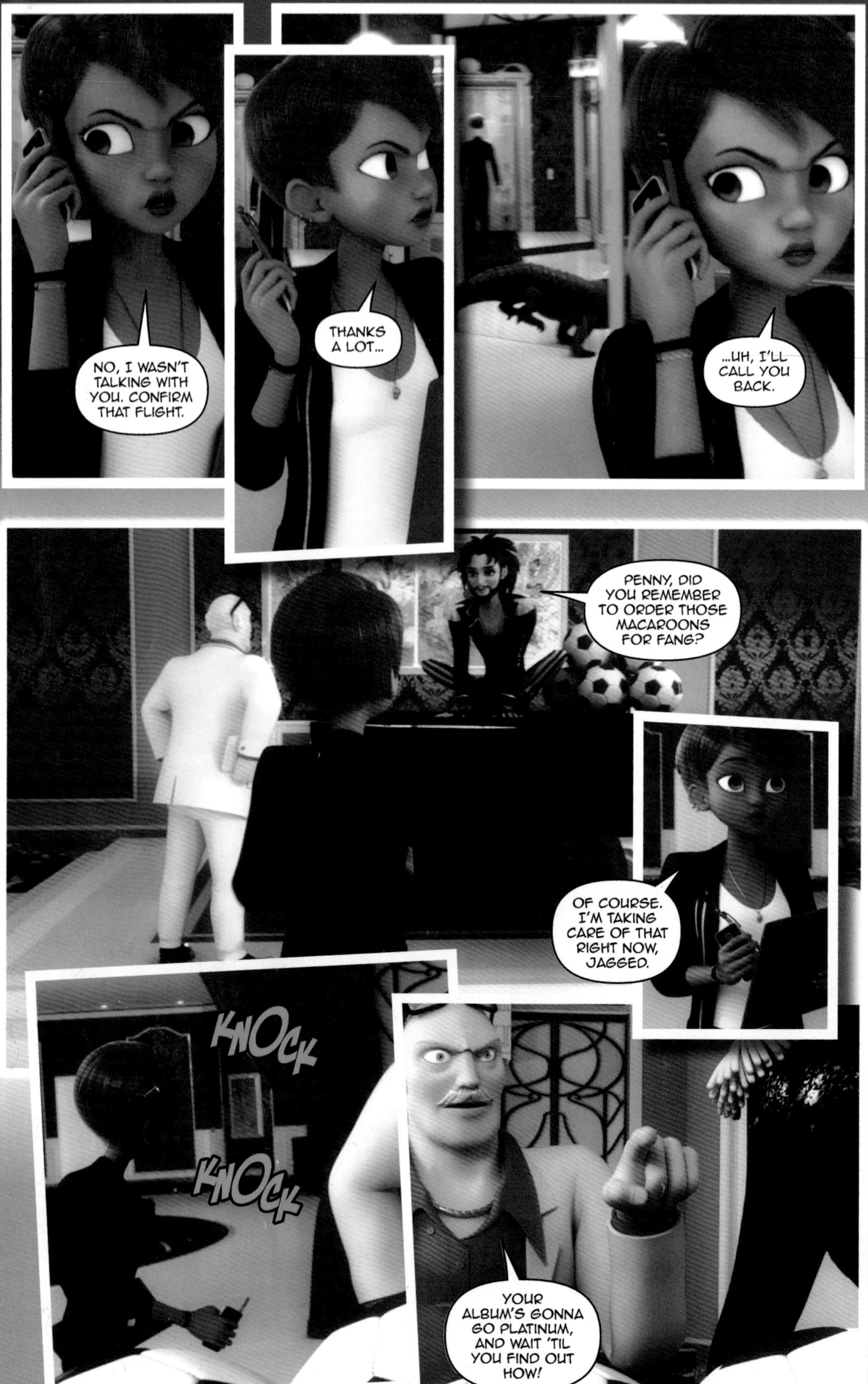
NO, I WASN'T TALKING WITH YOU. CONFIRM THAT FLIGHT.
THANKS A LOT...
...UH, I'LL CALL YOU BACK.
PENNY, DID YOU REMEMBER TO ORDER THOSE MACAROONS FOR FANG?
OF COURSE. I'M TAKING CARE OF THAT RIGHT NOW, JAGGED.
KNOCK
KNOCK
YOUR ALBUM'S GONNA GO PLATINUM, AND WAIT 'TIL YOU FIND OUT HOW!

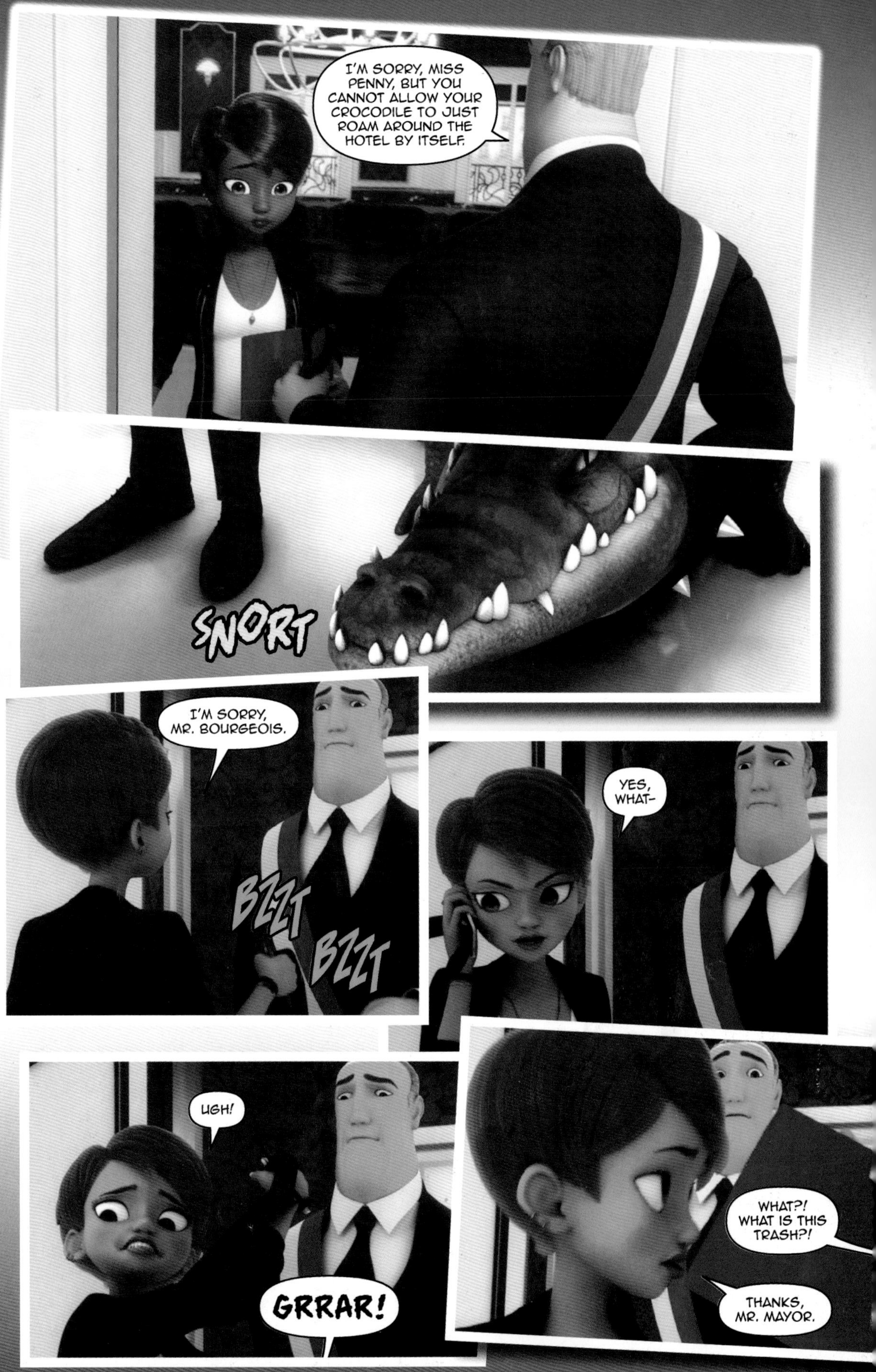
I'M SORRY, MISS PENNY, BUT YOU CANNOT ALLOW YOUR CROCODILE TO JUST ROAM AROUND THE HOTEL BY ITSELF.
SNORT
I'M SORRY, MR. BOURGEOIS.
BZZT BZZT
YES, WHAT-
UGH!
GRRAR!
WHAT?! WHAT IS THIS TRASH?!
THANKS, MR. MAYOR.

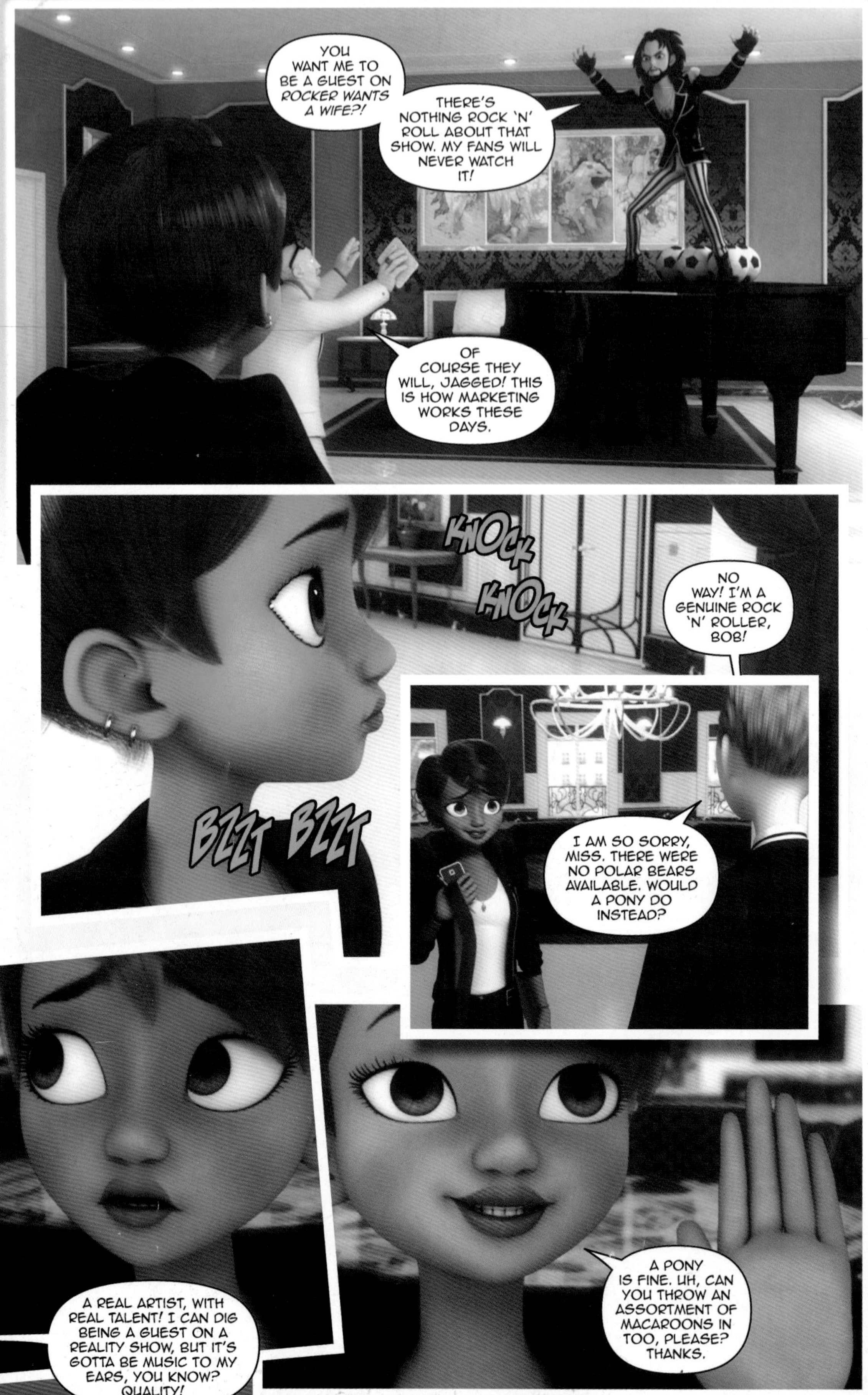
YOU WANT ME TO BE A GUEST ON *ROCKER WANTS A WIFE*?!
THERE'S NOTHING ROCK 'N' ROLL ABOUT THAT SHOW. MY FANS WILL NEVER WATCH IT!
OF COURSE THEY WILL, JAGGED! THIS IS HOW MARKETING WORKS THESE DAYS.
KNOCK KNOCK
NO WAY! I'M A GENUINE ROCK 'N' ROLLER, BOB!
BZZT BZZT
I AM SO SORRY, MISS. THERE WERE NO POLAR BEARS AVAILABLE. WOULD A PONY DO INSTEAD?
A REAL ARTIST, WITH REAL TALENT! I CAN DIG BEING A GUEST ON A REALITY SHOW, BUT IT'S GOTTA BE MUSIC TO MY EARS, YOU KNOW? QUALITY!
A PONY IS FINE. UH, CAN YOU THROW AN ASSORTMENT OF MACAROONS IN TOO, PLEASE? THANKS.

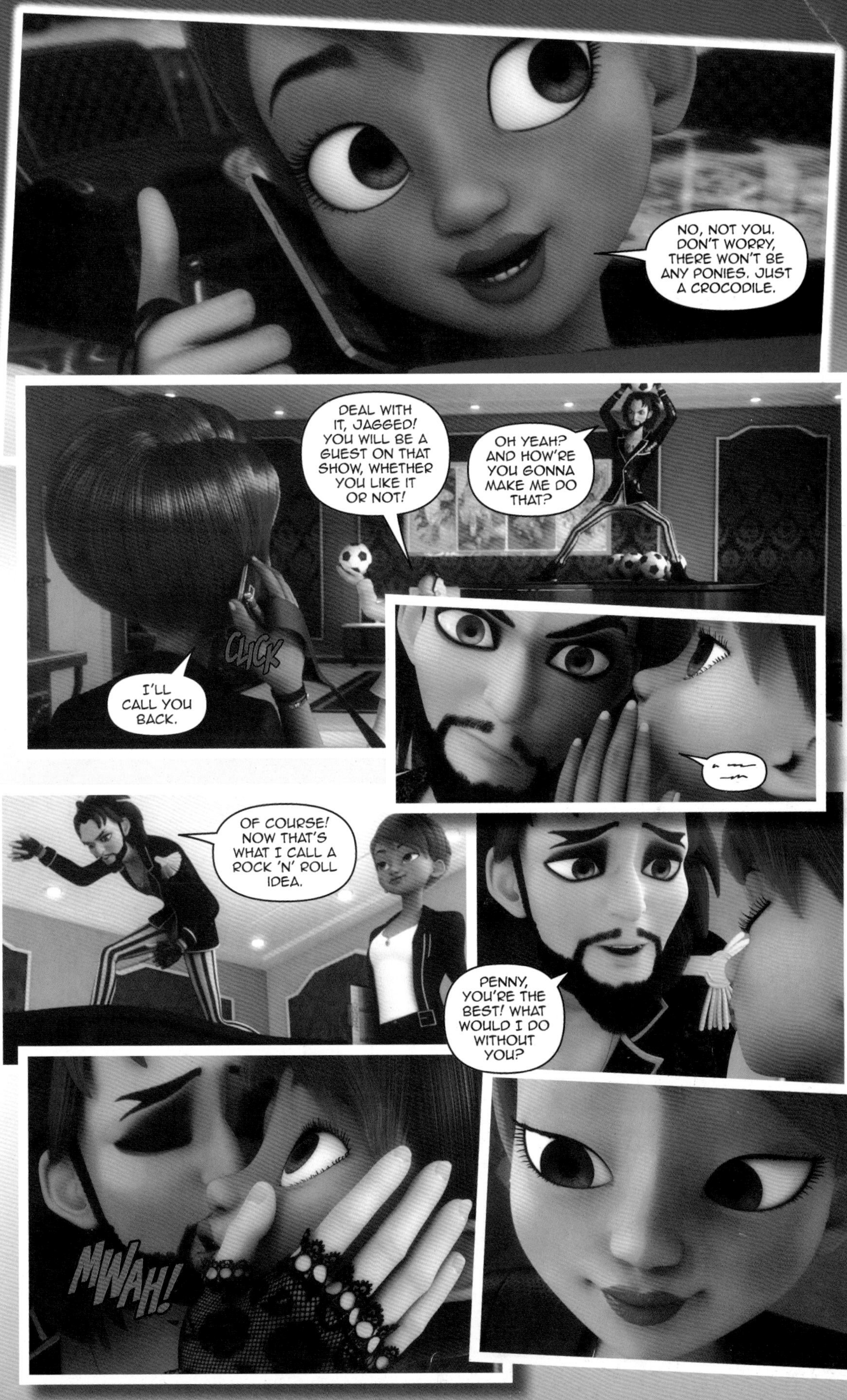
NO, NOT YOU. DON'T WORRY, THERE WON'T BE ANY PONIES. JUST A CROCODILE.
DEAL WITH IT, JAGGED! YOU WILL BE A GUEST ON THAT SHOW, WHETHER YOU LIKE IT OR NOT!
OH YEAH? AND HOW'RE YOU GONNA MAKE ME DO THAT?
CLICK
I'LL CALL YOU BACK.
OF COURSE! NOW THAT'S WHAT I CALL A ROCK 'N' ROLL IDEA.
PENNY, YOU'RE THE BEST! WHAT WOULD I DO WITHOUT YOU?
MWAH!

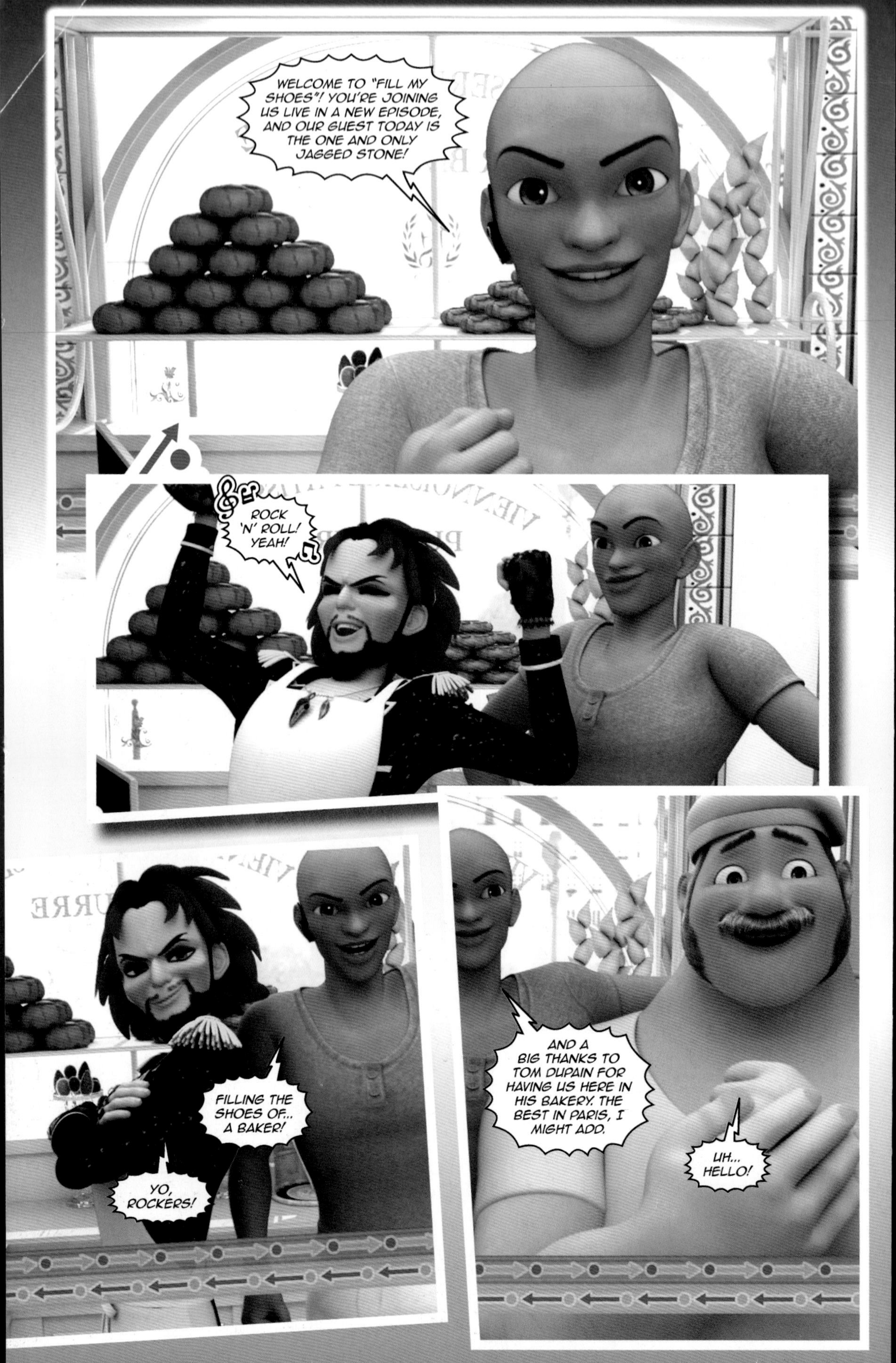
WELCOME TO "FILL MY SHOES"! YOU'RE JOINING US LIVE IN A NEW EPISODE, AND OUR GUEST TODAY IS THE ONE AND ONLY JAGGED STONE!
ROCK 'N' ROLL! YEAH!
FILLING THE SHOES OF... A BAKER!
YO, ROCKERS!
AND A BIG THANKS TO TOM DUPAIN FOR HAVING US HERE IN HIS BAKERY. THE BEST IN PARIS, I MIGHT ADD.
UH... HELLO!

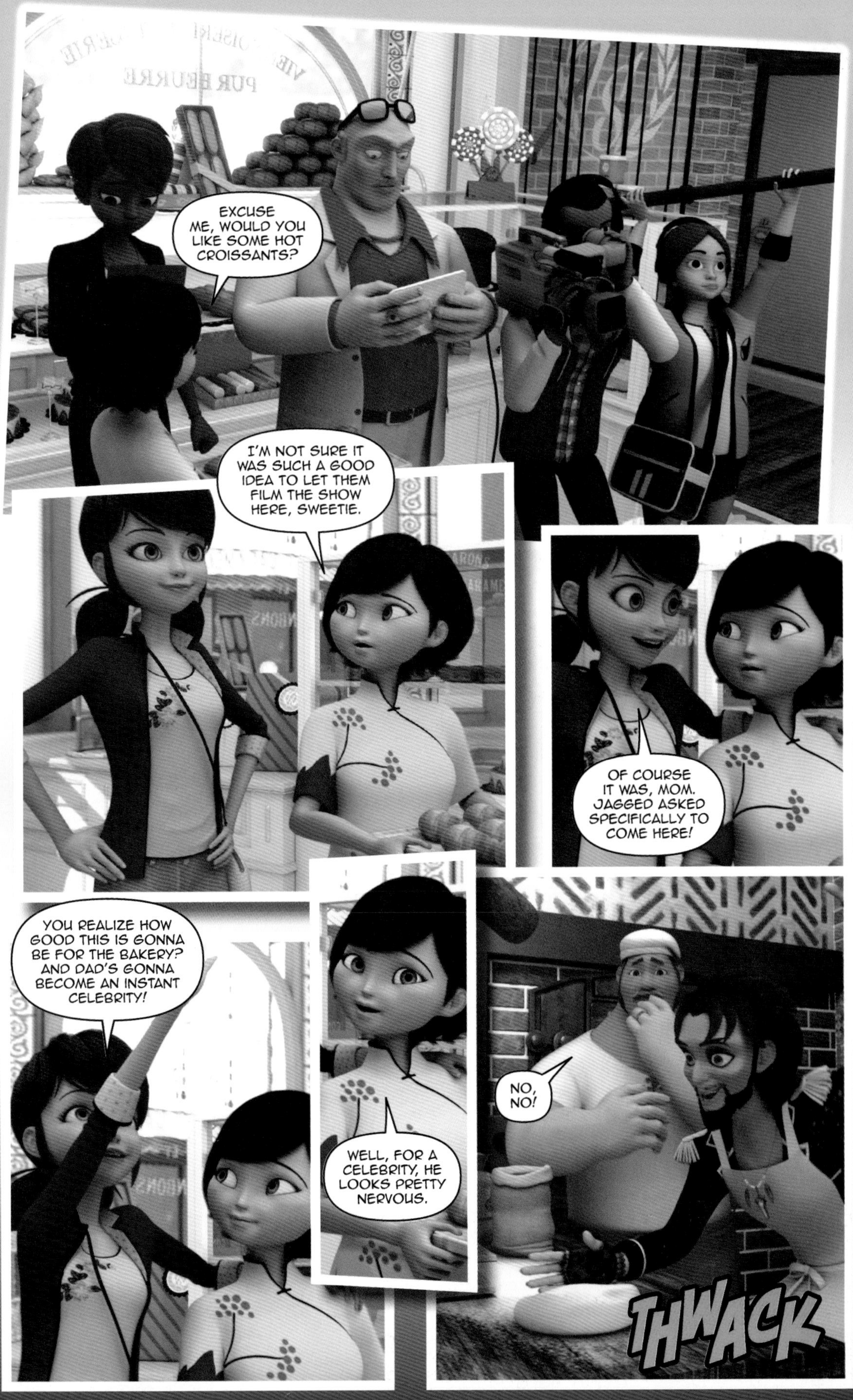

EXCUSE ME, WOULD YOU LIKE SOME HOT CROISSANTS?
I'M NOT SURE IT WAS SUCH A GOOD IDEA TO LET THEM FILM THE SHOW HERE, SWEETIE.
OF COURSE IT WAS, MOM. JAGGED ASKED SPECIFICALLY TO COME HERE!
YOU REALIZE HOW GOOD THIS IS GONNA BE FOR THE BAKERY? AND DAD'S GONNA BECOME AN INSTANT CELEBRITY!
WELL, FOR A CELEBRITY, HE LOOKS PRETTY NERVOUS.
NO, NO!
THWACK

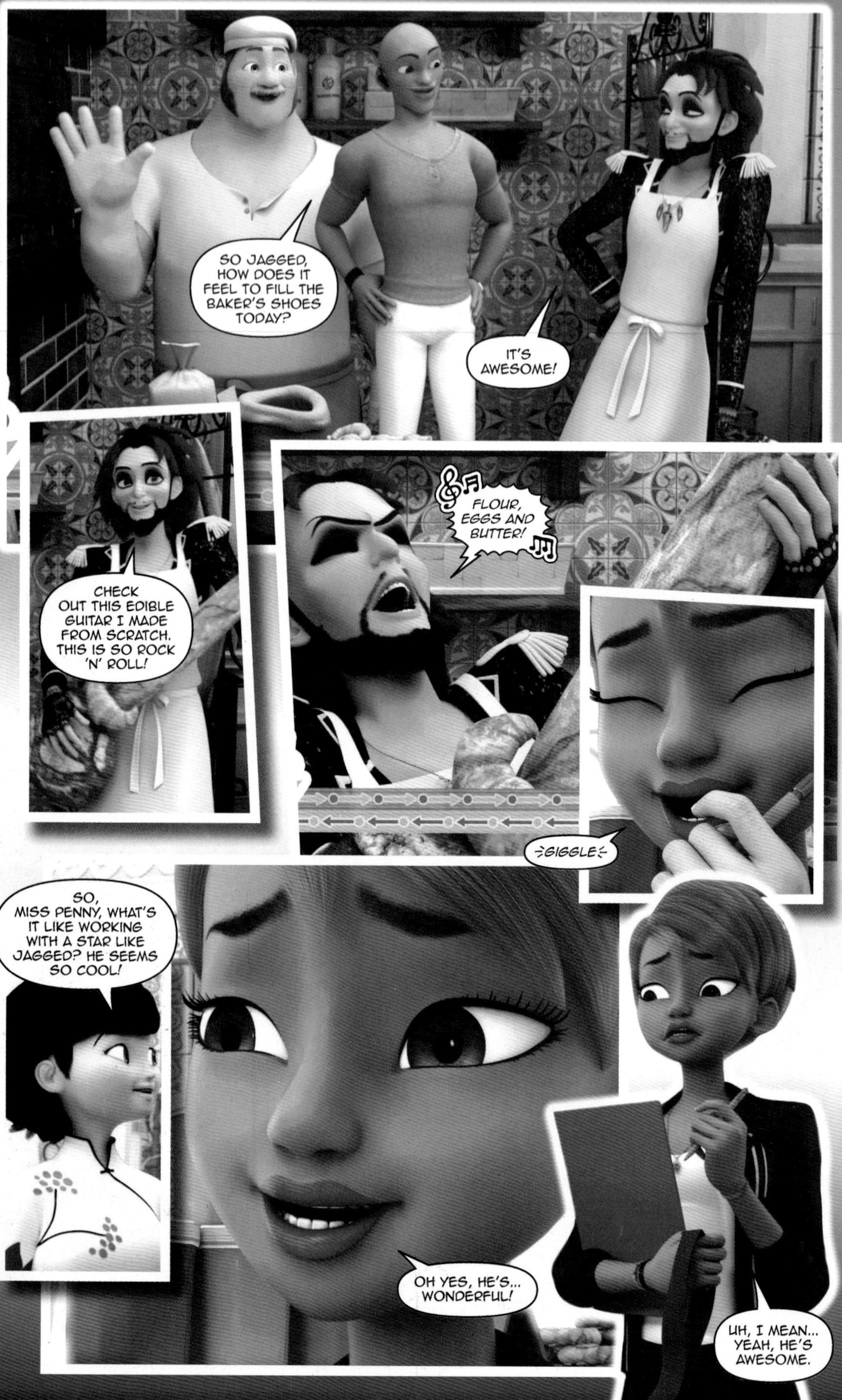
SO JAGGED, HOW DOES IT FEEL TO FILL THE BAKER'S SHOES TODAY?
IT'S AWESOME!
CHECK OUT THIS EDIBLE GUITAR I MADE FROM SCRATCH. THIS IS SO ROCK 'N' ROLL!
FLOUR, EGGS AND BUTTER!
GIGGLE
SO, MISS PENNY, WHAT'S IT LIKE WORKING WITH A STAR LIKE JAGGED? HE SEEMS SO COOL!
OH YES, HE'S... WONDERFUL!
UH, I MEAN... YEAH, HE'S AWESOME.

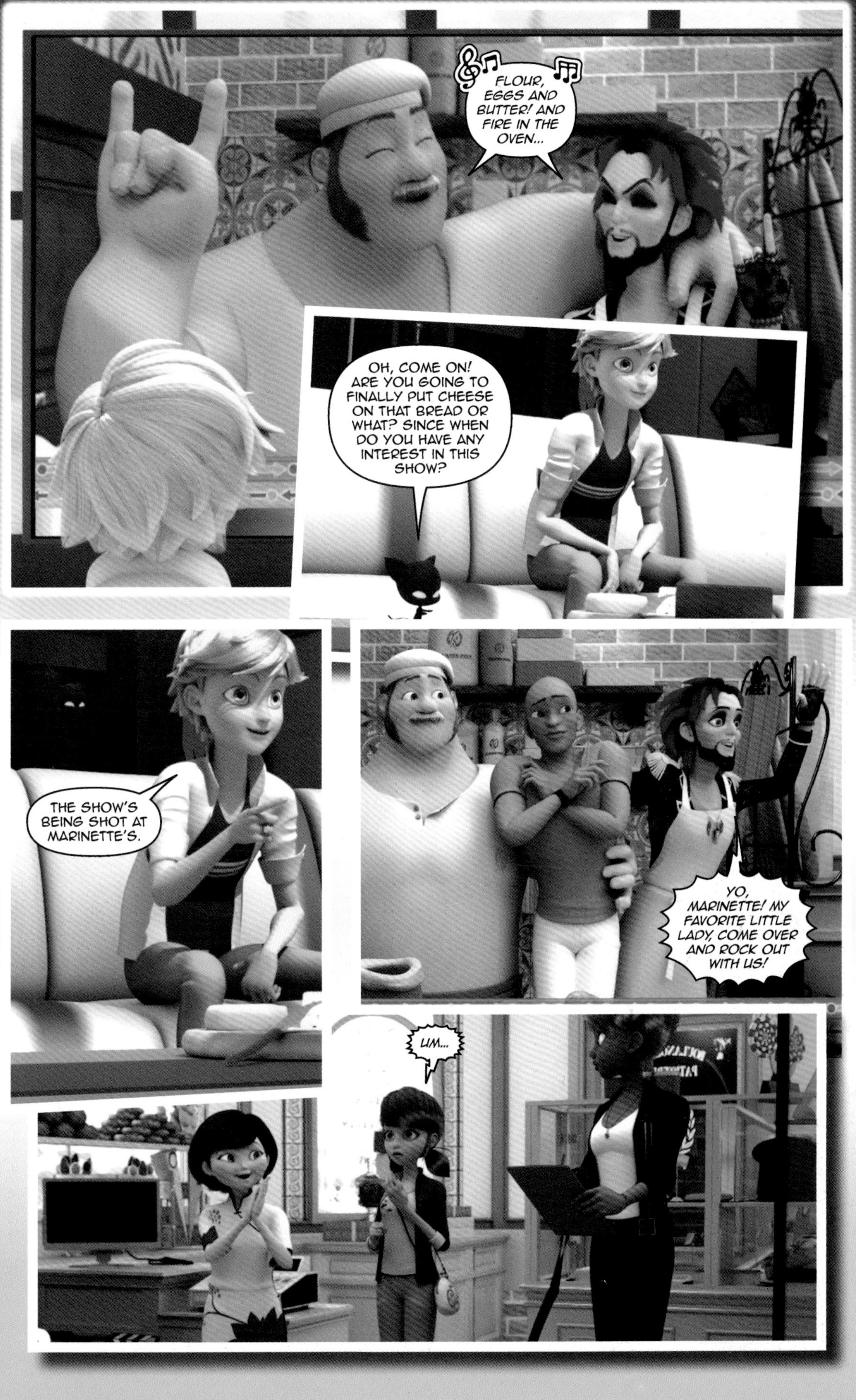
FLOUR, EGGS AND BUTTER! AND FIRE IN THE OVEN...
OH, COME ON! ARE YOU GOING TO FINALLY PUT CHEESE ON THAT BREAD OR WHAT? SINCE WHEN DO YOU HAVE ANY INTEREST IN THIS SHOW?
THE SHOW'S BEING SHOT AT MARINETTE'S.
YO, MARINETTE! MY FAVORITE LITTLE LADY, COME OVER AND ROCK OUT WITH US!
UM...

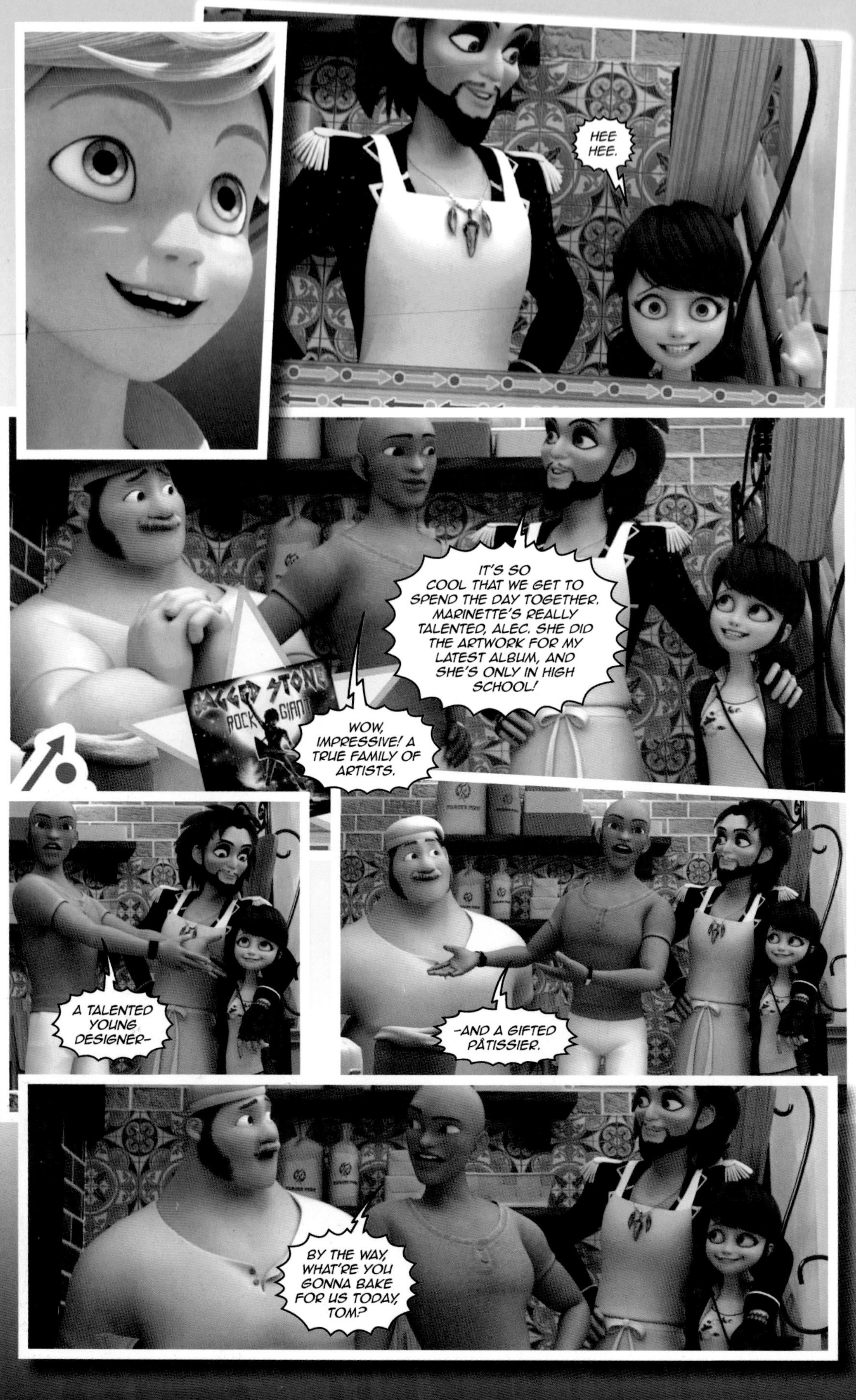
HEE HEE.
IT'S SO COOL THAT WE GET TO SPEND THE DAY TOGETHER. MARINETTE'S REALLY TALENTED, ALEC. SHE DID THE ARTWORK FOR MY LATEST ALBUM, AND SHE'S ONLY IN HIGH SCHOOL!
WOW, IMPRESSIVE! A TRUE FAMILY OF ARTISTS.
A TALENTED YOUNG DESIGNER-
-AND A GIFTED PÂTISSIER.
BY THE WAY, WHAT'RE YOU GONNA BAKE FOR US TODAY, TOM?

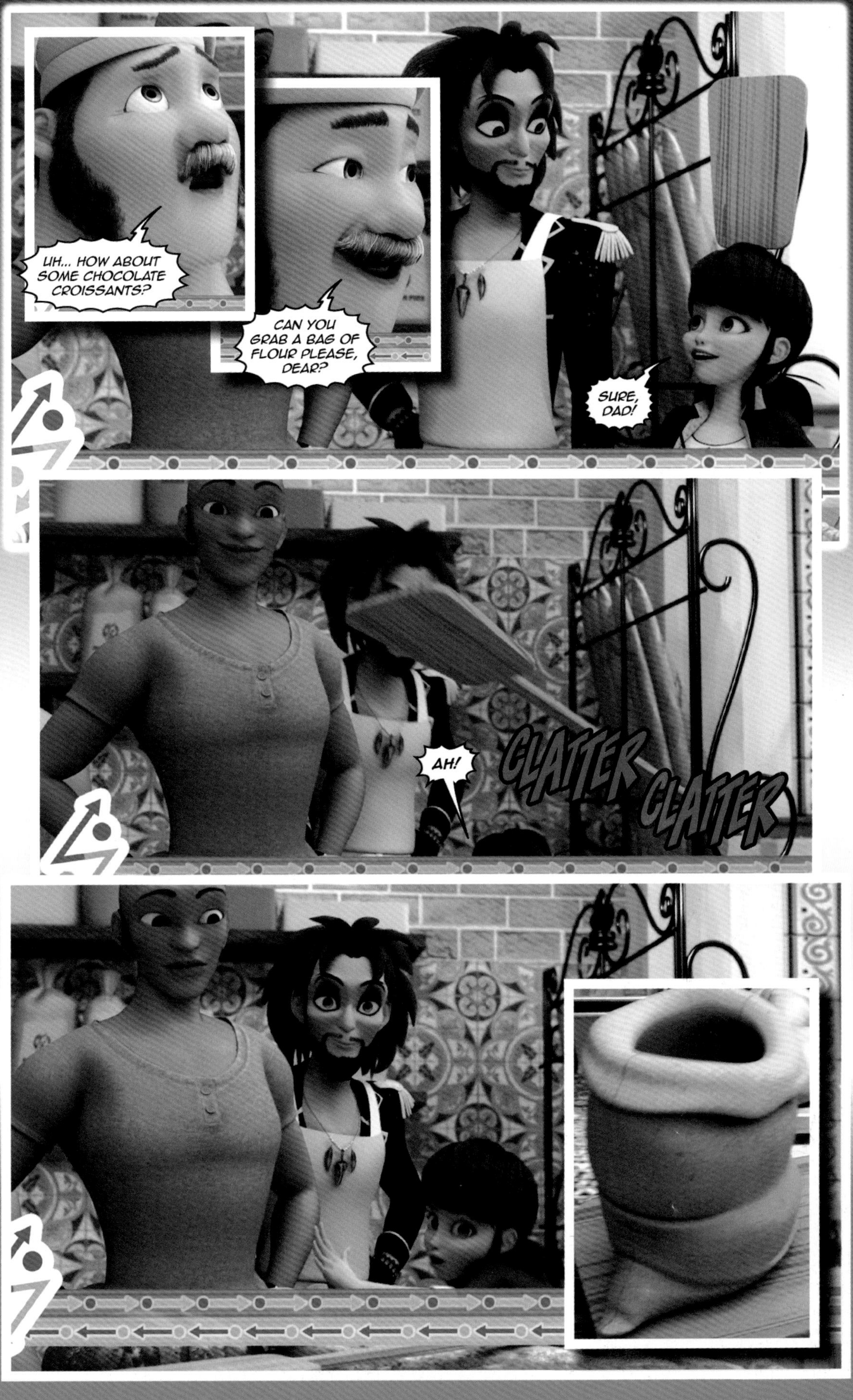
UH... HOW ABOUT SOME CHOCOLATE CROISSANTS?
CAN YOU GRAB A BAG OF FLOUR PLEASE, DEAR?
SURE, DAD!
AH!
CLATTER
CLATTER

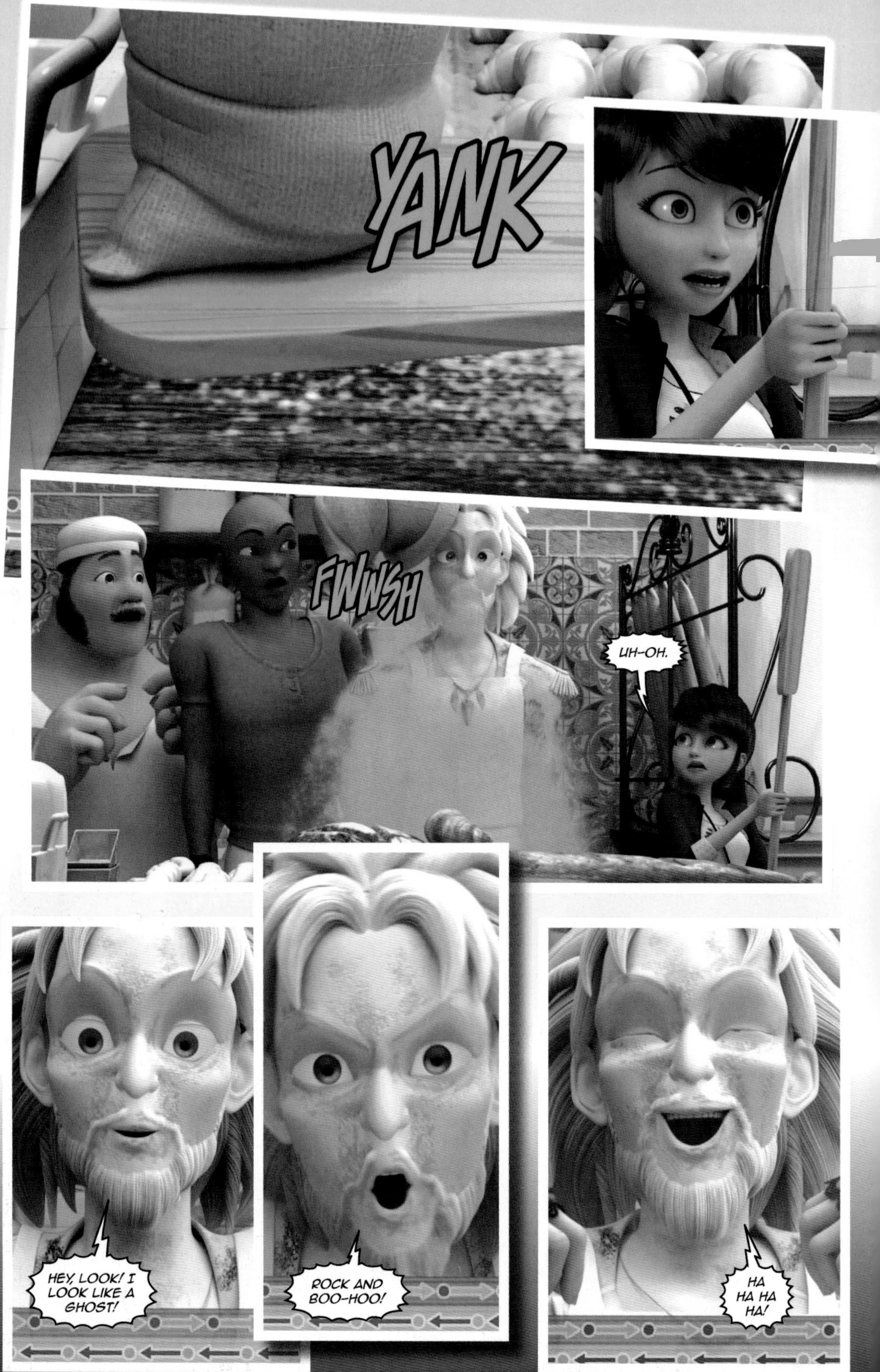
YANK
FWWSH
UH-OH.
HEY, LOOK! I LOOK LIKE A GHOST!
ROCK AND BOO-HOO!
HA HA HA HA!

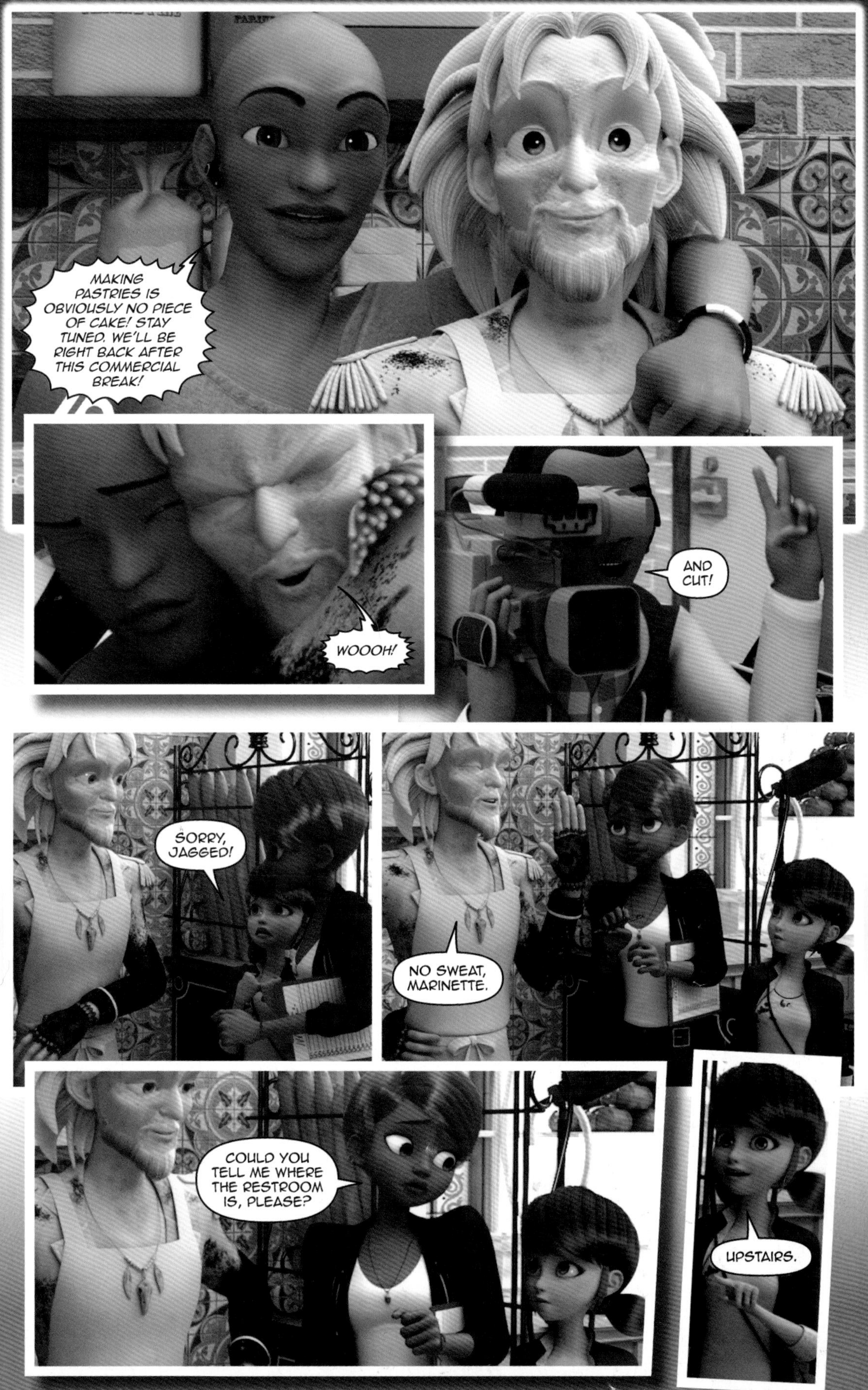
MAKING PASTRIES IS OBVIOUSLY NO PIECE OF CAKE! STAY TUNED. WE'LL BE RIGHT BACK AFTER THIS COMMERCIAL BREAK!
WOOOH!
AND CUT!
SORRY, JAGGED!
NO SWEAT, MARINETTE.
COULD YOU TELL ME WHERE THE RESTROOM IS, PLEASE?
UPSTAIRS.

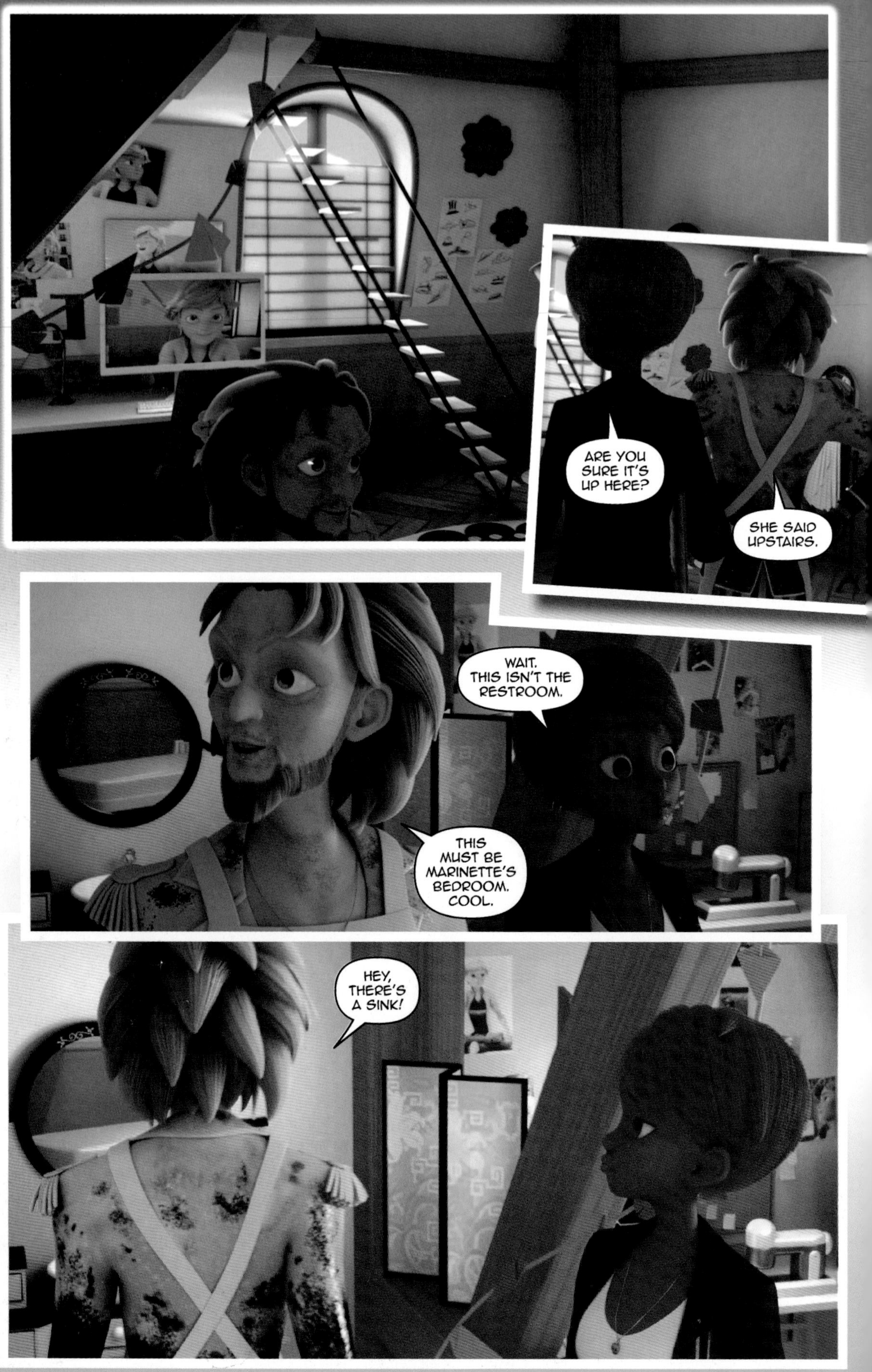
ARE YOU SURE IT'S UP HERE?
SHE SAID UPSTAIRS.
WAIT. THIS ISN'T THE RESTROOM.
THIS MUST BE MARINETTE'S BEDROOM. COOL.
HEY, THERE'S A SINK!

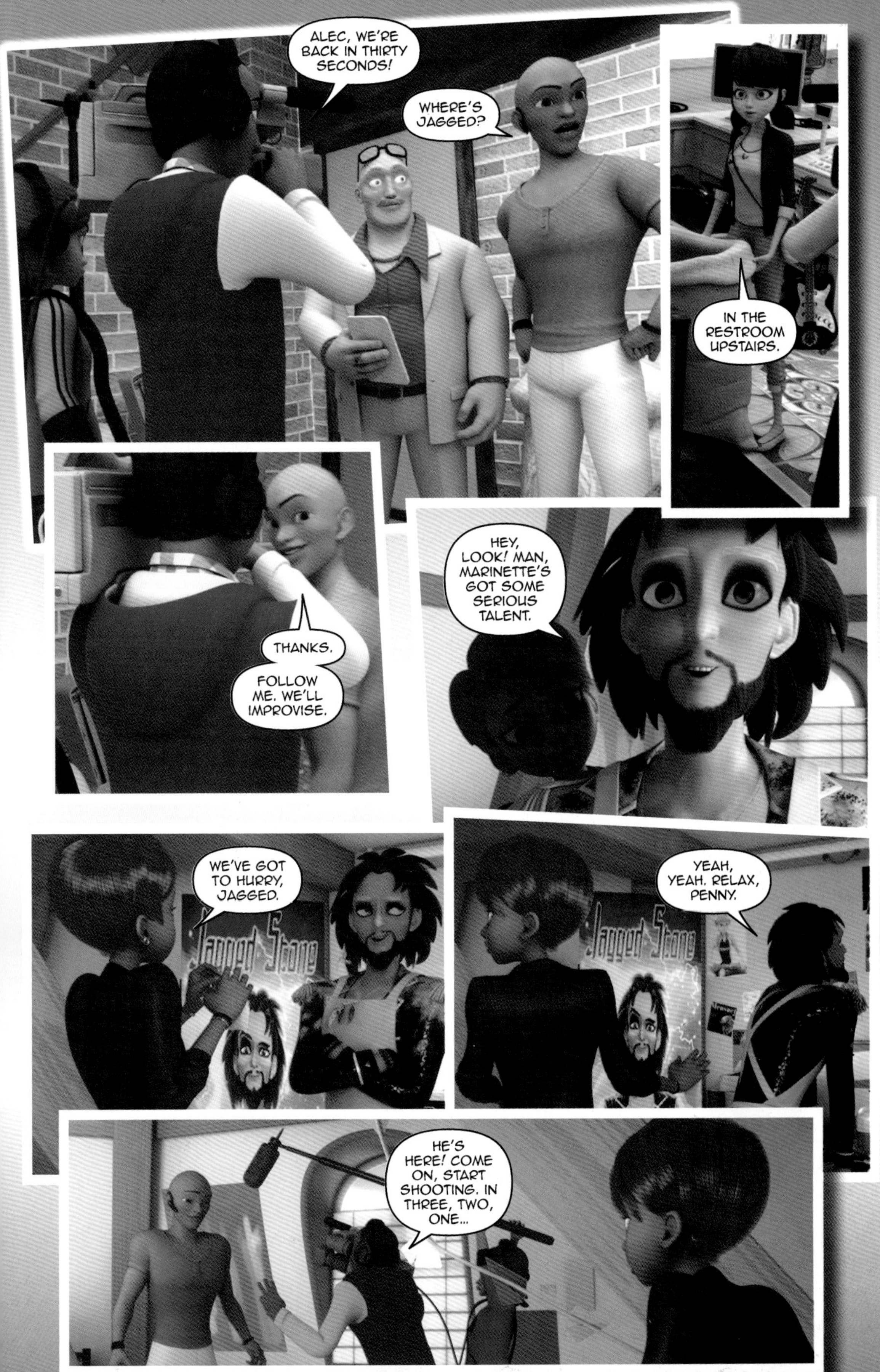
ALEC, WE'RE BACK IN THIRTY SECONDS!
WHERE'S JAGGED?
IN THE RESTROOM UPSTAIRS.
THANKS.
FOLLOW ME. WE'LL IMPROVISE.
HEY, LOOK! MAN, MARINETTE'S GOT SOME SERIOUS TALENT.
WE'VE GOT TO HURRY, JAGGED.
YEAH, YEAH. RELAX, PENNY.
HE'S HERE! COME ON, START SHOOTING. IN THREE, TWO, ONE...

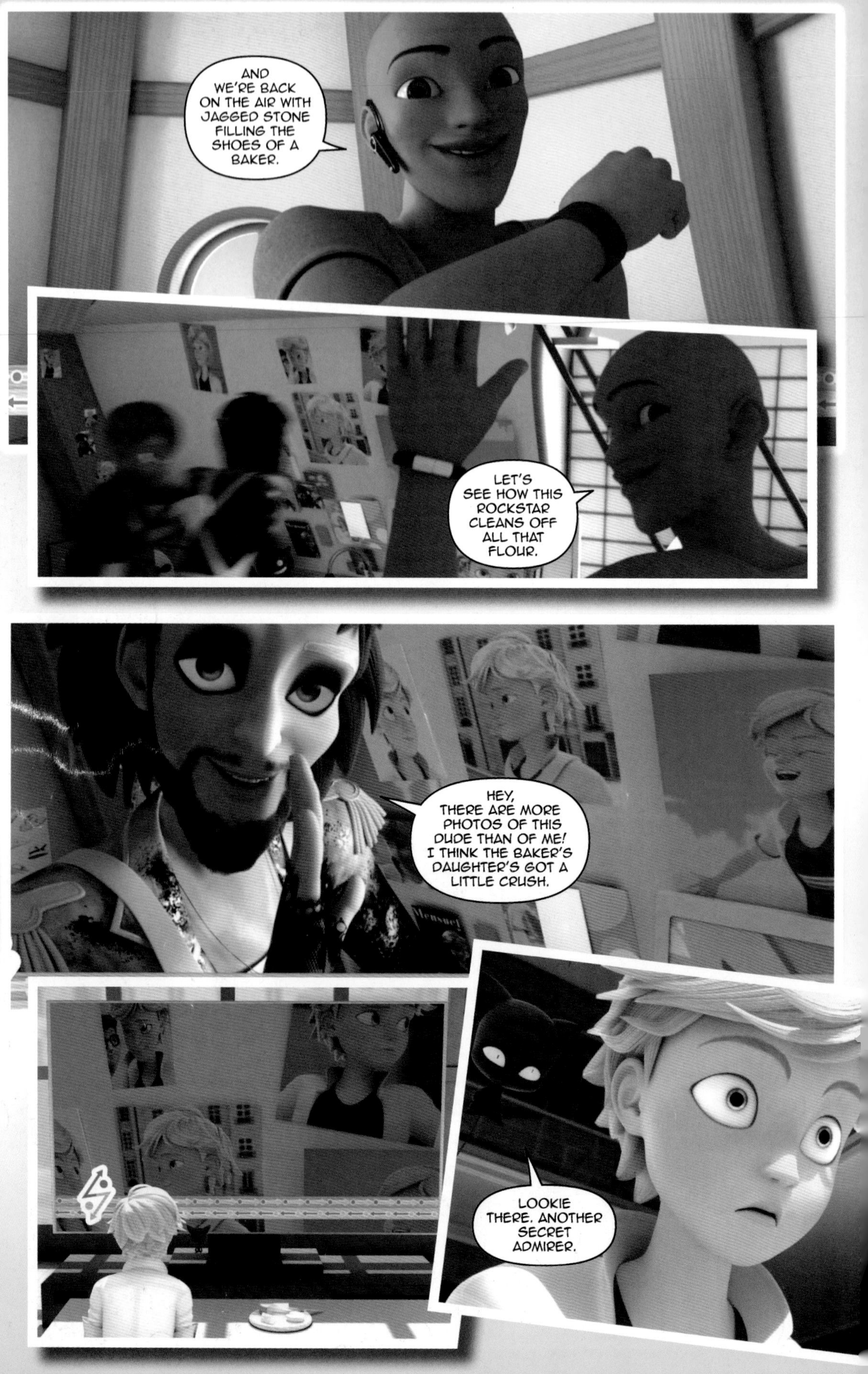
AND WE'RE BACK ON THE AIR WITH JAGGED STONE FILLING THE SHOES OF A BAKER.
LET'S SEE HOW THIS ROCKSTAR CLEANS OFF ALL THAT FLOUR.
HEY, THERE ARE MORE PHOTOS OF THIS DUDE THAN OF ME! I THINK THE BAKER'S DAUGHTER'S GOT A LITTLE CRUSH.
LOOKIE THERE. ANOTHER SECRET ADMIRER.

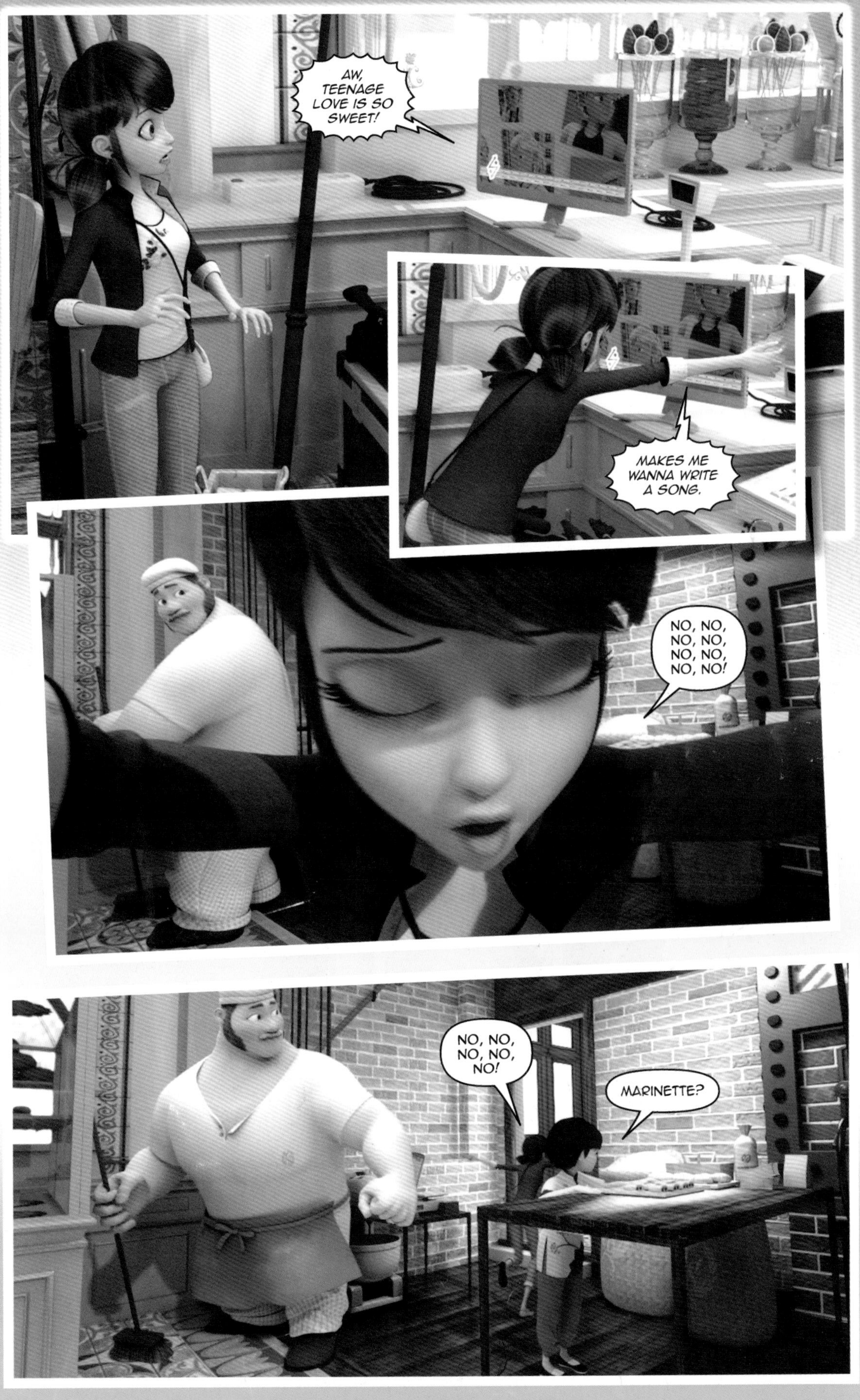
AW, TEENAGE LOVE IS SO SWEET!
MAKES ME WANNA WRITE A SONG.
NO, NO, NO, NO, NO, NO, NO, NO!
NO, NO, NO, NO, NO!
MARINETTE?

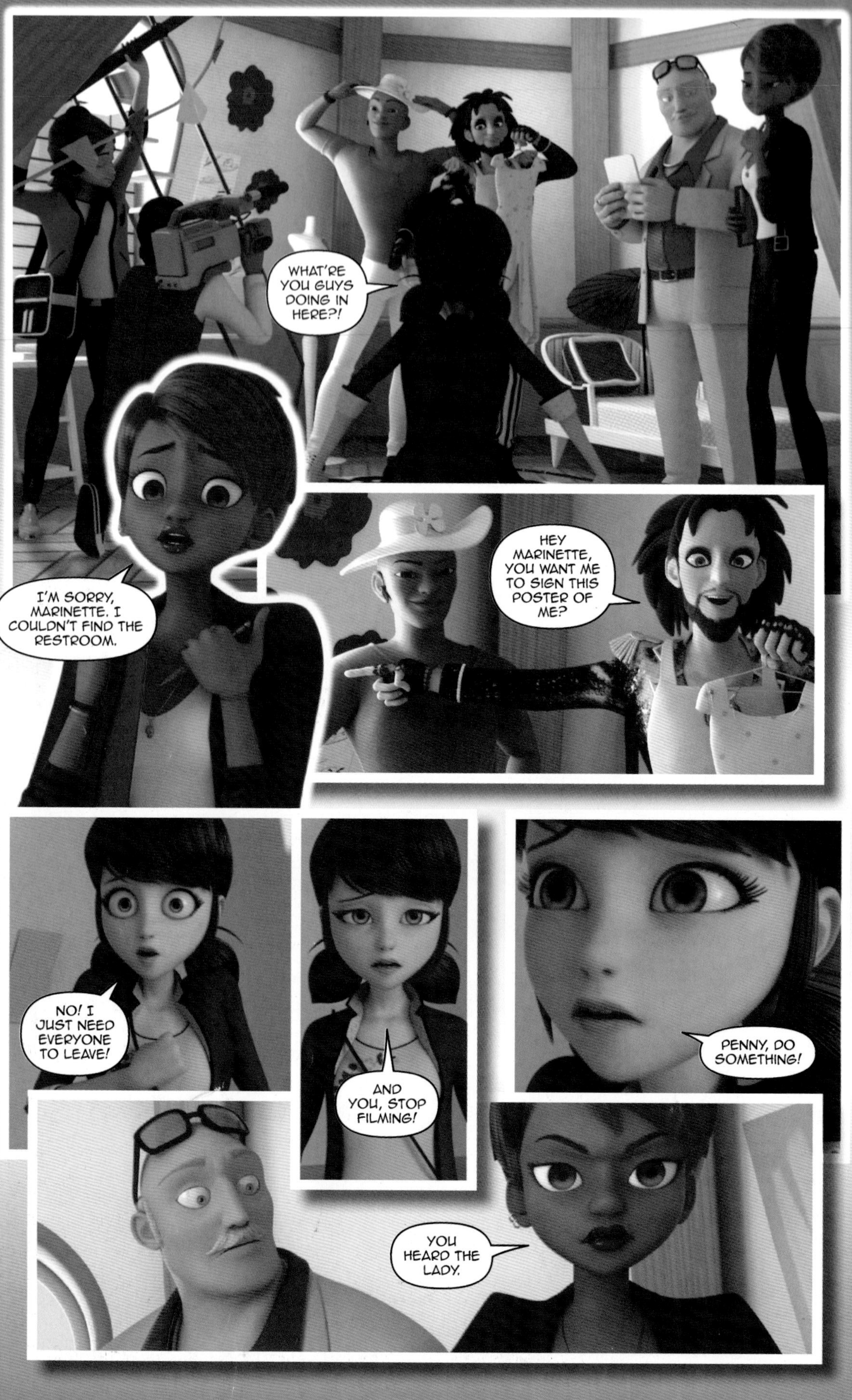
WHAT'RE YOU GUYS DOING IN HERE?!
I'M SORRY, MARINETTE. I COULDN'T FIND THE RESTROOM.
HEY MARINETTE, YOU WANT ME TO SIGN THIS POSTER OF ME?
NO! I JUST NEED EVERYONE TO LEAVE!
AND YOU, STOP FILMING!
PENNY, DO SOMETHING!
YOU HEARD THE LADY.

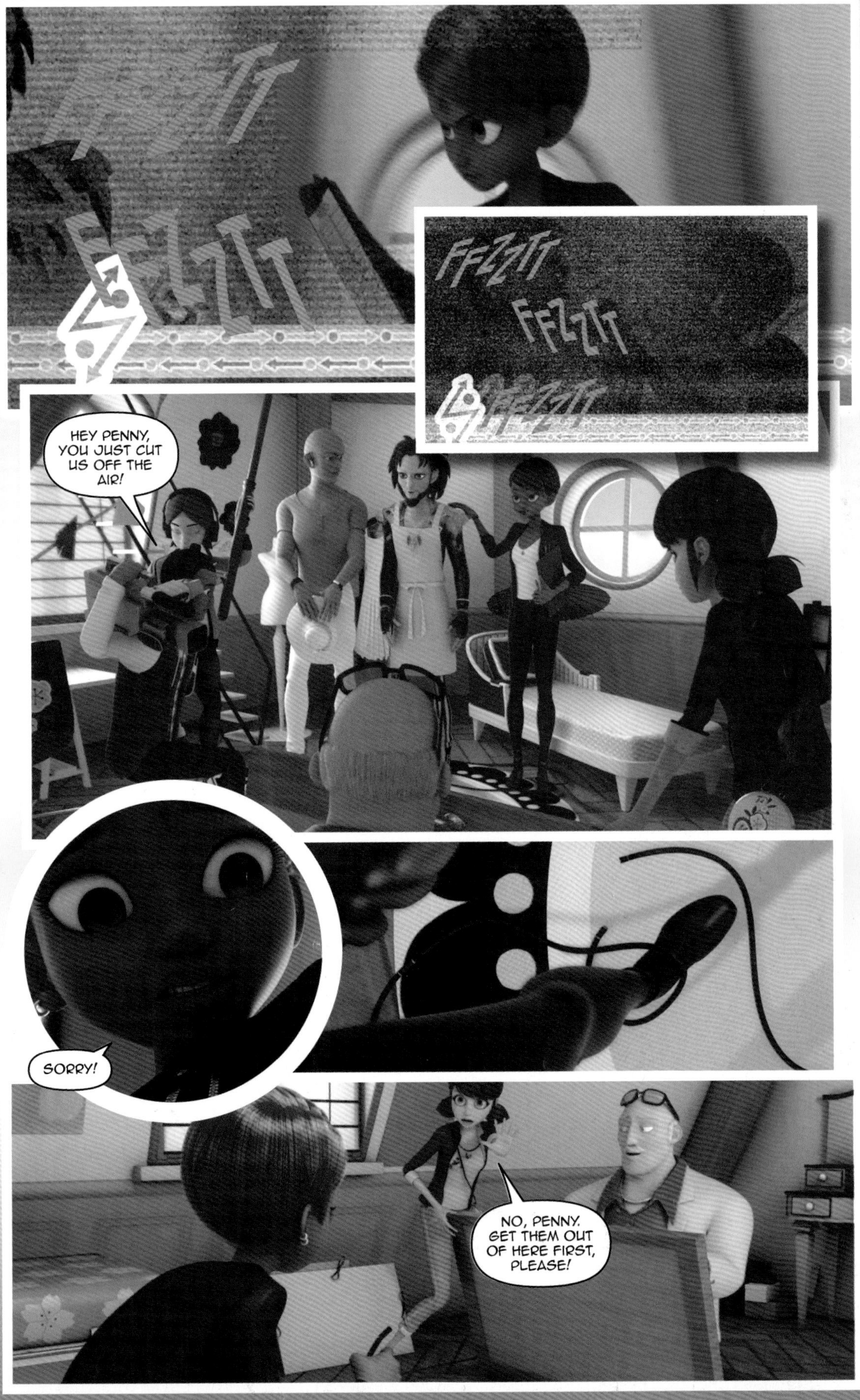

FFZZTT
FFZZTT
FFZZTT
FFZZTT
FFZZTT
HEY PENNY, YOU JUST CUT US OFF THE AIR!
SORRY!
NO, PENNY. GET THEM OUT OF HERE FIRST, PLEASE!

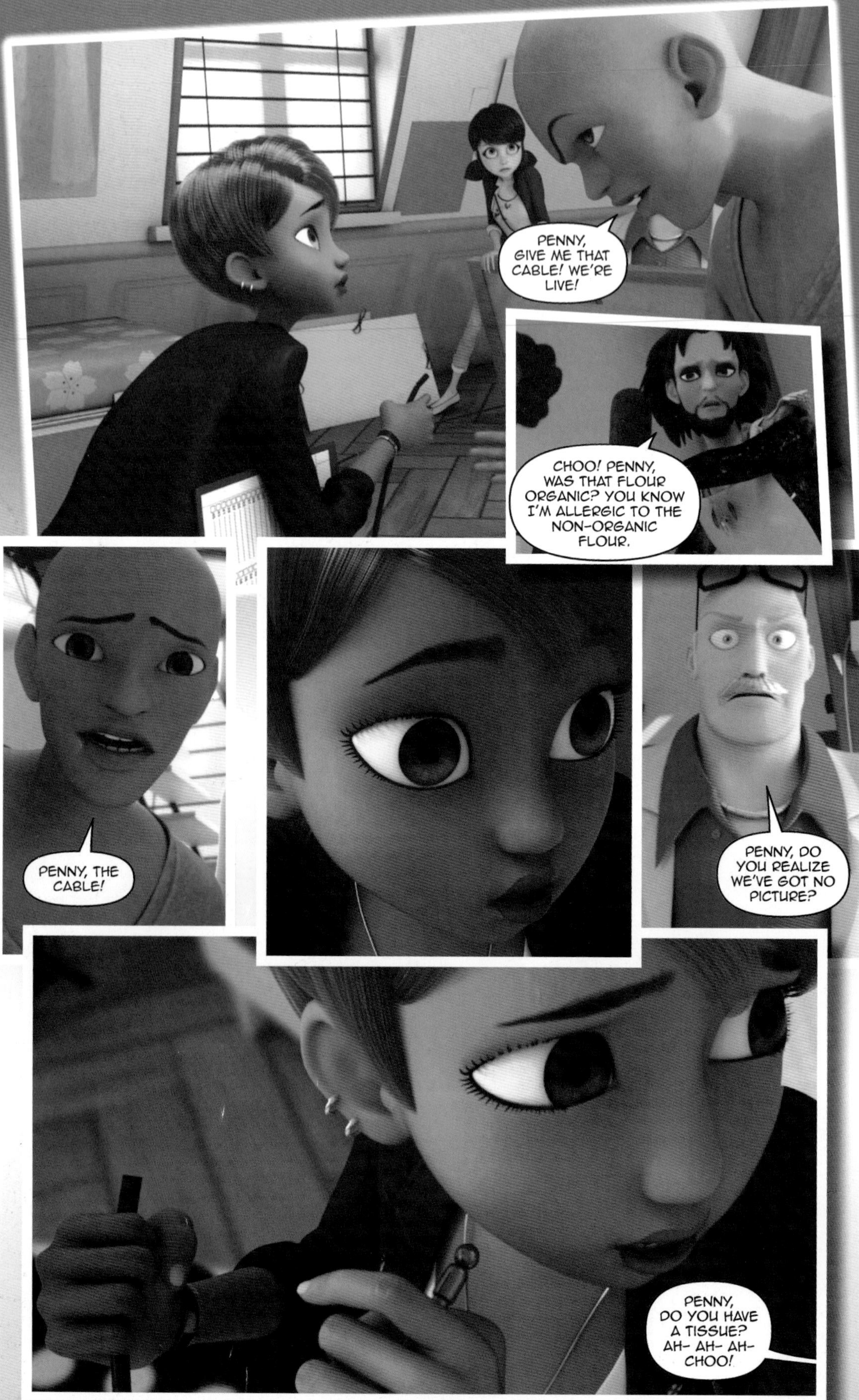
PENNY, GIVE ME THAT CABLE! WE'RE LIVE!
CHOO! PENNY, WAS THAT FLOUR ORGANIC? YOU KNOW I'M ALLERGIC TO THE NON-ORGANIC FLOUR.
PENNY, THE CABLE!
PENNY, DO YOU REALIZE WE'VE GOT NO PICTURE?
PENNY, DO YOU HAVE A TISSUE? AH- AH- AH- CHOO!

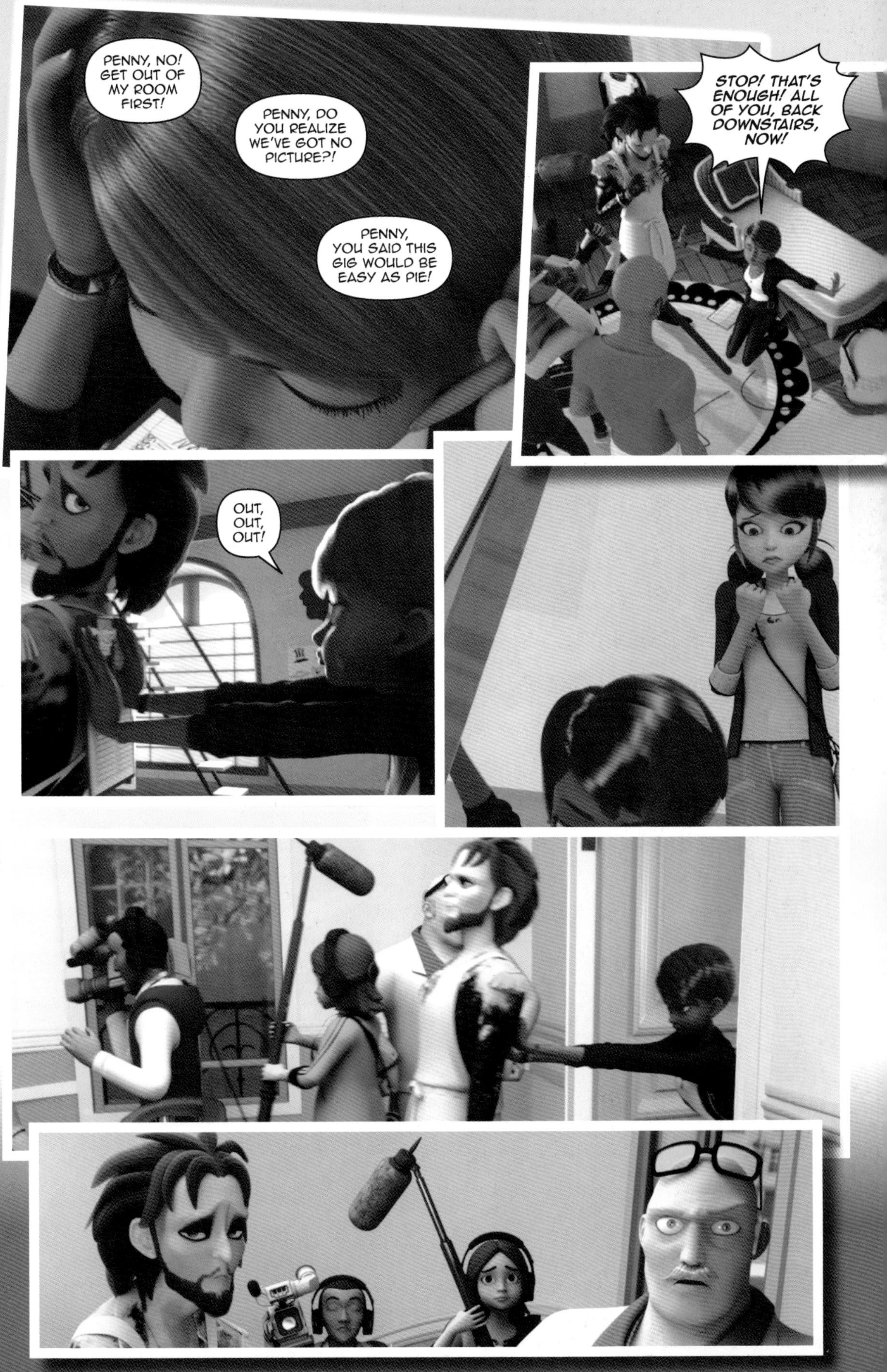
PENNY, NO! GET OUT OF MY ROOM FIRST!
PENNY, DO YOU REALIZE WE'VE GOT NO PICTURE?!
PENNY, YOU SAID THIS GIG WOULD BE EASY AS PIE!
STOP! THAT'S ENOUGH! ALL OF YOU, BACK DOWNSTAIRS, NOW!
OUT, OUT, OUT!

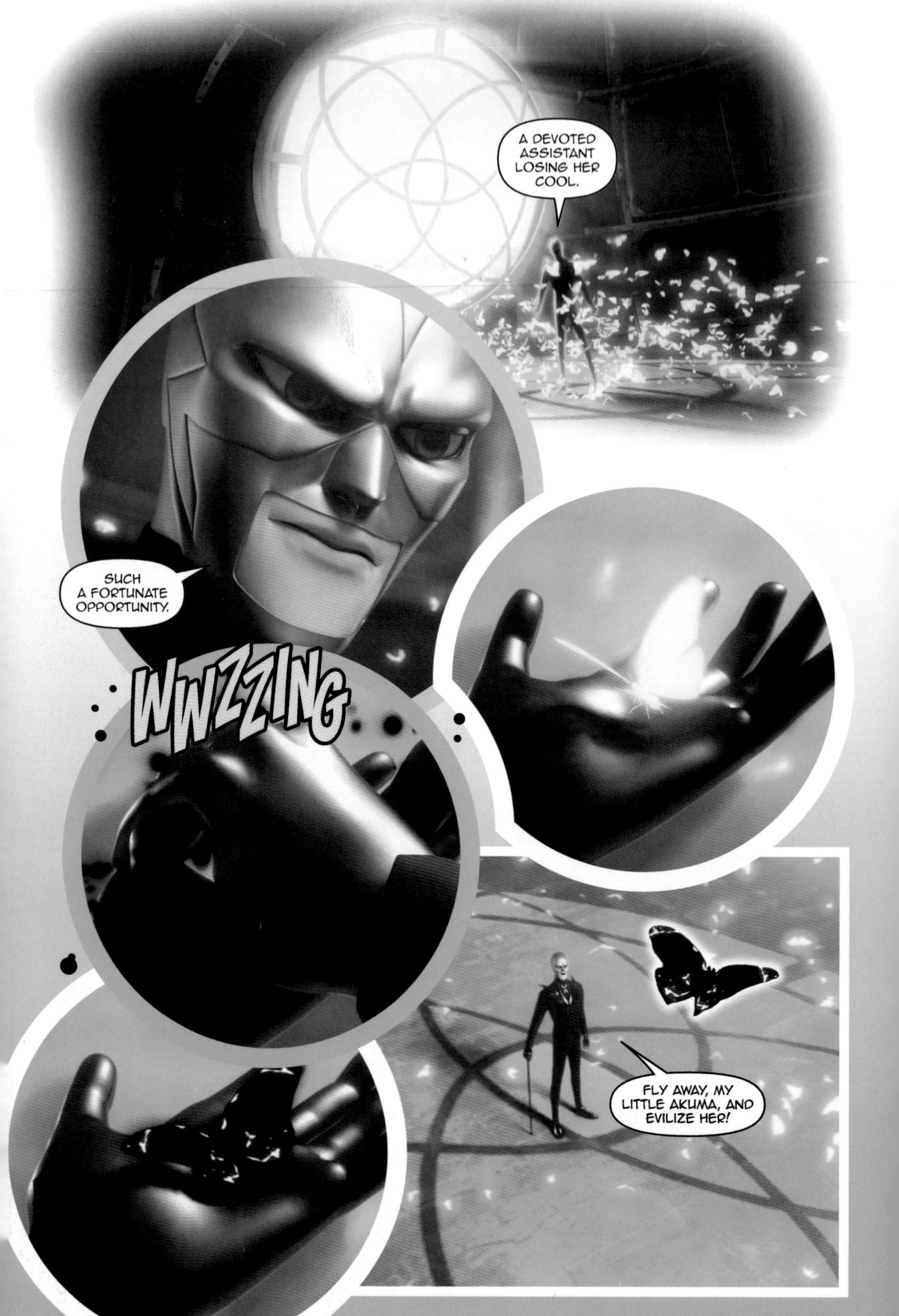
A DEVOTED ASSISTANT LOSING HER COOL.
SUCH A FORTUNATE OPPORTUNITY.
WWZZING
FLY AWAY, MY LITTLE AKUMA, AND EVILIZE HER!

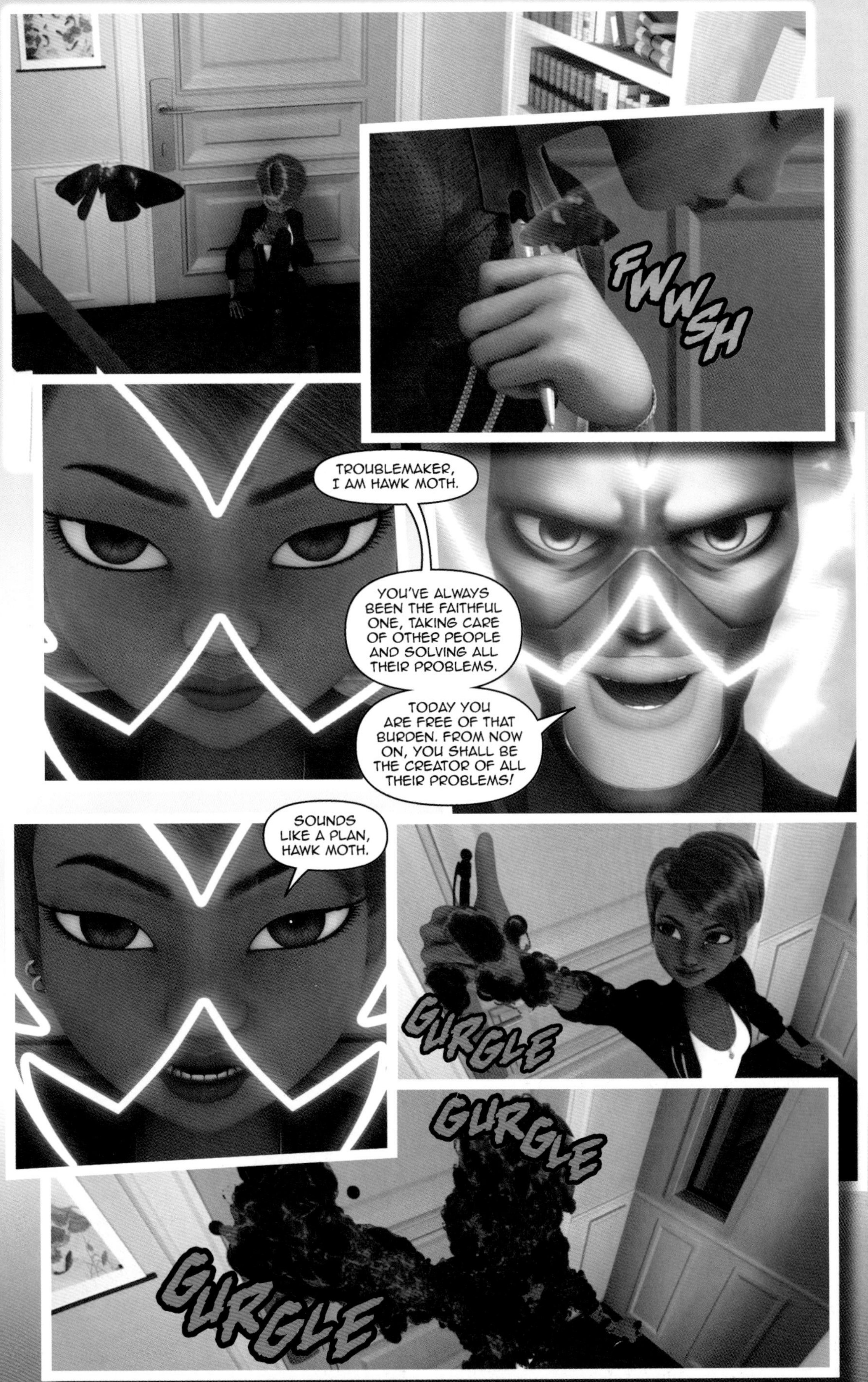
FWWSH
TROUBLEMAKER, I AM HAWK MOTH.
YOU'VE ALWAYS BEEN THE FAITHFUL ONE, TAKING CARE OF OTHER PEOPLE AND SOLVING ALL THEIR PROBLEMS.
TODAY YOU ARE FREE OF THAT BURDEN. FROM NOW ON, YOU SHALL BE THE CREATOR OF ALL THEIR PROBLEMS!
SOUNDS LIKE A PLAN, HAWK MOTH.
GURGLE
GURGLE
GURGLE

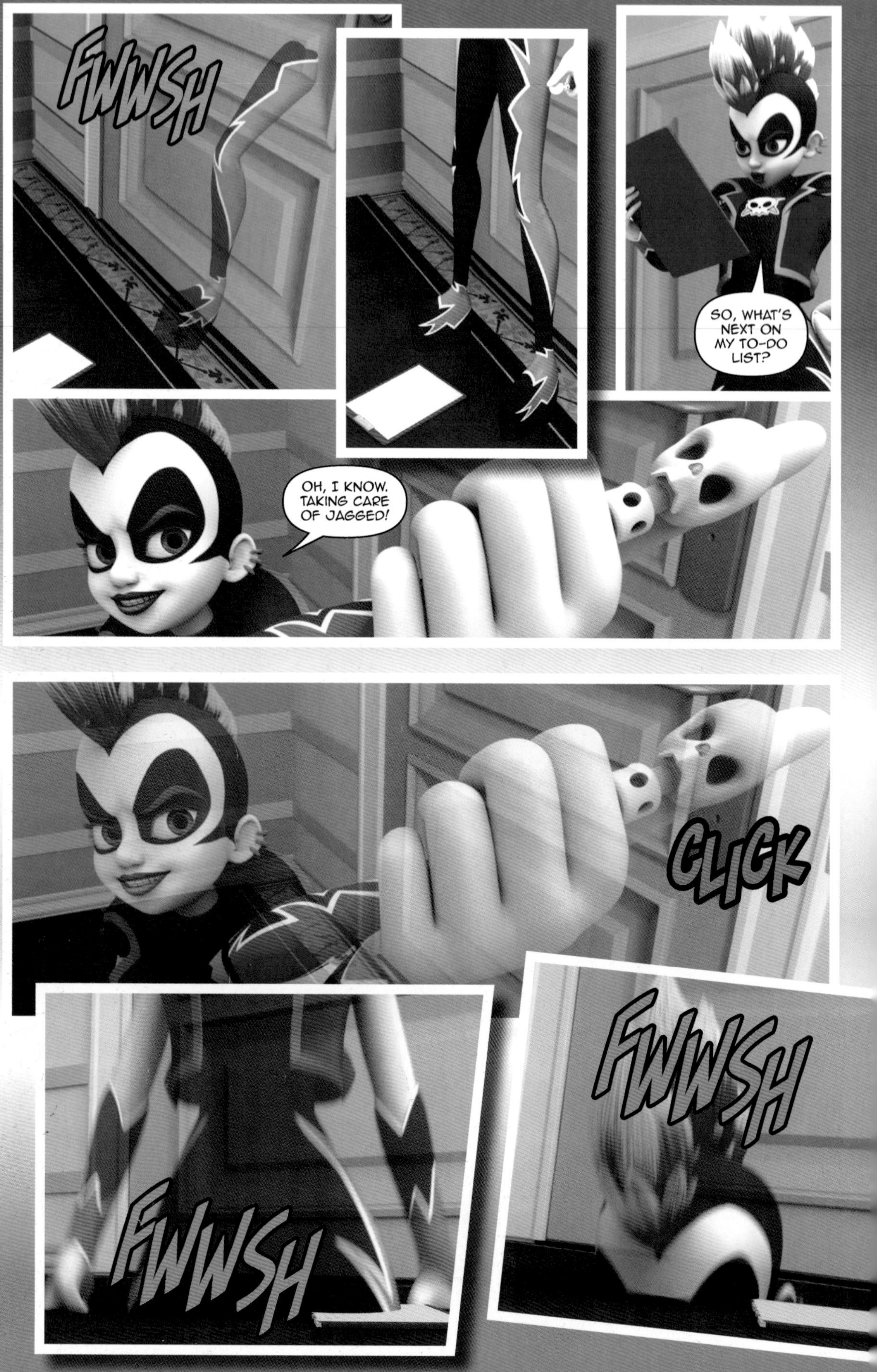
FWWSH
SO, WHAT'S NEXT ON MY TO-DO LIST?
OH, I KNOW. TAKING CARE OF JAGGED!
CLICK
FWWSH
FWWSH

WE'RE NOT COMFORTABLE WITH YOUR CAMERAS GOING EVERYWHERE AND INVADING OUR PRIVACY! OUR DAUGHTER IS UPSET BECAUSE OF YOUR SHOW. WE WON'T ALLOW THAT!

THE RATINGS ARE SKY-HIGH. THERE'S NO WAY WE STOP THE SHOW NOW. RIGHT, JAGGED?

11.58M

ACHOO!

AHA! SEE?

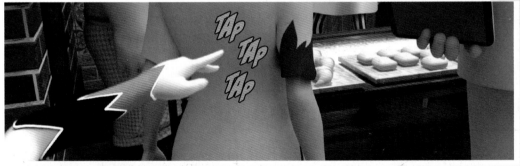

TAP TAP TAP

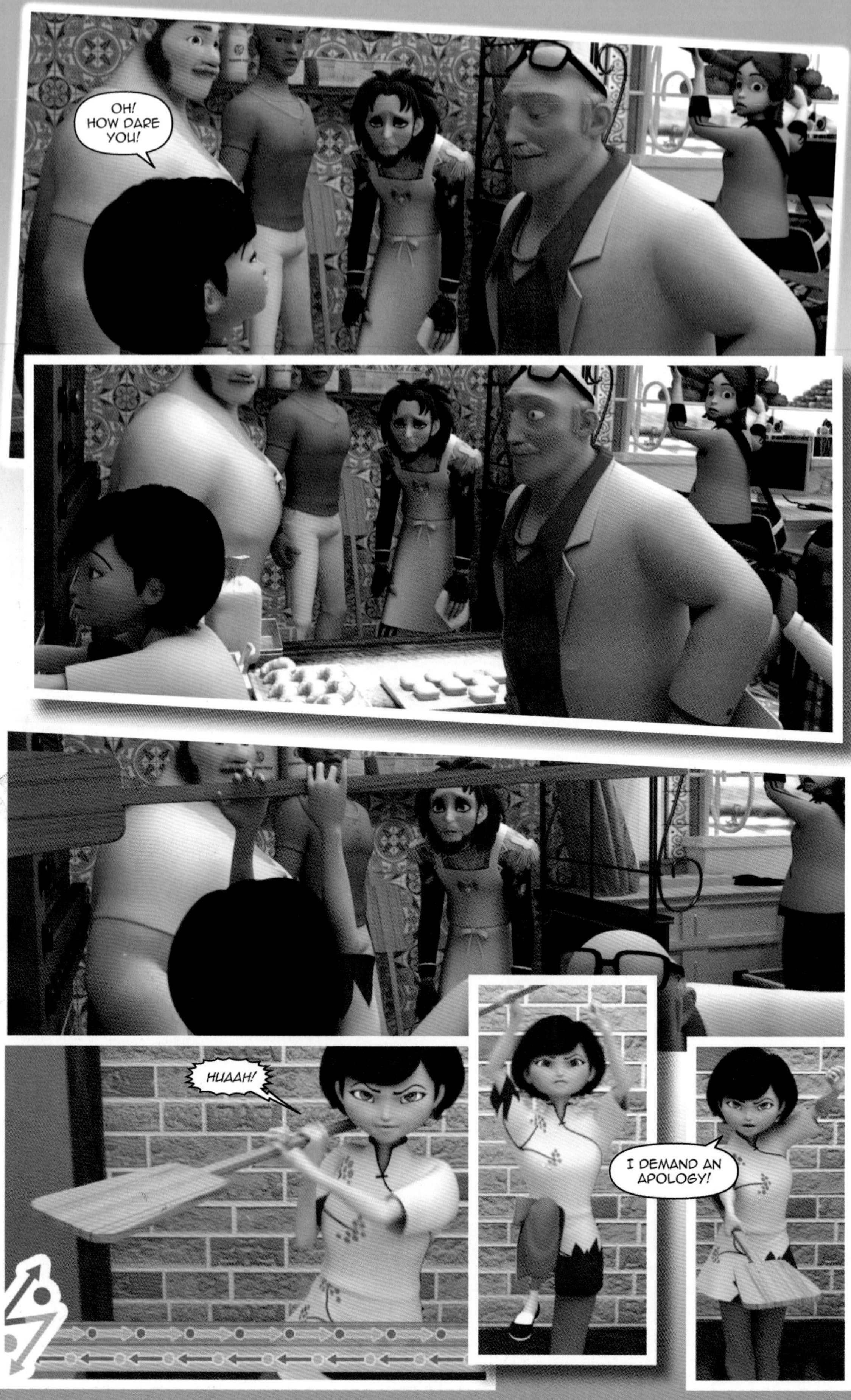
OH! HOW DARE YOU!
HUAAH!
I DEMAND AN APOLOGY!

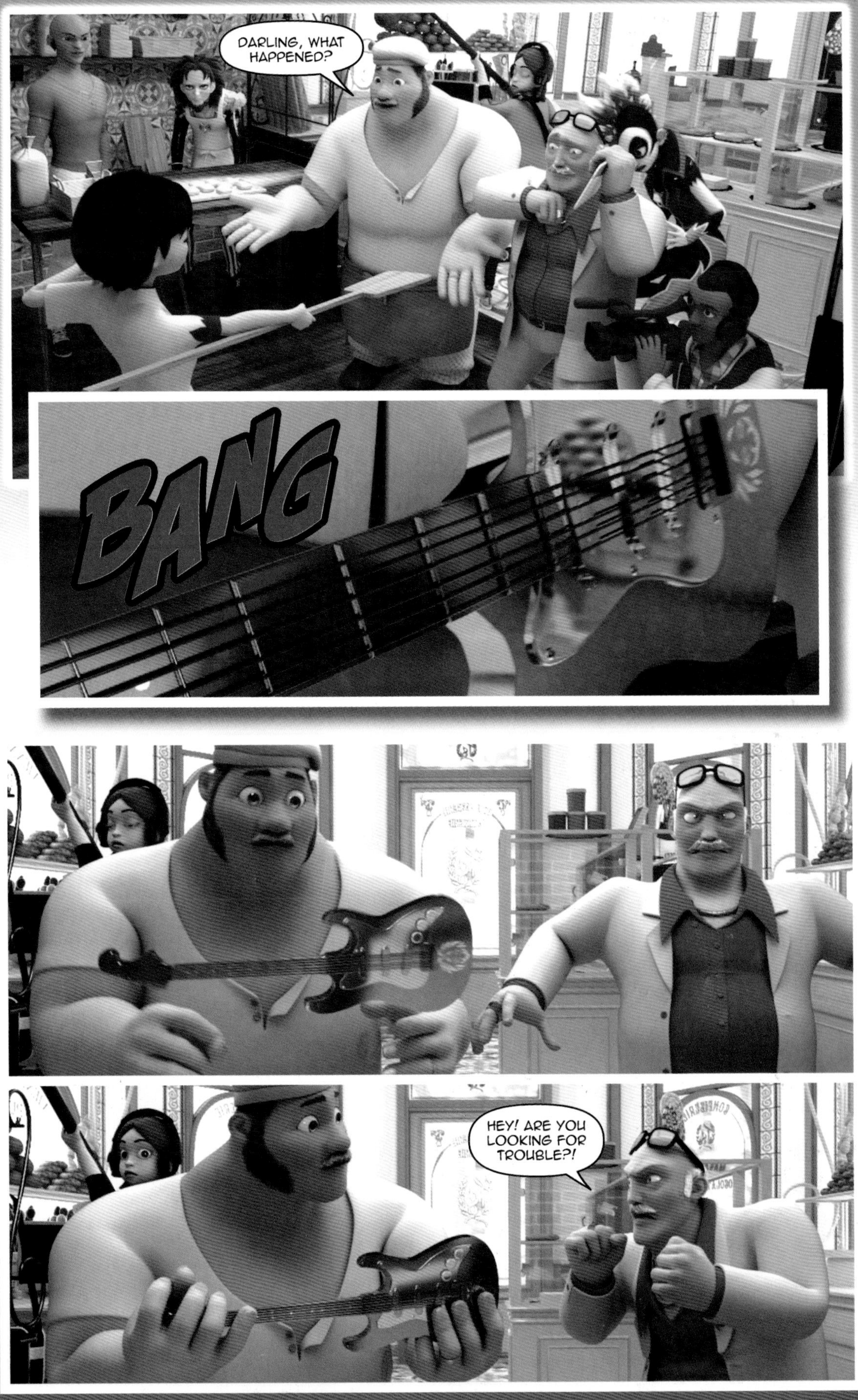
DARLING, WHAT HAPPENED?
BANG
HEY! ARE YOU LOOKING FOR TROUBLE?!

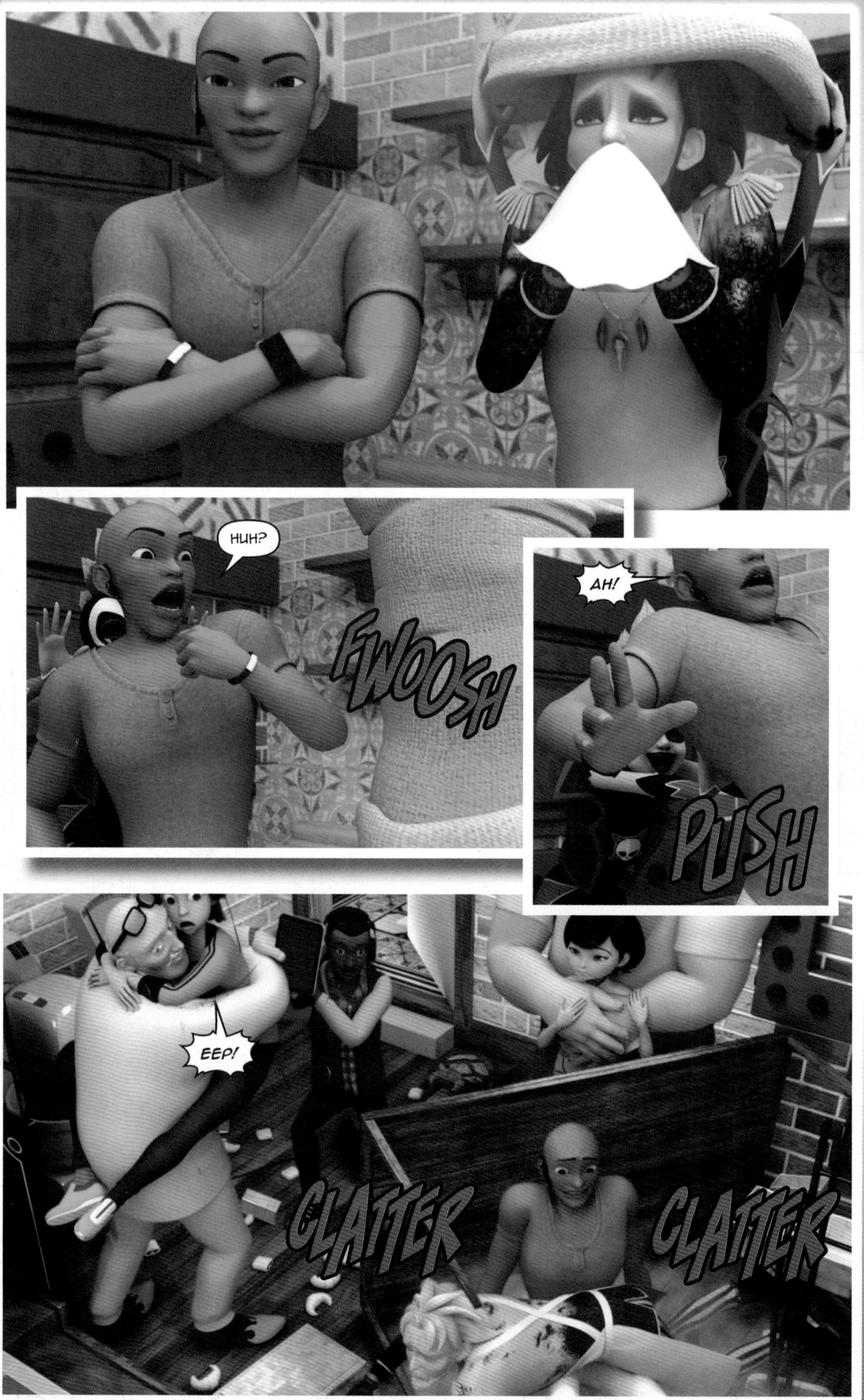
HUH?
FWOOSH
AH!
PUSH
EEP!
CLATTER
CLATTER

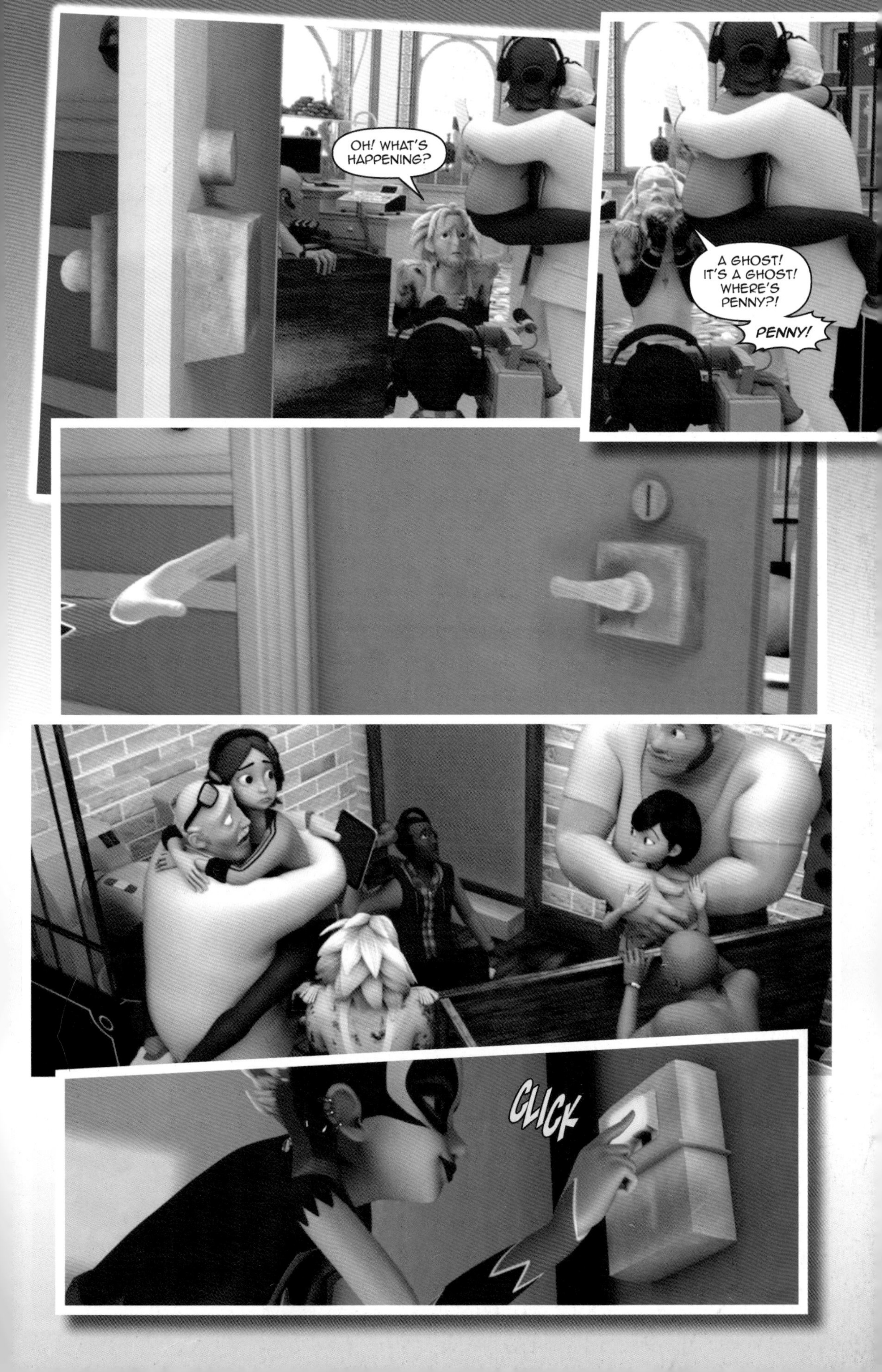
OH! WHAT'S HAPPENING?
A GHOST! IT'S A GHOST! WHERE'S PENNY?!
PENNY!
CLICK

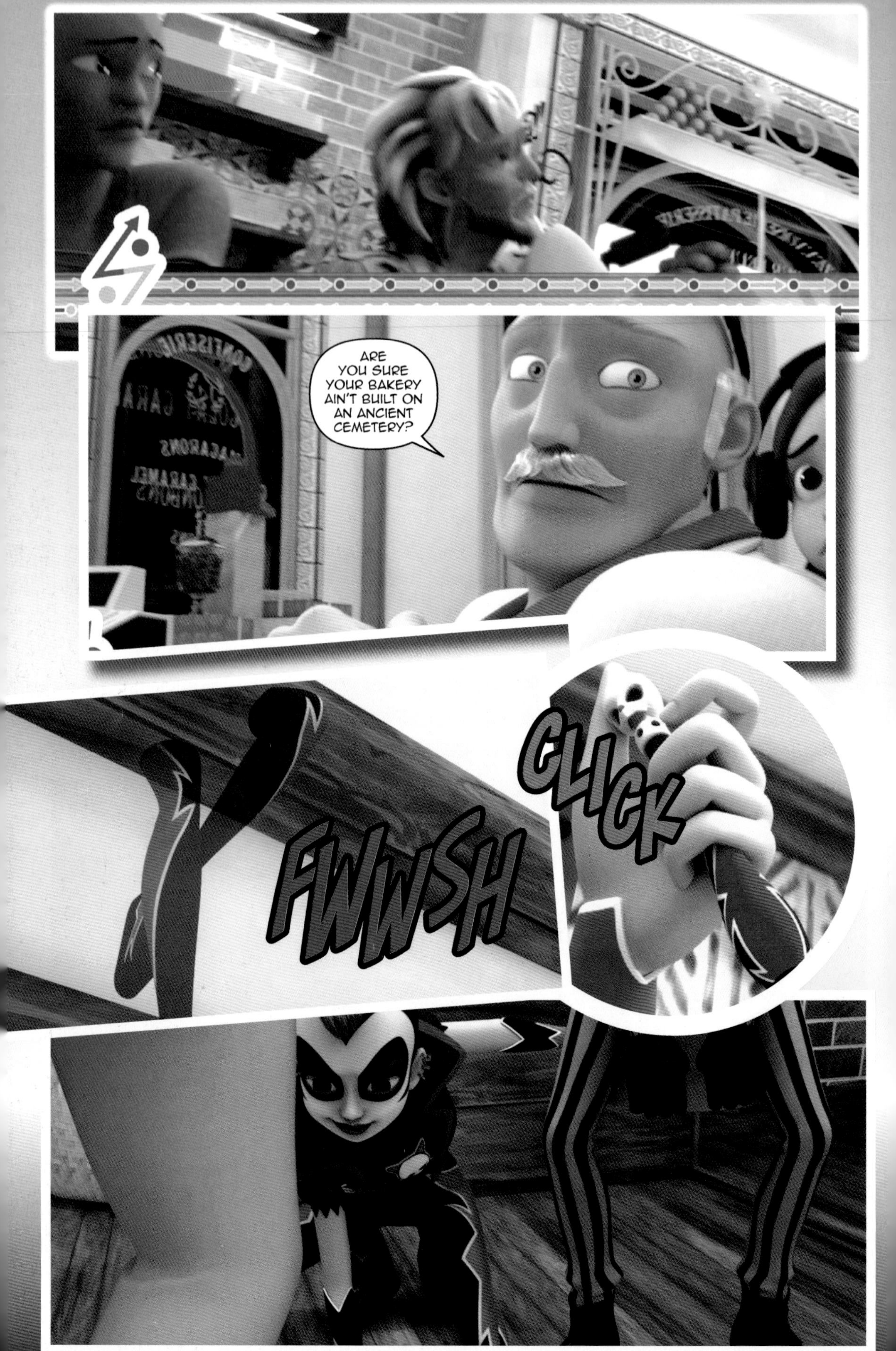
ARE YOU SURE YOUR BAKERY AIN'T BUILT ON AN ANCIENT CEMETERY?
CLICK
FWWSH

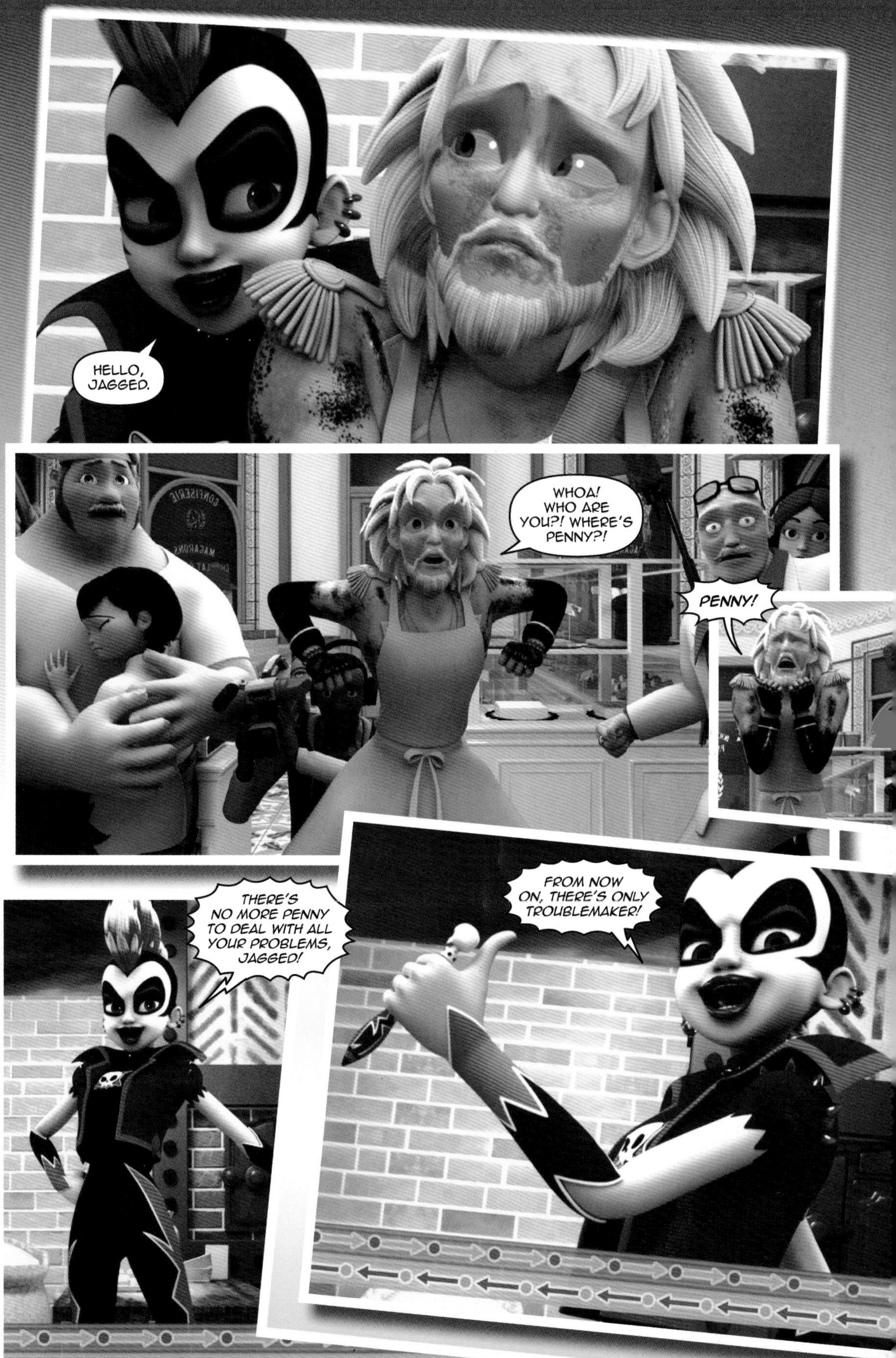
HELLO, JAGGED.
WHOA! WHO ARE YOU?! WHERE'S PENNY?!
PENNY!
THERE'S NO MORE PENNY TO DEAL WITH ALL YOUR PROBLEMS, JAGGED!
FROM NOW ON, THERE'S ONLY TROUBLEMAKER!

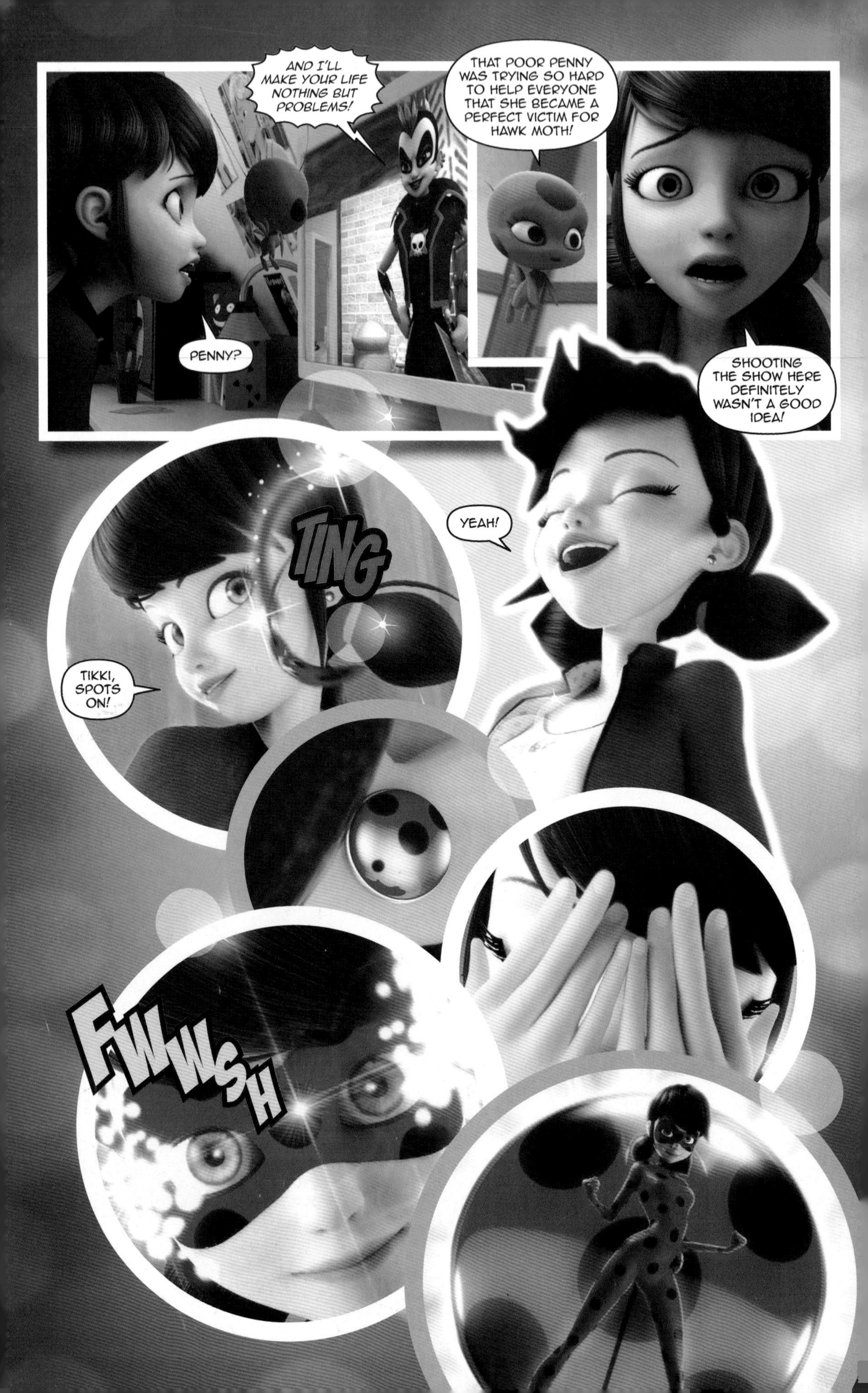
AND I'LL MAKE YOUR LIFE NOTHING BUT PROBLEMS!
PENNY?
THAT POOR PENNY WAS TRYING SO HARD TO HELP EVERYONE THAT SHE BECAME A PERFECT VICTIM FOR HAWK MOTH!
SHOOTING THE SHOW HERE DEFINITELY WASN'T A GOOD IDEA!
TIKKI, SPOTS ON!
TING
YEAH!
FWWSH

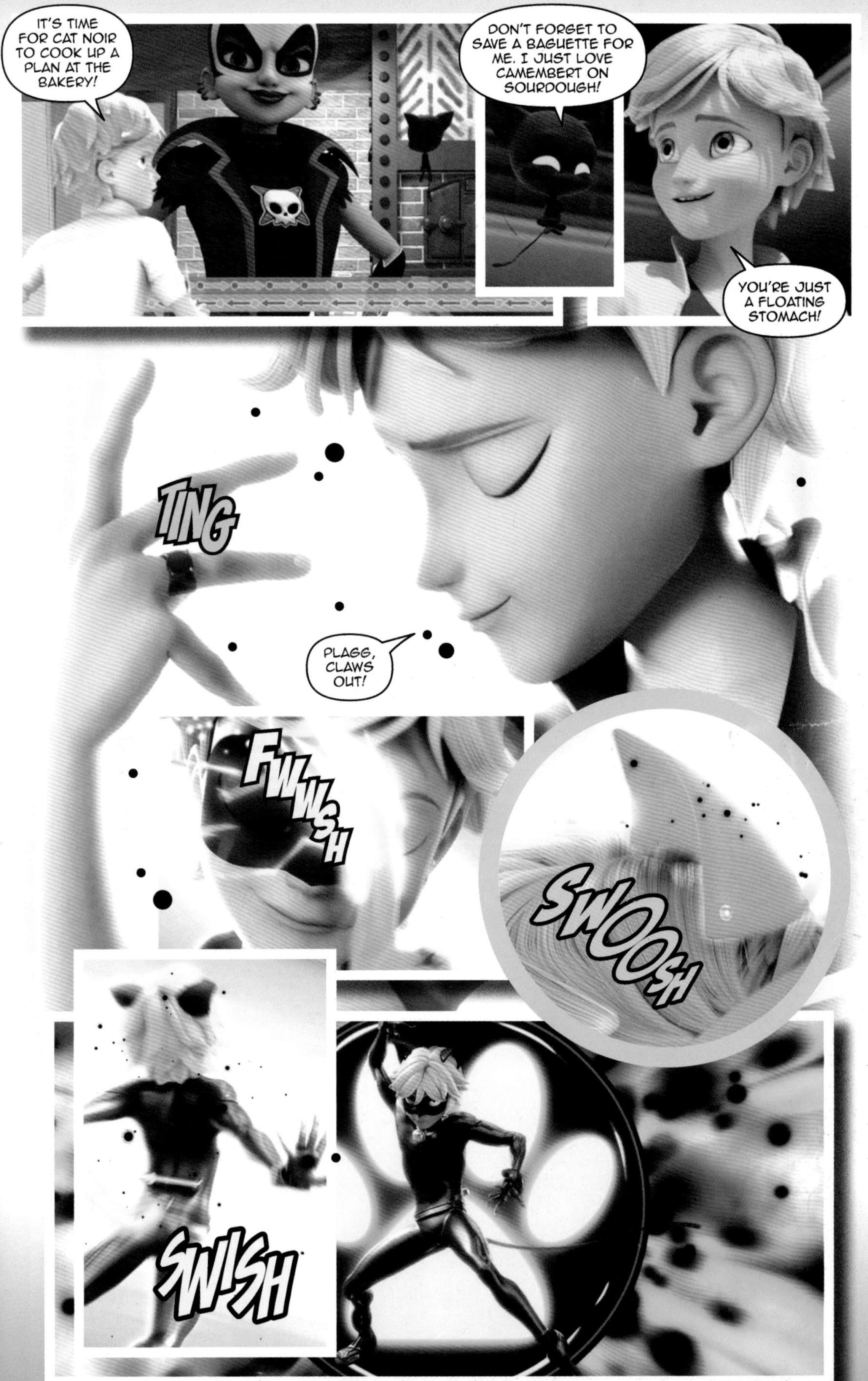
IT'S TIME FOR CAT NOIR TO COOK UP A PLAN AT THE BAKERY!
DON'T FORGET TO SAVE A BAGUETTE FOR ME. I JUST LOVE CAMEMBERT ON SOURDOUGH!
YOU'RE JUST A FLOATING STOMACH!
TING
PLAGG, CLAWS OUT!
FWWSH
SWOOSH
SWISH

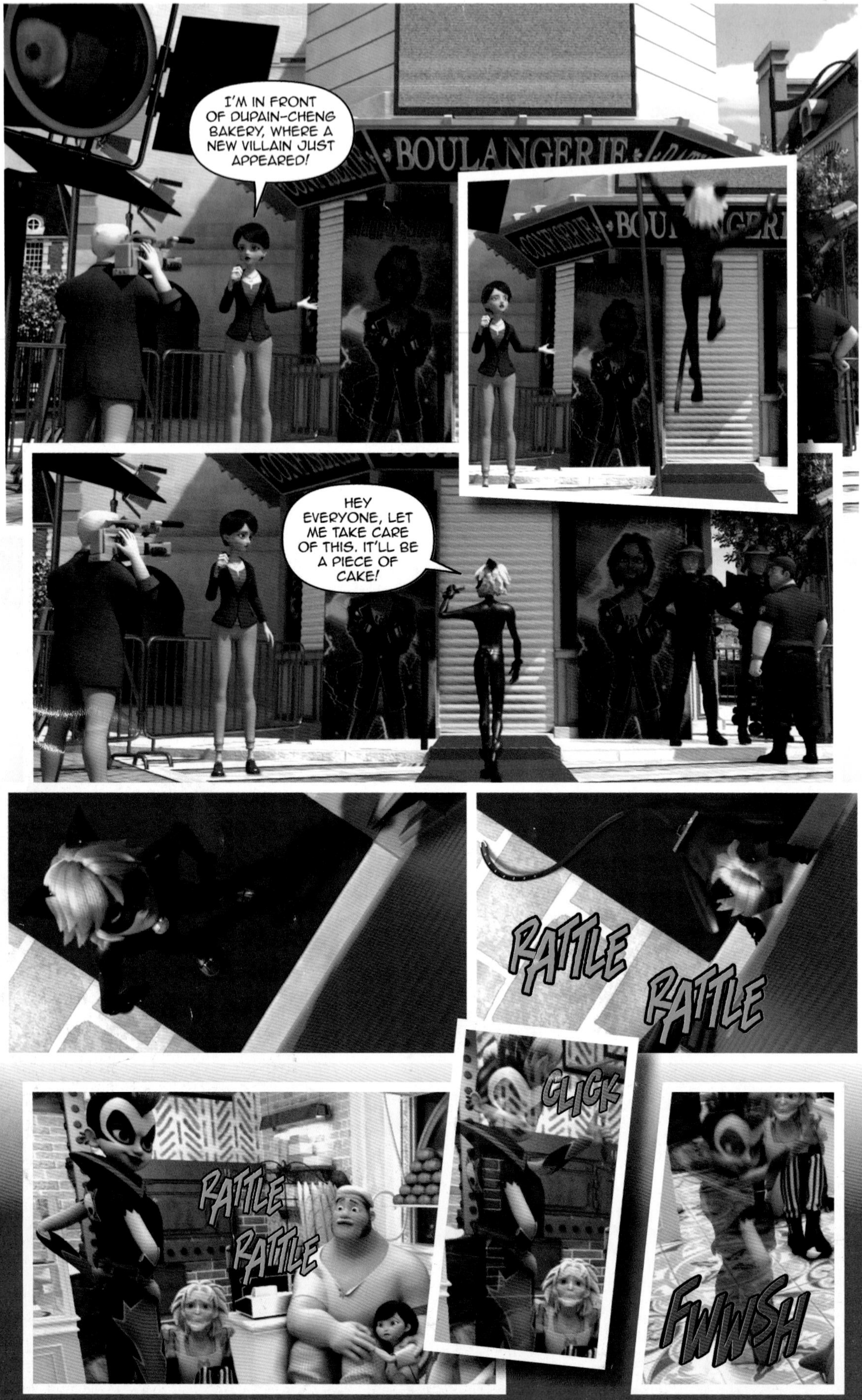

I'M IN FRONT OF DUPAIN-CHENG BAKERY, WHERE A NEW VILLAIN JUST APPEARED!
BOULANGERIE
CONFISERIE
HEY EVERYONE, LET ME TAKE CARE OF THIS. IT'LL BE A PIECE OF CAKE!
RATTLE RATTLE
RATTLE RATTLE
CLICK
FWWSH

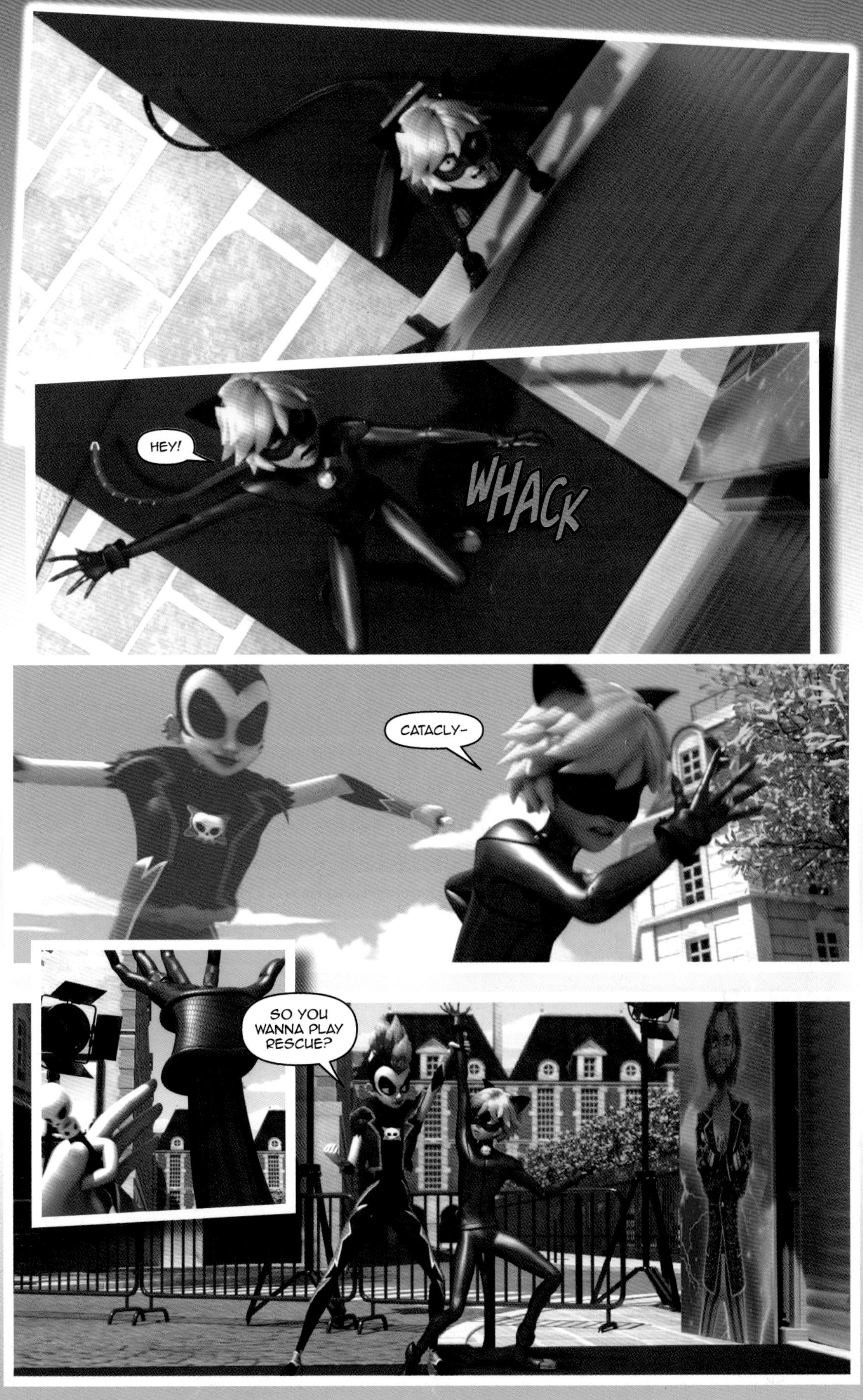
HEY!
WHACK
CATACLY-
SO YOU WANNA PLAY RESCUE?

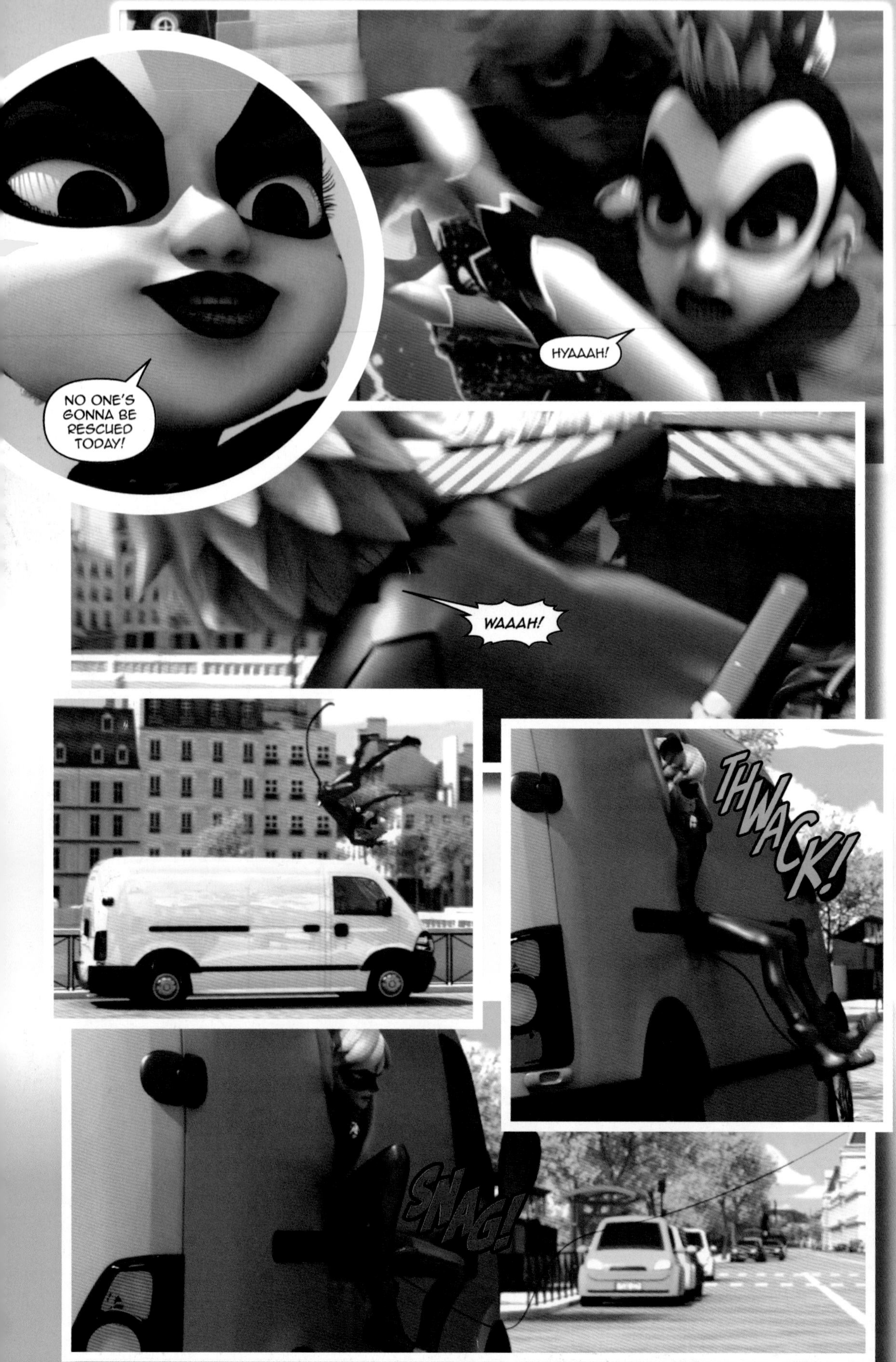
NO ONE'S GONNA BE RESCUED TODAY!
HYAAAH!
WAAAH!
THWACK!
SNAG!

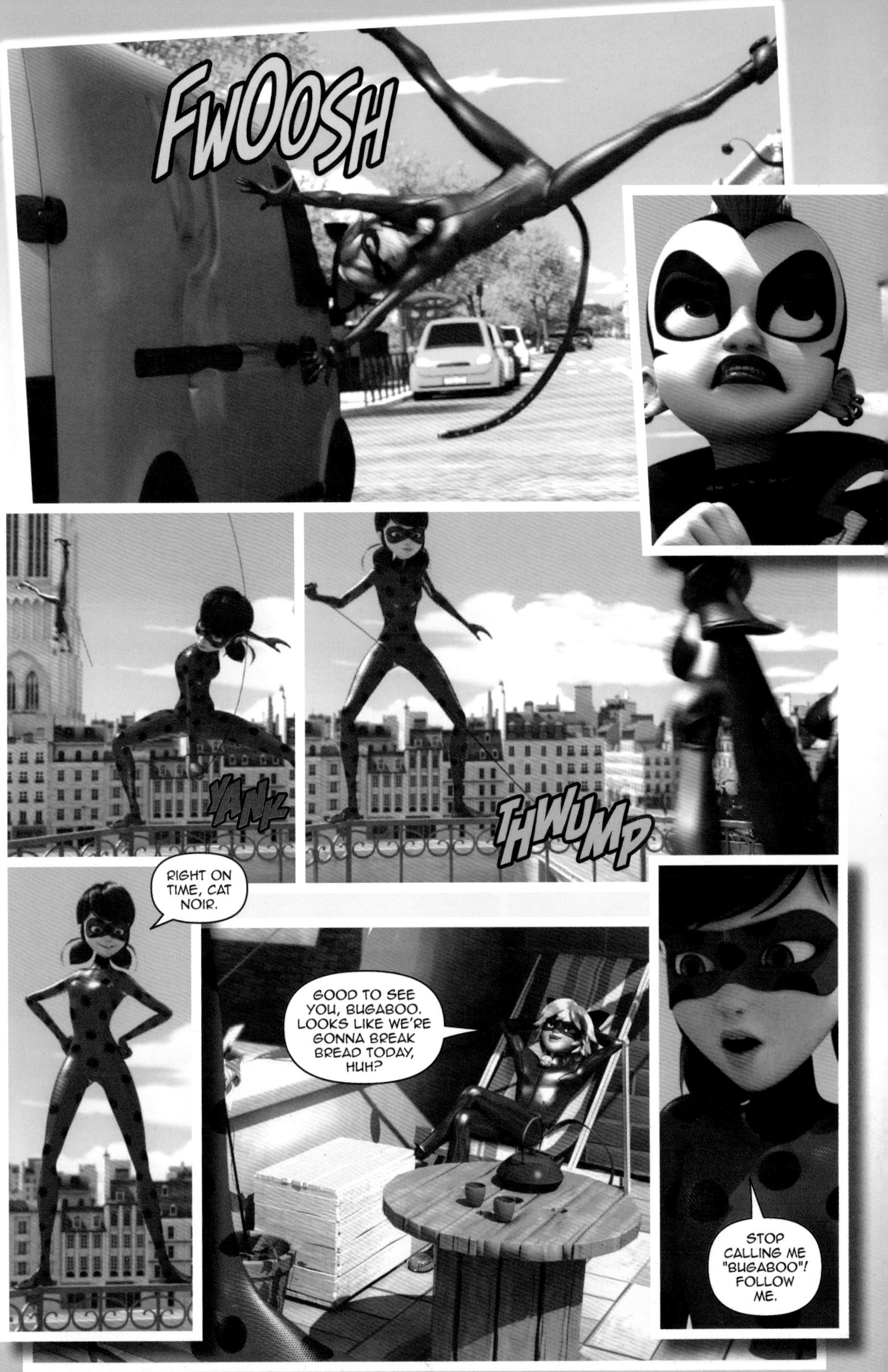
FWOOSH
YANK
THWUMP
RIGHT ON TIME, CAT NOIR.
GOOD TO SEE YOU, BUGABOO. LOOKS LIKE WE'RE GONNA BREAK BREAD TODAY, HUH?
STOP CALLING ME "BUGABOO"! FOLLOW ME.

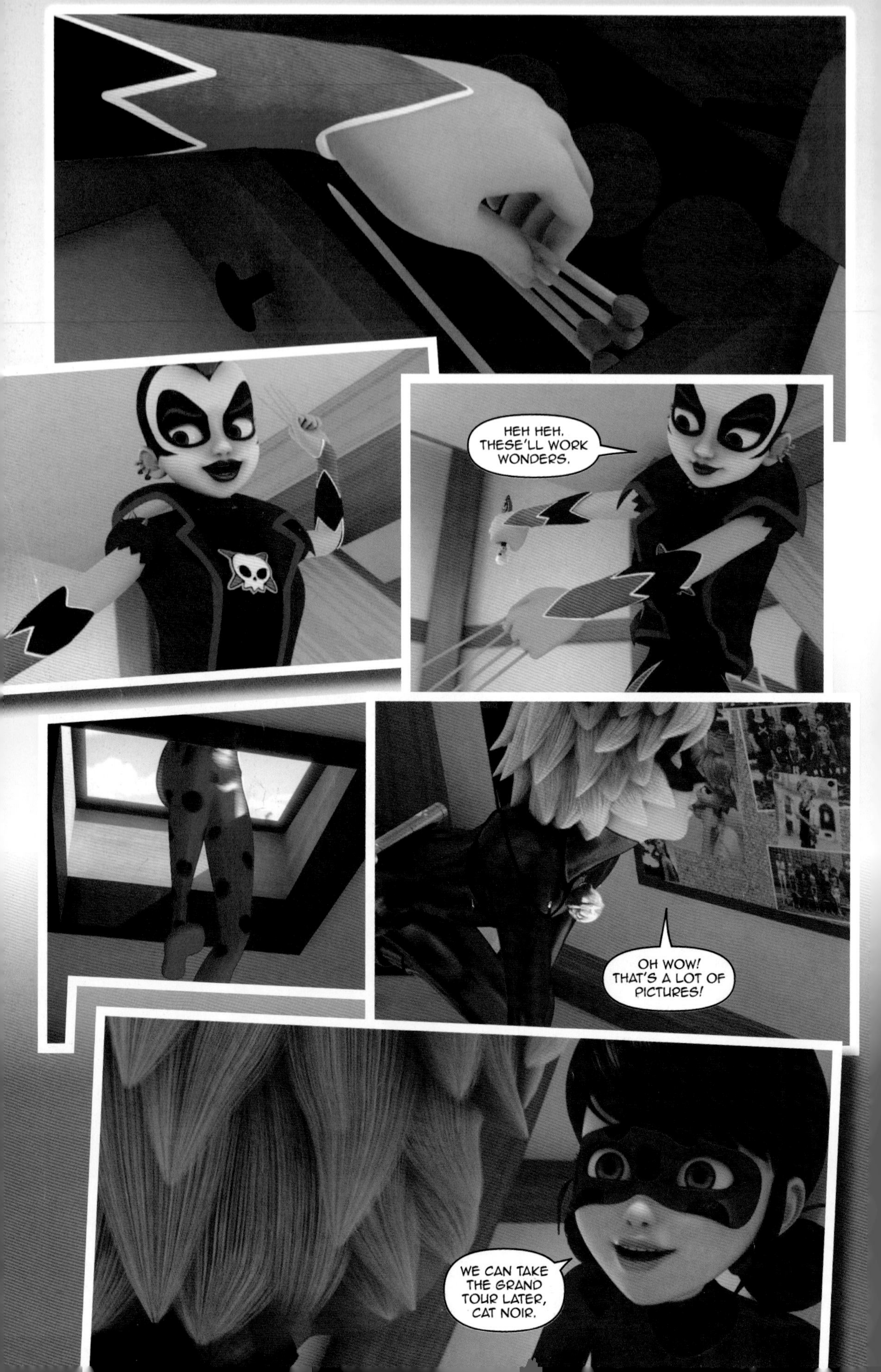
HEH HEH. THESE'LL WORK WONDERS.
OH WOW! THAT'S A LOT OF PICTURES!
WE CAN TAKE THE GRAND TOUR LATER, CAT NOIR.

FWIP FWIP FWIP

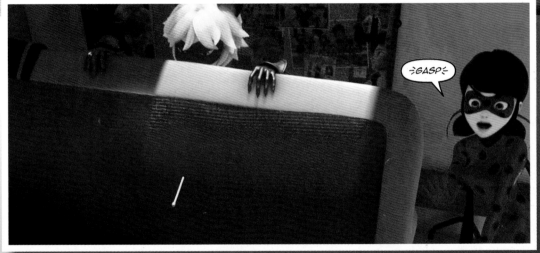

≻GASP≺

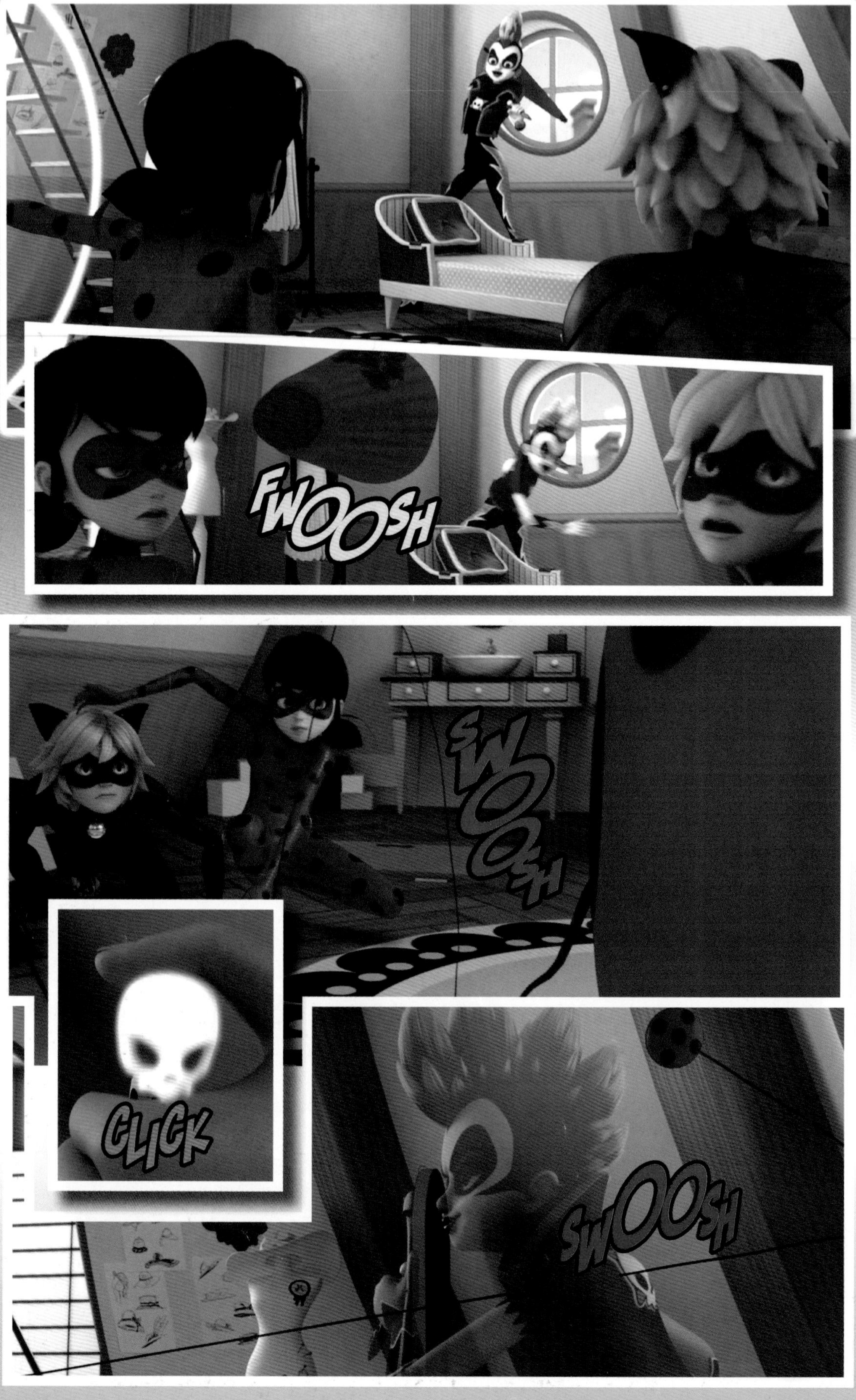
FWOOSH
SWOOSH
CLICK
SWOOSH

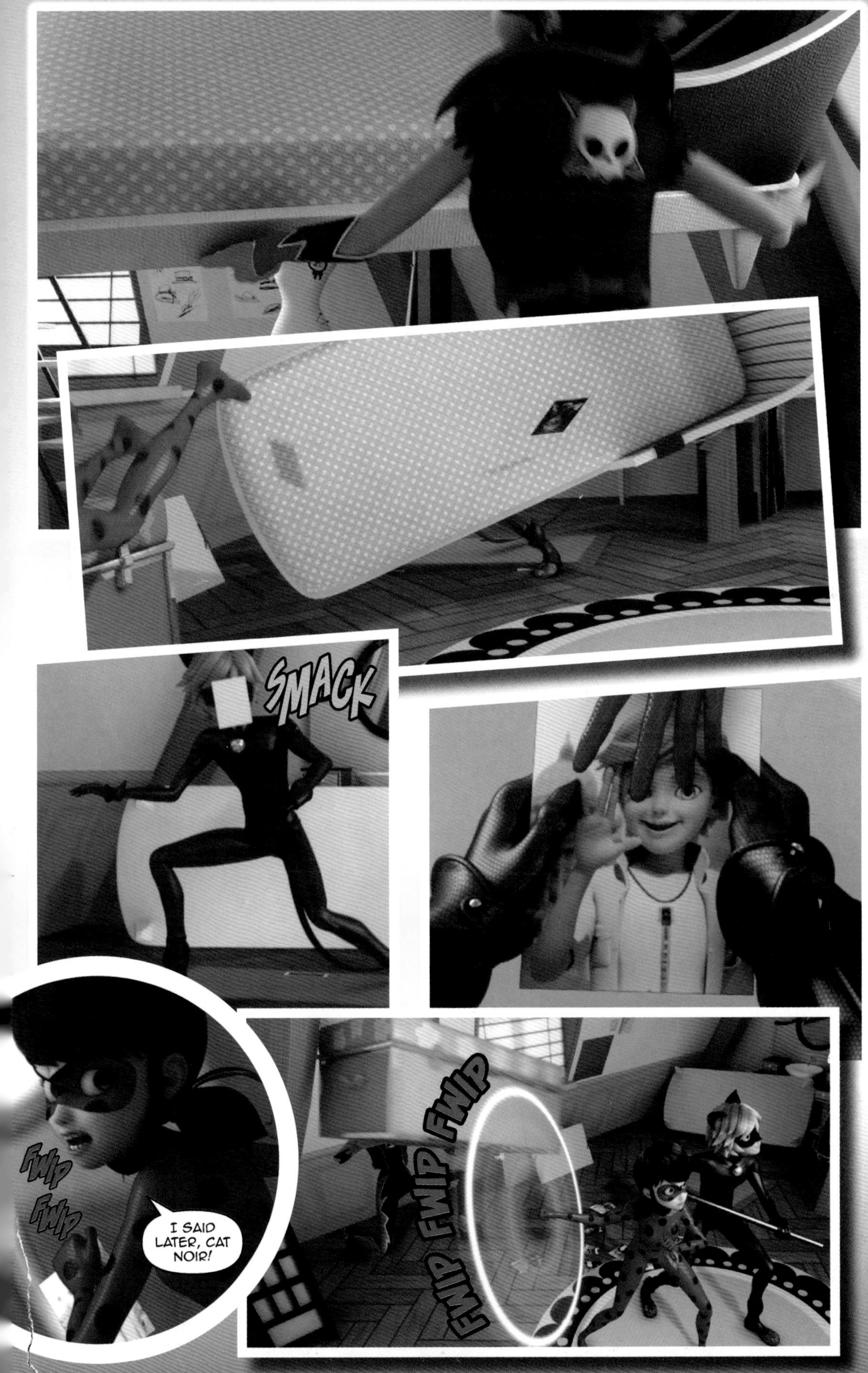
SMACK
FWIP
FWIP
I SAID LATER, CAT NOIR!
FWIP FWIP FWIP

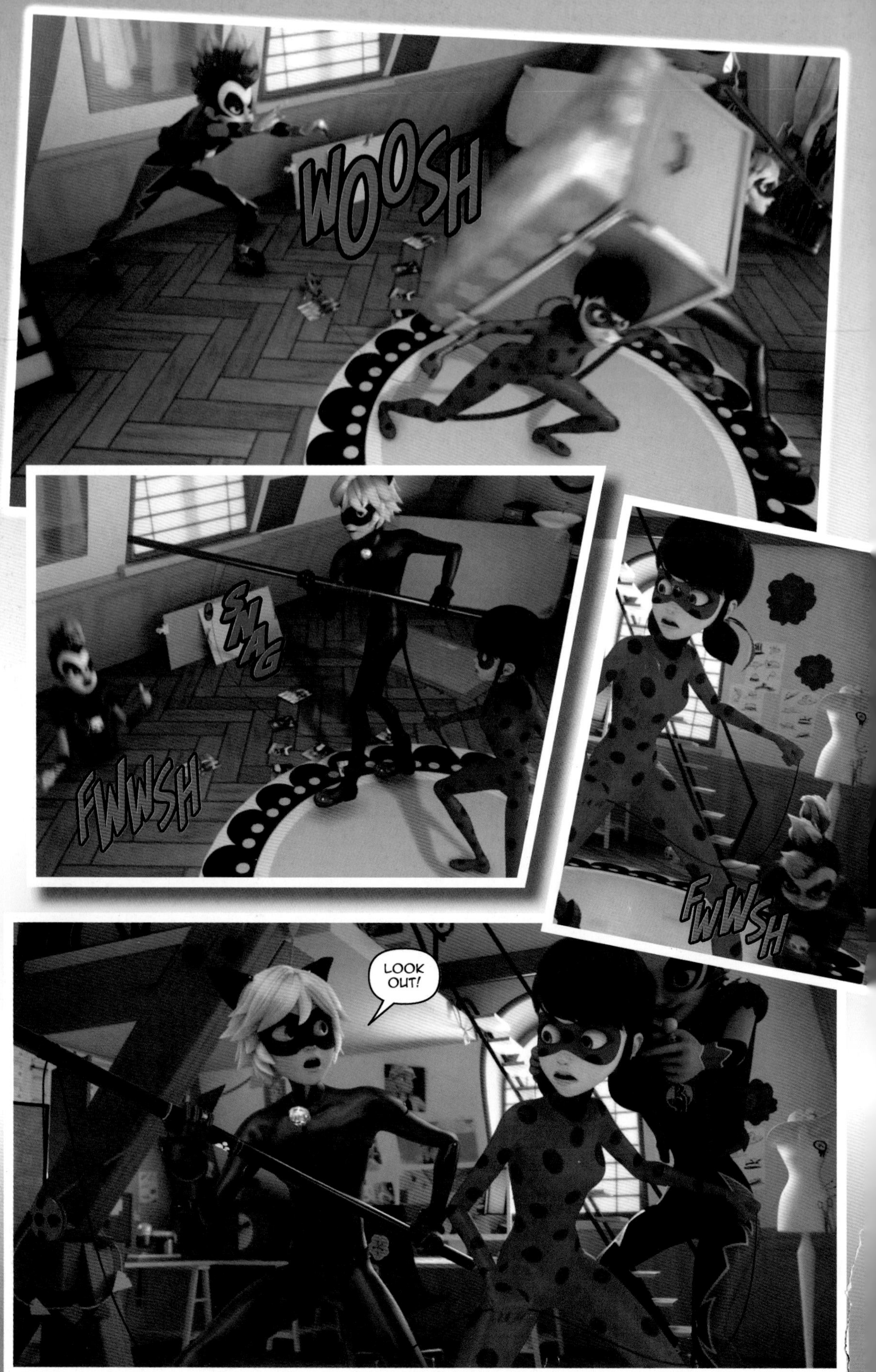
WOOSH
SNAG
FWWSH
FWWSH
LOOK OUT!

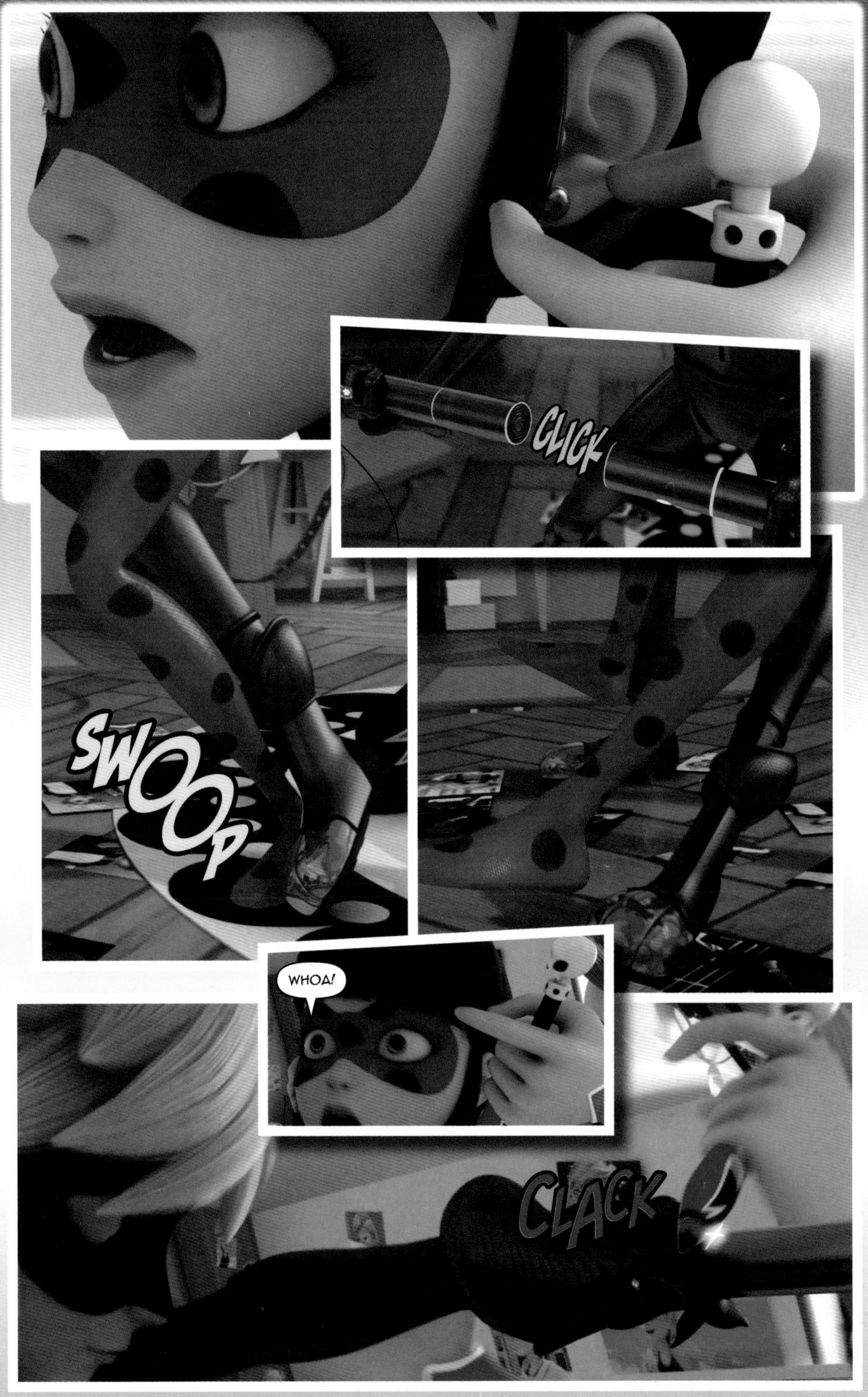
CLICK
SWOOP
WHOA!
CLACK

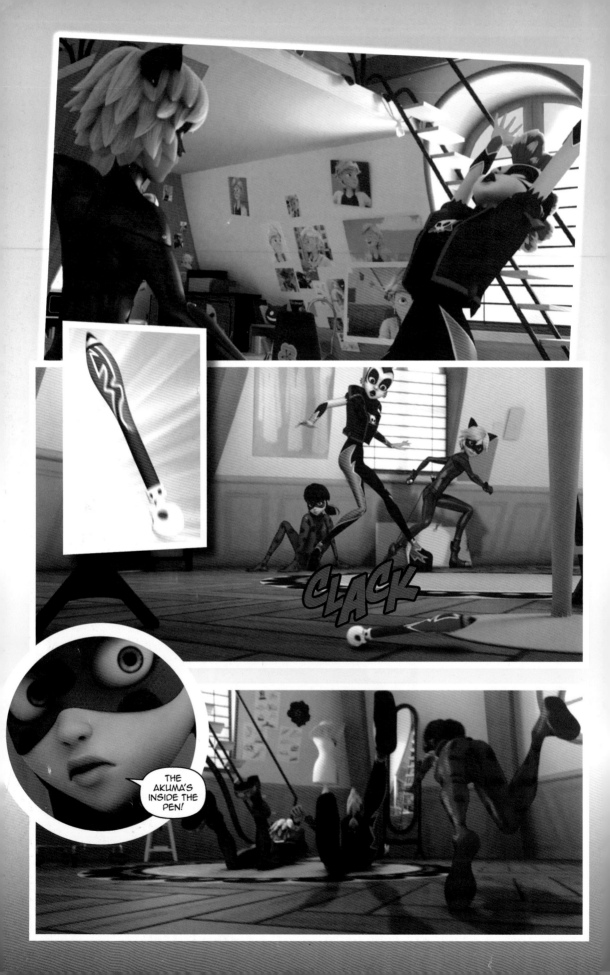

THE AKUMA'S INSIDE THE PEN!

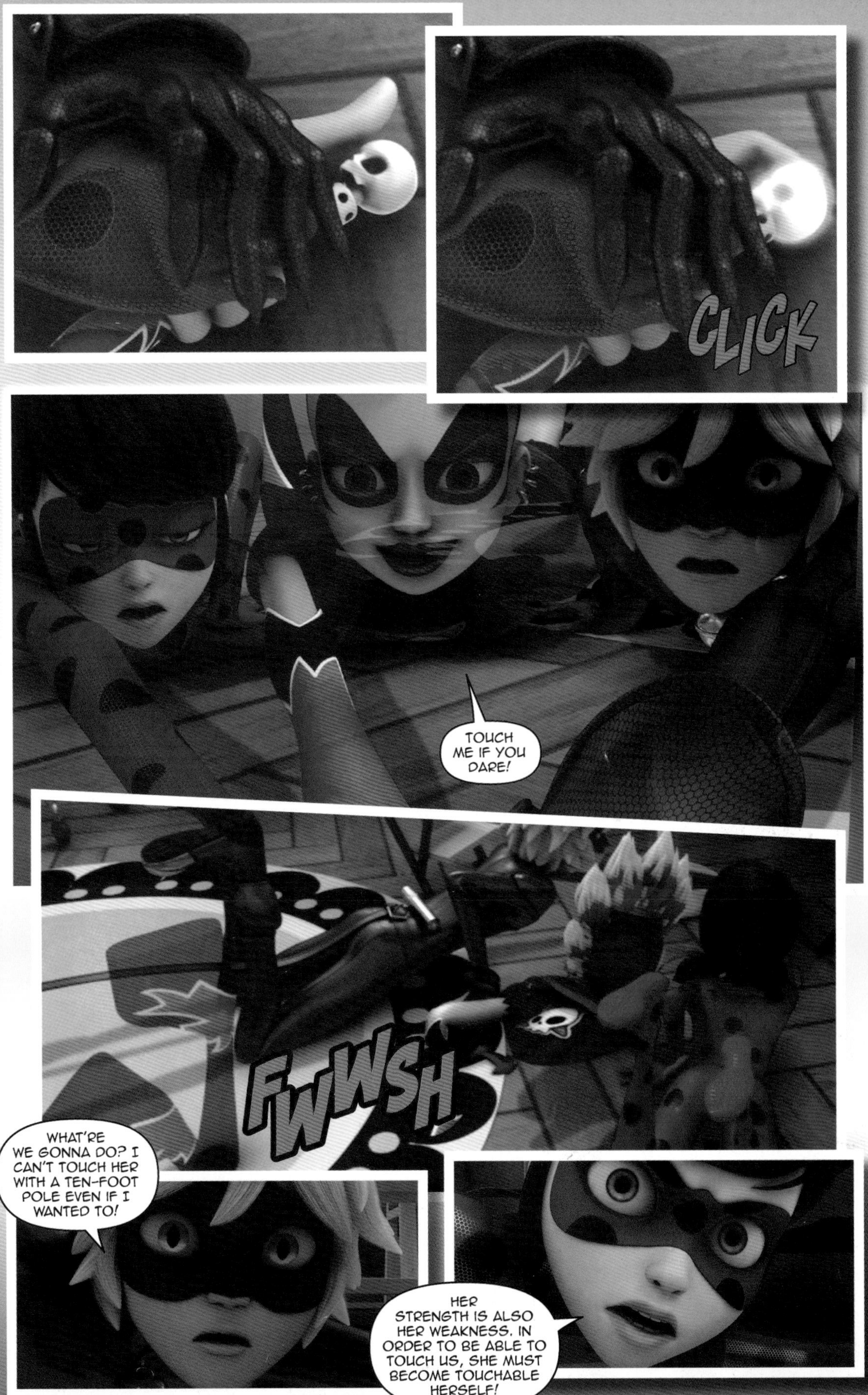
CLICK
TOUCH ME IF YOU DARE!
FWWSH
WHAT'RE WE GONNA DO? I CAN'T TOUCH HER WITH A TEN-FOOT POLE EVEN IF I WANTED TO!
HER STRENGTH IS ALSO HER WEAKNESS. IN ORDER TO BE ABLE TO TOUCH US, SHE MUST BECOME TOUCHABLE HERSELF!

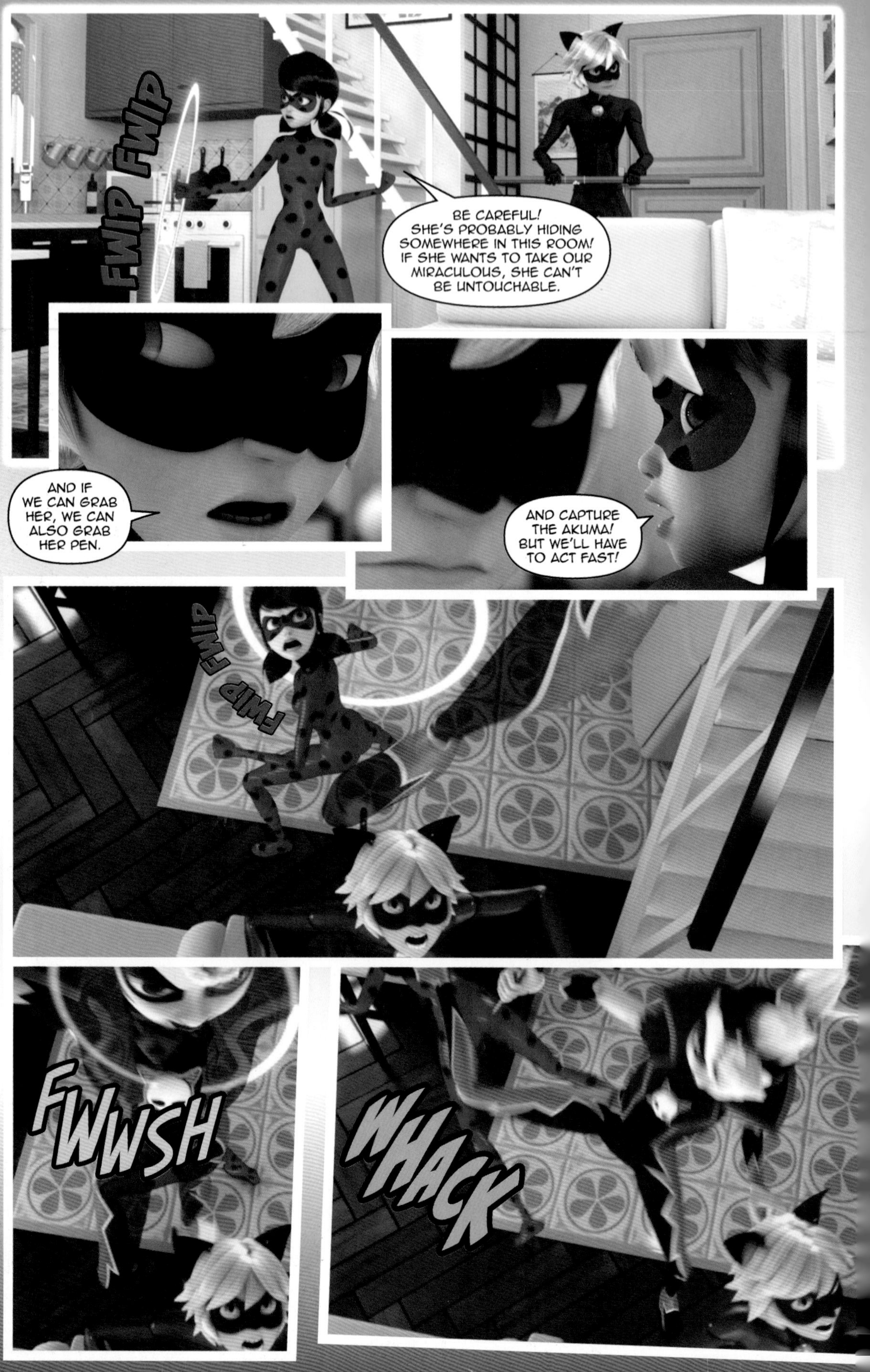
FWIP FWIP
BE CAREFUL! SHE'S PROBABLY HIDING SOMEWHERE IN THIS ROOM! IF SHE WANTS TO TAKE OUR MIRACULOUS, SHE CAN'T BE UNTOUCHABLE.
AND IF WE CAN GRAB HER, WE CAN ALSO GRAB HER PEN.
AND CAPTURE THE AKUMA! BUT WE'LL HAVE TO ACT FAST!
FWIP FWIP
FWWSH
WHACK

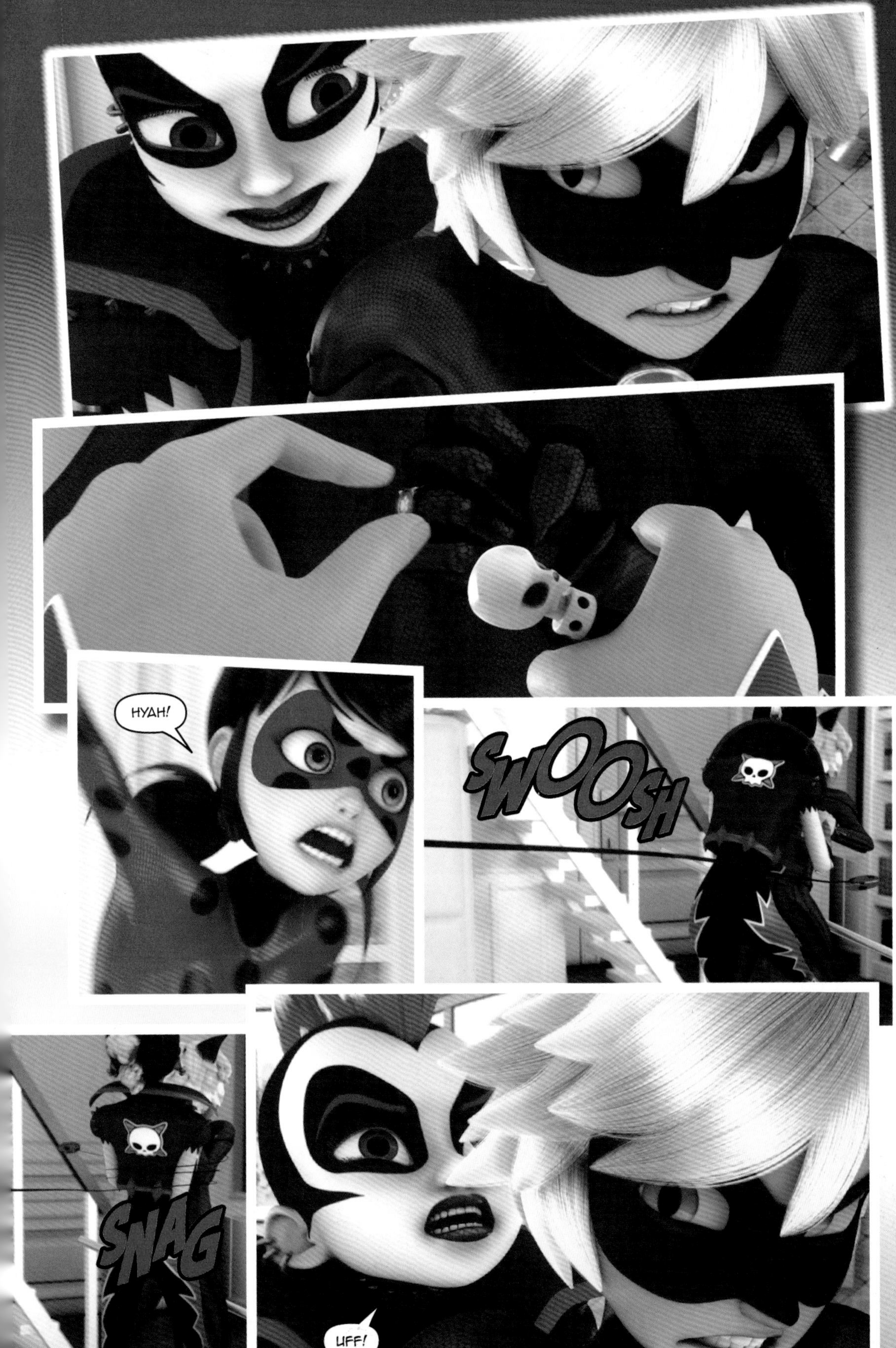
HYAH!
SWOOSH
SNAG
UFF!

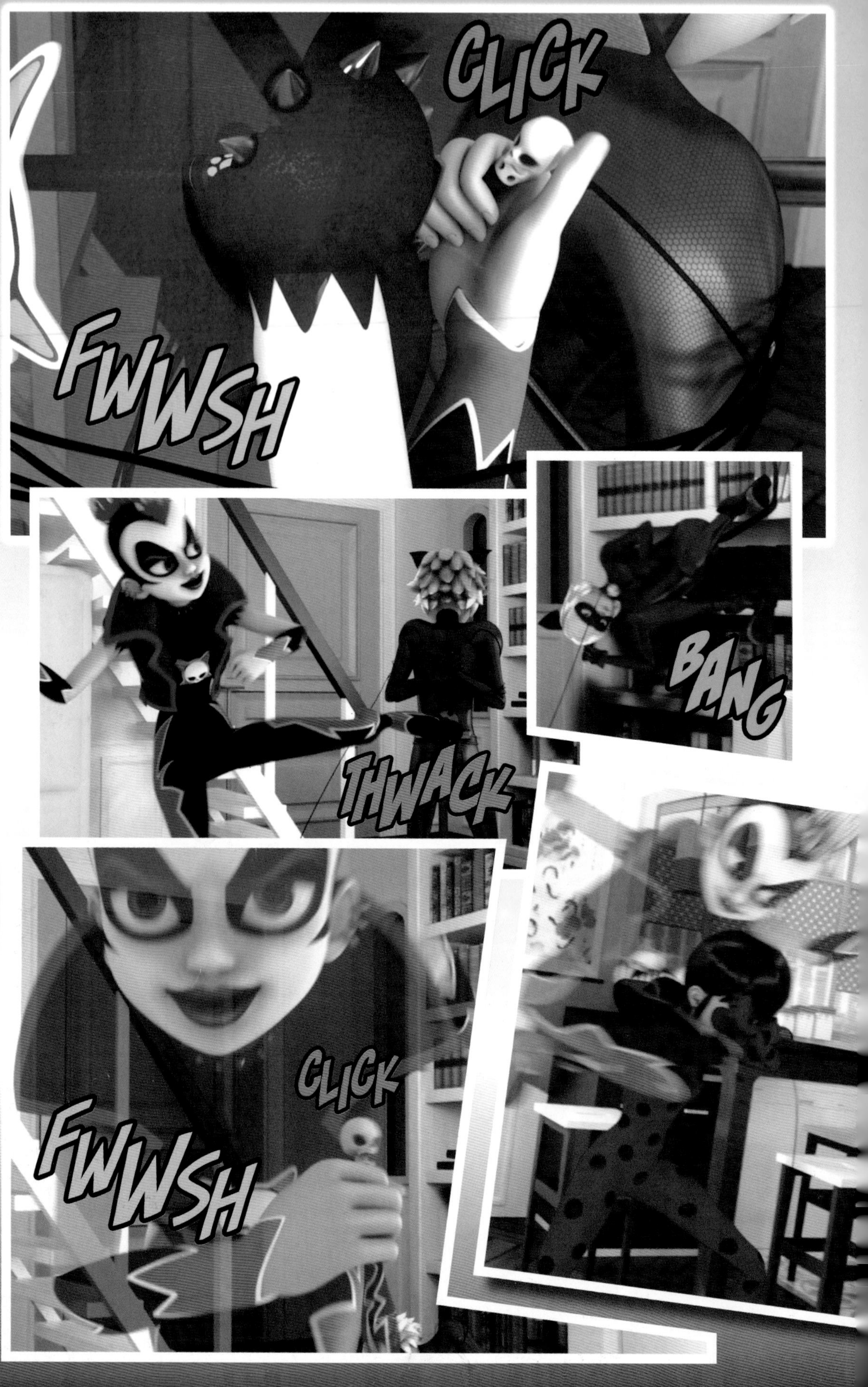
CLICK
FWWSH
BANG
THWACK
CLICK
FWWSH

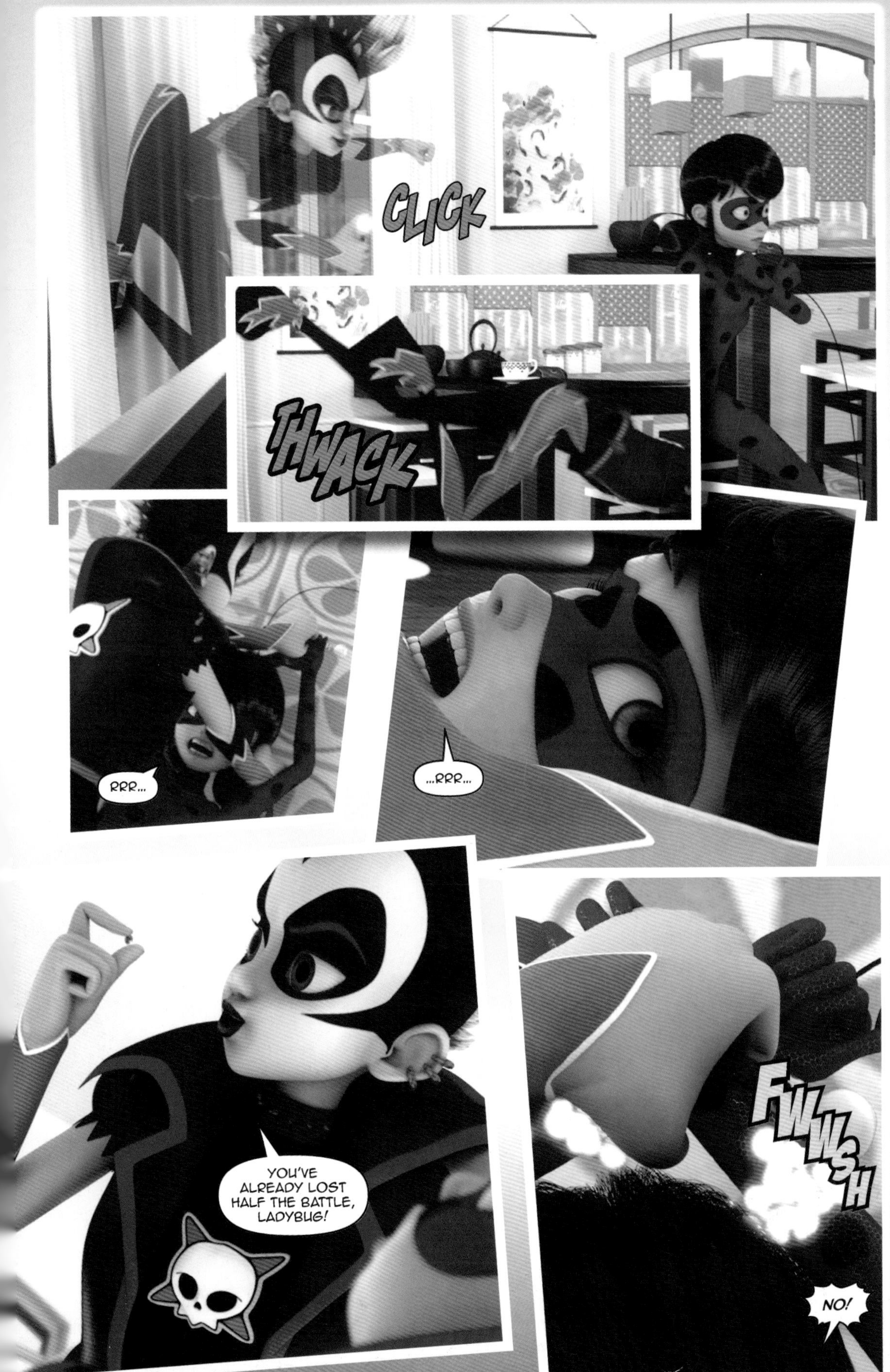
CLICK
THWACK
RRR...
...RRR...
YOU'VE ALREADY LOST HALF THE BATTLE, LADYBUG!
FWWSH
NO!

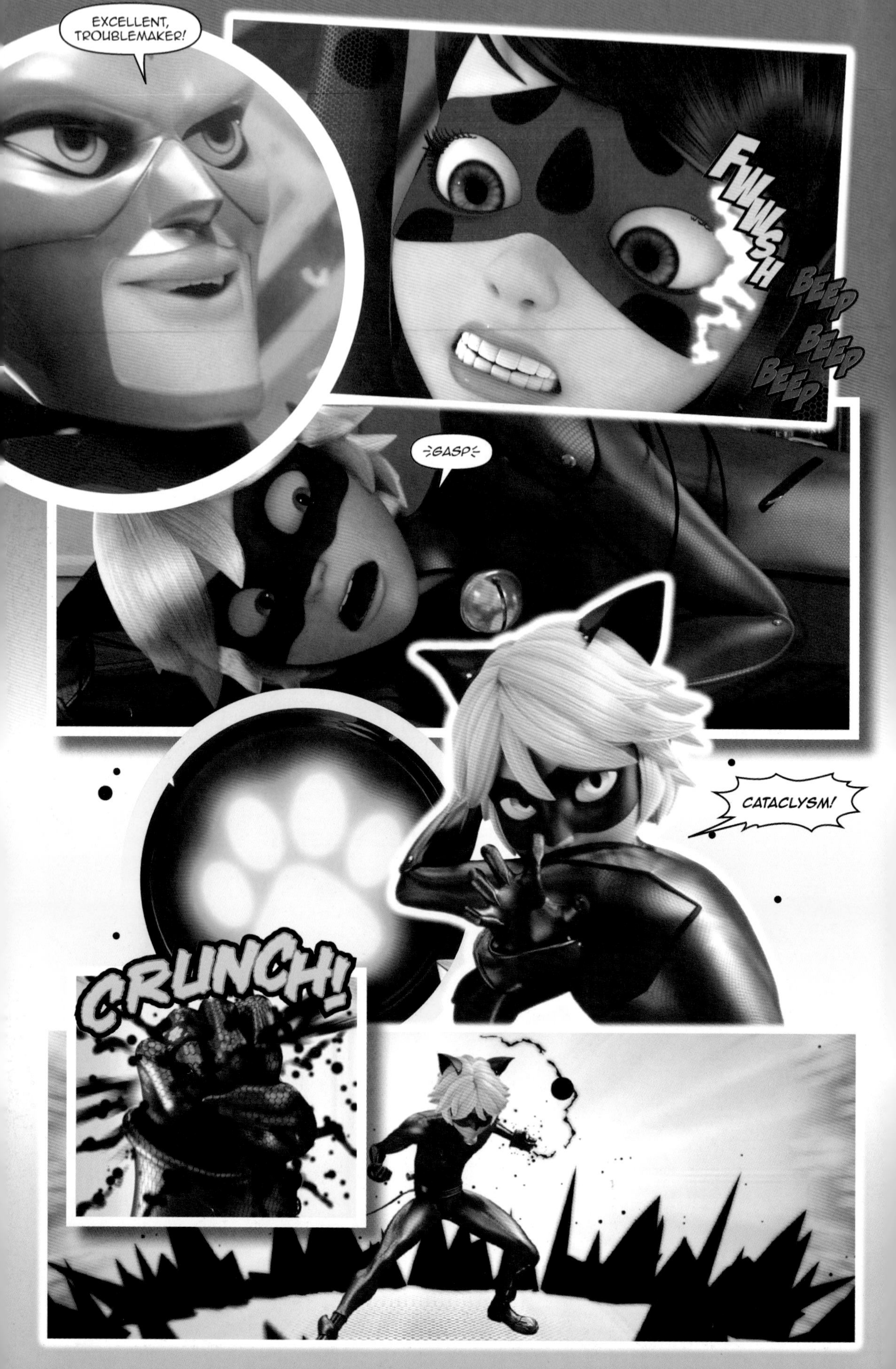
EXCELLENT, TROUBLEMAKER!
FWWSH
BEEP
BEEP
BEEP
GASP
CATACLYSM!
CRUNCH!

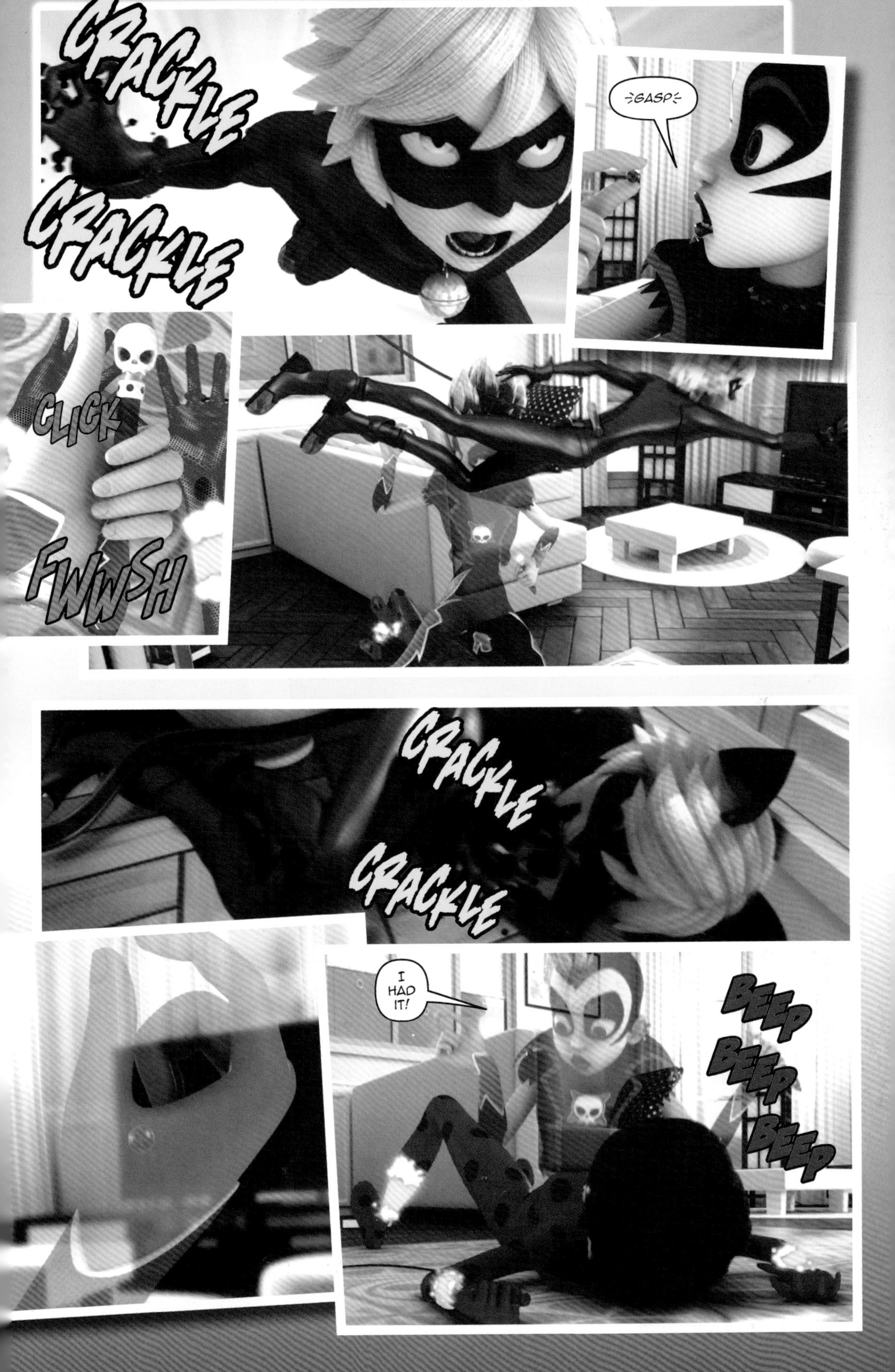
CRACKLE
CRACKLE
GASP
CLICK
FWWSH
CRACKLE
CRACKLE
I HAD IT!
BEEP
BEEP
BEEP

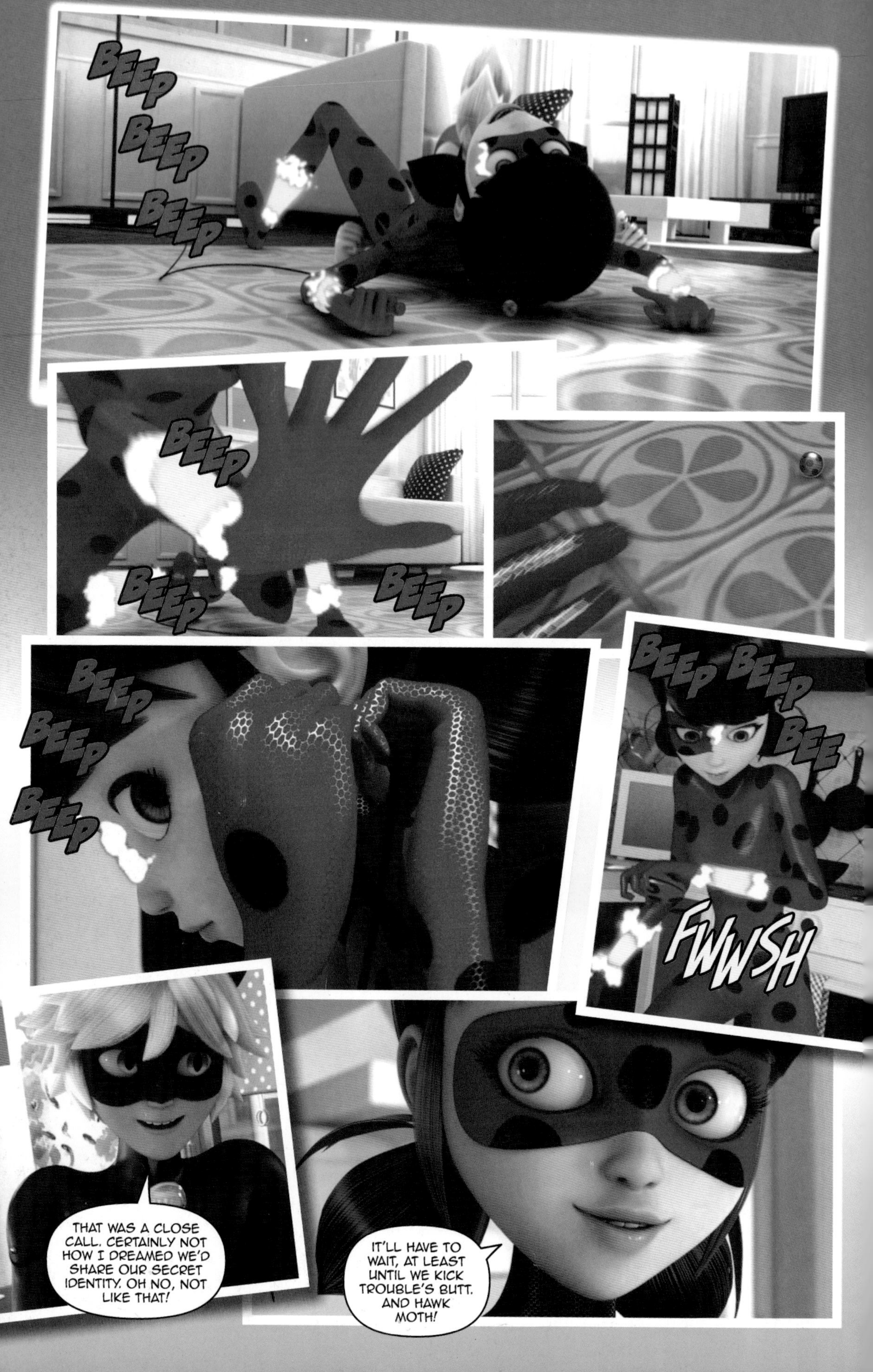
BEEP
BEEP
BEEP
BEEP
BEEP
BEEP
BEEP
BEEP
BEEP
BEEP BEEP BEE
FWWSH
THAT WAS A CLOSE CALL. CERTAINLY NOT HOW I DREAMED WE'D SHARE OUR SECRET IDENTITY. OH NO, NOT LIKE THAT!
IT'LL HAVE TO WAIT, AT LEAST UNTIL WE KICK TROUBLE'S BUTT. AND HAWK MOTH!

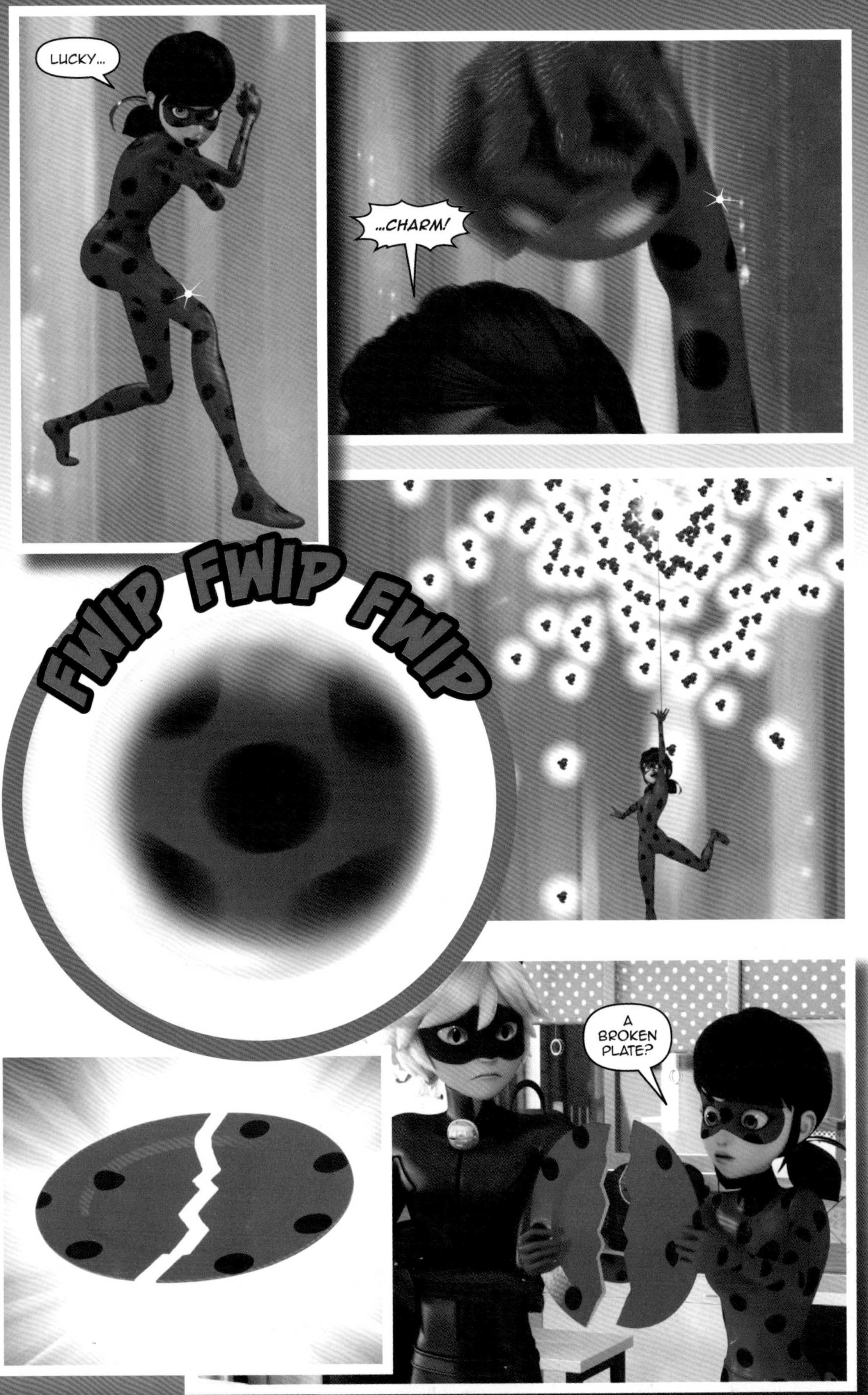
LUCKY...
...CHARM!
FWIP FWIP FWIP
A BROKEN PLATE?

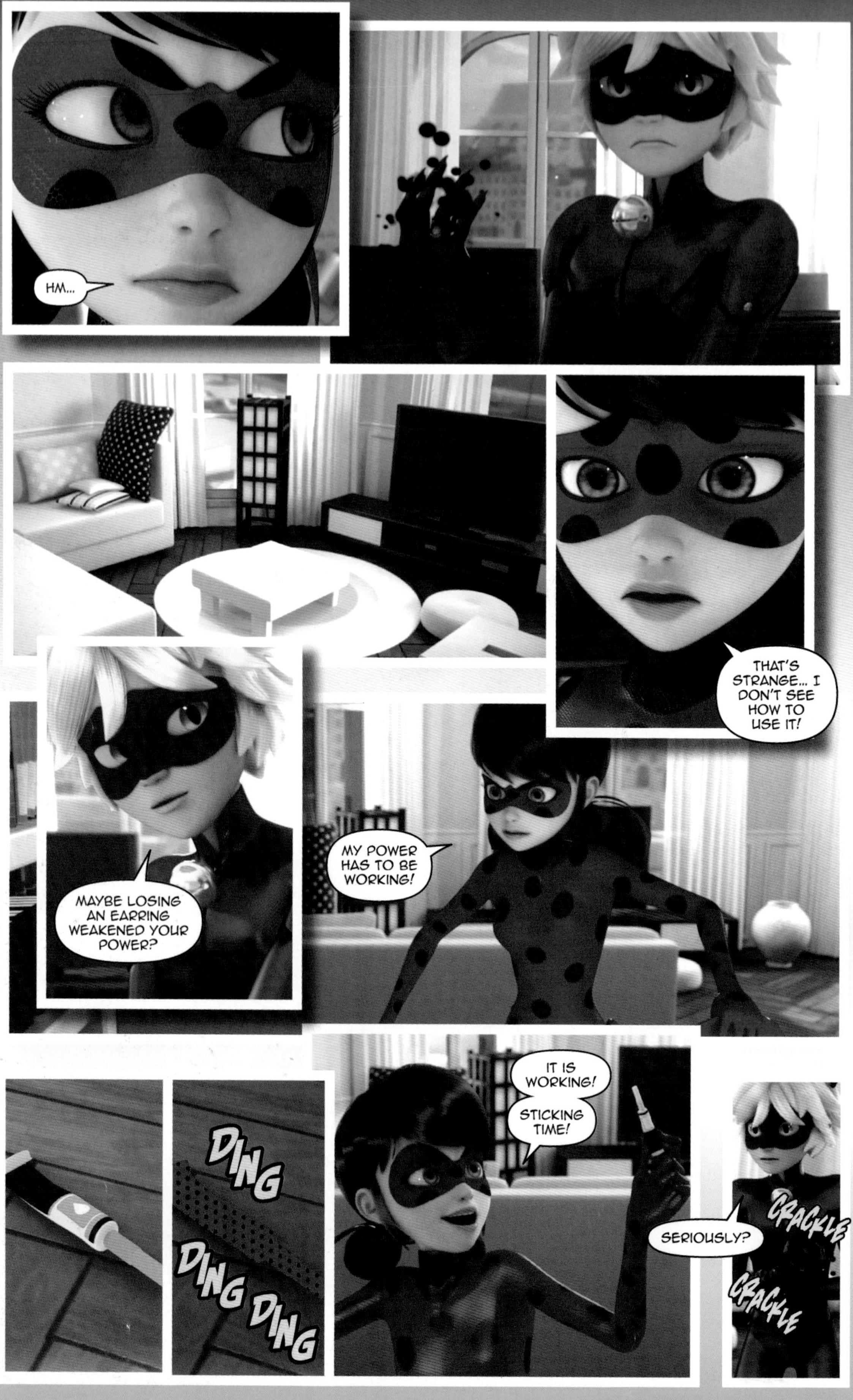
HM...
THAT'S STRANGE... I DON'T SEE HOW TO USE IT!
MAYBE LOSING AN EARRING WEAKENED YOUR POWER?
MY POWER HAS TO BE WORKING!
DING
DING DING
IT IS WORKING!
STICKING TIME!
SERIOUSLY?
CRACKLE
CRACKLE

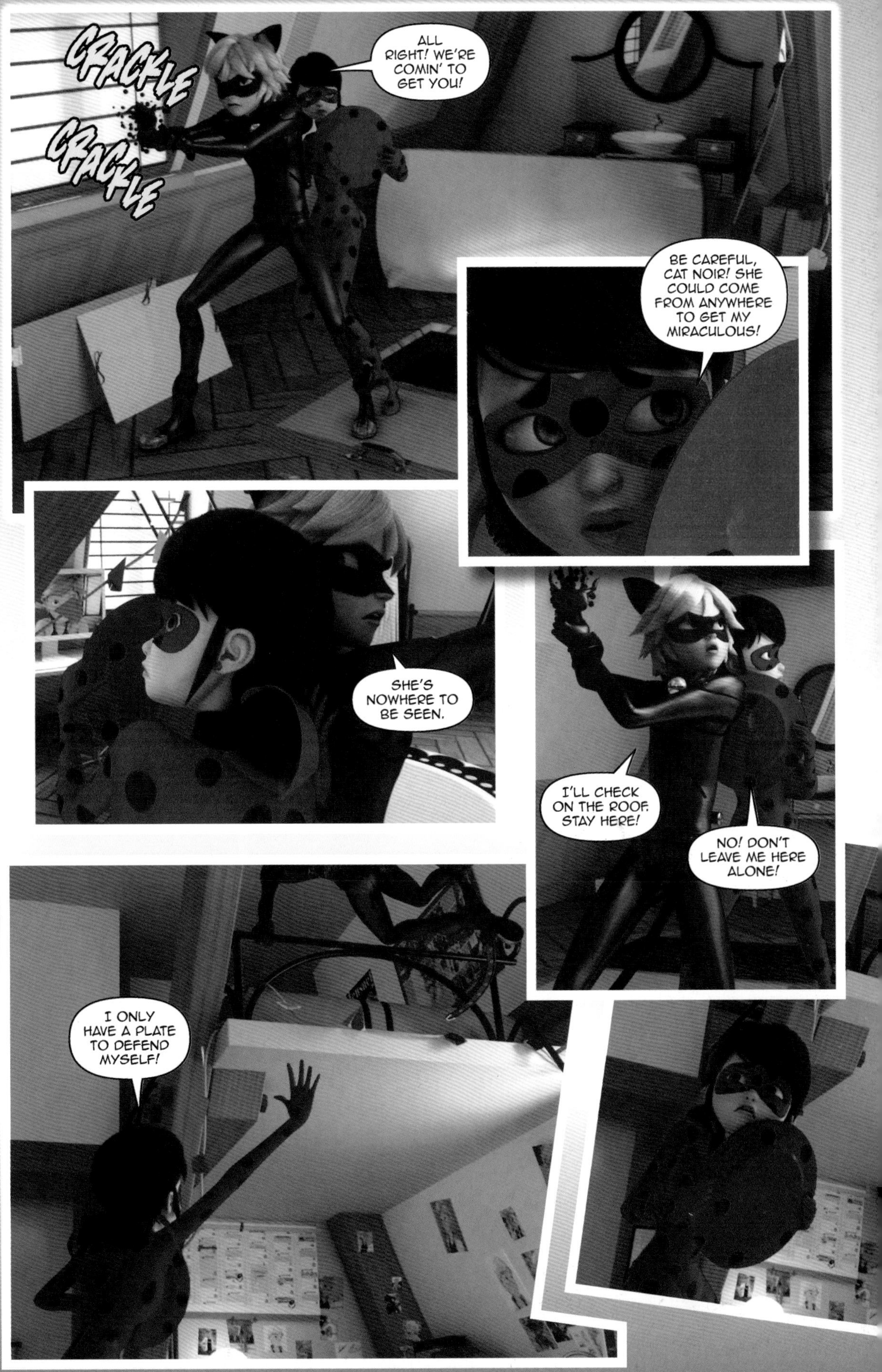
CRACKLE
CRACKLE
ALL RIGHT! WE'RE COMIN' TO GET YOU!
BE CAREFUL, CAT NOIR! SHE COULD COME FROM ANYWHERE TO GET MY MIRACULOUS!
SHE'S NOWHERE TO BE SEEN.
I'LL CHECK ON THE ROOF. STAY HERE!
NO! DON'T LEAVE ME HERE ALONE!
I ONLY HAVE A PLATE TO DEFEND MYSELF!

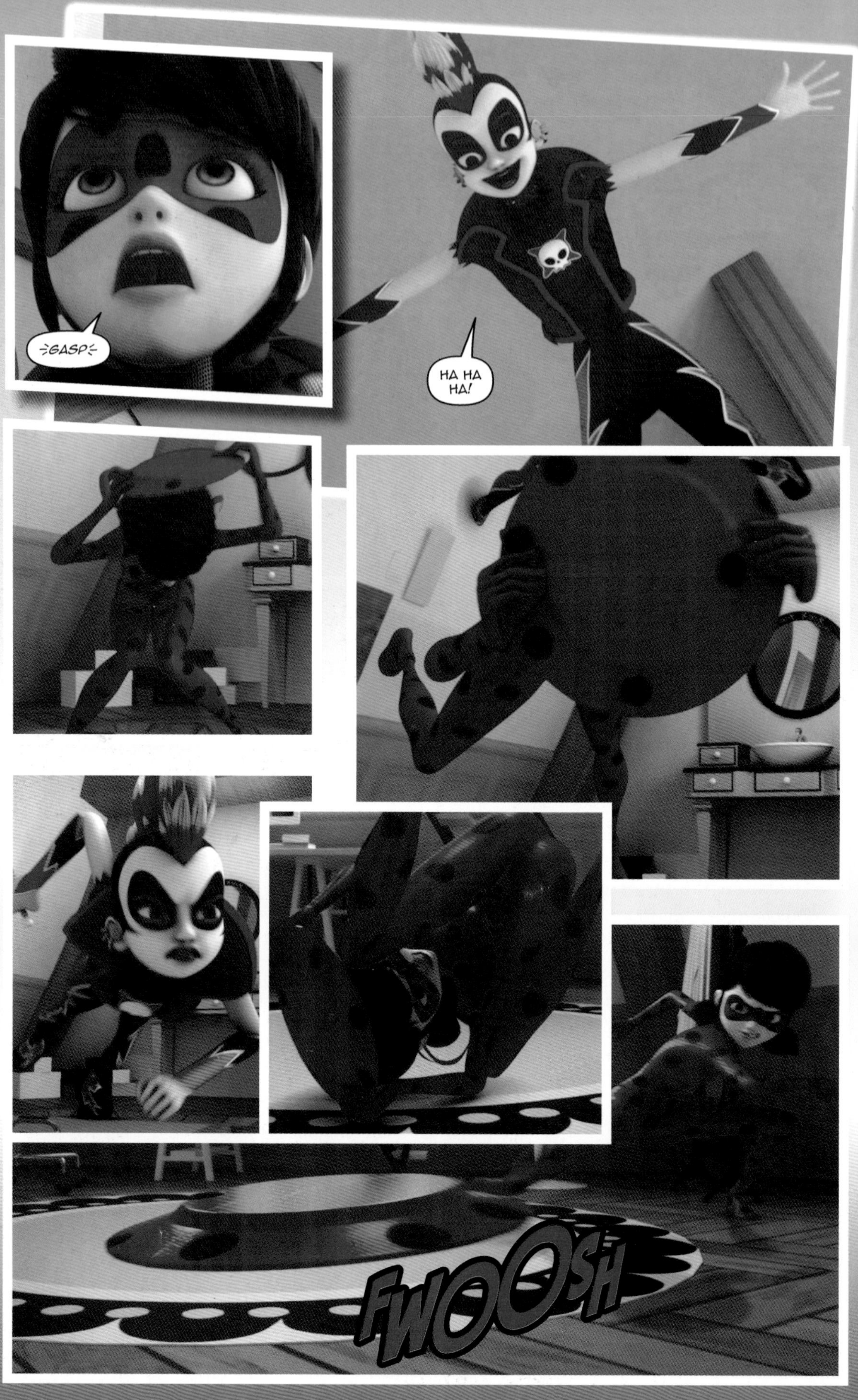
GASP
HA HA HA!
FWOOSH

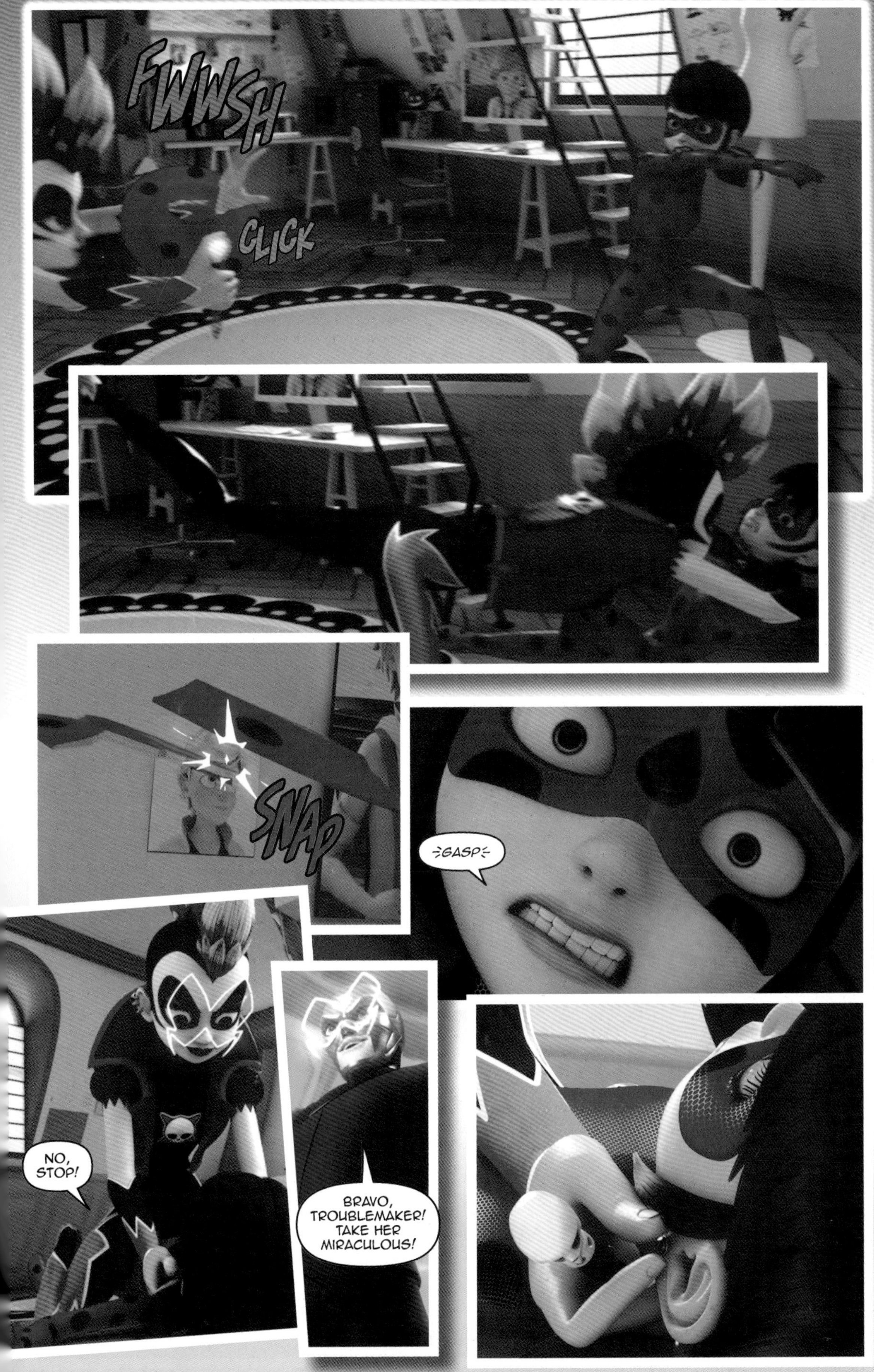
FWWSH
CLICK
SNAP
GASP
NO, STOP!
BRAVO, TROUBLEMAKER! TAKE HER MIRACULOUS!

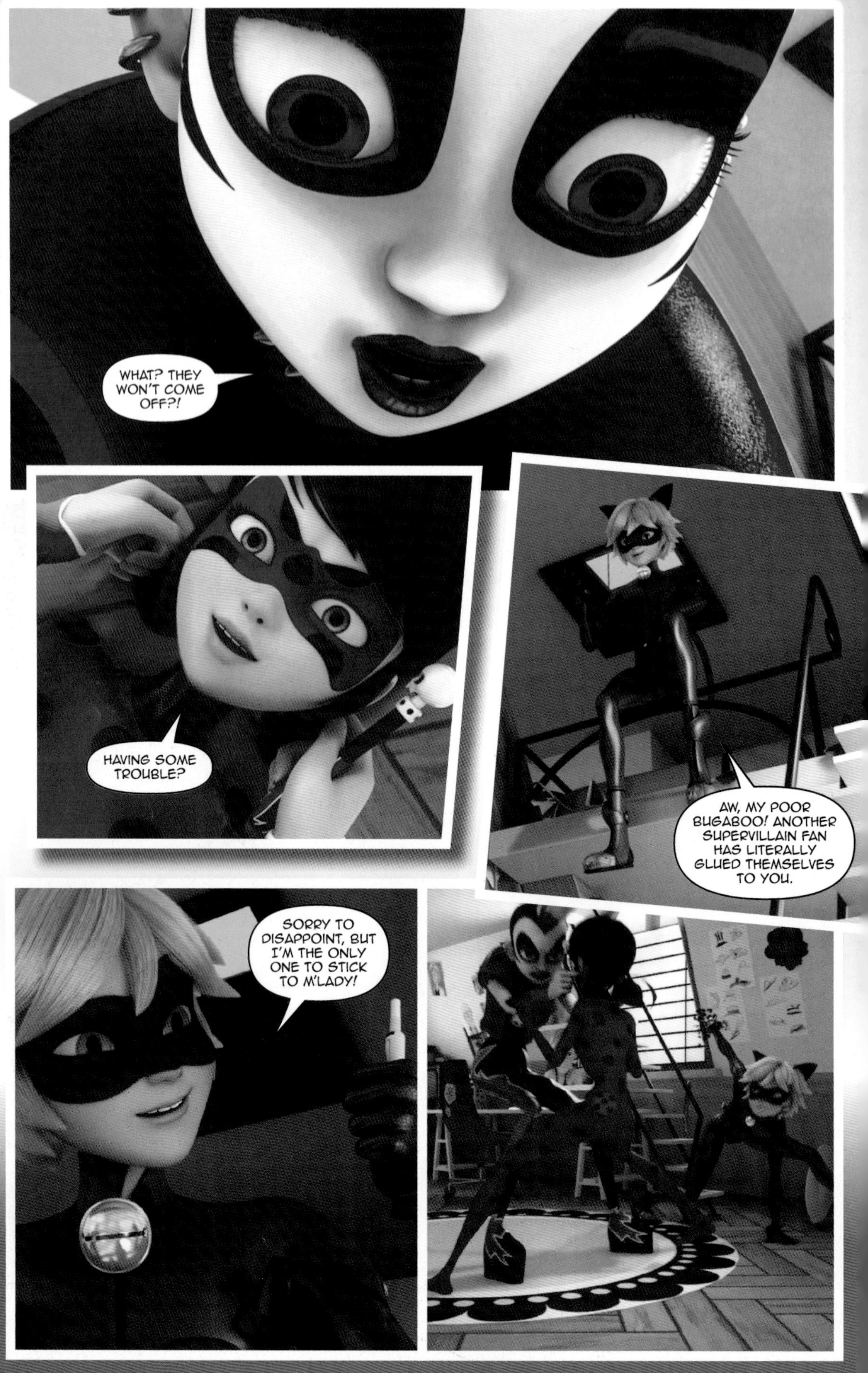
WHAT? THEY WON'T COME OFF?!
HAVING SOME TROUBLE?
AW, MY POOR BUGABOO! ANOTHER SUPERVILLAIN FAN HAS LITERALLY GLUED THEMSELVES TO YOU.
SORRY TO DISAPPOINT, BUT I'M THE ONLY ONE TO STICK TO M'LADY!

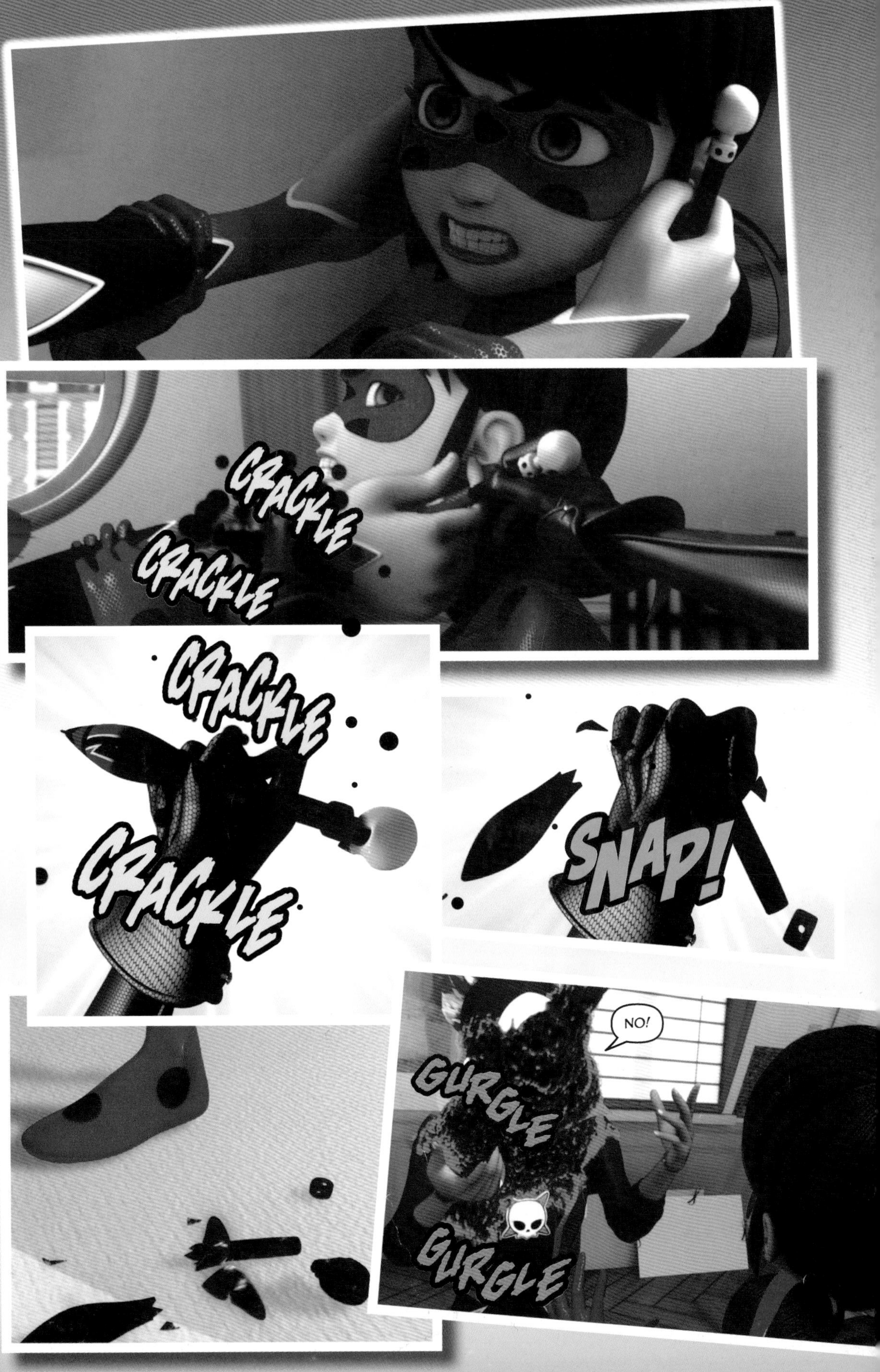
CRACKLE
CRACKLE
CRACKLE
CRACKLE
SNAP!
NO!
GURGLE
GURGLE

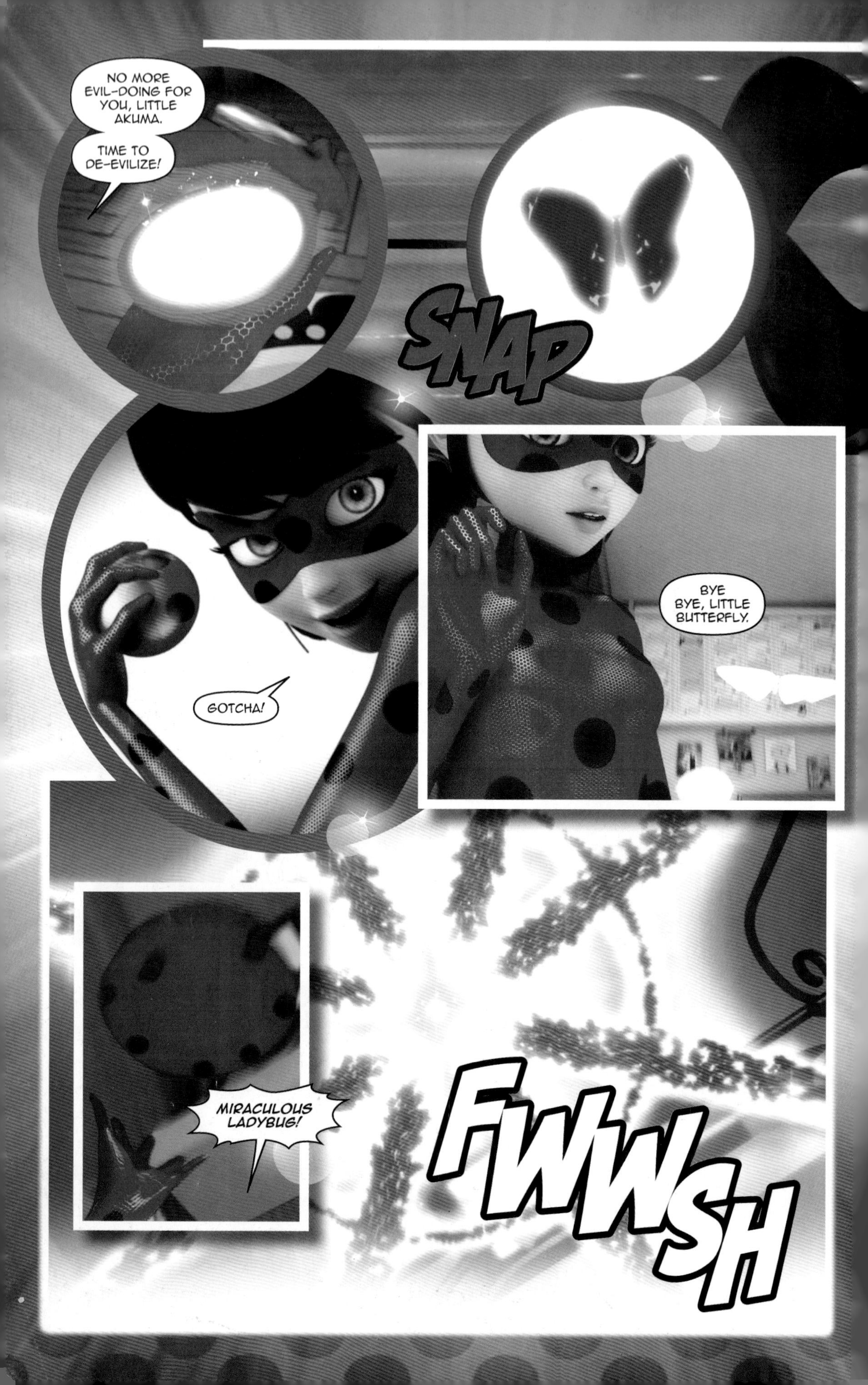
NO MORE EVIL-DOING FOR YOU, LITTLE AKUMA.
TIME TO DE-EVILIZE!
SNAP
BYE BYE, LITTLE BUTTERFLY.
GOTCHA!
MIRACULOUS LADYBUG!
FWWSH

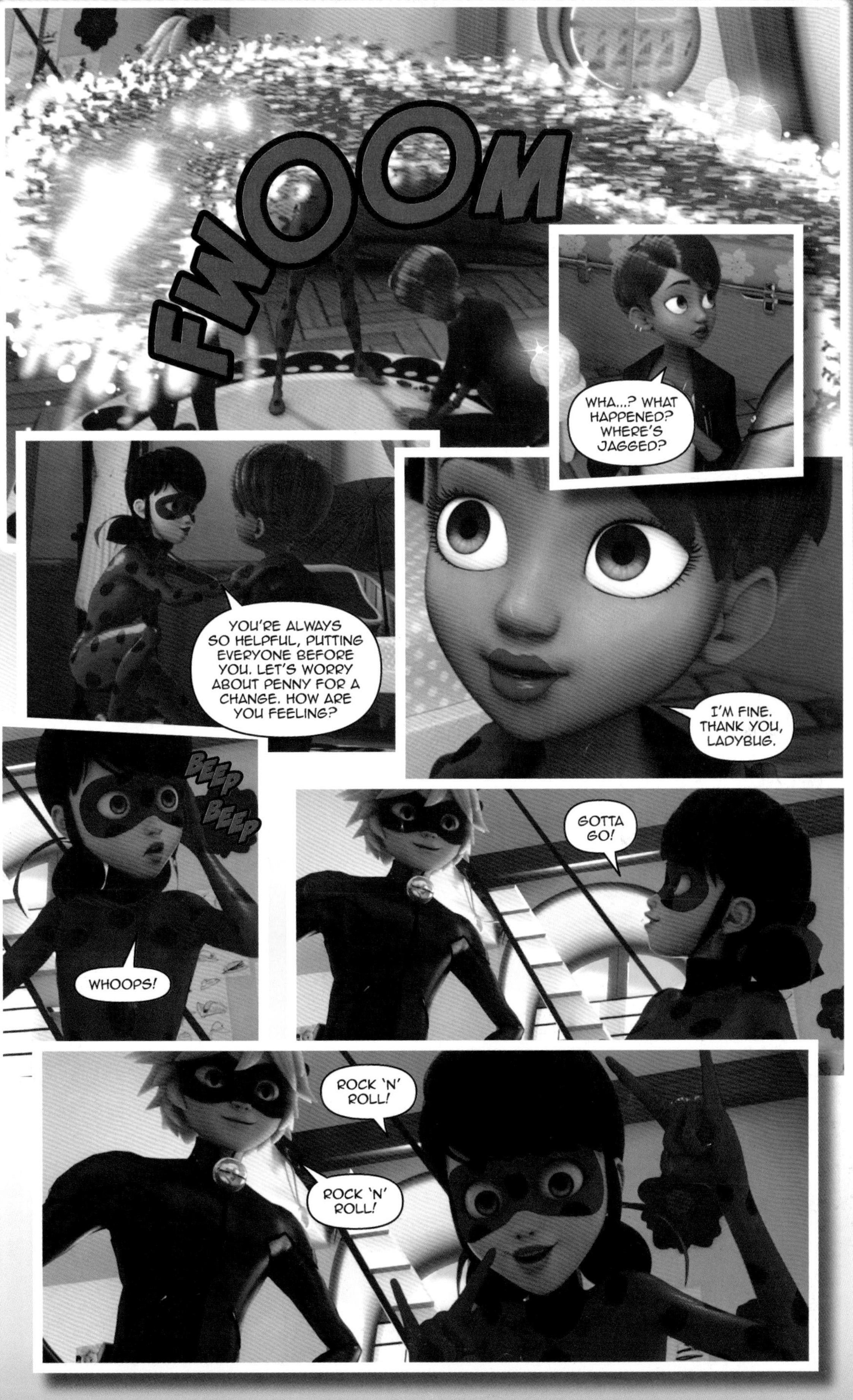
FWOOM
WHA...? WHAT HAPPENED? WHERE'S JAGGED?
YOU'RE ALWAYS SO HELPFUL, PUTTING EVERYONE BEFORE YOU. LET'S WORRY ABOUT PENNY FOR A CHANGE. HOW ARE YOU FEELING?
I'M FINE. THANK YOU, LADYBUG.
BEEP BEEP
WHOOPS!
GOTTA GO!
ROCK 'N' ROLL!
ROCK 'N' ROLL!

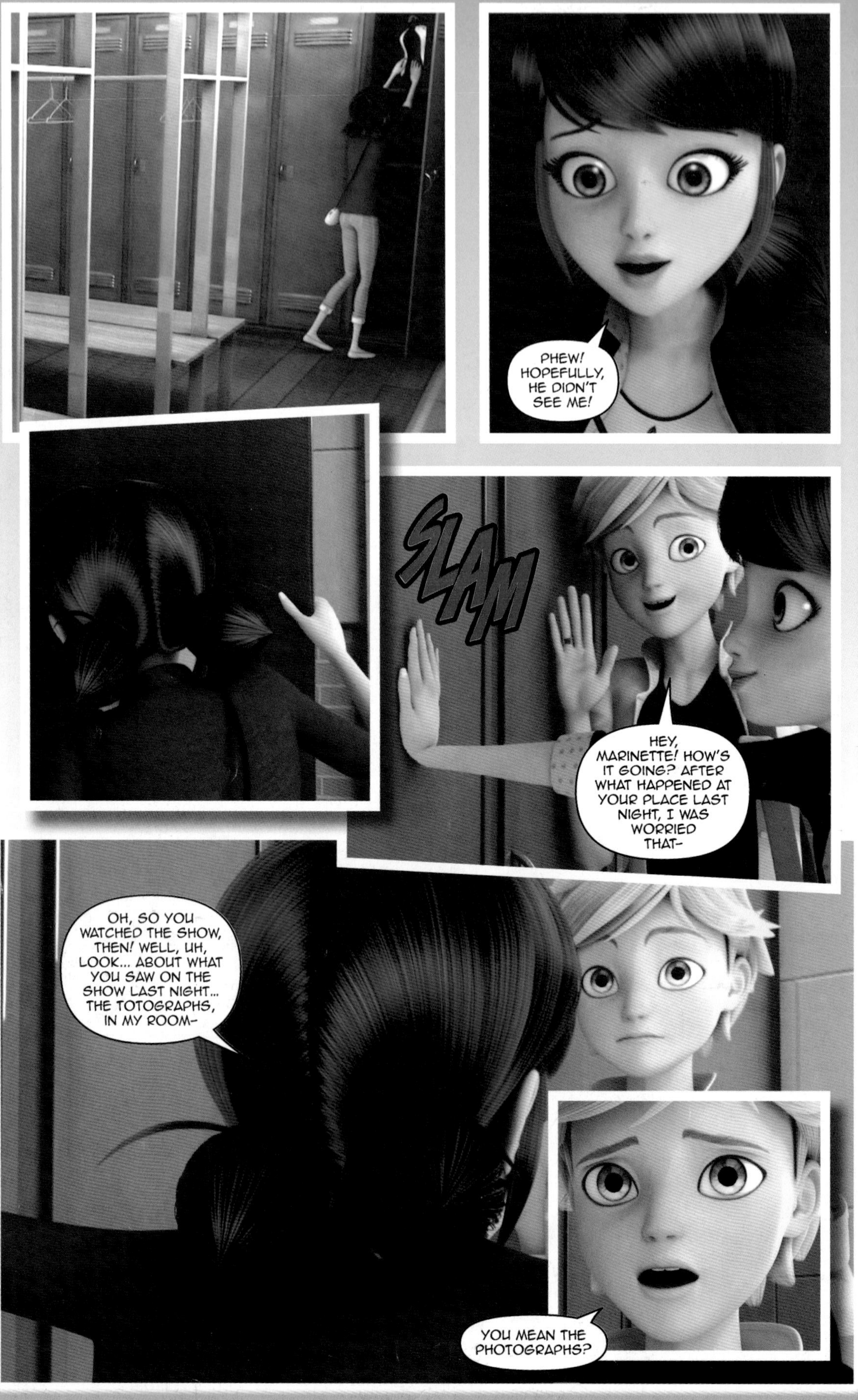
PHEW! HOPEFULLY, HE DIDN'T SEE ME!
SLAM
HEY, MARINETTE! HOW'S IT GOING? AFTER WHAT HAPPENED AT YOUR PLACE LAST NIGHT, I WAS WORRIED THAT-
OH, SO YOU WATCHED THE SHOW, THEN! WELL, UH, LOOK... ABOUT WHAT YOU SAW ON THE SHOW LAST NIGHT... THE TOTOGRAPHS, IN MY ROOM-
YOU MEAN THE PHOTOGRAPHS?

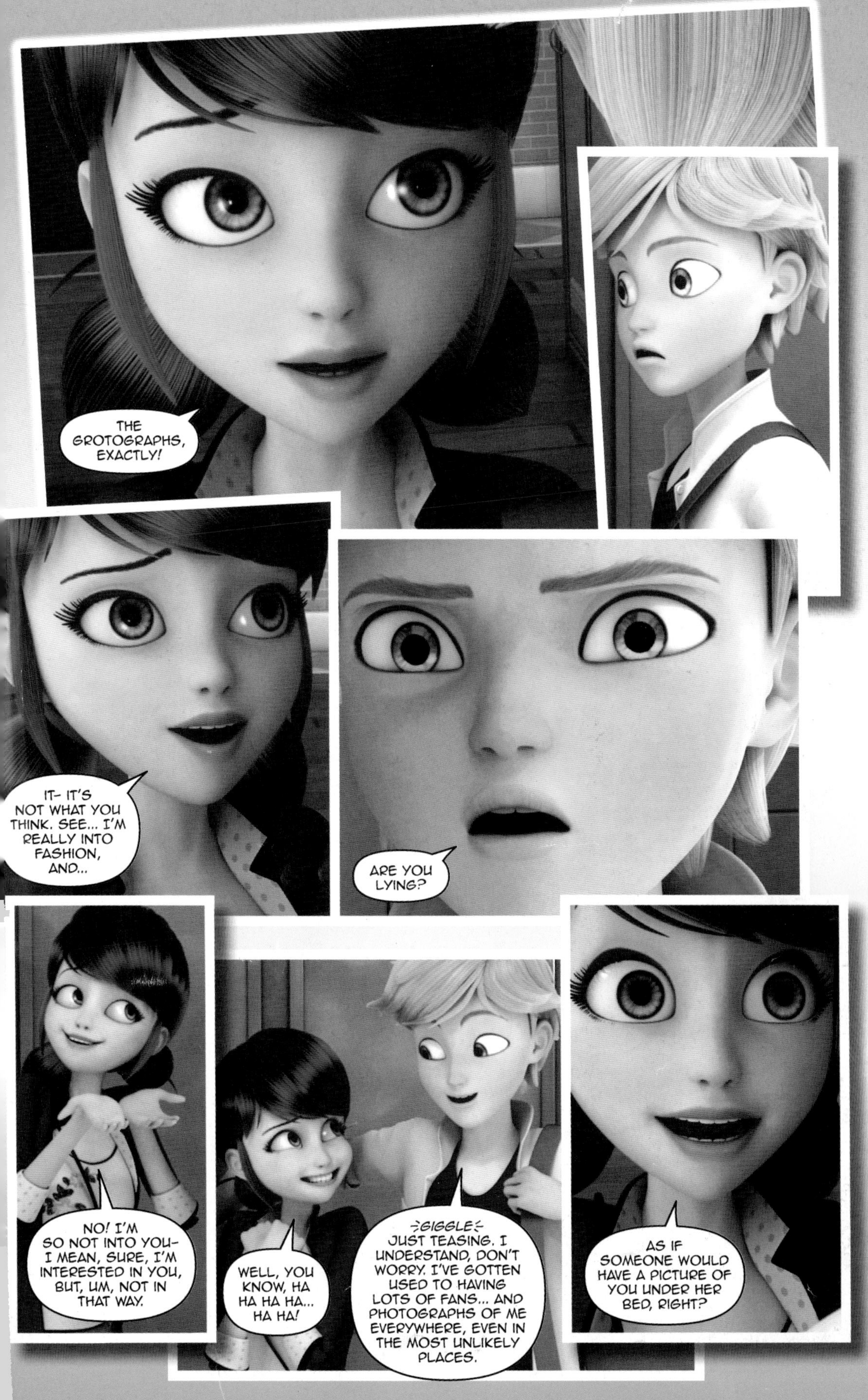
THE GROTOGRAPHS, EXACTLY!
IT- IT'S NOT WHAT YOU THINK. SEE... I'M REALLY INTO FASHION, AND...
ARE YOU LYING?
NO! I'M SO NOT INTO YOU- I MEAN, SURE, I'M INTERESTED IN YOU, BUT, UM, NOT IN THAT WAY.
WELL, YOU KNOW, HA HA HA HA... HA HA!
GIGGLE
JUST TEASING. I UNDERSTAND, DON'T WORRY. I'VE GOTTEN USED TO HAVING LOTS OF FANS... AND PHOTOGRAPHS OF ME EVERYWHERE, EVEN IN THE MOST UNLIKELY PLACES.
AS IF SOMEONE WOULD HAVE A PICTURE OF YOU UNDER HER BED, RIGHT?

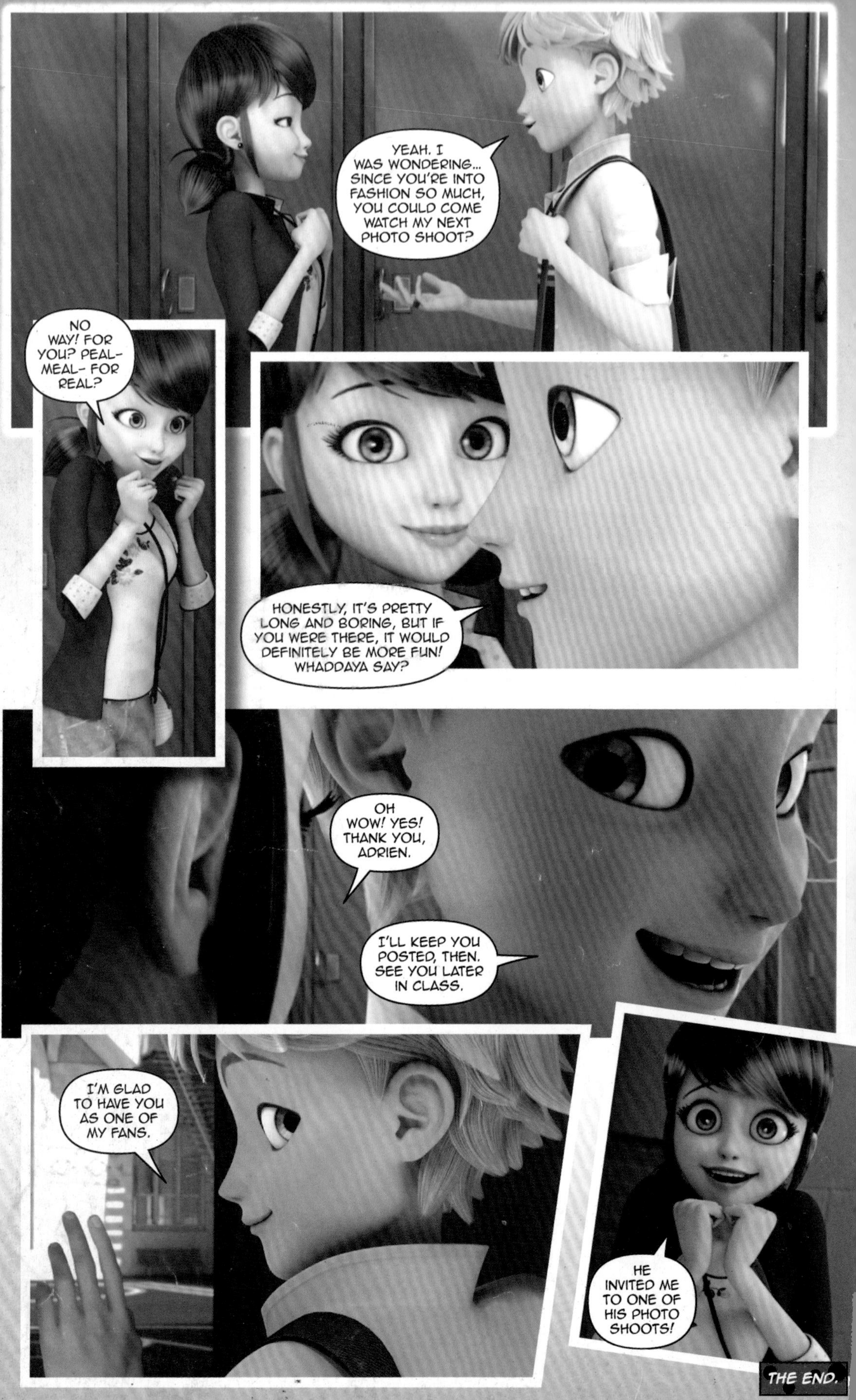
YEAH. I WAS WONDERING... SINCE YOU'RE INTO FASHION SO MUCH, YOU COULD COME WATCH MY NEXT PHOTO SHOOT?
NO WAY! FOR YOU? PEAL-MEAL- FOR REAL?
HONESTLY, IT'S PRETTY LONG AND BORING, BUT IF YOU WERE THERE, IT WOULD DEFINITELY BE MORE FUN! WHADDAYA SAY?
OH WOW! YES! THANK YOU, ADRIEN.
I'LL KEEP YOU POSTED, THEN. SEE YOU LATER IN CLASS.
I'M GLAD TO HAVE YOU AS ONE OF MY FANS.
HE INVITED ME TO ONE OF HIS PHOTO SHOOTS!
THE END.